T0150400

ROHZIN

ROHZIN

RAHMAN ABBAS

Translated from the Urdu by Sabika Abbas Naqvi

VINTAGE
An imprint of Penguin Random House

VINTAGE

USA | Canada | UK | Ireland | Australia
New Zealand | India | South Africa | China

Vintage is part of the Penguin Random House group of companies
whose addresses can be found at global.penguinrandomhouse.com

Published by Penguin Random House India Pvt. Ltd
4th Floor, Capital Tower 1, MG Road,
Gurugram 122 002, Haryana, India

First published in Vintage by Penguin Random House India 2022

10 9 8 7 6 5 4 3

This is a work of fiction. Unless otherwise indicated, all the names, characters, businesses, places, events and incidents in this book are either the product of the author's imagination or used in a fictitious manner. Any resemblance to actual persons, living or dead, or actual events is purely coincidental. This book contains sensitive content that may disturb some readers. It includes references to street slang, abusive language, sexual abuse, child abuse, violence, murder and suicide, and readers are advised to exercise their discretion. The author makes an attempt to deliver these messages in order to allow readers to prepare emotionally for the content or to decide to forgo interacting with the content. The objective of this book is not to hurt any sentiments or be biased in favour of or against any particular person, political party, region, caste, society, gender, creed, nation or religion. Neither the author nor the publisher advises/recommends/advocates the behaviour of any character as described in this book. Any liability arising from any action undertaken by any person by relying upon any part of this book is strictly disclaimed.

ISBN 9780670093861

Typeset in Bembo MT Pro by MAP Systems, Bengaluru, India
Printed at Replika Press Pvt. Ltd, India

www.penguin.co.in

MIX
Paper from
responsible sources
FSC® C016779

To my daughter, Mahira, and my son, Rumi Abbas

And to my beloved city, Mumbai

'He was still too young to know that the heart's memory eliminates the bad and magnifies the good, and that thanks to this artifice we manage to endure the burden of the past.'

—Gabriel García Márquez,
Love in the Time of Cholera

'It may have happened, it may not have happened: but it could have happened.'

—Mark Twain,
The Prince and the Pauper

CONTENTS

Let Me Acquaint Myself with My Being's Poison
(*Jo Zeher Hai Mere Andar Wo Dekhna Chahun*)

It was the last day in the lives of Asrar and Hina.

The sea that had its arms around Mumbai was ferocious. It desired to finally win the centuries-old battle, gulp the island and be victorious. Tall waves rose and fell, rose again and dashed against the shore. It had been raining for the past three days, so much that now the dark alleys, narrow lanes, the wide roads and the crumbling streets of the city were all submerged in knee-deep water. Black clouds veiled the sky. The city no longer remembered how the rays of the sun felt and looked. The sky was leaking through huge holes in its being, as if it had transformed into a never-ending waterfall. The waters of the sea had found a comfortable entry into the underground drains. The drains were a battleground for the unstoppable rainwater and the roaring sea, in a continuous struggle to make space for themselves.

This war had caused great damage to the embankments or the concrete sides of the newly constructed drains. The streams of water merged and made their way into the deepest layers of the soil. The residential areas around the inundated drains were submerging. The Mithi River was overflooded and the land around it lay submerged in deep waters. There were power cuts in most places. The condition of low-lying areas of the city reflected the wrath of rain and the destruction it had caused. All linkages between the city administration, government and the public had been snapped.

According to old dwellers of the city, it had never rained so heavily and destructively in the past. In the heart of the city an apocalyptic silence spread over the Mumba Devi's temple. Mumba Devi's deity looked sad. It was said that such sadness on her face was last seen by Brahma 6000 years ago when she had to counter 'Mumbaraka', an evil giant who terrorized the local population. After his defeat, Mumba Devi's temple was constructed and Brahma himself came to shower his blessings at the inauguration. When the deity was installed, there was an ambiguous and unexplainable silence on her face. Had Brahma already told her about the future Mumbai would soon have to face? Was there any other power in the universe except Brahma who knew the reason behind the transformation of Mumba Devi's natural smile into the sad ambiguous silence?

Asrar's father, Malik Deshmukh, along with his childhood friends Sajid Parkar and Abid Parkar, hunted for fish along the shores of the Arabian Sea.

They belonged to Mabadmorpho village and the name of their boat was the *Queen of the Sea*.

Everyone in Mabadmorpho knew the name of Malik's boat by heart. After extensive fishing in the turbulent waters, they returned to the shore each time and divided the catch among the three equally. Their wives sold it in the local fish markets. The sea, the fish and the boat were their lifelines. Their families lived off whatever little they earned from fishing. Happiness and food security were still a far-fetched dream for each of them. They were oblivious of the world and were very busy fishing in the seas. The sole aim for the three of them was to earn money, a lot of money. But fate had something else in store.

An unfortunate fate awaited them. The *Queen of the Sea* got caught in a severe whirlpool. All three friends were familiar with the movements, characteristics and various moods of the sea. They had spent most of their lives tossing over the waves. It wasn't the first time that they had seen a whirlpool. They had witnessed many, but the one which their beloved boat faced was so wide in circumference and so powerful in strength that they lacked the words to describe its intensity. Even their elders had never told stories of such a ferocious swirl in the waters. They stole a glance at each other but there was no time to even exchange words; all three jumped into the water to save their lives.

Only one made it to the shore.

Though the shores and the sea were thoroughly searched, Malik Deshmukh and Sajid Parkar were nowhere to be found.

Fifteen to twenty days later, a broken piece of the unfortunate boat found its way to the shores of Mabadmorpho. People were surprised to see that it was the very piece on which the name of the boat, the *Queen of the Sea*, was engraved. Immediately after this ill-fated incident, Mabadmorpho had to face one more inexplicable occurrence which kept it in a seemingly hypnotic state.

The day the broken piece of the *Queen of the Sea* was discovered, it was kept on elevated ground near the shore. Surprisingly, this coincided with the sighting of dolphins in the sea alongside.

Many felt that the dolphins were trying to catch a glimpse of the broken piece of the boat. Initially, no one believed the sighting. In fact, those who claimed to have seen the dolphins were rebuked and pulled up for being intoxicated even in broad daylight.

But the dolphins kept returning each day. When this went on for four to five days and the dolphins jumped out of the water, apparently to see the broken piece, people started believing the earlier story. Someone informed Abid, the sole survivor of the accident, about the dolphins. He immediately left his bed and went to the shore. More than half the population of Mabadmorpho was present there, watching the show of the dolphins. When people saw him coming, the crowd parted. He shook hands with a few and started looking in the direction of the dolphins. He kept staring at them attentively; his expression was ponderous. Then he climbed up to the elevated area and raised his hands in the air and waved at the dolphins. The onlookers stared at Abid and followed his gaze. They looked in amazement at the dolphins as they rose and fell into the sea. The rhythmic dance continued for nearly half an hour. Soon, they vanished into the deep.

Abid stepped down and the crowd surrounded him. A man named Karim Mujawar asked him in mock seriousness, 'Tell me honestly, do dolphins drink beer too?'

The mob chuckled. Some found it so hilarious that they had tears in their eyes. One more reason to laugh even louder was that everyone knew that Karim had just set up a liquor shop recently.

When seriousness returned, an elderly man asked, 'Abid, what is this all about?'

The man who had recently returned from the claws of death recalled that when they went fishing and were quite far in the sea, the dolphins would jump and dive around their boat and look at them. So, they also stopped to wave back. Having said that, Abid turned and walked away. The people who stayed back continued discussing and debating the dolphins. They finally concluded that what Abid had claimed was next to impossible. After all, he just had a close encounter with death and was not yet out of the shock. The silence of the crowd gave legitimacy to the idea that Abid was facing some severe mental issues after the accident. The dolphins were never seen near the shore again. This made people rethink what they had been told earlier.

After Malik Deshmukh's death, his wife Haseena earned a livelihood by selling dried fish. She also took the responsibility of continuing their son Asrar's education. Asrar was aware of his mother's difficulties and the hard work she had to put in. The day his tenth standard examination ended, that very evening he told his mother that he would go to Mumbai to acquire a new skill and to find work. Haseena tried persuading him to stay but he wouldn't budge. He told his mother that three of his classmates would also be accompanying him. They had planned to temporarily put up in 'Jamat Ki Kholi', which was a property of Mabadmorpho in Mumbai. Anyone coming from the village could find residence here at a very meagre rent. Such properties existed since the beginning of the twentieth century in Mumbai and belonged collectively to the villages in the coastal region.

After being satisfied with the necessary details, she gave her permission. A day before he had to leave his village, Asrar sat alone at the seashore for a long time. He stared at the beautifully scattered sunlight on the waves. There was a peculiar melody in the union of the waves and the rays. He had found that melody touching since childhood.

He used to go with his father to the sea on fishing trips. He had seen his village disappear from his sight, slowly, as the boat moved further away. He had seen the exclusive dance of the waves too. He was revisiting the moments spent with his father when the clouds appeared overhead, their shadows slowly spreading over parts of the sea. He was aware of the rush that lay hidden in these waters but had never enjoyed the serene beauty of the sea before in such a manner. He carefully observed the circles that the shadows of the hovering clouds made on the water's surface, those brown and black lines. Some dark and some faint. While deducing these shades and hues, his domestic problems surfaced in his thoughts. He could see the shadows of financial inadequacies reflect on his mother's face after his father's death. He also observed that his uncle's visit to his house had become more regular. His uncle often came to meet his mother around dusk and left at the time of the morning prayers.

He kept staring at the waves and his mind tried figuring out what lay buried in the depths of the water.

He dived into the sea and closely looked at the colourful and enchanting fish of all sizes that playfully swam around. When a fish came close to him, he felt it had something to tell, maybe a story. In fact, he usually felt that the sea was always ready to reveal its hidden truths to him!

The first of May was the first day of Asrar's life in Mumbai.

A superfast train takes at least seven and a half hours to cover the distance between Ratnagiri and Mumbai. His friends Suleiman Vanu and Qasim Dalvi were well-versed with this city. They vividly described the hustle and rush of Mumbai through stories to their friends. So, during the journey the city was like a floating dream in their intoxicated eyes. They were impatient to see the city, to embrace its speed and become a part of its business. Asrar had seen so many films made on Mumbai—*Bombay*, *Satya* and *Sadak* were his favorites. In fact, he had seen *Bombay* several times and heard its songs on the tape recorder. He used to hum one song from the film quite often:

> *Tu hi re, tu hi re*
> *Tere bina mein kaise jiyoon.*
> *Aaja re, aaja re*
> *Yunhi tadpa na tu mujh ko.*
> *Jaan re, jaan re*
> *In sanso mein bas ja re.*
> *Chand re, chand re*
> *Aa ja dil ki zameen pe tu.*
> *Chahat hai agar*
> *Aake mujh se mil ja tu.*
> *Ya phir aisa kar,*
> *Dharti se mila de mujh ko.*
> *Tu hi re, Tu hi re*
> *Tere bina mein kaise jiyoon.*

The train reached Panvel station at around nine in the night. They deboarded the train, kept their luggage aside, freshened up a little and drank tea at a nearby stall. They got into a local train after that. This was Asrar's first journey in a local. There were few people in the compartment. He took a window seat. A few youths on the platform who were chatting jumped in as the train started. Even before it reached Vashi station, tall buildings all around, shopping malls, huge hoardings on the streets and the red, yellow and blue lights seemed to be pulling Asrar towards them. Asrar had never seen so many advertisements and such blinding lights! Before he could get completely lost in the magic of this glamorous light, the train entered the next station. Through the window he saw an ocean of people on the platform, which scared him for a second. Then he immediately recalled the various scenes of Mumbai that he had seen on the television where the crowds of Mumbai were beautifully showcased. Even before the train could stop completely, people started shouting and pushing each other to board. The coach was overflowing with passengers. Asrar silently observed them.

An inquisitive-looking boy asked him, 'Where are you going?'

'Bombai,' Asrar replied staring at him.

Wherever his answer was heard in the coach, the tired faces started smiling. Some even laughed at it.

A man, with smallpox marks on his face, smiled and remarked in a Bombay accent, 'This is Bambai!'

A Gujarati boy who had just boarded the coach and had secured seats for his friends mocked, 'These "bhaiyyas" are going to ruin Mumbai.'

'I'm not a "bhaiyya"!' Asrar immediately snapped.

This unexpected answer made the Gujarati boys smile. 'The moron must be a Bihari then,' one of them said and the others started laughing loudly.

'I am from Maharashtra,' Asrar clarified.

The Gujarati boy spat the mawa he was eating out of the window and said, 'Nowadays even Chinesewala have started calling themselves Marathi!'

The Gujarati boys again burst out in laughter. Suleiman could not resist speaking. He said loudly, '*Apla manus aahe re* [He is one of us].' Asrar and his friends started conversing in Konkani delicately dipped in Marathi.

The Gujarati boys fell silent. One of them also apologized. 'You see it isn't written on anyone's face where they come from.'

Asrar did not say anything. As a matter of fact, he did not even understand what was going on. Seeing that the Marathi-speaking boys were in a majority, the Gujarati boys were now quite polite. They offered Suleiman water and said, 'We are true *sainiks* too!'

The crowd reduced after a few stations. But the congregation of passengers at the station made Asrar inquisitive. He asked Qasim, 'So many people even at this late hour?'

'Till eleven nearly all stations are crowded.'

'Everything shuts down so early back home.'

'My friend, this is Mumbai. It is overflowing with people. You will soon get used to this place.'

Asrar smiled and resumed looking out of the window. He looked at the slums along the railway tracks with dreamy eyes and craving in his heart. It was already ten in the night, and he was amazed to see how there was still music and life in those huts. Old men, women and children were sitting outside their houses and were chatting away or busy working. Some houses had dirty old curtains covering their doors. Some doors were open, and he could see the light of the television emitted from the rooms. In a few areas film songs were being played at a loud volume. Young men and kids were dancing away to glory. In a dilapidated house near the track he could see four or five eunuchs standing in the dark, wearing bright, provocative clothes. At a little distance near the senghat tree, he noticed a few shadows. Asrar wanted to see the scene closely, but the train moved ahead. For some time the shining clothes and faces with garish make-up floated before his eyes and later slept in his unconscious. When the train stopped at the Kurla station, Asrar saw many burqa-clad women and bearded men. The men were dressed in a white kurta pyjama. Asrar immediately inquired from his friend, 'Is this "our" area?'

'Yes, this is Kurla, this is the area of the Qasais.'

'What do you mean?'

'I mean that this area has a good population of Qasais.'

'But in our village, they generally wear lungis. Do they wear white clothes here in Bombay?'

'No, no. The ones that you see on the station are Chilyas,' Dalvi tried explaining.

Asrar was inquisitive. 'Who are Chilyas?'

'They don't watch television. They belong to Gujarat. Initially, they were in the taxi business, but now they have taken to the business of hospitality and hotels as well.'

Asrar didn't say anything. He resumed looking outside the train.

He was lost in the grandeur of Mumbai. He stared at every tree, house, building, road, hoarding and flyover. The city seemed like an ocean to him which had a lot of hidden secrets in its heart.

The thought of the ocean reminded him of how a day before he was sitting on the seashore. The music of the waves had slowly entered his soul and merged with it. For a few seconds he could no longer see Mumbai because his eyes had beautiful images of water in front of them. He saw the disturbed sea. The sea, that was hitting its head on the shores, as if in anger. And in an instant, it fell silent. But the silence had much more to it. It was a mysterious silence with a hidden conspiracy. He saw that on the surface of the silent waters, the *Queen of the Sea* was floating slowly. His father was engrossed in a conversation with his friends. Suddenly, the silent waters roared, and one could see water till the end of the horizon. A whirlpool opened its mouth right under the boat. The boat whirled and took seven spins before the water swallowed it.

Only Abid Parkar did not drown.

The first of May was a holiday. It was Maharashtra Day.

The inhabitants of the Jamat Ki Kholi were lost in deep sleep. At fajr, the muezzin coughed thrice into the mike and began reciting the azan and Asrar woke up. It was the muezzin's regular habit to check the mic by coughing to ensure that his voice was audible and clear.

It so happened that in the madrasa where he had studied, every Thursday evening, his teacher, Maulvi Abdul Haq Bijnori, would

take him to a secluded place to feed him strawberry ice cream and
would say, '*La yajub, la hujub* (It won't melt, it won't melt).'

As an after-effect of that hardened ice cream, his throat was
always in a bad condition the next day and his voice was terrible
too. He had stopped eating ice cream but the permanent sore
throat had made his life difficult and saddened his soul. Hence,
it was a routine to check his voice and throat every morning
before azan.

Asrar was amazed that as soon as the sound of the azan from
the nearby mosque rose, he could also hear some clear and some
not-so-clear azan merging into each other from near and far and
falling on his ears. Some voices were shrill, some strong, some from
the throat and some were nasal. This collage of voices continued
for a long time. One voice overpowered another and the one from
far away felt close. The mic system of one muezzin got stuck at the
'meem' of '*Assalaat khairum minun naum*', and continued buzzing
with coarseness.

The urge to see Mumbai in the daylight was dancing in his chest.
This was the reason he woke up a couple of times during the
night. Right in the centre of the room was a faint zero-watt bulb
that was dimly lighting up the place. Asrar's eyeballs looked at the
bulb and its yellow light reflected in his eyes, as if the bulb was
looking for its own reflection in his eyes. The films had carved
images of Mumbai in his heart. He was soon going to face the
reality that Mumbai was. His brain was going through a chemical
or hormonal reaction that prevented sleep from overpowering
him. He was awake even in his sleep. His eyes were fixed on
the ceiling. He noticed that the building was quite old. Two big
planks of wood were carrying the weight of the small planks.
Near the window was a small *mori*. On top of a slab was a steel

water tank. An earthen pot was kept right next to it with a steel glass on top. He stared at the pot for some time in the yellow light, then got distracted and looked away. There was a hanger on the door on which properly folded trousers were hung. For a moment his imagination made him believe that the clothes on the hanger were actually people and it was their souls that slept on the beds. This triggered a smile on his face. He said to himself, 'So many rubbish thoughts cross my mind!'

His mind involuntarily started thinking about those who were sleeping in that room. There were fourteen of them. Their beds were right next to each other with very little space in between. Some were snoring in their sleep. He stared at them and thought—are they alive? What if one of them has died and no one gets to know about it till dawn? Uncontrollable thoughts took birth in his mind. But he had a lot of control over his tongue.

His eyes were fixed on the clock. In fact, in the faint light, he could feel the presence of the clock on the wall. The hands of the clock were not visible at all. He was sure that it did have hands. However, it didn't matter if he could not see them at that moment.

Asrar was about to search his thoughts for something else when he felt as if some people were passing by the door. Before he could hear anything, their voices drowned. He was reminded of the seventh grade, when so many times he would feel that someone had peeped into the classroom and disappeared without being noticed. He failed to see that person each time. On a couple of occasions, when he would turn the pages of his notebook while the teacher was away, he felt that someone had crossed the door. But by the time he ran to look, there was not a soul to be seen. One day, after much disappointment, he shared this little secret with Aslam Dhamaskar, his old friend since first grade. Aslam claimed, 'I know everything.'

'What do you know?' Asrar inquired without hiding his amazement.

Aslam started talking discreetly in a secretive tone. He used words and phrases from the library books that he had read. These books spoke about the world of magic and magicians. They mentioned stories of djinns and devils. Aslam said that in the library and in the area to the left of the building where tall grass grew during monsoons and where squirrels lived, he had felt someone's presence who simply passed by the classroom. It was just a feeling, no one could see that person. Sometimes one imagined that the mysterious person was covered in white, had a long white beard and his face shone brightly. Aslam had also told his father about this. His father used to clean the mosque and head the prayers in the absence of the imam. Aslam said that because his father knew every person in the village and in the surrounding villages and went for special congregations organized by the Tablighi Jamat, he knew of many such incidents.

Asrar seemed interested and agreed with Aslam, thereby giving him the confidence to speak further. He put his hands around Asrar's shoulders and told him that there used to be a small mosque a hundred years ago on the land where the school stood now. Djinns offered namaz in that mosque. The British rendered it empty and useless and gave it away to one of their rich loyalists who claimed to be Sir Syed Ahmad Khan's friends, for building a school. The year the school was inaugurated the man died a painful and mysterious death. Some say that the djinns took him to the hills near the sea and threw him in the deep waters. His body was found after many days on the shores of Mabadmorpho. The elderly say that his entire body had no wounds or any other signs except a huge hole in the place of his heart. The police was called. They sent his body to the government hospital. Some villagers went to the hospital and on returning told everyone that the heart was missing from the body. This traumatized the villagers.

There was a wise old man who lived in the village during that time. After his death, his mazar was built adjoining the school. Everyone in the village called him Peer Sahib. They related the story of the rich man to him. He remained silent for some time and then quietly said, 'The djinns eat the hearts of those who destroy their dwelling.'

His words spread like wildfire and reached the house of the rich man. Before the fortieth day of his death, his family constructed a mosque in the school campus. For many years, people kept offering namaz in that building. A few years back the mosque was taken down and a bigger one was built to accommodate the growing population of the village. And this was the mosque where good djinns lived. 'We see them sometimes, but they never harm anyone,' Aslam said, concluding his story. After hearing the narrative, Asrar regretted not offering namaz at that mosque ever. From then on he started offering namaz in that mosque every Friday and instead of listening to the sermons, he would stare at the walls, the ceiling and the chandeliers. He felt that it was possible that a djinn was sitting somewhere around listening to the cleric's sermon.

When this story of the past crossed his mind, he was forced to think, was it a djinn who had just crossed the door of this room?

'Why will Mumbai have djinns, it'll have ghosts!' These words involuntarily fell out of his mouth.

Aslam was lying right next to Asrar. He turned towards him and said, 'Get up, it is nearly morning!'

'Aslam, are you listening to me?'

Aslam did not open his eyes. Asrar understood that he was in a deep sleep; an attempt to wake him up would be futile. He turned over and closed his eyes. Coincidentally, he fell asleep. When he woke up, he was the only one lying down. The rest were having breakfast.

The door and windows were open, and there was light in the room. The sudden exposure to sunlight was blinding. Asrar shut his eyes in reflex. That very moment he realized that he had just seen a dream. But what was it that he saw? He could not recollect. The only thing that he remembered was that he was an ascetic, wandering in a jungle. He was old and everything around was black. Black, tall trees reached up till the sky. The sun's rays were incapable of finding a way through those giant trees to enter the jungle. The black soil had scattered grass growing on it, which was also black. He saw a few butterflies flying, they happened to be black in colour too. He was amazed and worried at the same time. He started reciting some verses from the Quran. He was convinced that the verses had a lot of power. He started reciting the Surah Yaseen and continued walking in one direction.

After walking a little further, he saw black liquid flowing on the ground and realized that it was a river! The water was black! Disappointed, he sat on the bank when he saw a white boat-like thing approaching him, slowly, from a distance. It was a boat indeed. When it came closer, he saw a woman seated on it. She was clad in a green sari paired with a saffron blouse. When he could clearly see the woman, he noticed a mark of kumkum on her forehead, heavy silver bangles around her wrists and a golden necklace around her neck. She wore a nine-yard sari. The sari, delicately tucked at the back, reminded him of the enchanting portraits of goddesses Lakshmi and Saraswati that adorned religious calendars.

For Asrar, this woman was a godsend and the only ray of hope to help him escape this jungle. He started waving his hands in the air to grab her attention. The woman did not answer or wave back. But Asrar was content that the boat was coming towards him. In a few moments, it reached the shore. He stood spellbound. The woman left the boat and came to Asrar. Her facial expression was a mix of happiness and seriousness. She asked him, 'How did you manage to get to this place? There is no way which leads to this jungle.'

He looked at her and answered, 'I did not come on my own.'

'Whoever got you here has to be a resident of this place. No outsider can bring a stranger in here.'

'This place scares me. I really want to get out of here,' a scared
Asrar pleaded.

'I realize that you do not belong here and want to leave.'

'Yes. But who are you?' Asrar inquired.

'My name is Mumba. I am the keeper of all secrets that belong
to islands, oceans and jungles. When a resident, out of greed or
want, brings someone in here, it is me who rescues him,' she
answered in a comforting tone.

This made Asrar think. He did not see anyone there and he
told her so.

'You are an outsider, hence you cannot see anyone. Only the
inhabitants of this place can see each other.'

Before she could complete her answer, Asrar had another
question ready. He asked her why everything around was black in
colour, even the river.

Her eyes looked at the surroundings, and then she remarked,
'Your eyes have not yet opened enough to see the enchanting
beauty of this place!'

'What is so beautiful here?' He wished to know.

'Just look at this river. It is a river of the sweetest honey, the
taste of which remains embedded on the taste buds for seventy
years. The tree that gives you shade produces fruits that can destroy
a human being's hunger for the next thousand years. The floor has
no pebbles but precious gemstones and jewels whose sparks are like
a balm to the sore eyes.'

'But I can't . . .'

'Ah, I know that you cannot see all of this. This world reveals
its beauty only to its inhabitants. The butterflies that you see are
nymphs. Anyone who has had the opportunity to witness their
beauty will lose his mind. The words that I have to describe these
enchantresses do not belong to your language.'

'Anyway,' Mumba stopped. This was the only description that
she gave. She saw the wonderment on his face and asked him to sit
in the boat. 'This boat will take you to the place you've come from.'

He moved towards the boat, but his eyes were fixed on Mumba. As soon as he got into the vessel, he asked Mumba, 'But I can see you, as well as the colours of your clothes. Do you not belong here?'

She laughed but did not reply. He was still looking at her when he realized that the boat had left the shore and moved away. After a while, he could no longer see the shore. His heart wanted to see Mumba once more. He squinted his eyes to look harder and the view took him by surprise. The spot where Mumba was standing was now occupied by a white-clad woman. Her face shone like the brightness of the full moon. He immediately recalled that she resembled the djinn that had crossed his door in Jamat Ki Kholi. Before he could see her to his heart's content, someone had pushed the door of the room very loudly, waking him up. And this was the time when all the others in the room were having breakfast.

Seeing that Asrar had woken up, Aslam called out, 'Brother, you slept off during your attempt to wake me up?'

He looked at Aslam and recollected that he tried waking him up during the time of the morning azan.

Suleiman had a cup of tea in his hand. He turned towards Asrar and instructed him, 'Boy, get ready immediately, we need to go on an outing!'

'I suggest you bathe first, before the water stops running in the tap,' said Saleem, who had been living in the kholi for years and in some way or the other had become a caretaker of the place.

'Remember, you need to queue up for the toilet outside, so better hurry!' Qasim added while pressing an omelette between a bun. This made everyone smile.

Saleem remarked with annoyance, 'We have to stand in a line for everything—a line for the toilet, a line for this, a line for that.' He added an expletive towards the end of the sentence to substantiate the pain caused by queues. Asrar noticed his opened mouth. Saleem had a gold tooth, the tooth next to it had turned yellow, almost as if it was trying to replicate its neighbour's colour.

Asrar wondered how great an impact could an artificial tooth have on a natural one?

A boy entered the room and went on to wash his hands. He then turned towards Saleem and with utmost annoyance complained how the residents don't even flush after using the toilets and leave it dirty. Saleem replied, while pulling out with his fingers a strand of meat that was stuck in his teeth, 'Brother, this is exactly what these bastard bhaiyyas do.'

'Saleem Bhai, how do you possibly know who flushes and who doesn't. You did not see it for yourself!' said Mohammad Ali, who was rumoured to be in love with a Shia girl from northern India.

Qasim laughed at the latter part of the remark. 'You did not see it for yourself!'

Saleem looked at Qasim and said, 'He has relations with the bhaiyyas; that is exactly why he gets offended!'

Then he looked at Mohammad Ali and asked, 'Tell me honestly, isn't it true that . . .'

Mohammad Ali gave a crooked smile and put his hands in his pocket to take out the packet of *haathi-chhaap* tobacco. He started rubbing it on his other hand. He asked Saleem if he should prepare tobacco for him too.

Saleem wanted to continue with the previous conversation. 'Do not take me to be a fool!'

Mohammad Ali asked again, 'Tell me, should I make for you too?'

'Yes, sure,' Saleem replied.

All this while Asrar found this exchange very amusing.

Qasim again reminded Asrar that if he wanted to use the toilet, he'd better do it now or else take a bath because the taps would soon stop running.

'Oh yes, I will. But let me freshen up a bit before that.'

He advanced towards the door, then halted and asked Qasim for directions to the toilet.

'Go straight towards your left and you will find it,' instructed Mohammad Ali while handing tobacco to Saleem.

'Aye hero, take water from the *mori*,' said Saleem, putting tobacco in his mouth.

Asrar filled a plastic vessel with water and left the room.

The passage was dark. A little further to the left were two toilets. The door of one was open. He entered and, trying to close the door from inside, noticed that it was old and decaying. The bottom of the door was decomposing. The nearly perished bottom was covered with an iron sheet which had rusted over time. He tried latching the door again but in vain. He kept the water aside and in absolute darkness, attempted again, when he noticed a rope. He was reminded of his school washrooms that had such ropes tied to the nails of toilet doors to lock them up. He tied the rope in the same manner and sat down. It was dark around him. The stench that rose from the commode and entered his lungs via his nostrils was terrible. He had never faced such foul smell before. The stench maimed his intestines along with his heart and brain. He was trying to build up as much pressure as he could so that he could empty his bowels and rush out to breathe in fresh air again.

The darkness was slowly fading. In the little light that was now around, he noticed a used candle with half-burnt matchsticks lying in a corner. There were marks left by extinguished cigarette buds. He saw white insects crawling over each other on the decayed part of the door. Then he started staring at the commode. It looked like an ulcer. The ulcer had burst open at various places and was blistering now. Tiny, white insects were crawling over the blisters. One, two, ten, twenty, god knows how many! One of the white creatures was now attempting to crawl over Asrar's slippers. He immediately poured water over it. The insect was swept off. But the moment this water went into the commode, a burst of stench rose from it. It was as if the waves of the stench were hidden deep under the dump. He blocked his nostrils with his fingers and looked away. He was astonished. There were many obscene figures drawn on the wooden door in front of him. Some words in Hindi were also carelessly scribbled. At one place a genital was drawn with small and big circles. At another place a couplet had been inscribed:

Is anjuman mein aap ko aana hai baar baar
Deewar-o-dar ko gaur se pehchan lijiye

He started looking at another obscene drawing with great concentration. One corner of the door was adorned with the drawing of a woman's breast, one small and the other one larger with, 'only for the purpose of looking and not sucking' written next to them.

The face of Jamila Miss popped up in front of his eyes. She was his class teacher in the tenth standard and taught maths and science. Her house was nearly two kilometres from the school. Once, when the peon was absent, Asrar had carried the geometry notebooks to her house. Miss had corrected the notebooks in three or four days. She then asked Asrar to bring them from her house. She was a very hard-working and talented teacher, and her husband was also an educated man. He was the headmaster of a government school in some other district. Her only son was pursuing a course in hotel management from Mumbai. None of her relatives lived around this area. She herself was very busy with the job at the school and therefore many of her chores remained incomplete. She started calling Asrar regularly to assist her. Getting entries made in her bank passbook, paying the electricity bill, booking the gas cylinder, etc., were the chores that Asrar would do for her. Miss would make tea for him quite often. She served delicious glucose biscuits along with it. Asrar would generally refuse them, but while watching a television programme or film, he never realized when the biscuits vanished from the plate.

When Miss started trusting him completely, she asked questions about his personal life and family. Asrar elaborately explained everything about his family and household to her. His eyes watered while talking about his father's death. Miss Jamila also became emotional. Then she had put her head lovingly on Asrar's head and consoled him. From then on, whenever he went to Miss Jamila's house, he divulged all the stories and details of events that took place in Mabadmorpho. Sometimes he carried fresh fish along with him too. Once Miss pressured him into eating at her place and he gave in. He was interested in watching television at her house. He had told her that he didn't have a TV at home. It had broken down a couple of months ago and was yet to be repaired. Miss smiled and advised him to bring his schoolbag with him when he came to her house so that he could watch television and simultaneously study.

August was the month when it rained heavily in Ratnagiri. The thunder and lightning were terrifying.

Miss Jamila was cooking in the kitchen and Asrar was completing his homework in the drawing room. Miss felt that it was getting dark outside and it might rain. She asked Asrar to bring the clothes inside and shut the doors and windows. While closing the windows he stared at the old-fashioned houses of Mabadmorpho which were now shrouded in a mysterious darkness. The sea looked black, as if it were merged with a sky made of coal tar. The grey clouds were spreading in the sky and the west winds were dancing through the trees. A few birds flew and vanished between the mango and tamarind trees. There was a jamun tree adjacent to the window. A bat lived on it. On one branch sat a tiny, golden-feathered bird. She would sing softly at short intervals. Her voice made the body of the bat vibrate. It was widely believed in Mabadmorpho that the tree where bats dwelled was a meeting place for the wandering souls of the dead. Asrar looked at the bat and started thinking about the golden bird. What if she was a soul waiting for someone?

He closed the window and predicted, 'Jamila Baji, it looks as if it is going to rain quiet heavily!'

'Yes, it has suddenly got dark outside.'

Before Asrar could continue the conversation, the wind became stronger, and it started pouring.

He drew the curtain aside and looked outside the window. Jamila Miss lived on the hill. Mabadmorpho started from where the slope of the hill ended. The boundary of the small village merged with the Arabian Sea. From the window he could see the dancing waves of the sea as well as the drenched roofs of the houses in Mabadmorpho, but it was dark outside, and everything was a blur that day. He moved on to stare at the bat on the jamun tree. When the wind changed its direction, the raindrops could be seen falling on the windowpane. When he turned towards the television, he saw black dots covering the screen. 'Miss, the cable is gone,' he said in a loud voice. 'Then switch off the television,' instructed Jamila.

Asrar switched off the TV and started reading his book. The sound of the rain was getting increasingly louder. His concentration kept slipping as he wanted to look out of the window. The book felt like a burden to his eyes. He kept it aside and drew the curtains of the window again. Miss also came into the drawing room. He sat on a table, gaping at the beautiful and blurred sight across the glass window. Jamila put a chair next to the table and went back into the kitchen and returned with a cup of tea and a plate of bhajiya. She called out to Asrar. He turned and immediately jumped off the table to grab the plate from Jamila's hands and said, 'Miss, *aap bhi na* [Why did you have to take the trouble?]!'

She smiled.

'Arre baba, look how it is raining. The taste of the tea will be enhanced by the bhajiya,' she said and went towards the kitchen. She got herself a cup of tea. They were sitting next to the window, sipping the chai and enjoying the fries. The change of weather and the drop in temperature actually made the snack taste even better. She told him all about her village in Sholapur. Every summer vacation she went home, where her four sisters and two brothers lived. Her father had passed away and her old mother lived with her eldest brother. He listened to her attentively. He had known her since seventh grade and thoroughly enjoyed her teaching, but it was his first encounter with her personal life. He started asking her questions. These questions opened up some old pages of her past. A little later, when the evening azan was faintly heard, she covered her head with a corner of her sari and said with a smile on her face, '*Jitna sunaw kam hai baba* [The stories are never-ending].'

Asrar smiled too.

The intensity of the strong winds and the heavy downpour could be seen through the falling trees and the huge raindrops. Suddenly, a loud thud was heard. Asrar peered out of the window. It sounded like something had fallen down. Jamila also stood up. '*Arre baap re baap*, the mango tree right next to the jamun has fallen,' Asrar said in a worried tone. '*Ya mere Allah!*' she uttered in reflex. She looked down from the window and remarked, '*Barish bhi kaisi ho rahi hai, kya tufan bifan aata kya* [What kind of rain is it? Do you think a storm is approaching]?'

'It seems so. The road towards Mabadmorpho has been blocked because of the fallen tree. Should I go downstairs and check?'

Miss pointed towards an umbrella and asked Asrar to carry it with him. He went out of the door and saw that a lot of water had collected on the stairs. He descended the stairs carefully and left the building. He opened the umbrella and proceeded towards the gate. The road that went to Mabadmorpho was now blocked by the fallen mango tree. The tree was quite old. A few more people came out of the building. One of them had a torch with him. He could now see a little light near the gate. The shower was heavy. The winds were overturning the umbrellas. A man, whose face Asrar didn't see clearly, advised that they wait for the rains to subside and then come back and take a look at the fallen tree.

Another man readily agreed and said, '*Hau master, abhi to bhotich barish ho rahi hai* [Yes, master, it is raining heavily]. We'd better get back to our homes!'

They returned. Asrar went near the gate and tried looking in vain for a small opening, hoping that might make it possible for him to reach Mabadmorpho in spite of the blockade. No sooner had he turn towards the building than a strong gust of wind overturned his umbrella. Before he could get the umbrella back in shape, he was already drenched. He ran towards the building. While climbing the stairs he could hear more trees fall. He had witnessed such rain three or four years ago when the intensity of the winds had blown away twelve to thirteen temporary tiles from the roof, turning his house into a small pond. He paused at the first floor to look at the jamun tree that was dancing in the wind.

In a few moments he realized that the tree was not just dancing but it also smelt sweet. This smell entered his nostrils. But the rain and storm did not allow him to fully enjoy the fragrance. He rang the bell to Jamila Miss's house but started knocking once he realized that there was a power cut in the building. Miss opened the door. The room was dimly lit by a faint candle in the corner.

'Miss, I got drenched.'

She picked up the candle and looked at Asrar from top to bottom. Water was dripping from his clothes.

She asked him to wash himself in the bathroom. He entered the house. Miss took the umbrella from him, and he started taking big strides towards the bathroom. It was dark in there.

Miss closed the main door and took out a candle from the box near the television. She lighted the candle and gave it to Asrar to put inside the bathroom. When Asrar bent to fix it on the floor, the candle went off. 'Wait, I will get the matchsticks,' her voice echoed in the darkness. His drenched body stood silently in the dark. It is said that the eyes of the body are powerful.

Miss was searching for matchsticks near the gas stove in the kitchen, but the eyes of her body too were staring at the quiet and drenched body of Asrar. The drenched body stood silently in the darkness. Physical attraction is impromptu and unscripted. It could be felt at any moment. The realization of this attraction sent a strange shiver through Jamila's body, though her mind discarded the thoughts immediately. Asrar's body was a closed dome, oblivious to external murmurs.

However, it was also true that right then the locks of the dome had loosened and could break any moment.

Miss lighted the matchstick and asked Asrar, 'Where is the candle?'

'Right here in my hand.'

Miss entered the faintly lit bathroom. 'Keep the candle in one corner.'

Asrar sat down. The matchstick in Jamila's hand went out.

She sat next to him and took out another matchstick to light. In its light she saw Asrar sitting on his knees. He was holding the candle in his hands. She let the matchstick light it. Then Asrar placed the candle on the floor. While getting up she told Asrar that she would get him a T-shirt and a lungi. He said nothing in reply and kept sitting there, in silence. Miss took out her husband's clothes and gave it to him. Asrar immediately shut the bathroom door. The situation perplexed him very much. The running tap was pouring water into the bucket. He could hear the music of the raindrops through the glass panes of the windows.

The candlelight made it possible for him to see all the things in the bathroom. His eyes fell upon the hanger. On it were two blouses and a bra that belonged to Miss. His hands involuntary moved to touch the bra. He had never held one in his hands before. He felt a weird desire. He was oblivious of the depths and layers from where these desires arose. While touching the protruded part of the bra, his thoughts began to race. Jamila Miss slowly began entering his imagination like the light which slowly spreads from a little fire. He rubbed that area on his eyes and kissed it. Suddenly, the incorrectness of the situation made him scold himself, 'You call her baji and then think of her in such a manner?' The bucket was now full. He removed his clothes and poured water on his feet; then he realized that there was no towel in the bathroom. He immediately wore his clothes and opened the door thinking that he would ask Miss for a towel. He opened the door and saw her standing there with a towel in her hands.

'Arre, Miss, *shukriya*,' he said and shut the door again. Miss had a smile on her face. The door was closed but she kept standing there for a while. What did she have in her heart? How much was she able to recognize the stirrings of her inner self? To what extent did she feel her overpowering desires? She didn't know, but she was definitely surprised. She was surprised that desire didn't have a religion. It was so powerful that all excuses of morality were destroyed within a few moments and the heart responded to bodily passions.

She smiled and said to herself, '*Bachcha hai abhi, kachcha hai abhi* [He is a child and still naive]!' She went back to the drawing room and sat down. Her face was blushing at the thought that her mind could still nurture such absurd ideas. Asrar was still bathing inside. While applying soap on his body, his hands reached where there was a stream of desires, from where all the passions arose. He had risen, drowned and sailed on the waves of desire since last year. He placed his hands on his member and tried imagining those waves of desire that he had tested the previous year through the intoxication of masturbation. Suddenly, he could see the jamun tree, the bat and the golden bird that he had seen that day. In that one moment his mind had millions of thoughts encompassed within itself. He was in the bathroom for not more than ten minutes, but those minutes seemed to last for a thousand hours in his mind. Innumerable faces, scenes, imaginings and thoughts walked through his brain like a caravan in the light and vanished in the darkness of the unconscious.

He was a little hesitant in sitting near Miss Jamila in a T-shirt and lungi. She was well aware of this and made an attempt to overcome the awkwardness of the situation and asked, 'To which side did the mango tree fall?'

'Right in front of the gate, Miss. The entire road is blocked. It can be cleared only once the rain stops!'

'All right.' She looked outside the window. It was pouring.

'Miss, I hope god stops the rain soon.'

'If it doesn't stop then . . .?' she said in a mischievous tone.

'*Meri watt lag jayegi*,' he replied.

'What do you mean?'

'I meant to say that it will be a problem for me to go back.'

'Is there a telephone in your house? Or anywhere near your house? You can make a call from my mobile phone and inform them that you will be late and if the rain doesn't stop, you will spend the night here.'

Asrar informed his neighbour and asked him to convey the message to his mother.

Miss went to the kitchen to cook dal.

Asrar sat comfortably on the sofa and fell asleep.

The innocence on his face was accentuated by the dim light of the candle. Jamila peeped twice from the kitchen to steal a glance at him asleep. After finishing her cooking, she came and sat near Asrar. She felt happy seeing him dressed in her husband's clothes. The torrential rain had not rested yet. Nor did the thunderous winds contain themselves. The music of the heavy drops was echoing in her ears. In this music there was a magical calm. After many days, in fact, many years, she felt vibrant. She had no justification for this, nor did she have any clear understanding of it. It was just a feeling. In this state of her mind, she was just a woman. All the dust around her had vanished and she was of her own being. The solitude of being in a womb of desires. Jamila was overwhelmed by that vibrant feeling in her womb at that moment.

The food was ready, but Asrar was still asleep.

Jamila at times leaned on the window and looked outside at the rain or looked at Asrar while he slept. A few moments later, there was fierce lightning which woke Asrar up. The sound scared Jamila too. Asrar was amazed that he had slept for so long. 'Sorry, Miss, I fell asleep. It sounds like thunder and lightning.'

'Good that you took some rest. Yes, there was a thunderbolt,' she said while seating herself in the chair.

The dark sky, which could be seen through the windows, now had remnants of the recent lightning. Some bolts spread themselves in the sky and some came so close as if to touch the buildings. They stood near the window, witnessing the fearful circus in the sky.

The candle kept on the table went off. The bolts of lightning in the skies were playing a very dangerous game of firecrackers. Suddenly, a bolt darted towards them, as if to strike the window. Jamila responded in a reflex of fear. No sooner had she turn from the window than her foot slipped. Asrar held her or else she would have fallen on the floor. 'Do not be scared, Miss; this is a very common occurrence. The lightning bolt has fallen somewhere far.'

'I got really scared!' Jamila said, pulling herself together. She stood again, leaning on the window. Her hand was in Asrar's hand. Together, they looked at the havoc-causing bolts and sparks in the sky outside the window. They could also feel the thunder within themselves which made the soul float. The windows to the body were opened up by the warm desires of the being. This warmth had a hidden magic to it. The desires of the being found their own course.

The two were under the misconception that the feeling that had sent sparks through their respective bodies, and the thoughts that were like bolts to them were hidden from each other. There still existed an innocent distrust between the two. Maybe they were unaware that desires find a home in each body, in each soil. Those who know are aware that desires have no specific season to be born in. When desires rise from their slumber, they can cross the highest walls and boundaries. Desires are the essence of the mud dough that made Adam. Desire leads to a metamorphosis of the body. The being transforms into varied symbols, characteristics and appearances. The man transforms into an animal of an unknown epoch, while the woman changes into an archaic bird or some other phenomenon. The being searches for its pinnacle and satiation in other beings. Desires are very opportunistic. The poison of desire is very overpowering. The heart stops and the brain sleeps under the veil of oblivion. The 'self' drowns in complete darkness while the being changes its attire. In this darkness, the soul participates in this transformation.

Asrar turned towards Miss, she lifted her eyes. Their eyes were warm. Miss also turned towards him. Desire was alive in each soil. Jamila's fingers intertwined involuntarily with Asrar's. Their eyes were searching in each other for the pinnacle of their being. The rain outside was deafening. There were lightning bolts, and the west winds were encircling the building with fearful groans. The winds were spirited and mad. They were revolving around trees and branches, uprooting them.

Miss came closer to him. Desire leads to a metamorphosis of the body. Their noses touched, and in the warmth of their eyes red sparks rose and drowned as if in a whirlpool. Desires acquainted the being with the taste of metamorphosis. The taste of each other's tongues made them forget their existence. They sat on the floor. Miss transformed into a fierce lioness. She entrenched her paws into Asrar's back and started chewing on his bones. She felt the taste of his heart's nectar on her lips which, like a wave of light, intoxicated her soul.

They lay there till morning, smashed with the defeat of their being. When Asrar woke up and looked at Miss, who was lying next to him, he noticed that one of her breasts was smaller than the other. He smiled. He got up and went to the bathroom. The candle there had already melted. He looked out of the window. The rain had stopped. Very light rays of the sun could be seen scattered in the sky.

A lot of other things were also written on the latrine door. He read them all. During this time, he had forgotten the innumerable insects in the commode. The foul smell had already lost its strength. The reminiscence of Miss Jamila had silenced the chaos inside him a little. When he exited the toilet, he saw a man standing there. He had a tiny container in one hand which was filled with water and a beedi in the other. He looked at Asrar and said in a condescending tone, '*Kya be, so gaya tha kya* [Were you sleeping]? I knocked at least thrice!'

Asrar lowered his gaze and apologized, 'Sorry!'

'*Sorry ka bachcha, aa jate hain saale* [What use is your sorry? God knows where these people with their sorrys come from].' The man entered the latrine groaning and mumbling to himself.

2

Will I Find a Way to Return if I Wish?
(*Mujhe Bhi Rah Na Milegi Jo Lautna Chahun*)

Jamat Ki Kholi was on the ground floor of a very old and dilapidated three-storey building. All the residents living there had followed the *pagadi* renting system for the last five decades. The owner of the building belonged to a business family and was a pious man. The building was decaying but the residents didn't want to get it reconstructed.

When Asrar came out of the building, the summer sun of May dazzled his eyes. There were two more boys with Asrar who had come to Mumbai for the first time. The moment they exited the kholi, it seemed as if they had turned into statues. They gaped at the tall buildings, the windows, curtains on the windows, the roads, the people on the roads and the clothes that the passers-by were wearing. Along the road and on the footpath, till their eyes could see, there were hawkers and vendors lined up. The one in front of them was selling children's clothes, rosaries, zamzam (holy water), various books of prayers, toothpaste, caps and copies of the Quran.

A black dog slept comfortably under the stall. Asrar looked at the dog. Half of its body was submerged in the dirty water collected near the footpath. Its eyes were closed and a big, fat, lazy fly sat on its nose. The nose was like a tunnel for the petty fly. Mumbai itself seems like a tunnel to newcomers.

Asrar spotted three or four holes dug in the footpath. The dog suddenly waved its tail and shooed away the mouse that was nibbling at the trash stuck to its tail. The mouse ran into the nearest hole. At the same time, two mice, fighting with each other, came out of the second hole and used the dog as a bridge to enter the drain. The fly had flown after this commotion, but the lazy dog lay there unperturbed. Maybe this was his everyday life. While spending his life on the footpath, he had risen above avenging the small transgressions of the lowly mice. When Asrar's eyes accustomed themselves to the brightness, he saw a few perfume shops nearby. Their signboards were written in Arabic calligraphy. One shop was named 'Khalis Atariyat-e-Jameel-ul Aasam'. The shop was open. Small and beautiful glass bottles of varied shapes and sizes filled with attar adorned the shop.

'Where are you lost?' Mohammad Ali wondered, putting his hand on Asrar's shoulder. 'There is so much more to be seen.'

They would not have walked more than a few feet when the sight of the Minara mosque stopped them. Saleem uttered a few lines in its praise and told them how the area would be lit up during the month of Ramzan and would overflow with people. So much so that there would be no place to even put your foot down on the ground. Qasim playfully remarked, 'So if there is no place to put your feet, then where do people put their feet?' This made everyone laugh. Saleem stayed silent but later followed it up with a brief smile. Mohammad Ali bought three paans from the shop around the corner. The beauty of the inscriptions and engravings on the Minara mosque had filled Asrar with awe. He kept gaping at them for a long time. He was unaware that those minarets had been witness to the springs and the dark nights of this city. They had witnessed the elaborate gatherings and long processions, the chaos and the political battles. They had watched the discriminations of creed and religion.

They knew the uniformed policemen who had killed many barbarically in the 'Umar Ali Usman Lungi Cut Bakery' riots but were left unpunished by the court. These minarets had also seen Imam Mehjural Bukhari al Maaroof Hijrul Ghilman in the dark nights helping put RDX boxes on the silent roads. No one ever knew whose work it was but for the minarets. This matter remained the subject of many debates till the imam was murdered a few kilometres away from the mosque. Asrar was intrigued by the mosque. He was sure that the facades and minarets were home to a number of djinns.

Asrar was unaware of the doom that the surrounding areas had witnessed repeatedly, such events as had made these minarets ashamed and sad. They remembered the day when thousands of Muslims had gathered protesting against 'Salman *vald* Mansoor al Halaj aka Kitabul Tawaseen' and the police had blindly opened fire on the crowd. Dozens of young men had been pushed into the dark tunnel of death. The drain that ran below the minarets had been overflowing with blood. The bloodshed was the result of the firing by the police, which had fired not just bullets but hatred. It is said that blood in dirty water loses its smell but the devs and djinns have the ability to smell this fresh blood. It is also said that when there is bloodshed of innocents on Mohammad Ali Road, the blood flows underground through the drains to reach the temple of Mumba Devi before heading to the sea.

It is believed that the demons dance a disturbing *tandav* in the courtyards of the temple. It is possible that these demons belong to the same lineage of blood-drinking demons who had been defeated by Mumba Devi. This dance of annihilation is done to add on to the sorrows and grief of Mumba Devi. After the dance, these demons enter the drains which carry the blood. They enter the tunnels under the ground and separate the water from the blood and drink the blood of the innocents that comes from Mohammad Ali Road. They come and dance again in front of Mumba Devi's temple after drinking the blood. This aggravates her anger but because she has promised Brahma never to attack the demons till the seven islands of Mumbai are in their original state, she suppresses her anger. Mumba was told by Brahma that it would rain for forty nights and days on the seven islands and everything will be destroyed. All islands would submerge. Even history would end. The submerged islands will reappear as one big island. After forty years of this happening a demon named Gujaratam Desham Kaladam would rule it. When all limits of barbarism, cruelty, injustice would reach a pinnacle, the walls of the Mumba Devi temple which had stayed intact even after being submerged would break open and Mumba Devi would rise to defeat the demon. Brahma had foretold the battle between the devi and the demon but had not predicted the result of the battle. That is exactly why there is anger and fierceness on the Devi's face along with deep thought and wonder.

Mohammad Ali gave Saleem a paan, which he put in his mouth. The lime that had come gratis with the paan was placed on the tongue.

They moved ahead.

Cars, taxis and buses were crawling on Mohammad Ali Road. People were crossing the street by running in front of these vehicles. The horns were being relentlessly blown. A few people were talking loudly at the turn of the road. Below the JJ Flyover, two hand-rickshaw pullers were sitting on their vehicles and smoking. A taxi driver was arguing with a Bohra woman. A crippled man standing opposite to this woman, wearing a green cap, was waiting in anticipation of alms, as if his wish would be granted immediately after the argument ends. Even the beggars in Mumbai seemed to be very hopeful. Asrar really liked the red, green and blue beads around the beggar's neck. The argument had not ended when a young girl also joined the beggar in spreading her hands in the hope of alms. The lame beggar did not like the girl's presence. He hit the girl on the hip with his crutch. She ran but before crossing the road hurled a few abuses at the beggar which were drowned in the noise of the traffic. No one noticed this incident. Asrar kept staring at the flyover which looked like a sleeping anaconda in the sunlight.

On Mohammad Ali Road, the smell of delicious sweets from the Umar Ali Usman sweet shop, filled the air. They looked at the nankhatai. A boy wearing a lungi entered the shop with a tray of sweets on his head. The smell of the fresh sweets attracted Qasim's attention the most. He immediately asked the boy, 'Which mithai is this?'

'Aflatoon,' the boy replied.

Mohammad Ali asked Qasim, 'Do you want to try it?'

Without waiting for his answer, Mohammad Ali bought half a kilo of aflatoon and offered it to the newcomers.

After spitting out the betel juice, Mohammad Ali showed off his knowledge of various kinds of sweets in Mumbai. Saleem added that even the sweets at the Dum Dum shop were very delicious. They were relishing the sweets when a few kids rushed towards them with outspread hands, asking for a share. One boy was only wearing trousers. The oldest boy wore a torn cap. Saleem spat his betel juice on the footpath and irritably said, '*Kya re kaam dhanda nahi hai? Chal hat* [Don't you have any other work? Get lost].'

When the older boy pointed towards the younger one's mouth, probably to indicate hunger, Mohammad Ali said, '*Abe saale, tu idharich piche ki footpath par rahta hai na* [Don't you live in these parts, on the footpath behind]?'

The boy stared at Mohammad Ali. He told the newcomers that these kids were actually drug addicts. They beg and eat and are found sloshed. On hearing this, the boys ran away. There was routine traffic on the roads. Two buses going towards Churchgate arrived. They were still indulging in aflatoon when Saleem said, 'The buses are empty, we should catch them.'

They boarded a double-decker bus which had empty seats on the top floor. Asrar sat next to Mohammad Ali on the front seats. Both belonged to the same village but were meeting for the first time. Ali told Asrar that he worked with a diamond businessman and if Asrar wanted, he could put in a word for him. Asrar said that he would discuss it with Qasim before making a decision. The bus reached Haj House. The engraved verses from the Quran on the building made Asrar happy. He asked Mohammad Ali, 'Such a tall mosque?'

'It is the Haj House.' Mohammad Ali smiled.

'What do you mean by Haj House? Don't people go to Saudi Arabia for the pilgrimage?' Qasim inquired.

'You idiot, the entire world knows that the pilgrims go to Saudi; this place makes all the arrangements for them,' Mohammad Ali explained.

Asrar silently kept looking at the grandeur of the building. He had never seen something as beautiful as this. Mohammad Ali had shown him the buildings of Churchgate station, Anjuman-e-Islam and the *Times of India* and gave him the little information that he had acquired. Asrar was impressed with Mohammad Ali's knowledge.

The Mumbai that he saw after crossing the Churchgate signal was very different from the Mumbai he had seen on Mohammad Ali Road and at the Umar Ali Usman sweet shop. But he did not ask any questions; his eyes widened as he gaped at the Mumbai that can take your heart away.

They deboarded the bus at a little distance from the Taj hotel. The newcomers looked at the Taj hotel from the Gateway of India with much intensity, as if to carve and save it in their memories forever. Before the magnificent building they felt small and inconsequential. The intimidating sight of the hotel only seemed to enhance its grandeur in their hearts. The place where they were

standing would be the same spot from where the world media
would report the terrorist attack on the hotel five years hence. At
that point these friends would remember this memorable journey
to the Gateway of India and the Taj hotel.

Seven years later, during the last days of July, on a Sunday
afternoon in the room of the jamat, Mohammad Ali dreamt of
Asrar. They talked for long about life. In the dream, Asrar lived in
some other country. He started talking about the barbaric terrorist
attack in detail, to which Asrar replied, 'I am no longer there
where the terrorists live. What will I do with all the information?'
This saddened Mohammad Ali. He opened his eyes and felt the
tears. He intensely missed Asrar. He got up and hired a taxi to
Haji Ali dargah. He sat in a corner in the courtyard of the dargah,
engrossed in Asrar's memories. He cried for long.

Saleem narrated the history of the Gateway of India and bought
them ice creams. After that, he said there was a surprise in store for
them that day. All of them asked in unison, 'What, what, what?'

Saleem smiled and repeated in Arabic, '*Innalllah ma'as sabreen*
[God is with those who keep patience].'

'To hell with patience, please tell us!' Qasim snapped
impatiently.

'Aslam Bhai might invite us for dinner,' Dhamaskar said.

'We can make food at the room itself,' said Saleem.

'Are you taking us to the movies?' Suleiman asked.

'These kids are coming to Mumbai for the first time, tell
them quickly,' Mohammad Ali said to Suleiman before Aslam
could react.

'Come with me, all of you,' instructed Saleem.

They followed him to the back of the Gateway of India where
the concrete stairs descended into the sea.

Saleem's friend had four ferryboats that took tourists for a ride. Saleem had arranged this ride on the sea for all of them. They climbed into the boat, and when it was fully packed, the journey started. They were now enjoying the city, brightly lit by the sun, from the water. Mumbai was retreating from their vision. To see the city from the coast as one goes further into the sea was an experience. To piece together the facades and domes of the Taj hotel into one's vision was a novelty. The breeze from the sea carried with it salt and coolness. The sea gave rise to grief in Asrar's heart.

That grief turned the water into a whirlpool in front of his eyes. It was small, but the water that fed the whirlpool was blood red in color. In fact, it wasn't water—it was blood. This blood was not just whirling but gave rise to thousands of smaller whirlpools of blood within. He could see his father's face in each one of them. For more than four minutes, these whirlpools kept dancing in front of his eyes. He wanted to drill his retina so that the blood in his eyes spewed out like fountains. At times, the wish to be covered in his own blood filled his heart. Though Jamila Miss may have helped in making this wish fade away, it would sometimes come back. He smiled. He could now see Jamila Miss in his eyes. The short journey with her on the sea was treasured in the casket of his heart. It was fresh again.

What had happened on that evening of torrential rain had changed the equation between Jamila and Asrar. Every second or third day, Jamila Miss simplified the complexities of chemistry, biology and algebra for him. She taught him from the textbook *The Life Cycle and Mapping Our Genes* in the most interesting way. She had made topics like menstruation, reproductive system and other difficult ones easy and explained the importance of each. Ovaries, uterus, fallopian tubes and vagina—she had explained these difficult terms to him. She had also expressed her disagreement with the function and characteristics of the vagina and the penis narrated in the book. The function of the vagina in the book was explained as 'the area for release of menstruation, of childbirth and the area through which the sperm passes'. And the function of the penis was given as 'to help sperms reach the ovaries'. Jamila Miss said that these organs were not just for reproduction, but also to express the passionate desire of love. They were the bridge between the soul, body and emotions.

One day Miss told him that she wanted to go sailing to the sea to witness how fish were hunted.

'Fish get themselves captured on their own,' was Asrar's immediate response.

She looked shocked.

He realized that the sentence he'd uttered had hidden meanings which he had not intended to express.

He wanted to explain when Miss said, 'The weather should also be appropriate for it, eh?'

She had said it with a lot of passion and mischief!

He smiled. Her smile followed.

In spite of that, he elaborately told her what he meant. She enjoyed his unnecessary justification.

Asrar shared with her the nuances of fishing at sea, with his head on her lap. He told her how his father had worked on other boats as a *tandel* (apprentice) before starting his own business. He knew by the flow of water, its temperature, waves and movements where to find what kind of fish. This extensive knowledge that Asrar had of the sea made her want to experience the water even more. Asrar promised her a sea journey soon. He told this to his mother and asked her to talk to his uncle. His mother spoke to his uncle, and he agreed.

After a week, on a Saturday evening, Jamila Miss, his mother, uncle, two servants and Asrar boarded the boat. The fuel-driven boat had been purchased by Asrar's uncle on a bank loan a year ago. It had a cabin where five to six people could be accommodated. Near the cabin was a window-like door through which the servants had loaded the basement with necessities. The front of the boat was unusually spacious. There was enough space for fifteen to twenty people to stand. On that day, instead of fishing, they were on an excursion. Jamila Miss and Asrar's mother and uncle were chatting away standing at the front of the cabin. Asrar sat inside. The boat moved from the jetty after the anchor was lifted.

It was a memorable experience for Miss to sit on the boat and watch the centuries-old fort at Ratnagiri from the sea. The fort was built on a mountain. It was impossible to climb the mountain from the side of the sea. Her eyes could see a tunnel under the mountain. Who knows, it may have been a secret escape route in days gone by? She wondered if one could see the blue and green shades of the sea water standing on the walls of the fort and looking down. On the left of the fort there was a large stretch of red soil. The rains would transform it into a layer of greenery. She had been to the fort many times. Once she had spent five hours under a weak wall of the fort with Asrar. Now she was looking at the fort from a very exclusive angle. She was filled with surprise and happiness. Awestruck. When the boat took a turn, it looked as if the lighthouse stood against the sunlight. Her eyes met the sunlight spread on the waves and was dazzled by its intensity. She took out her sunglasses from her purse and wore them. Asrar's mother liked her glasses and told his uncle, 'These glasses look really good on Madam.'

'*Madam bhi achchi dikhti hai* [Madam also looks good] . . .' He stopped midway and touched his beard before remarking, 'Subhanallah!'

Asrar's mother headed towards the cabin, smiling. The servants were busy talking while chewing tobacco at the back of the cabin. The boat entered the coastal strip of Rajiwade. Asrar's mother came out of the cabin with a thermos and plastic glasses. Asrar was carrying biscuit packets. Rajiwade was an old residential area. The sea took the shape of a bay here. The water looked muddier. Most residents in this area were in the fish business. The majority among them used small boats to catch crabs. The string of small houses on the mountain looked heartwarming from the sea. There was a small island that was covered with sea flora. Asrar's mother poured tea into the cups while Asrar laid out biscuits on the plate. The large red sun was coming closer to the horizon. The green bushes on the small island sparkled in the red rays of the sun. The breeze blowing had its own rhythm and salty tang. It gave a special flavour to the tea. They discussed the surrounding areas and scenes while sipping chai.

Asrar's uncle told Jamila Miss that there was a popular story about Rajiwade. According to the old folks, the area was habited by Prophet Muhammad's companions who left Mecca after his demise to spread Islam in other parts of the world. Asrar immediately interrupted and said that his English teacher, Abbas Dhamaskar, had said that those old Arab men who migrated to the coast of India were actually very disillusioned by the political and social happenings in Mecca. Looking at Jamila Miss, Asrar added that after the Prophet's death, Mecca was going through difficult times and the struggle for power which followed led to a lot of bloodshed. The people who came to India were those who refused to continue staying in an environment of hatred and violence. Asrar's uncle was confused. 'How can there be bloodshed in Mecca?' he wondered.

The previous summer, Jamila had read a book on Islamic history which confirmed what Asrar had said. 'History books tell us that there was immense bloodshed for twenty-five to thirty years after the Prophet's death,' she told Asrar's uncle. The information came as a shock to Asrar's uncle. Jamila was known for her intellectual capabilities and was respected for her responsible statements. The uncle became silent. He continued talking about exotic varieties of fish, but the conversation was still stuck into his heart like a thorn.

Apparently, he put this question to the mufti of Mabadmorpho's Jama Masjid a few days later. The mufti had graduated from Azhar University and was considered knowledgeable by most. His answer was: 'To call the events bloodshed and acts of violence was not received well among people, hence it was labelled as the war between good and evil. But the reality was that there was bloodshed.'

Meanwhile, the red and yellow sun was comfortably resting on the sea off Mumbai. After taking one round of the bay, the boat turned again towards the sea. It seemed to be approaching the sun. The sky had no clouds. Flocks of birds were heading back home. An island-like elevation suddenly had thousands of cranes sitting on it. Their presence was accompanied by many small, brown birds whose hopping and chirping delighted the heart.

Asrar stood in one corner staring at the island-like elevation. He was so lost in memories that he had taken a long time spotting it. Suddenly the strand of memories broke as Saleem offered him a plate of vada pav. He smiled on realizing how easily he gets carried away by memories. The boat took a round of the Mumbai dockyard from the west and turned towards the Gateway of India. Near the dockyard, huge commercial vessels were anchored. Mohammad Ali put a paan in his mouth and, grabbing Asrar's shoulder for support, stood up. Aslam Dhamaskar looked at the huge ships and asked, 'Do they catch fish in such huge boats in Mumbai?'

Mohammad Ali playfully tapped his head and said, 'Oh, idiot! They do not catch prawns but sharks with these boats!'

They all laughed.

Aslam joined in.

Saleem enlightened them with all his knowledge about the dockyard and the navy. He told them about a small residential community of fishermen a little further from where they were. It was the same place from where, a few years later, Ajmal Amir Kasab would enter India with his accomplices.

The boat moved towards the Taj. Asrar stared intently at Mumbai with eyes full of desire. In the purest of sunlight Mumbai looked extravagant, alluring and breathtaking from the boat. The glass front of the huge skyscrapers reflected the brightness of the sun. Evening had not yet set on the city. The boat came back to the Gateway of India. They deboarded and sat under the shadow of the Gateway for some time. Qasim bought two water bottles from a shop nearby. The cold water rejuvenated their souls.

The crowd had increased around the Gateway. Tea, snack and water vendors were roaming about. People were getting their photos clicked with loved ones and families. A boy was getting a photo clicked with his arm around his beloved's shoulder and a broad smile on his face, as if it was his first love. The girl was blushing. At a little distance a girl sat sticking to her lover. Qasim could not take his eyes off that couple. Mohammad Ali grabbed the bottle from Qasim's hand and said, '*Abhe kaiko pareshan ho raha hai*? [Why are you getting worried unnecessarily?]'

'*Ye log ko sharm nahi aati* [These couples aren't ashamed]?' said Qasim.

'*Unki marji, teri kaiko jal rahi hai* [It's their wish, why are you getting so offended]?'

Qasim felt silent.

A tea vendor came, and they all had chai. The crowd had grown. Many couples could be spotted in the area. Lots of youngsters could be seen roaming about. At one end, a middle-aged woman sat with a young boy. She wore mogra flowers in her hair. After spotting a mangalsutra on her neck, Qasim Dalvi told Mohammad Ali, 'She looks like an aunty.'

'Like your aunty?' Mohammad Ali asked.

'He could not find anyone in school, even though he tried a lot,' Asrar said.

'I didn't try a lot, just winked once,' Qasim said, correcting him.

'You winked directly?'

'What happened next?' inquired Mohammad Ali, sipping his tea.

'*Kuch nahi, saali bohat bhaw khati ti* [Nothing at all. She was quite full of herself].'

'She hit him with her slippers,' Asrar said laughing out loud.

Qasim was embarrassed.

Before he could say anything, Aslam Dhamaskar said, 'She was very outgoing. She had a dark complexion but a huge heart. She was once caught with a teacher in the science lab.'

'Why, what happened?' Saleem asked with a lot of interest.

'*Hamare PT teacher us ki lete they* [Our PT teacher used to sleep with her],' Suleiman explained.

Saleem looked at Mohammad Ali in anticipation to hear more.

Qasim Dalvi said, 'Sir didn't sleep with her, she let him sleep with her.'

'And you thought she would let you sleep with her too?' Aslam asked loudly.

'These boys are experts. I thought they were still kids,' Saleem told Mohammad Ali.

'*Aslam Bhai, khane khujane mein expert rahnach padta hai, nahi to item rafuchakkar samjho* [It is extremely important to be vigilant in these matters, or else opportunities will vanish],' Mohammad Ali told Saleem. He knew that Mohammad Ali was saying this to him because his seth's wife had tried making advances towards him and had called him to her house in her husband's absence. But being self-righteous, he had ignored her or found excuses each time. She was not amused and called another servant home for 'cleaning up'. This new servant was not just good at his work but also well experienced in the matters of women and their needs. He finished his work, went to the seth's house to complete the task which the madam had desired for so long. This servant had secretly revealed to Mohammad Ali what had transpired. He had said, 'She is one of those women who will never take the first step. When you make a move, she will try to act as if she isn't interested and will say things like it is a sin and is not allowed in our religion, etc. She will swear and take God's name. But she will do all of this in a manner to turn you on. Her methods can put wet grass on fire.' He also told Mohammad Ali that after the 'work', she said, 'I am destroyed, I got carried away by emotions.'

Mohammad Ali asked, 'Then what did you do?'

'Oh! I had already understood her style, I asked her, "When are we meeting next?"'

'And then what did she say?'

'I'll call you when I see an opportunity.'

'But she just told you she was destroyed?'

'Drama yaar, every woman has a style. They all want to hunt but with full safety.'

'What do you mean by safety?'

'*Eda ban kar peda khane ka, aur kisi ko hawa bhi lagne nahi deneka* [The "work" should be done, there should be pleasure, but no one should ever come to know about it].'

'Aah. You've become an expert now!'

'You are no less of an expert. You have captured Bhaini. *Tera mal bhi ek dam kanwla hai* [Your booty is no less].'

Mohammad Ali smiled at his friend's remark but said, 'She loves me.'

The friend laughed his lungs out.

The laugh was deep and layered. He laughed with him too. And the only word they uttered while laughing was love . . . love . . . love. They continued to laugh. Mohammad Ali could not

have imagined that after a few months, he would come face to face
with a new meaning of love altogether. Such a meaning that would
open his previous life and leave marks on the path of his future. In
the past he had several relationships with women, which could be
called consensual sexual alliances. But for the last 5–6 months, a
Shia girl living on the third floor of the kholi had been head over
heels in love with him. The girl lived with her mother. The mother
was in the business of clothes. She bought clothes from Surat and
sold them in Mumbai. She had to be in Surat for fifteen days each
month on business. When she would be away, her daughter would
call Mohammad Ali over. And sometimes he would go to No. 8
in the red-light area where he had a casual relationship with a girl.

It was after a very long time that Mohammad Ali told Saleem
about the physical relationship between his boss's wife and
the worker. And he said it with a heavy heart. This grief was
not caused by the success of his friend, the worker, but by his
own failure.

'Absolutely correct, boss!' Aslam bowed down.

Right then a boy with a camera around his neck came to them
and pestered them to get photos clicked in front of the Gateway or
the Taj hotel. This was a good way of making money. He agreed
to click for Rs 100. They got two photos taken, one in front of
the Gateway and the other with Taj as the background. The photos
were developed in a few minutes. They were extremely happy
to see the pictures. Especially the newcomers. For them it was a
precious memory of their first day in Mumbai.

By evening, the crowd had grown so much that if any of the
newcomers had got lost, it would have been impossible to find
them. Hence, Mohammad Ali advised them to hold hands. They
moved away from the Gateway along the sea wall. They stopped at a

place, sat on the wall and looked at the floating boats. Many foreign tourists were also getting photos clicked. A white-skinned girl in shorts was standing and enjoying the cool breeze from the sea. Her perfectly shaped legs were more attractive than her golden hair and white skin. Each of them skipped a heartbeat looking at her. But after every glance they would look here and there to hide what their hearts felt about the fairy from the West who had created the desire for sin in their hearts. Two smooth-skinned, clean-shaven men came and stood near them.

Seeing them, Mohammad Ali suggested, 'Let's walk a bit now.'

They walked to Kala Ghoda. The walk left them tired and speechless. The city seemed impregnable to them. There was a sea of beauty, money and power which they could just watch from a faraway shore.

On a lot of persuasion from Asrar, Mohammad Ali told them about the smooth-skinned boys encountered earlier. '*Ye log dhanda karte hain, lekin bohat sare fukat mein bhi dete hain* [They do that business and get money out of it, but a lot of times they do it for free].'

Then Qasim asked an idiotic question, '*Fukat mein kya dete hain* [What do they do for free]?'

Mohammad Ali smiled and started observing the statue installed in front of the Jehangir Art Gallery.

Saleem Ghare was also curious about the answer that Mohammad Ali would give to the question.

Seeing the faces of Mohammad Ali and Saleem, Aslam addressed Qasim and said, 'They give what the hoor can't give in heaven!'

They laughed for long. So did Qasim. They laughed to their heart's content.

They reached their room at around 10.30 p.m.

Asrar, Mohammad Ali and Aslam went out after having dinner. It was eleven. The shops in the building had shut down. When they had come out in the morning, there were few street vendors but now there were many—with stalls of sherbet, samosas, bhajiya, kebab, chicken tikka, cosmetics, caps, etc. These stalls had few customers but more beggars, people clad in dismal clothes, looking old and haggard, and children.

An old man covered in dirt was sitting at a closed stall. It looked as if he had cut himself off from the present world and was living in a parallel universe. He stared blankly and kept whispering. Suddenly, this oblivious man stood up and raised his hands towards the heavens and screamed, '*Haq Allah* [God is the absolute truth].'

The vendors made fun of him and got back to their work.

A Pathan buying chicken tikka from a vendor turned and abused the old man, '*Gandu ka bachcha, charas sir mein gus gai kya* [Bastard, have the drugs done in your brain]?'

The vendor smiled at what the Pathan had said.

'This is his routine. When the effect will die down in the morning, he will say that he talked to the djinns the entire night,' the vendor said, placing chicken pieces on the fire. 'He must have made the djinns addicted too!' the Pathan said wittily. After shouting 'Haq Allah', the unknown man sat again on the footpath. Mohammad Ali said that the area had a huge population of those who bought and sold drugs. He advised the newcomers to beware of such people. That was when a twelve-year-old boy came and stood in front of the khichda stall. He held out one hand and pleaded, 'I am hungry since morning.'

'*Bhag bhenchod* [Get lost],' the vendor shouted.

Asrar asked Mohammad Ali, 'Why did the vendor abuse the boy?'

'He is a beggar but a bastard too! He will find his high and will soon be sloshed on one of the footpaths. Everyone knows such people in this lane. But the visitors and those who come here for shopping do give these people some money.' Ali then explained all about whiteners and thinners which were sniffed and known as 'handkerchief addictions'. As marijuana and heroin were very expensive, these drug addicts sustained themselves on whiteners and thinners.

After hearing all this, Qasim replied with a lot of innocence, 'Indeed, Allah takes care of all.'

Mohammad Ali immediately responded, 'Is Allah that . . .?'

'If Allah doesn't give them, then who does? He is the provider. Isn't he?' Qasim said in his defence.

'Allah has also given us brains. Understood?' Ali responded.

Asrar interrupted Mohammad Ali and reminded him that he had to talk about his employment. Mohammad Ali took out the Haathi-chhaap tobacco and licked a little choona and stuck it in his mouth on one side. He started talking about his work.

He told them that his boss was a businessman who dealt in artificial diamonds. He imported them from China. Cubic zirconia was the most exotic artificial diamond which looked exactly like the real one. Looking at the inquisitive and confused eyes of Asrar, he repeated that cubic zirconia was an artificial diamond, also referred to as CZ. It had the same shine, hardness and look as real diamonds. Asrar shook his head. Mohammad Ali said that CZ was so like the real diamond that it was very easy to fool people. Only an expert or a jeweller could spot the difference. Qasim also listened to Ali with the utmost interest. He added that after CZ, moissanite is the second kind of fake diamond. It was used to fool those greedy to buy diamonds at a lower price. Asrar replied with a simple 'Okay'. Mohammad Ali looked at them for a moment and said that his boss said that the fake diamonds, even though similar in appearance, could never lower the value of a real diamond.

Every real diamond had its own uniqueness. It had its own rays of light that touched the heart. Every diamond had its own spirit. After praising real diamonds, Ali told them ways to recognize an artificial one. Qasim seemed more interested in knowing the methods of recognizing a fake rather than knowing more about real ones. He impatiently asked, 'Tell, tell.' Ali spat out the tobacco and explained that the diamond had to be placed on a newspaper. If it was a CZ, reading the print would not be a problem but if it could not be read then it was a real diamond. Asrar was impressed by Mohammad Ali's knowledge.

Seeing curiosity in the eyes of Qasim, he continued explaining that real diamonds did not hold steam for more than three seconds on their surface, whereas fake gems could be recognized by the shining colours inside them when fogged with steam. But CZ and moissanite could cut glass like real diamonds. 'Ali Bhai, you have solid knowledge!' Qasim interrupted. Ali smiled and continued. He said that the size of the diamond could also tell its worth. In the market the diamond is generally measured in cents. There is a weighing scale that measures it in carats too. Big diamonds weigh from one-fourth of a carat to one and a half carats. The latter weight means that the size of the diamond is equal to a corn seed. Bigger and heavier diamonds are extremely precious and expensive. Hence, if a diamond was larger in size than a corn seed, one should be very careful.

Qasim and Asrar were not just impressed by this knowledge but decided to learn the skill of diamond polishing too. They realized that learning this under the guidance of Mohammad Ali would make it easier. The unknown man sitting on the footpath stood up again. He raised his hands towards the sky, murmured and went and lay down near a closed stall. Most vendors had already packed their goods. The number of people on the road had decreased considerably. The footpaths had become a pile of rubbish where rats and cockroaches were enjoying themselves. Some dogs were relishing on the scattered chicken bones in the garbage dump.

Mohammad Ali praised his employer's attitude and greatness and told them that he treated his workers like family. He was always there in case of any difficulty.

Their conversation lasted till half an hour past midnight.

When the newcomers woke up the next morning, there were only two boys in the room.

Usman was writing something in a diary and Haider was having breakfast. Usman and Haider were brothers. They were acquaintances of Qasim and Suleiman from the village. Usman had just completed his MA and was about to enrol in BEd. Haider was doing a diploma in computer science from a polytechnic. Asrar had seen them in the village a couple of times but had had no interaction with them. This was their first meeting. He told them that along with work he wanted to continue his education through distance learning. Usman and Haider promised every assistance they could provide. No one, at that time, knew how short Asrar's life would be.

Usman and Haider told Asrar that there was a vacation in their college but because their cousin was coming from Bahrain, they had delayed their visit to the village. Asrar told them that when he and his friends left the village they had other plans and ambitions, but after meeting Mohammad Ali and hearing about the diamond business, they had decided to take it up. Usman appreciated their decision and advised them to make sure to learn the skills of recognizing, sharpening, cleaning and polishing the diamonds. The acquiring of a skill was always profitable. Usman told them that Mohammad Ali was more skilled than his own boss was in this business. And that was the reason why his boss treated him so well. Haider added, 'Mohammad Ali is a pure-hearted man. He himself would want to assist you boys in acquiring the skills.' One could sense the closeness between Usman, Haider and Mohammad Ali.

The afternoon call for prayer was resounding in the air. Usman asked the newcomers if they had to offer namaz.

'No,' they replied in unison.

Usman had to buy a few books from Mohammad Ali Road. He thought that if the newcomers accompanied him, it would be a good pastime for them. 'Let us all go to Mohammad Ali Road,' Usman said and after a pause added, 'A restaurant in that area serves delicious kebabs.'

They all got ready and came out of the building. The sun was at its brightest.

They stopped near the Dum Dum sweet shop. Aslam went on to the paan stall at the turn of the road and got himself some mawa. They crossed the footpath and started moving towards JJ Hospital. There were a lot of small shops there. Concrete shops and vending stalls. A lot of vending stalls had changed into shops. In one such stall, along with newspapers, files and books were also laid out neatly. They all stopped at the newspaper vendor's shop. Haider pulled out an English newspaper. Aslam and Asrar were busy looking at detective novels. Qasim found the theme of one book particularly interesting. Seeing his friends flip through books, he told Usman that he wanted to buy that book. Usman shot a glance at the book and asked Qasim why he required the book at this time. Qasim snapped, 'I could need it anytime!'

He peered deep into Usman's eyes and added, 'It is mandatory to acquire knowledge in our religion.'

Usman smiled at this justification and asked the vendor the cost of the book. After much bargaining, they bought it for Rs 40.

Qasim murmured the title of the book: *Islamic Ways of Sexual Intercourse.*

His face bore a victorious smile.

The book vendor had seen this smile on the faces of all his customers who had bought that book. This sixty-eight-page paperback edition of the book was no less than a treatise. Qasim stuffed the book into his trouser pocket and smoothed his kurta. Usman noticed him and smiled. Aslam picked up a book which was titled *The Dangerous Love of a Djinn* and started looking at its cover. It had a girl on it and in the background was the picture of a smiling, beardless djinn whose one hand was on the girl's shoulder while the other held a knife to her throat.

Haider asked, 'Do you believe in djinns?'

To which Aslam replied, 'In our society there are djinns. Even the Quran talks about them.'

'But can a djinn fall in love with a girl?'

'A djinn once fell in love with a woman in our locality.'

'Tell me the details of the story in the evening,' Usman said. 'Let's go before the kebabs get over at the hotel.' They were all hungry and hence they moved ahead. Near the Mandvi Post Office, on an archaic elevation, was a s*abeel* (water kiosk) below an old tree. They halted under its shade. Suleiman was thirsty.

The elevation had two earthen pots of water and two steel glasses secured with chains. Suleiman quaffed down a glass of water in one go. Asrar's eyes began observing the surroundings. There were bookshops behind the sabeel. There was a mosque nearby with white minarets. There were shops selling clothes, commodities of daily use, etc., around the mosque. One- or two-storey buildings stood in the vicinity. Just a glance at these buildings was enough to tell that they were from another era. Time had withered many windows. Just a few yards from these buildings, two skyscrapers were under construction. The tree under which they sought shelter near the post office was also quite old.

Under the same tree, many years back, the don Dawood Konkani had partied and made merry. A road goes towards the Mumba Devi temple and Kalbadevi from here. A monster living on the old trees near the Mumba Devi temple had revealed to the tree that the boy Dawood who made merry with his friends here and repeatedly uttered to them '*Abhe chutiya hun kya?*' would become the don of Dongri and would swiftly create terror in the entire world.

He would flee from Mumbai when the dawn of the new century would be short of thirty-eight solar eclipses. He would rule another island and would become a member of a secret espionage agency that would terrorize the city of Mumbai. Many would call these acts of terror—his revenge. The intelligence agencies of the world would be in search of him. He would find shelter in a cave provided by another secret agency.

For the tree, all the information provided by the monster was gibberish, and hence it never took him seriously. The tree asked the monster, 'So, from where do you collect these rumours?'

The monster snapped, 'This isn't a rumour!' He then started justifying what he had predicted. He told the tree that once an angel grieving the death of a Sufi at Haji Ali stopped by the Mumba Devi temple. Mumba Devi addressed the angel as Mikhail Singh Mikhail. According to the monster, Mikhail had also told Mumba Devi about the mystery around Dawood's death. But this information was cautiously whispered and hence he couldn't make much sense of it. He also shared more details and told the tree that Mikhail complained a lot about Azrael Singh and considered him a prick who had started enjoying his own vanity. He had started bullying the other angels over the past hundred years or so. Mumba then asked why Azrael was being such a terror? Mikhail said this was so because since the time of the two world wars his department was involved in the duty of shifting souls from here to there. This work had made him very close to God. The increase in the number of deaths had given him a reputation in heaven. Shia, Sunni, Wahabi, Barelvi and other smaller beings who worship God were thrown by him mercilessly in some corner of hell. No one interrogated him any more. His work had increased so much that it was impossible for anyone to keep records and establish accountability.

The tree listened with the utmost attention. Two white pigeons sat on that branch of the tree which bent over the sabeel. They became alert to the conversation. One of them suddenly flew and went towards the imambara. The monster

reported that Mikhail said that most of those who died met
an unnatural death. They died because of hatred. Their deaths
were not in keeping with the record register and hence Azrael
was not bothered about record-keeping any more. Mumba Devi
then asked how Azrael captured their souls when many people
died at the same time.

Mikhail laughed.

'What makes you laugh?' Mumba Devi asked.

'It is a matter of grief, but I couldn't control my laughter. Those
souls that escape the clutches of Azrael are captured by djinns and
devils. They use these spirits to fool humans or make fun of them.'

The monster said, 'Let me tell you a story.'

The tree was all ears.

'Once a Tibetan djinn captured the soul of a known jihadi
from Afghanistan. The jihadi had concluded a suicidal attack on
an American convoy in Nooristan. Dozens of American soldiers
were killed in the attack. Unfortunately, his spirit entered the
shell of a hand grenade and fell far into a drain. Azrael's team
gathered the spirits of all Americans and left. The soul of the
jihadi remained in the drain. The fierce sound of the blast had
gathered the attention of the djinn who was crossing Nooristan
to reach Bamiyan. He immediately utilized the opportunity of
enslaving the jihadi's spirit.

'The intensity of the blast had rendered the spirit unconscious.
The soul came back to its senses coincidentally at the same time
when the djinn was standing in front of the destroyed Buddha in
Bamiyan. The djinn lay the soul on a flower. The jihadi's spirit
was clueless about the reality. At the time of the blast, he had
expected that his eyes would close here and open in the arms of
hoors in paradise. Such nymphs wore no burqas, no clothes and no
lingerie. Now that his eyes opened before the demolished idol of
the Budhdha, he experienced a condition of confusion and shock.
In complete astonishment and suspicion, he said, "Such an Allah
was in Bamiyan too!"

'The Tibetan djinn smacked him on his head and said, "There are forty thousand million years left for you to go to Allah. Right now, you happen to be in my captivity."

'The djinn captured the jihadi in the gemstone of his finger ring. On returning to Tibet, he made the soul of the jihadi enter the body of a fox cub. The soul became healthy and fresh inside the fox and regained its fervour in a few days. The fox rebelled against its pack and started a revolution against the laws of the jungle. When the elves and bats told it that the laws were made by the family of the lion and a mere fox could not bring any change, it managed to create an army of foxes and announced jihad till the death of the Barbary Lion. This show of confidence and bravery by the spirit made the djinn fall for it. He knew that this jihad would have no result but the jungle would turn into a ground of terror. He put the spirit inside a balloon and asked the balloon to carry it back to Nooristan, or else Tibet would also turn into Afghanistan.'

After telling the story, the monster said that when Mikhail and Mumba were talking about heaven and earth, he was eavesdropping from the window. 'When they were discussing the blasts in Mumbai, Mumba had tears in her eyes.'

The tree was grief-stricken for long. Then it finally spoke, 'It is the responsibility of Mumba Devi to plead to Brahma and ask for the protection of this city.'

The monster laughed loudly and flew towards Chor Bazaar.

They reached the JJ signal while chatting away.

They crossed the street just a little before the signal. At the turn of the road was a small eating joint with kebabs being smoked on a coal fire at its entrance.

The smell of smoke and meat permeated their nostrils. They entered the restaurant. The floor was wet. There were a few beggars relishing the kebabs. A boy was cleaning the floor. Rubbish was scattered under the table at which they seated themselves. Usman ordered kebabs. Their disappointment at the condition of the eating joint was overcome by the flavour of the seekh kebabs. The newcomers praised the kebabs while sipping a Thums Up.

'The hotel doesn't have an agreeable appearance, but the kebabs are fantastic!' Usman said.

'Thank you, Usman Bhai, you showed us a good place,' Asrar acknowledged.

They stood near the signal for long, talking while observing the environment around.

Usman entered a bookshop, collected the desired books, paid at the counter and left. Asrar remarked, 'We had books like these in our school library.'

'They are books of *adab* literature,' Usman said.

'Are they books to learn etiquette from?' Qasim asked.

Usman and Haider smiled. Asrar said, 'Don't you remember our Urdu teacher telling us to read books of adab to learn *aadaab* [etiquette]?'

Usman put his arms on Qasim's shoulders and said, 'Your Urdu teacher was mad. The function of adab books is very different!'

'What is their function then?' Qasim asked.

Ali could not gather what to say; hence he replied, 'Literature is a disease, and its cure is also reading literature.'

'I didn't get you,' Suleiman interjected.

Asrar was not listening to all this. He was in his own world looking at the footpath—the JJ flyover, vehicles crawling on the roads, people peeping out of the windows of double-decker buses, a crowd of people approaching the area and surrounding buildings. The flyover seemed like a huge snake to him. A wish arose in his

heart to see the view of the city from this flyover. He was intrigued
by the chaos of life that Mohammad Ali Road had brought him
face to face with. He had heard stories of the busy streets, fast life
and the hustle-bustle of Mumbai since childhood. Now he was
witnessing all of it through his own eyes. He wanted to capture
these images in his heart.

The debate on the literary books had ended by now. Usman
and Haider told Suleiman and Qasim about Chor Bazaar. Both
showed interest in seeing the market. Asrar was walking a few steps
ahead. Qasim called out to him and informed him that they were
all headed towards Chor Bazaar.

Chor Bazaar proved to be a museum. Asrar was astonished
at the kinds of items that were being sold. Old and exotic coins
from various countries, old currency notes, radios and television
sets he had never seen, furniture, toys, parts of vehicles, clothes,
pretty vases and ornamental and etched showpieces, paintings—
some real and mostly fake—magazines and books, expensive pens,
gramophones, video cassettes—none of which he had seen before.
A donkey stood nearby. Qasim gaped at it and asked, 'Do they sell
donkeys here too?'

'You ask a lot of donkey-like questions,' Usman said, smacking
Qasim on the head.

Asrar saw an old man who looked like a Sufi selling rings, gems
and colorful stones. He wore turquoise beads around his neck,
rings on his fingers and had a messy beard. Stones in varied colours
attracted Asrar's attention. They were blue, shiny blue, red, blood
red, white as coconut, orange and light-yellow stones. He sat down
to look at them when the old man said, 'The red stone will change
your fate, boy.'

Asrar looked up and said, 'Fate is in the hands of Allah!'

The man smiled and said, 'Show me your hand.'

Asrar stood up and opened his palms. The Sufi narrowed his
eyes and stole a glance. He stayed silent for a few moments. He
suddenly bent down and took out a magnifying glass and looked at
the palm again through it. He lifted his eyes and stared deep into

Asrar's. Asrar could sense a lot of intensity on the face of the Sufi.
He said in a loud voice, 'Maulabax!'

An aged man came out of a nearby shop clad in white kurta
and trousers. Contentment and the experience of age reflected
on his calm face. When he came near, the Sufi said, 'Look. Look
at this,' and pointed towards Asrar's palm. The man also looked
at it through the magnifying glass. Finding it all very interesting,
Asrar's friends gathered around him. After studying the hand for
long, the aged man said in a morose tone, 'Almighty is behind
every design!'

Before Asrar could say anything, Usman pulled him out and
took him away, saying that this was Chor Bazaar and customers
were fooled here. But Asrar's heart was telling him that the Sufi
was not putting up an act. There was definitely something. They
had moved away, but the Sufi and the aged man still stood there,
talking. In fact, that evening, they turned the pages of many old,
archaic books. The aged man had a precious ancient manuscript
in the form of a book titled *Kitab-ul-Hikmat Bain-ul-Aafaq* (The
Book of Knowledge of All Worlds). This manuscript had travelled
through Iran, Iraq, Hijaz and Syria before coming into the hands of
a Mughal prince in the twelfth century. This prince had lent it to
his concubine to read for a few days.

The concubine was murdered by thieves who looted a lot of
things from her house, including this book. For them this was
nothing more than a bundle of papers. One day a poet bought it in
the seventeenth century in Delhi at a throwaway price. The book
stayed in the house of the poet for the next three generations.
In the first decade of the twentieth century, a maulana borrowed it
from the poet's grandchildren. When he realized the importance
of the book, he started his research. It revealed such information
that sleep started eluding him. He started living in a parallel
universe altogether. The maulana bid farewell to Delhi and
without informing anyone left and settled in Mumbai. He kept
himself immersed in hash and alcohol for twenty years. During
that time, he translated a few parts of this 1500-page book into

Urdu. He had done this translation to understand the actual purpose of the words written in the book.

The aged man who met Asrar was the maulana's son. He had acquired knowledge and wisdom from his father and had command over Persian, Arabic and Urdu. The maulana had talked to his son at length a few days before his death. He had explained to him some tenets of wisdom and warned him that the book should not reach the hands of any religious man ever. He said: 'This is that truth which the evil truth wants to destroy. Keep the book like a treasure close to your heart.' He also handed over the Urdu translation and said that it was the most important book in the world but if it became commonplace, then the world would submerge in blood. He did not share a lot of details of his research with his son. He was sure that this book was written by Yakrab Abu Kuhan, who had the knowledge of all the worlds. He had given this knowledge to his daughter, Turab Kuhan.

The daughter had revealed this secret to one of her lovers. He profited through that knowledge and was able to establish his empire before the death of the Saryo River. This empire had established control over many countries of the world. She had revealed many secrets to her lover about the world, life, human nature, history but did not hand over the book to him. She had given it to her brother's son, Jalal Hikmatyar, and made him vow that he would not open the book till her husband died. He fulfilled his promise. But after the death of his uncle, the disintegration of the empire started and there was chaos all around. Once, when he was leaving his house, a poison-dipped arrow hit him in the chest.

His wife, Tilism Shabyar, after the burial, crossed the Saryo and after a long journey across the desert reached Hijaz. She camped there for seven days. It came to her knowledge that there was a civil war on in Hijaz. People of various clans and tribes were killing each other and hanging severed heads and limbs in lanes and streets. They cut off the genitals of honourable women and spat on them. And those who did not join them in the spitting were considered traitors and enemies. The terror struck fear in Tilism's heart. She went to Damascus. Her husband had beseeched her to carry the book to a safe place immediately if anything ever happened to him. She had lived up to her husband's expectations. The book kept wandering. It is said that the clan to which Tilism belonged had rumours doing the rounds that the *Kitab-ul-Hikmat Bain-ul-Aafaq* had been lost.

The book contained signs of those who were privy to revelations of life, death and secrets of death and soul while they were alive. The Sufi-faced man had heard similar things. A line on Asrar's palm had intrigued him and hence he had called the aged man.

Meanwhile the newcomers and their friends reached Pydhonie enjoying the labyrinth that Chor Bazaar was. They drank sherbet from a stall and returned to the kholi.

A week was spent in roaming and exploring the various parts of old Mumbai. It didn't take much time for Asrar to acquaint and associate himself with this area. He was now well versed with the names of surrounding areas as well as streets and directions. He found this area very kinetic, busy and attractive. He had relished the paav, khichda, biryani, kheer, phirni, ragda, seekh kebabs and beef to his heart's content. Mohammad Ali pleaded and requested his boss Moosa Patel to employ Qasim and Asrar.

One day Moosa Patel was to meet Qasim and Asrar. Mohammad Ali acquainted them with the possible questions that Moosa Patel might ask. A formal meeting took place and they got their jobs. It was a very special day for Asrar. He called up on his neighbour's phone and spoke to his mother. That evening he called Jamila Miss from Saleem's mobile. He spoke to her for long and shared the details of his job. She asked a few questions about Mumbai and expressed anger at the fact that he had gone away without informing her. He promised her that he would return soon and explain the reasons to her face to face.

It was a Saturday evening and those who lived in other parts of the city started gathering in the kholi. The room was overflowing. A round of tea was served. There was random talk and discussions.

Mohammad Ali gestured to Asrar to get ready. When everyone had
had their tea, he collected the cups and washed them under the
water tank. Then he freshened up and changed his clothes. When
Ali and Asrar were leaving the room, Saleem asked them when they
would return. Ali told him that they were going to meet a friend
near JJ Hospital. They said they would return around ten, but told
him not to wait for them for dinner.

Mohammad Ali and Asrar crossed the road and caught a taxi.
Asrar said, 'We could have walked to the hospital.'

Ali didn't reply and chewed on mawa. Once in the taxi,
Mohammad Ali said that he was giving a surprise party to celebrate
Asrar's new job. This made Asrar happy. He inquired about the
nature of the party he should expect. Ali asked him to just wait
and watch, and promised that it would be a memorable day of his
life. Asrar tried making sense of what Ali was saying but could not
understand what it was all about. The road to JJ Hospital had a
lot of traffic. The taxi crawled. The vehicles often stopped while
people crossed. If a passer-by came in front of the taxi and it started
moving, choicest abuses would be hurled at the driver. The double-
decker bus behind their taxi was continuously buzzing its horn.
The taxi driver pulled his head out of the window and shouted,
'Motherfucker, there is traffic ahead!' Another taxi driver smiled.
Then their cabbie explained to the smiling taxi driver, 'Fucker is
continuously honking unnecessarily!'

Ali had already told the driver their destination before boarding
the taxi. A little before the JJ Hospital signal, the driver turned off
the engine. The jam was such that it was difficult for the taxi to
even crawl. Ali took out another mawa from his pocket and offered
it to Asrar. Asrar nodded in refusal and stuck his neck outside the
taxi window. He stared at the moving crowd. His eyes were cold
towards the people he was looking at, but his heart had the warm
spark of the moments spent with Jamila Miss.

The boat trip with Miss came rushing back to his memory.
It was nearing sunset. He could visualize his mother, Jamila Miss,
his uncle and the servants chatting in one corner while he sat in

the dark in the other. For some time, Jamila Miss kept talking to his mother and uncle. During the conversation, his mother told Miss that Asrar generally remained aloof and sat in the darkness. Jamila Miss said she would talk to him. The night was having its effect and the lights from far away had dimmed and disappeared. The sound of the waves and the noise of the boat's engine were competing with each other. Jamila Miss got up, stared at the waves and walked towards Asrar.

Asrar stood up when he saw her in front of him. She glanced briefly at everyone else from behind the deck. They were all busy in conversation. She pounced on Asrar and hugged him. Asrar was shocked. They stood near the deck from where they could see everyone on the boat, but no one could see them. They were facing each other. Asrar's mother thought that Jamila had gone to have a talk with Asrar. Jamila Miss's back faced the others on the boat. They were both silent. Asrar moved back a little into the dark. She looked at the waves. The water was smashing against the sides of the boat. She felt as if the temperature of the sea had risen. The temperature within her also rose in the presence of Asrar and spread all over her body. This was a unique feeling. She felt aroused—as if mercury would spill out of her body. Asrar knew well the smell of that mercury. He could gauge from her eyes the secrets of her heart. The smell of her fluids had found its way into his nose many a time, but he had never in his wildest of dreams imagined this intense flow of heat in Jamila Miss's eyes, now sensuous with a desire coming from deep within her.

He placed his index finger on Jamila Miss's lips. As she closed her eyes and opened them, she experienced an intoxicating happiness. Such intoxication can convince a human being to descend the stairs of forgetfulness and rebellion. His finger slid to her chin. She softly held Asrar's toe captive between her thumb and index toe. The awakened intoxication of the spirit and the gushing blood in the body sent vibrations to her toes. Asrar cast a glance at the others in the boat. His uncle was smoking a cigarette.

His mother was preparing a paan. Asrar's fingers were now on Jamila's throat, and he mischievously applied pressure to it. She found it difficult to breathe. He then moved his finger to the spot where her ribs separated into two parts, even as he tightened his grip around Miss's toe. She closed her eyes and when she opened them, she saw Asrar up close, as if he was trying to capture the moist image of her body in his memory. She opened her eyes at the touch of Asrar's finger, which had travelled from her chest to her navel. A chill ran down her veins and her spine felt as if she was responding to a sorrowful song. Her aroused state seemed to have mingled with the cold of the water. The black surface of sea was the interpreter of the sea's sorrow.

The loneliness and unfulfilled desires of the being had come together, and they seemed to be whispering within Jamila. She realized that she had been deprived of thousands of moments of pleasure. She had no wisdom of this deprivation as such, but her soul was in conversation with it and had aroused an intoxication which had further awakened the memories of innumerable, unknown and old deprivations and desires within her. She felt that her husband had never absorbed her moistness in his memories. He had never experienced the warmth of the burning fire within her behind the wet of her soul. Why was the man who was her husband not someone else? Someone who could arouse intoxication in her soul. Someone who could drive warmth and passion in her veins. Someone who could capture her fluids on his tongue, heart and memories.

Something glistened on the surface of the sea. Asrar remained standing there. The boat had reached that place where the rawas and surmai fish were in abundance.

'Get down! We have arrived,' Mohammad Ali said, prodding him with his elbow.

It was as if Asrar had woken up from a very long dream. He immediately opened the door of the taxi and stepped out. The streetlights were dim. Many poles had unlit bulbs. They entered a narrow lane. There were four–five paan shops at the turn of the lane. A few young men stood around these shops. Ten to twelve people were eating seekh kebabs around a makeshift shop. A man was selling tea from a kettle in his hand. Two boys standing near the tea seller were talking in loud voices and interrupting their talk with even louder laughs. A little further, film CDs were being sold at another makeshift shop. Asrar was shocked when he noticed that the covers of these CDs had sexually explicit photographs of Western men and women. Then he glanced at one cover, and it showed the private parts of a male and female. He was immediately reminded of his textbook detailing the 'function of the vagina and penis'. But along with that memory, the words of Jamila Miss resonated that these organs were not just for reproduction and biological processes but also to express the passionate desire for love. They were the bridge between soul, body and emotions.

He asked Ali, 'What place is this?'

'Paradise, my brother, this is paradise. This area is called Kamathipura.' They walked further ahead. Asrar saw that along the way, on both sides, stood adolescent and middle-aged women. Some wheatish, some darker and some fair. They had powdered their faces, wore lipstick and a few had flowers in their hair. Their features indicated that some belonged to the North-east, some were Nepalese and a few Maharashtrians. They went even further and turned right. Here there were two- and three-storey buildings with a few women standing near the staircases. On the opposite side was a restaurant where a bearded man, clad in a white kurta pyjama, sat at the counter. There was a framed photo of the Kaba on the wall. Some people were sitting and having tea in the restaurant. A Nepalese woman was drinking Pepsi at the counter. There was a neem tree nearby. A vulture sat on its branch. Two adolescent boys stood under it, gaping at the Nepalese girl. The bearded man at the counter was staring at the boys. Behind the girl was a blue drum

at the back of which lay a nearly dead pigeon. The vulture had its
eyes on it. It sometimes took a break to look at the Nepalese girl
but would soon turn its neck to look at its prey. Ali bought two
chocolates from a nearby paan shop and offered one to Asrar while
putting one in his mouth. 'You will start working from tomorrow,
so have fun today.'

Asrar said nothing. He had realized that many of the women
he saw were sex workers. He had also seen a movie made on
prostitutes and red-light areas. That movie was playing in his head.
Ali threw the chocolate wrapper into the nearby drain from which
two fat mice were peeping out. They were staring at a discarded
chicken piece which a drunkard had thrown a few moments ago.
Mosquitoes had alighted on the chicken piece. Flies were also
competing to get access. No sooner had the chocolate wrapper
been thrown in the drain than the flies headed towards it. The
mice attacked the piece of chicken together. The mosquitoes flew
away. A cricket that was lazing on a rice grain seemed to regard
the mice with the utmost indifference. The chaos in the drain
made the vulture cast his eyes on it. He looked down upon the
mice with a sense of superiority and went back to looking at the
Nepalese woman.

The pace of Mohammad Ali's heartbeat increased, and his feet
shivered. He entered the building opposite the restaurant. Two girls
standing at the main gate of the building tried to stop him and strike
up a conversation. One of them wore jeans, a white T-shirt and
scarlet lipstick. The other one wore a sari and a body-hugging blue
blouse with buttons in the front. She tried holding Mohammad
Ali's hand. He touched her cheek, whispered something and
moved forward. Asrar noticed that two buttons of the blue blouse
were undone and a Rs 100 note was carefully tucked into it. When
Asrar passed the women, one of them spat out betel juice and told
the other girl, 'Madhuri's customer!'

The other one said, 'Madhuri gets them by doing French.'

The other one disagreed and said, 'Do not talk rubbish.'

The one in the jeans answered with silence and raised her fingers to her throat as if to swear. There were many rooms in the building, but all of them were engulfed in darkness. A small 40 watt bulb hung in a corner but it was covered with spider webs. In fact, a few dead spiders hung from the bulb. At the end of a saffron light, a lizard slept comfortably on an open electric wire which had snapped from the switch.

On the second floor, in the veranda, on the door of the last room, stood a woman clad in a purple sari. Mohammad Ali said something to her. Asrar noticed that the woman had two roses stuck in her hair bun. She had applied a very strong perfume. The woman drew the curtain aside and shouted, 'Madhuri!' Asrar raised his eye to look at the door where a picture of Lord Ganesh adorned a tile. A horseshoe hung from a nail below the tile. Ali entered the room. Inside the room, along the walls were small-sized diwans which one could not call charpoys. On both ends of the diwan stood out teak poles that supported the curtains which covered the diwans. There were four beds in the room with little space in between. Madhuri moved towards Mohammad, looking pleased on seeing him. They talked for a minute or two. Asrar realized that they were well acquainted. Madhuri had a broad forehead, wheatish complexion and a bright face. She wore a red lehenga, which she had paired with a tight green blouse. Asrar noticed that there was a window in the room. It was curtained but light entered through the cracks.

When Asrar's eyes adjusted to the darkness in the room, he saw three girls sitting on a bed. The girls looked at them with smiles on their faces. The wall right across from the women had four photos hung on them. One picture was that of Goddess Lakshmi, but Asrar wasn't aware of who the other goddess was. She was dark, had an elaborate nose ring and big eyes. It felt as if the goddess was staring at Asrar. The third picture was that of Lord Krishna and the fourth was of the grave of Haji Malang Baba. All the four pictures had garlands made of pink paper flowers. When the conversation between Madhuri and Ali ended, she turned towards Asrar and said, 'This is the best place for your first time!' She said it with a lot of mischief in her voice. Mohammad Ali smiled. Madhuri called out to a girl. The girl seemed to have just entered her adolescence. She was either the same age as Asrar or one or two years older than him. Her name was Shanti. Asrar looked at her. She stared back. Her facial features were proof of her Marathi origin. Her ears had four piercings each and she wore three pairs of earrings. Her nose wasn't prominent, but her eyes were white and big. She was two fingers shorter than Asrar and had large breasts, which had formed arches. The string of her lehenga hung outside. She wore a silver toe ring in her second toe. Mohammad Ali looked at Shanti, too, with a passing glance. Shanti smiled looking into Asrar's eyes. Ali gestured to Madhuri that the girl was acceptable.

Madhuri called out to Shanti, 'He is new, be careful.'

Shanti grinned and shook her head. Mohammad Ali gestured Asrar to accompany Shanti to her bed.

3

For Want of a Voice, in Answer of My Own
(*Mein Ab Sada Ke Sile Mein Koe Sada Chahun*)

Asrar held his second month's salary in his hand. The notes reminded him that two and a half months had passed in the kholi so quickly that he didn't even realize it. He decided to take two days off and visit his village. He shared this desire with Mohammad Ali, who took permission from Moosa Patel and Asrar got the leave approved for Monday and Tuesday. He decided to go to Ratnagiri on Saturday evening by train.

In the two months that Asrar had spent in Mumbai, he had tried understanding and adjusting to the culture and chaos of the city. Sunday being a holiday, he spent it on recreation and visiting the houses of his fellow villagers who lived in Mumbai with his friends. Now he knew places like Churchgate, VT, Haji Ali, Dadar, Andheri, Malad, Borivali, Mumbra and surrounding areas. He had seen these places innumerable times. He was well acquainted with the routine and weekend schedules of Mumbaikars. He also knew the dressing styles and cultures of the people and communities who came from various Indian states to find employment there.

One day he read a few pages from Haider's textbook. He really liked this paragraph from the book:

> Mumbai is a magical city. Time passes in its lap without being noticed and without much realization. Mumbai swallows up days. Years pass by and suddenly the people wake up only to ponder where years of their lives had vanished. The morning sun rises and then the evening arrives, so do weeks, months and then salaries. Morning happens again, followed by evening, a year and then many years. Salaries happen and in want of these salaries, lives are spent. Mumbai eats life like rust. It can be said that a person transforms into a prostitute in Mumbai. One can earn as much as they want to spend, they can be as successful as the hard work they put in. Mumbai is a well. It quenches all thirsts. It is true that so many simply drown in this well. It won't be wrong to say that Mumbai turns a person into that hungry whore who becomes a victim of Aids and proceeds towards a painful death. Mumbai is as benevolent as cruel and indifferent. Mumbai does not have a single face, a single identity. All faces and identities that belong to her are false. It has no face, no identity. Mumbai is a mirage.

He read this paragraph over and over again, and pondered over it.

There were two days left to go to the village.

After returning from work he went shopping with Qasim and Mukhtar Thakur. Mukhtar knew the markets in the surrounding areas very well. They went to Manish Market first where Asrar bought clothes, electrical appliances and chocolates.

From there they proceeded to the Crawford Market on foot
but there was nothing which Asrar needed or wanted to buy. Then
they went to Abdul Rehman Street to buy pistachios and almonds.
They kept walking through Zaveri Bazaar after that. They stopped
to drink tea at a makeshift shop and started conversing. Mukhtar
showed him the area where a bomb blast had happened a year back.
Asrar asked a lot of questions about it. Mukhtar answered as much
as he could and suggested that Saleem and Mohammad Ali were the
best people when it came to information about these things. Asrar
had a lot of questions in his heart, and he wanted to find answers to
them. He kept the empty cup aside and looked at the shop in front
of which the bomb had exploded. In a while, they boarded a bus
from there and went to Kalbadevi. He bought a beautiful flower
vase from a shop in Kalbadevi for Jamila Miss. While showing him
around, Thakur took him to Mumba Devi's temple and asked,
'Do you know whose temple this is?'

There was a gate on the main road which opened into the
temple's courtyard. An idol of Mumba Devi was at the gate. On
the opposite side of the road was a gulmohar tree. There were
shops selling garlands and other temple and prayer essentials near
the gate. Thakur told Asrar and Qasim a few stories about Mumba
Devi. Asrar expressed his desire to enter the temple and see it for
himself. Qasim said that he would wait outside while the other
two went in to take a look. Maybe he wanted to have mawa. Asrar
and Thakur entered the temple. It was old-fashioned, with four
saffron flags. Asrar was amazed to see Mumba Devi's idol. The
face of the Devi showed anger and ferociousness. Her eyes were
wide in anger. Asrar was reminded of the 'Ek Veera Devi' temple
near the shore in Mabadmorpho. He had gone inside that temple
with his friends a couple of times. The deity was worshipped
by the Kolis. Her face reflected motherhood, love, serenity and
seriousness. Her idol did not instil fear in one's heart, as Mumba
Devi's face did.

There was a huge crowd in the courtyard. Many peepal trees had found their way to grow through the cracks in the walls. Several pigeons sat on the roof. When the bomb blast took place between Zaveri Bazaar and the temple on 25 December 2003, another one had taken place near the Gateway. Nearly twenty-four people had died in the blasts. Most of them were identified. There were four unfortunate people whose bodies were burnt to ashes in the explosion. Their souls had cracks too. These cracks had appeared because of their sudden death and the sudden separation of the soul from the body.

For many days these mortified souls sat hidden in the drains below the temple. Mumba Devi was given this information by a dev. Mumba Devi gave him a mantra, a spell, and said that he should bring the souls in front of the temple and then chant the mantra. He obeyed her. The mortified souls transformed into beautiful white pigeons. Since then, these pigeons have stayed on the temple premises. They were distinct from the regular, common pigeons. The common pigeons keep expressing love all the time, whereas these pigeons were love-deprived. They stared at the skies with blank eyes and the skies stared back, because the skies have stars which don't just carry wounds of the 25 December blast but also know of the 31 July 2011 blasts. They are also aware of the 2006 train blasts, the 26 November sea attack on Mumbai, the Ghatkopar and other blasts. Were these supernatural calamities responsible for Mumba Devi's immense grief? Had Brahma already informed her of these unfortunate incidents which had spread an ambiguous silence on her face?

A pigeon bent to look at Asrar and gestured to another one. They had felt something after seeing Asar's soul. Soon, all the pigeons were looking down at Asrar while he stared at the children who carried red, orange and yellow garlands for Mumba Devi.

They hired a taxi from Kalbadevi to go to Bhindi Bazaar, where Asrar bough tea powder, dates, rusks, cups, saucers, glasses and other household items. They reached the room at nine in the night.

Mohammad Ali was waiting for him.

He informed him that they had to go to their boss's house. Asrar rested for about ten minutes and then they left the kholi.

It was raining outside. Ali wore a raincoat and Asrar took an umbrella. Moosa Patel lived on the twentieth floor of a skyscraper in Colaba. His wife opened the door. They entered the house and Patel's wife served them water.

Moosa Patel emerged from his room, exchanged greetings and then handed them an envelope. He told them that Yaqoob Umar Ibn Maqallab Mahayat's maternal cousin, Ranjeeda Maqallab, would collect this cheque from them the following day in the office. Moosa told them that he was going to China to attend a diamond exhibition. Then he looked at Asrar and said, 'Do not go and stay put at the village, do return. And convey my wishes to your family.' Asrar replied with a smile, 'Of course not, sir, will return soon.' Moosa Patel accompanied them till the door to say goodbye. Before shutting it, Moosa said, 'Yaqoob was such a brilliant man once, but circumstances . . .' And he stopped. There was disappointment on his face. He took a deep, cold breath and uttered, 'May God bless us.'

As soon as Mohammad Ali left the building, he hung his bag around the neck and wore the raincoat over it. Asrar opened his umbrella. It was still raining. They stood under a banyan tree for shelter. Asrar was holding on tightly to the umbrella and looking at Ali when he told the entire story of Yaqoob and his brother Sadiq. Moosa Patel had told Asrar of things which were only known to Yaqoob's family and nearest friends. Asrar could clearly hear the story over the sound of the heavy rain and the rushing cars.

The conversation included the information that during the
1992 riots, police had sided with the rioters and turned a blind eye
towards the 1000 murders and more than 3000 people who were
wounded. Yaqoob's heart was broken because of those planned riots.

Nobody knows how a broken heart could respond and react.
Ali said that extreme barbarism and cruelty were perpetrated.
Places were set on fire. Houses were marked and then locked
and burnt in the midnight. Mumba Devi had witnessed the fires,
bloodshed and communalism. During those days Mumba Devi
had heard the rishi's soul who lived on the neem tree across from
her window, telling the demons that 'violence breeds violence and
revenge breeds revenge'. A demon had said that the soul of the
saint was that of a warrior who was famous in Shivaji Maharaj's
army for his bravery. The saint had also said that Shivaji was an
honourable man under whose flag both Hindus and Muslims
were united like two bodies in one soul and fought against the
foreign enemies.

A taxi stopped in front of Asrar and Mohammad Ali. Asrar
closed his umbrella and sat inside the vehicle. Ali told him that one
day that same year an incident took place. He was sitting with a
relative at Moosa Patel's shop. His relative was a servant at the shop.
Silence had engulfed Mumbai by the evening except the sound of
police sirens and ambulances. The boys who worked at the shop
were relieved at around 4 p.m. Ali continued, 'Moosa Bhai, my
relative and I went to Moosa Bhai's old house which is in our area.
He had not bought the new house by then. His wife still likes
that area. Moosa Bhai told his relative, "*Sala, Yaqoob ko jab andar
se khabar mil gai thi ke Gallu ne police ke kaan mein haag diya hai to fir
jhanjhat cancel karna chahiye tha, abhi kitne mein padga malum hai? Sab
ko . . . sala* [When Yaqoob became aware that Gallu had tipped off
the police, he should have cancelled the plan. Now do you know
how much it cost everyone]?" This relative had worked with Moosa
Bhai for years. He was his secret keeper. Moosa Bhai switched on
the television. There was some news about an incident but then
I wasn't as aware and couldn't understand a thing. The relative

asked, "*Apna kuch lagela hai kya seth* [Is something of ours at stake boss]?" Moosa Bhai said, "No, but these people are friends. And this boy, Yaqoob. What a smart chap he is. May God bless him." That night we stayed at Moosa Bhai's house for long.'

Ali asked the driver to stop the taxi a little before the VT station near a restaurant. They had chilli chicken and fried rice at the restaurant. During the meal Ali told him more about the Mumbai serial blasts. Soon they were done with eating and paid the bill. While getting up Asrar said, 'Still, it is wrong to kill innocent people.'

Ali remarked, 'If they hadn't been killed, we wouldn't have been alive. The situation was very dangerous then, idiot!'

Ali stood up, Asrar opened his umbrella. It was still drizzling. Ali bought two paans from the nearby shop. Asrar said that they could have had food at the room itself when Ali said, 'Cross the road and I'll explain it to you.' Across the road there were British-style buildings that were under construction, below which were arched and shaded footpaths for pedestrians. They headed towards the station. The shops were closed. The small lanes in this area of Mumbai were very pleasing to the heart. They were an example of the same architecture which was reflected in the British-style buildings. The walls of the covered lane, *raahdari*, were made of large bricks. During the day the place was crowded with stalls and makeshift shops that sold stationery, books, toys, clothes, etc., but after sunset the area saw another world altogether. A mysterious world of entertainment and recreation. Asrar had never seen the area in such a spirit of revelling before. He was amused and amazed at seeing beautiful and ravishing women in the shades and shadows of the raahdari's walls. Two playful girls were talking to a man. A girl in body-hugging jeans stood in the darkness. Her face was hardly visible, but her attractiveness wasn't hidden. Ali pressed Asrar's hand and said, 'Isn't she hot?'

She had sharp ears and turned towards them. 'Want to come?'

Ali stopped. Asrar pulled his hand to drag him away, but in vain. The girl approached them. Asrar stared at the girl. She was beautiful.

She had a sharp, long nose and lips that looked like juicy mulberries. The girl repeated, 'You want to come? The hotel is quite near!'

Ali whispered, 'How much will you charge?'

'Five hundred, extra for the hotel.'

'I have one more guy with me,' he said looking at Asrar. Asrar was both amazed and scared at the same time.

'His charge will be extra,' the girl said.

'Tell us the combined rate,' Ali said.

The girl looked at Asrar and said, 'Seven.'

'Will you come for five?' Ali bargained.

'*Chal, hawa ane de* [Get lost].' The girl refused and turned away.

Ali and Asrar moved ahead. Ali said, 'I knew she wouldn't agree but I still tried just to teach you how to deal with these women.' Asrar said nothing. He walked in silence. Till VT railway station he saw beautiful women selling their bodies. They took a taxi. Asrar said, 'The girls here are really pretty.'

Mohammad Ali looked at him and chewed on his betel leaf, 'This is the area for rich people. Pretty women and high rates.'

They talked randomly for a while.

When they reached the room, everyone had already slept. Qasim opened the door. No sooner had they hit the bed than they fell asleep.

Asrar's train to Ratnagiri was at midnight. He boarded it.

There were five to ten minutes left before the departure of the train. The crowd in the general compartment was comparatively thin on that day. A twelve-year-old boot-polish boy with a ragged bag on his shoulder entered the compartment. Asrar sat on the first seat near the door, next to the window. The moment the boy entered he shouted, 'Boot polish, sir, should I polish yours?'

Asrar looked at him with sleepy eyes and yawned. 'I am wearing slippers, walk ahead, kid.'

'So what? Let me polish your chappals,' snap came the reply. Asrar was impressed by his confidence and wit. He said, 'Leave it' and handed him Rs 5. The boy took the coin and raised his hand in a quick salaam and moved forward. A man with a cardboard box full of water bottles boarded the train and shouted, 'Paniwala, pani.' Asrar stopped him and bought a bottle of water. He took two gulps. The train moved. Asrar had been feeling very tired over the past few days. When the cold breeze touched his face, he fell asleep. He had closed his eyes, but it was not sleep. For now his eyes opened in the same bed where Ali had taken him two months ago. He had felt that the room was congested. He went there for the sake of Mohammad Ali's friendship. On the other hand, that area, those women, the ambience, gave rise to feelings that fuelled carnal desire. This passion, this desire and need is a self-feeding want. No one guides anyone on how to quench this thirst. The paths unfold themselves. Like the passion of love, the desire of sex moves, unstoppable, towards Nimrod's fire! Once the ambience was set, Asrar had simply flown along.

Shanti had drawn the curtains of the diwan. The curtains were made of red cotton. The light that sieved through the red colour cast its shadows on their skin, making their complexion alter its colour.

$$O$$

Shanti had had more than twenty to thirty customers daily since the age of fourteen. Drunkards, rogues, pious, communal, respectable, noble men with established status in society would all come to her and pour the heat of their blood into her and return to their civilized society. This was the routine. She wasn't interested in who crawled on her in what way, who trampled her with all his might. She kept lying like the ground beneath one's feet. Does a whore symbolize the downtrodden earth? Was she the dying sound of creation and fertility? God only knows. But Shanti was that ground within which life and creation were taking their last breath.

It is said that destruction is necessary for evolution. Shanti was very aware of the fact that her existence was also a necessity. All the secret routes to her soul that emerged from her vagina and uterus were now maimed. Her womb was a dark moon. Asrar lowered his gaze and scratched his nose with his left hand. Shanti sat with her back resting on the wall. She saw Asrar lowering his gaze. Asrar's eyes stayed focused on the bed. Shanti's experience had taught her that the moment the curtains dropped, the customer utters two–three formal and made-up praises of her beauty and immediately puts his hands on her breasts without caring for her reaction. There were some who asked her about her well-being. Twice or thrice, there were customers who came only to hold a conversation. They asked questions about her life and clicked a few photographs.

Once a British novelist had come over. His eyes were small, and he sported a long beard. He asked Shanti a few questions in a Mumbai dialect. Shanti really enjoyed this interaction. The novelist had given her a Kashmiri shawl before departing. Shanti really loved the present. Sometimes she took out that shawl from her box when the smiling face of the novelist flashed in front of her eyes. Once a rich Gujarati had come over, had given her a Rs 1000 note and ordered her to turn over.

She returned the note immediately and said, 'I'm a whore, not your wife.'

The man was shell-shocked and immediately left the place.

Two or three minutes had passed. Neither did Asrar make any advances, nor did he try to strike a conversation. She saw that he had shut his eyes. She was reminded of what Madhuri had said, 'He is new, be careful,' and she smiled. She was amazed at her own smile. She was reminded of her first time.

Shanti's childhood was spent in the Killari village of Latur in Maharashtra. One week was still left before her fourteenth birthday when her luck showed its true colours. Her parents were sleeping inside, and she was sleeping with her grandmother on a charpoy outside. In the middle of the night, they heard loud bangs and in front of their eyes the entire village was reduced to a rubble. She held on to a neem tree and realized it was shaking too. She had learnt about earthquakes in school and was sure this was an earthquake. In a while, her ears were witness to loud shouting, weeping, calls for help, running, wailing, grief-stricken voices and much more that wrenched her heart.

The earthquake had destroyed everything in Latur. More than 10,000 people died, 16,000 were wounded, and more than 20,000 domestic animals were eaten up by the earth. Her parents and younger brother were victims of this disaster. Her maternal uncle gave her courage and support. She had no one left in this world but her Ashok Uncle. He always looked upon Shanti with a lot of care and love. Shanti was aware of his kindness. Ashok made her sit under a mango tree at a distance where she sat crying her heart out. In the afternoon people started pulling out dead bodies from the rubble and putting them out in the open. This was when Shanti went towards the destroyed houses. The bodies were so many that one could not count them, and even more difficult was finding the dead bodies of the loved ones. Many wounded people were trying to lift the bodies and putting them in order without caring about their own injuries. These volunteers had advised children to stay away from the site of destruction. The children, ignoring this, cried and looked for their loved ones. A schoolteacher whose head was severely injured asked people to take the children away, for this terrible sight would become a lifelong trauma for them. They scolded and drove the kids away.

Shanti came and sat under the mango tree again. Before dusk, government employees had also reached the spot. The children were injured, traumatized and scared. The wailing cries of the children rose and fell with short intervals. Somewhere some woman cried and beat her chest in grief. A traumatized woman tore open her blouse and kept shouting at the top of her voice while beating her chest. Killari village looked like Karbala with innumerable dead bodies, open wounds, traumatized children, destroyed houses, wailing women and crying men. Shocked birds were perched on tree branches. The animals that managed to stay safe during the quake were now so terrified that they looked near-dead already. Dogs were howling and cats searched for familiar terraces and walls. Those who had died were gone, but those alive were in no better condition. Close to sunset, Shanti's uncle informed her that he would be taking her away from this disaster to another city. She was broken-hearted and silent. Her uncle told her that dead bodies were all kept in the government hospital and would be handed over to the relatives after a few days; it was no use staying back in the village. Shanti had no other option and so she held on to her uncle's hand and accompanied him. She had realized that Killari was now the graveyard of the living. Before the arrival of government representatives and NGO volunteers in the village, Ashok Uncle had already left with Shanti.

He booked a lodge near the Aurangabad depot. He tried explaining to Shanti throughout the day that the village was destroyed forever. She had to be courageous to start a new life. The untimely and sudden demise of her parents was the worst sorrow of her life. Tears flowed down her cheeks constantly. Ashok would try to hug and console her. She kept weeping for three to four days. On the fifth day Ashok took her out for a visit to a historical monument in Aurangabad and bought her two new frocks and a maxi. He took her to a nice restaurant. They returned to the lodge in the evening.

After a while Ashok told her that he was going out for some work. Till then she was to bathe and change into fresh clothes. Shanti had grown up. She blushed at her own image in the mirror clad in the brightly coloured frock. She combed and parted her hair. She stared at that parting and wondered how fortunate she would be if Ashok put vermilion in this parting and made her his wife. This elated her grief-stricken heart. She liked him. Ashok had graduated four years back and was a contract clerk at a government office. Shanti had felt that Ashok looked at her through the eyes of a man rather than her uncle. He had many times stared at her body with the eyes of a hungry lion. As it is, a lot of women in Maharashtra got married at a very young age. Marriage between uncles and nieces was also common among some tribes and communities. Shanti, dressed in her new frock, lay on the bed. She had already slept by the time Ashok returned. Ashok had got rice, kebabs and Pepsi from outside. Seeing Shanti fast asleep he took out a Romanov vodka bottle and mixed it with Pepsi. Romanov vodka was his favourite drink since college days.

Shanti woke up in short while. She sat up. Ashok smiled and said, 'It's good that you took some rest.'

She got up and went to the bathroom. She washed her face, redid her hair and moved closer to the bed. She looked at herself in the mirror. 'You look pretty in this frock,' Ashok complimented her. Shanti blushed but did not reply and kept looking at the mirror and putting clips in her hair. 'Did you hear what I just said? You look pretty in the frock.' She turned and replied, 'I am so dark, do not make fun of me, Uncle.'

'*Arre pagal*! Who said that you are dark? You are just like Sridevi.'

She was embarrassed. She turned to look in the mirror and was immediately reminded of her mother. Many more memories came rushing back to her mind. She had some grievances with her mother. She fought a lot with her father and when he went out of

the village, she went away with the local Shivam Senav chief. Her
grandmother had abused her mother a couple of times, 'You go
there to fuck in the jungle?' Shanti thought that this abuse was out
of anger and moreover, such abuses were common in the village.
Her mates at school also abused each other. In fact, they were
expressions commonly used.

One day she returned early from school. The door was closed.
Her grandmother and father had gone out of the village. She climbed
up the ladder placed at the back wall of the house and peeped inside
and was shocked to see her mother and the Shivam Senav head in
an objectionable position. This had happened one month before the
earthquake. She had then climbed down the ladder and gone towards
the jungle. She sat under the trees there for about an hour or more
and when the school got over she went back to her house. Her
mother was busy cooking food. Shanti hid her emotions and grief.
This disloyalty of her mother had wounded her heart.

Even though her mother had been disloyal, when the mirror
reminded her of her mother, her eyes let loose a string of tears.

Ashok got up and walked up to her. He stood pressed against
her back and absorbed her tears in his handkerchief. She could
feel Ashok's touch against her back and hips. This touch made
her conscious. Her heart was full of a mélange of emotions.
She stopped crying. Ashok made her sit at the edge of the bed.
He conversed with her for a long time and tried to console
her. He told her about the obstacles she would face in life and
gave her motivation and courage. He held her hand between
his own. He made her swear that she would never cry again.
He told her that they would return to the village in two days.
The government might have completed their work by then and
hopefully the hospitals would begin handing over the dead bodies
to relatives. He said that after performing the last rites, he would
take her to Pune, and rent a house there and take care of her.

Shanti thought that Ashok was indirectly trying to say that he would soon make her a part of his life. This misunderstanding or illusion gave her great satisfaction.

At around 10 p.m. Ashok served food in two plates and poured the Pepsi into glasses. He offered one glass to Shanti. She drank half the glass in the first gulp. They continued talking while eating kebabs. The dinner got over and by that time alcohol had found its way into Shanti's blood. She could feel sleep in her eyes. Thoughts came to her heart with great speed. She remembered Ashok intentionally leaning on her back. When her entire being was intoxicated, she declared to herself, 'I'm in love with Ashok Uncle.'

Ashok turned up the fan. They lay on the bed and fixed their eyes on the ceiling fan. Ashok's fingers intertwined with Shanti's. She was enjoying the feeling. For her love was that feeling, the feeling that aroused from brushing against each other. She had just crossed the bloody line of female adolescence nine or ten months back. After her first menstruation, her mother had explained to her the relationship between the womb, uterus and the deep red blood. She had shared her secret with her friends. Girls who were older than her by four or so years increased her knowledge on the same. Most of the information was exactly what Jamila Miss had taught Asrar from the class nine biology book. There was a girl named Rakhi who was around nineteen years of age. She had already slept with twelve bachelors, two married men, two boys younger to her and a close relative. She interrupted what the other girls were saying and said, 'The womb is the Kurukshetra of a woman and a man's love.'

All the girls burst out laughing after hearing that. She also told them that the womb was a spell of God through which the universe was created. Perhaps, this was what her relative had explained to her on having sex. She told them that there was a spot inside the vagina where the universe and nirvana rested together. To make sure that making love didn't end up on a funeral pyre, it was important to reach that point. She had read this line in some Marathi book and had memorized it. She had made most girls around her aware of themselves and they wished to enjoy the pleasures of making love deep inside their hearts.

Shanti was silent. Ashok said, 'I really like you.'

She turned towards him without replying and looked into his eyes. Her eyes were intoxicated. Ashok turned towards her too. The fan suddenly speeded up. Maybe the voltage had increased. He placed his palm on her cheek. His gesture was met with her silence. He turned off all the lights. That very moment Shanti could see nothing but darkness. Before Shanti could adjust to it, Ashok bent over and whispered into her ears, 'You are my wife now.'

Her overwhelmed emotions translated into tears.

She could feel the warmth that was oozing out of Ashok's fingers and lips touching her. The intensity and passion sparked desire within her. She was ready to move ahead but the lack of experience had created clouds of anxiousness within her. Rakhi's words resounded in her ears, 'The womb is a spell of God through which the universe was created.'

She said in a lowered voice, 'Yes, I am your wife,' and closed her eyes.

Asrar's closed eyes reminded her of her own closed eyes. She thought that there was fear in the boy's heart. She moved ahead and placed her head on Asrar's shoulder and said, 'Say something . . .'

Asrar did not speak up. She sat across from him.

Asrar said, 'I'm not here to do anything. Just to see.'

'Aah, tell me what you want to see,' Shanti said seductively.

'Just to see how this world is like.'

'This isn't a world. It is hell,' she snapped.

'A man enters this hell out of his own will and a woman by God's will.'

'You look educated.'

They remained silent for a long time and then Shanti said, 'If you don't feel like right now, don't do it. Whenever you do, come over.'

Asrar smiled and she reciprocated his smile. He shook hands with her and stared at her in the scarlet light for a few more minutes. Shanti now spread herself on the bed. Asrar kept sitting beside her. After ten to twelve minutes, the room echoed with Ali and Madhuri's loud conversation. Shanti got up. Asrar whispered into her ears, 'It should look as if we did have sex.'

She pulled him to the bed and said, 'Lie down, shake the bed a little, act and then get up and leave.'

Mohammad Ali gave Rs 400.

Madhuri shoved the notes in the cleavage of her blouse and looked at Asrar. 'Keep visiting, boy.'

Asrar shook his head. By then Shanti had also returned. Madhuri handed over her share of the payment.

Shanti looked at Mohammad Ali and said, 'Your friend is nice.'

'Trying to flirt, eh?' Madhuri remarked playfully.

Shanti laughed.

Asrar addressed Madhuri and said, 'Shanti has become an expert!'

Shanti was impressed by the compliment. Taking the credit, Madhuri proudly declared, 'I have trained her.' She paused to look at Shanti and continued, 'She used to be so difficult and hesitant in the beginning.'

Shanti smiled and Madhuri wrapped her arms around her neck.

'Farewell, I will return soon,' said Ali and headed towards the door.

Asrar followed.

This brief fusion between memories and dream occurred in such a flash that it didn't feel like a memory. It felt like an elaborate film of each moment. When he opened his eyes, the train was passing the bridge over the Vashi creek. The same boot-polish boy was sitting in the space between the compartment door and the washbasin. He was smelling a handkerchief. Asrar realized that the boy was taking drugs. He wanted to stop him and explain the ramifications to the kid, but then he was reminded of the sex workers of Kamathipura. His conversation with Shanti came rushing back to his mind. He said to himself, 'Some intoxication is necessary to continue living life.' He looked out of the window. The water in the creek below looked mysterious in the moonless night. He drank some water from the bottle. He kept reflecting on why he could not convince himself to sleep with Shanti. There was no specific reason coming to his mind. He decided to go and meet Shanti again someday.

The train stopped at Panvel station.

The stalls on the platform had shut. Two dogs were sleeping, and an old man was selling tea. Three boys deboarded the train and went to the tea seller. He served them tea in plastic cups. Asrar remembered that while coming to Mumbai, they had stopped at this station and had tea from a stall which was at a small distance from where the old man stood. The excitement to see the city had rushed through him when he had boarded the local train here. It was as if Mumbai was a black hole which was pulling him towards it. Oblivious of all realities around he felt he was also falling into the vastness of that black hole. He was getting acquainted with the realities of the city and in the past two and a half months, he had already seen and visited many areas of Mumbai and around. But his thirst remained unquenched. He wanted to see each part of the city, absorb its scent in his veins and adorn its colours on his brow.

Asrar had made good friends in the kholi. They let him accompany them wherever they went. This was also because

Asrar was an ardent listener. He would listen to whatever they had to say and never utter it to any other soul. He would forget what had been said. He was trustworthy and people felt at ease while sharing their secrets with him. He had great control over his speech. He never indulged in a wasted conversation. His skin had become lighter during his stay in Mumbai. A layer of red had covered his lips and his eyes shone brighter. His eyes were light greenish, which attracted people. On the first meeting itself people couldn't resist praising his eyes. The wish to be independent and stand up for himself had given rise to a peculiar satisfaction within him which not just reflected in the seriousness of his tone but also in his eyes.

The train started moving. Not more than five minutes had passed when it began to rain. Asrar immediately shut the window. Another fellow traveller got up and closed the door through which water was entering the compartment. The boot-polish kid had deboarded the train at Panvel station. The compartment was a little dark. Most travellers were sleeping with quilts wrapped around them. It was getting cold. There was a view of the jungles from the window after Panvel. The weather here was generally pleasant and during the rains it became exceptionally beautiful. The train crossed a river. The river was at its best. Asrar stared at the moving waters. A little distance away from the river were a few houses which had yellow bulbs lit at their entrances. One could see the play of smoke and raindrops in the yellow light. Asrar slept off with this image and that of the river in his eyes. He rested deep in the arms of sleep, cutting himself off from his physical and spiritual existence for about an hour or two. After the deep sleep, slowly some elements of his subconscious translated into grey, purple, deep pink colours and engulfed his dreams, and searched for faces to reveal themselves. Deep inside the being there were numerous faces, experiences of the soul, which only few experts could skilfully explain and interpret. The being tries to convert these faces into dreams because ignorance of them could be the main reason behind the soul's sorrow and the convulsions of the being.

Asrar saw a dream. He was sleeping in a dark room. Although there was no lamp inside the room, his heart was lit up and this light was decreasing his fear of the darkness. There was no door or window in that room. It felt as if there was nothing else inside. He had no clue about how he found his way inside. The room had no roof. When he opened his eyes, the sky had a different feel to it altogether. In that dream, he opened his eyes at short intervals and successively fell asleep soon after. He felt he had been sleeping in this room for a long time. He had seen the moon turn crimson four times and once break into two halves. He could see a black moon, or something covered in black right next to the moon, which had a bright halo around it.

This scene shook his heart with fear, but whenever he saw the moon turn red, he felt happiness from within. In the light of the red moon, he saw the light from his own heart become redundant. In his short intervals of consciousness, he realized that his room was wandering in the dark universe without any other room to give it company. Everything in the sky, and their secrets were flying away from him. He saw an extravagant display of firecrackers in the sky at least six times. Many stars were broken and scattered in the universe as if celebrating their own end. The rays of thousands of colours were traversing the universe, but before eyes could preserve the rays they crossed the distance of centuries. In that room Asrar had been help captive for eternity, but time had no access to it. He had no idea why he didn't get up or try to get out of the room and search for someone. He did not know.

Once he noticed that a woman descended from the heavens and sat on his lap. She had a magical wand in her hand and her face shone green. She wore a mask on her eyes which shone with golden glitter. She waved her wand and suddenly the dark room transformed into a royal bedroom. They were on a grand charpoy across which was kept a teak table. A blue glass tray was kept on it. The tray had cashew, almonds and hapus mangoes on it. A red-coloured wine bottle also found space there. The woman took a sip from the wine bottle and poured it into Asrar's mouth through her lips. The wine was so intoxicating that it made him lose all connection with his existence. He could feel himself transform into a handsome prince. There were two glittering bead necklaces around his neck and his fingers adorned exotic gems. He was healthy and his chest was broad. The woman kissed his chest, eyes and lips. He held her tightly in his arms. She was silent. He had no thoughts to share too. It was as if she had known him for years and he too knew who she was. It flashed through his mind that this woman could be Shanti, but he discarded the thought because Shanti was a young adolescent girl whereas this woman seemed older and experienced. He smiled and thought that this woman was no other than Jamila Miss. The woman waved her wand again. That very moment it started raining rose petals on the bed and over them. They had no clothes on their bodies, which now smelt of fresh rose. The woman kissed him on the bed of petals. Her kiss left a permanent mark on a corner of his heart. He was involved in the act too. After the act of love, she kissed his forehead. He removed the mask from her eyes. He recognized her. He had known the woman for years. He then kissed her on her arms and held her close. She waved the wand again to change the ambience.

He opened his eyes. The train was at Mangaon station. It was 6 a.m. He pressed his mind to remember the dream but could recollect only a few parts. The part which did not vanish from his mind was the fact that he remembered who that woman was. He could not share his dream with anyone. He thought that no one else in the world could see such dreams except him. He did not know why he saw such dreams. In the past four or five years he had seen similar dreams and always remembered the woman. He felt no embarrassment in the course of the dream but when he opened his eyes, he felt a little ashamed.

A few months later, when Shanti shared with him her secrets and related a similar dream, he also told her about the woman he had seen.

Three tea sellers and two vada pav vendors entered the compartment. He bought one vada pav and sipped his tea while looking out of the window. The remnants of rain clouds were still there.

The train started again. Most passengers were now awake. Some were brushing their teeth near the door. A woman was chiding her child for having peed on the berth. An old Madrasi man sitting next to him took out a box from his pocket which contained his artificial teeth. He placed them in his mouth and looked at himself in the mirror on the box lid. He seemed very proud of his shiny white teeth. His wife said to a fellow lady passenger in a mischievous tone, 'He thinks he is nothing less than Rajinikanth.' Everyone around started laughing. Another bearded man who apparently was a Bihari was travelling with his wife. His wife had been complaining about being bitten by something on her stomach for quite some time. She faced the other side and took off her burqa. Her husband shook and dusted her veil near the window and returned it to her. She kept it aside and called out to a tea seller. She apparently wanted to be free from the black veil for a while now. Some young French boys sat on the opposite berth. They were headed for Goa. They had been gaping at the veiled woman for quite some time. So, she wanted to remove her veil to reveal her age to them. Two dusty-eyed girls walked from the other compartment and stood by Asrar's seat to look out of the window. They were wearing shorts and had attracted the attention of the entire compartment. Asrar cast a passing glance at them and resumed looking outside. They had pretty legs. Looking at them, he was reminded of Jamila Miss's legs. The only difference was that Jamila Miss had silky golden hair from below her knees to her ankles.

The sun spread its rays on the green stretch of the mountains outside. The tamarind, jackfruit, peepal, mango trees stood drenched in the rain. Wild grass had grown around their roots. There was greenery as far as one could see. The drops of rain on leaves, branches and the grass shone in the first rays of the sun. Waterfalls tumbled down a few hills. There were small drains around the train tracks. The water reflected the red soil. These drains surely met some rivers which emptied themselves into the Arabian Sea. The red flowing water retained its identity while flowing through the salty green waters, although the sea gently diluted the distinction. The sea, after all, had a reputation to maintain. 'The sea engulfs everything, even memories.' This thought ran in Asrar's head. He was reminded of that night when Jamila Miss had accompanied them to the sea.

They had eaten dinner around midnight. His mother had fried freshly caught pomfret on the gas stove. He had no clue that his mother had carried the spices with her to fry fish. Jamila Miss was happy. His uncle, too, talked a lot with her. Her mother slept off around three in the night. He could see the desire for sleep in Jamila Miss's eyes too. The servants were smoking bidis. His uncle instructed Asrar to spread a sheet on the deck so that 'Miss can rest for a while'. He went and returned. 'Come on, Miss. Go sleep on the deck. I will wake you up before morning.' Asrar helped her climb the deck. She turned and he said, 'You can sleep comfortably without any tension.'

'It would have been a pleasure had you and me been the only travellers on this boat,' she whispered.

Asrar didn't reply and left the deck.

When he was separating the fish from the net in the open air, Jamila Miss's whisper, 'It would have been a pleasure . . .' echoed in his ears. He wondered what was this word 'pleasure' all about? Why was it that there was pleasure in whatever he did with Jamila Miss, pleasure in all the time he spent with her, all the work he did for her, pleasure in every moment he was with her. He was drowned in his thoughts when another question occurred to him: Why is it that pleasure changes into 'wetness' so easily?

The boat started its return journey around 5.30 a.m. A round of tea was already over. After a few minutes the sky started lighting up. There was still time for the sun to rise. His uncle asked him to wake up Miss so that she could witness the sunrise. There was a small island nearby. 'We will anchor the boat there so that she can see around,' Uncle said. Asrar went to the deck.

He bent towards her face and whispered, 'Miss.'

He got no answer. He patted her arms and said, 'Miss, wake up. It is about to be dawn.'

Miss caught hold of his hand. He could only utter, 'Miss, it is about to be morning.'

She looked at him and said, 'I'm not asleep. I'm awake.'

'Why? Didn't you sleep at all?'

'No. It felt nice to think about you,' she confessed while getting up. He looked at her attractive eyes. They were not just dreamy but were intoxicating at the same time. She came out on the deck. He stood still. He could not understand what to do or say. This confusion made him lie down on the bench that had a sheet spread on it. He could feel the warmth of Jamila Miss's body on that sheet. He felt her through her closed eyes and entrenched her odour within himself. The smell had a faint, unspeakable sadness. He opened his eyes and kept the sheet aside. The orange, yellow and pink colours of the rising sun decorated the horizon. His mother, servants and uncle were having tea.

Jamila Miss looked at the rising sun with a sense of longing within her.

In half an hour, the boat was anchored near a small island spread over ten kilometres. The island had sky-kissing coconut trees. There were also amla, karvanda trees, squirrels, butterflies and chameleons. There was a well, constructed by the villagers, nearby. Asrar drew water from the well so that everyone could freshen up. Then his uncle brought out the gas cylinder, stove, sugar, tea leaves and a kettle for making tea.

Asrar told Jamila Miss that some years back a team of archaeologists from the Archaeological Survey had stayed on the island for some months. They had carried out digging at many spots.

Asrar's uncle joined the conversation and said that he had visited the island during those diggings. He had spoken to government officials who had told him that they believed that this area was part of a coastal kingdom called Paus and their king had his palace here. The team was searching for the remains of that palace. But the artifacts they found here culturally belonged to Sindh. Jamila Miss found all of this interesting, even though she had no prior interest in history or the history of cultures. She expressed her desire to see those excavation sites. Asrar said that he would show her around after tea. When they got up to leave, Asrar's mother warned, 'Do not go very far in. People say that there are a lot of snakes.'

He smiled and said, 'We'll return soon.'

Asrar and Jamila Miss followed a narrow path and reached the centre of the island where coconut trees stood sticking to each other. There were beer bottles, cigarette butts, broken glass and plastic pouches lying around. They turned right from there and arrived at the wall where the excavations had been done. The two vanished from everyone's sight. The sound of the waves hit their ears and the cold breeze touched their bodies. A little further the excavations suggested the presence of a few rooms. It was possible that in the past there had been a palace here. They descended the stairs nearby and realized that the excavation was done along such lines that the skeleton of the structure was clearly noticeable. Asrar walked in front and Jamila Miss followed. They reached the ground floor and looked towards the sky.

'Isn't this splendid, madam?' Asrar said.

'Yes, perfectly round.' She smiled.

He looked into her eyes and gathered the courage to utter, 'That line you said at night was pretty solid.'

'Which line?' she asked casually.

'It would have been a pleasure had you and me been the only travellers on this boat,' he said mimicking her tone.

She laughed out loud. He stood in silence.

He ran his eyes on the surroundings.

He was amazed and confused at her laughter. His face wore a faint smile. After a pause Jamila Miss said, 'It was not a line, pagal. My heart really desired that.' He said nothing and kept staring in her direction. He could not bring himself to tell her that till morning he had pondered over that sentence from all perspectives. Seeing his silence she said, 'Let's go and see what lies ahead.' She pulled him by his arm and climbed a slope. The moment they reached the top, there was some movement in the grass. Jamila Miss let out a scream and Asrar couldn't control his laughter. She stared at him while he kept on laughing. She searched the grass but couldn't see anything. Then she saw that a packet lay near the wall, the sight of which embarrassed her. She stared at the picture on the packet which was that of a scantily clad, seductive woman and the text read 'Delux Cobra for Lasting Pleasure'. Miss's eyes darkened and Asrar became quiet after seeing her expression change. The sound of the waves could be heard still. They stood silent under the open sky. There was a centuries-old palace beneath their feet. For centuries the craving, the belongingness and the surrender that gave birth to the desire of meeting each other in loneliness had grown in their hearts. They moved towards the last room of the dilapidated palace. It was faintly lit. There was a banyan tree on the other side, the branches of which had entered the room. They were now facing each other.

When a man and a woman stand across from each other with a desire of surrendering their hearts and soul, the condition of their being reflects in their eyes. A dreamy feeling of intoxication surrounds their eyes. They were captives of that feeling. This feeling isn't a slave to any relation that needs to exist between the man and woman. The only necessity is the presence of a man and a woman. To be each other's need is the only relation required.

Asrar wasn't aware of what happens when love accompanies this feeling. Asrar's soul was yet to experience *ishq*. And on the other hand, it was as if a cobra had bitten Jamila Miss and its venom had spread in her entire being. She searched for the antivenin in

Asrar's stretched veins. Asrar's fingers could feel the venom inside
her. It had a distinct warmth, a unique smell and flavour. Jamila
touched his eyelashes with her tongue. He poured his antivenin on
her soft petals, on the rosy tongue of her being. The warmth of this
was like raindrops on her soul. With the soil of her soul drenched
in those raindrops, the venom subsided. She kissed Asrar's forehead
and ran up the slope and stood under the open sky, leaning against
a coconut tree. The sound of the waves kept competing with her
soul. Asrar joined her in a few minutes. He held a banyan branch
and hit her playfully. She kept running and he pursued. This
playfulness continued for long.

It was already past an hour when they returned to the boat.

The train stopped at Khed.

A few people boarded the train. A student asked him, 'Shift a
little and make some space, please.'

Then Asrar surfaced from his ocean of memories.

He made space and the boy seated himself. Asrar looked out of
the window. Clouds were gathering again in the sky.

The train passed a long tunnel on its way to Chiplun from Khed.
He had been to Chiplun a couple of times. This small town
was a valley. He remembered coming to Parshuram Ghat with
his schoolmates to witness the beautiful landscape of Chiplun.
He drank a cup of tea at Chiplun. When the train reached
Ratnagiri, it was 8.20 a.m. by his watch. The sky was covered
with clouds. A yellow dot made space for itself in the black
clouds. It was the sun.

He took out his umbrella from the bag and stuffed it under
his arm. He exited the station carrying his bag on his shoulder.

He spent the entire Sunday at home. He told his mother all the details of his life in Mumbai, his friends and the kholi. He praised Moosa Patel, Saleem and Mohammad Ali a lot.

Haseena ardently listened to whatever her son had to say. After his stories were over, she told him about the events and incidents that had happened in Mabadmorpho. He reciprocated his mother's attention. There were some reports that left him astonished—a djinn had taken over a girl. The girl kept talking to him all the time. No one knew the language she spoke. The people were astonished because it rained coins from the windows of the second floor of her house. At times the girl disappeared for some days and when she returned it didn't seem as if she had been absent. When she returned there was no sign on her body. Her mother said that she didn't vanish but stayed at home, and that because of the effect of the djinn she had become invisible. Moreover, the witches of Mabadmorpho were really angry lately. They were taking away clothes from people's cupboards and from their clotheslines. These clothes were found in their actual condition, ironed or otherwise, on the shore. But now they were fine as a peer baba was invited to calm the witches down. The third incident was that a Hindu girl had eloped with her teacher, but their dead bodies were found three days later at the house that they had rented. A letter was found in their house which read, 'We are killing ourselves of our own will because this world is not made for those who love.' The girl was a Brahmin, whereas the boy was a Dalit. One more sensational incident had taken place while Asrar was away, but Haseena did not talk about it.

A teacher of Madarsa Ahle-Abu-al-Farja-ul-Baladat-ul-Arbiya in the neighbouring village was caught molesting a white goat in the fields. When the panchayat had asked him the reason for such an obscene and shameful act, he had replied that the face of the goat resembled that of his late wife and he believed that her soul had entered the goat's body after her demise.

People laughed at his answer for a long time. The sarpanch was part of the organizing committee of the madrasa and liked the teacher. He gave a long speech on the social importance of a goat. While the speech continued, a few members of the panchayat dozed off on stage. The crowd also lost all interest and started conversing with each other. The sarpanch shot a shrewd glance at the crowd and slipped his last sentence out of his mouth. 'My wife passed away four years back and I know the pain of separation,' he said.

The teacher asked for forgiveness and the matter subsided.

After four days the corpse of a white goat was found on the shore of Mabadmorpho. Its head had been severed.

People came to visit Asrar, and he met them very formally. His neighbour's daughter, who studied in seventh grade, had been finding reasons to come to his house again and again, but Asrar wasn't interested. Even before Asrar went to Mumbai, she had been trying to get casual with him but he found her to be just an innocent, young child. After the sunset prayers, his neighbour called out to him. When he returned from the neighbour's house, he looked surprised. Jamila Miss had called. He told his mother about the call. His mother said that she had met Jamila Miss at the market and had informed her about his visit. Asrar told her mother that he might get late for dinner as Jamila Miss had invited him over. After the prayers he went to his uncle's house and had a short chat with his aunt. He then proceeded to Jamila Miss's building. When he reached near, he paused and looked at the jamun tree. He also looked at the bark of the mango tree which had fallen that night when all the curtains between Jamila Miss and him had been taken down. They were just man and woman at that moment.

The primary relation between man and woman was without promises, aims and conditions. Man and woman are each other's alchemy needs. Everything else is a journey of etiquette. A journey which has successfully destroyed this primary and innocent relationship between man and woman. In spite of this, men and women, even for a moment in their lives, discover this relationship and search for its manifestations. At times this bridge is constructed in a week, a month, a year or many years.

At that point, such was the relationship that existed between Asrar and Jamila Miss. He knocked at the door. Jamila Miss's face brightened as she saw him. He smiled and entered the apartment. She shut the door behind him and kept standing. She then switched off the tube light. She leaned against the wall, and he moved forward. He placed his hand on her forehead and was about to kiss her when he noticed that she was crying. He did not know what to do or what to say. He asked in a soft voice, 'What makes you cry?'

She didn't answer. Her warm tears ran down both her cheeks.

'Did you have a fight with Sir?'

She didn't reply. He wiped her tears with her palms. He kissed her forehead and her eyelashes. He licked her eyes. He put his hands on her shoulders and said, 'Tell me why you are crying.' It was the first time that he had overlooked the honorifics he would use while addressing her.

She wrapped her arms around him and said, 'I love you.'

It was the first time that Jamila had also changed the language she used with Asrar.

'Oho! What is there to cry about then? I love you too.'

After uttering this sentence, he felt a weird languishing feeling within himself. His soul told his heart that he was lying. This was when his heart became curious about what love was. What did love mean? He immediately regained control over himself. Jamila Miss had said that those who loved each other also cared about each other, but he had only called her once after going to Mumbai. He thought that this apparent lack of communication had made Miss think that he didn't love her. He patiently listened to all her grievances. He held his ears and apologized and promised not to repeat these mistakes in the future. Jamila Miss liked the way he held his ears. He hugged her tightly.

They chatted for a long time. Their conversation was interrupted for tea and sweets. Jamila Miss tried to persuade him to stay back for dinner, but he said that there was dinner at home with some of his relatives coming over. They stood near the window. The moon shone brightly. Both were reminded of that night when passion filled the gaps between their bodies.

'Jamila Miss, that night was like the end of the world,' he said, reminiscing about the past.

'Yes, you left scratches all over me,' she replied with a smile.

Their continuously stared at each other, and they shared the pleasure of silence for some time. Asrar finally decided to bid farewell and promised to return the next day. Jamila Miss escorted him to the door.

He went to Mohammad Ali's house the next morning. His house was fifteen minutes from Asrar's place. Mohammad Ali had given him a parcel to deliver. He knocked at the door and was welcomed by a beautiful woman in her mid-forties. She said, 'Mohammad Ali had informed me over the phone that you would come.' He entered the house. No sooner had he taken two steps than he realized that he had forgotten to take off his slippers. He felt embarrassed. He removed his slippers immediately and re-entered the room. There were a few chairs and he sat on one of them. A girl served him a glass of water. This girl was the same age as him. The woman introduced the girl, 'She is Ali's younger sister, Saira.' Asrar greeted her and she reciprocated and went back to the kitchen. The beautiful woman asked many questions about Mumbai and Mohammad Ali and Asrar patiently answered. She told him that Ali's father was at sea. The girl served tea. She told him that Ali's father served as a *khalasi* on a boat. She drank tea and inquired about Asrar's mother.

Asrar gave details about his family, and she happily remarked that she was acquainted with his mother. Sometimes, they met at the fish market. Asrar had no prior knowledge of this. She also said that she and Asrar's father were classmates in school. Two girls in school uniform entered the house that instant. The woman introduced them as Maryam and Rukhsana. They were Ali's younger sisters who studied in sixth grade at the English-medium school. They wished Asrar. The phone rang. The woman picked up the receiver from the corner of the showcase and started talking. It was Mohammad Ali on the line. The woman told Asrar that Ali wanted to talk to him. They spoke and Ali insisted that he should have lunch at his house. Asrar had to give in to Ali's persuasion.

During the conversation, Asrar came to know that the name of the beautiful woman was Rehana Begum, and she was Ali's father's second wife. Ali and Saira were children from his first wife, while Maryam and Rukhsana were Rehana's children. But it was the result of Rehana's good nature and compassion that the kids never felt this difference. They had food after the noon prayers. He ate surmai fish and fried bombil to his heart's content. While biding adieu, Rehana gave a small parcel for Ali which Asrar took with him.

The weather outside seemed pleasant. Clouds were rushing to cover the sky again. People were enjoying the weather in their courtyards. All shops except the ones selling cigarettes and paan were open. Asrar saw one of his schoolteachers and stopped to wish him and chat with him. When Asrar returned home his mother had already slept.

He lay down next to her.

By the evening relatives started arriving. Amusing stories were being exchanged. The people of Mabadmorpho were experts at telling stories when they got together.

Asrar told one of his relatives about Rehana Begum's good nature and warmth. The relative added to those praises. He also said something about Ali's mother Rashida, which left him grief-stricken. He started seeing the manifestations of this tragedy in Mohammad Ali's personality. He realized that Ali had a huge wound in his heart which he tried to cure through his wanderings in Mumbai. These thoughts about Ali made him wonder about himself. Was there any part of his life which he couldn't recollect or did not have the strength to recollect? Could it be that the incident had been submerged so deep into the subconscious that he had to put in extra effort to dig it open? He tried pondering it over but each time his mind travelled to some other thought, and he tried in vain to bring it back. He was at an argument with himself about why he could not focus on what he really wanted to think.

Existence seemed like a riddle, the ends of which were intertwined and lost. His heart was a blackboard on which there was an inscription, but the dust of time had made the text illegible. The more he thought about the text and tried to recollect it, the more it became obscure. It was this text which was the main cause of the melancholy of his soul. The dilemma of his soul shoved him rather into melancholy, but he was not able to understand his situation. The same thing happened to him that day.

Everyone had food at around 9 p.m.

Asrar told his relatives that some of his friends were waiting for him. He told his mother that in case it got very late, he would stay over at a friend's place.

When he left his house, his heart was gloomy. His feet were proceeding towards Jamila Miss's house.

His heart was asking him again and again, 'Why is the heart so treacherous?'

This thought was fatal. It rose in his heart like a shark on the surface of the sea. He submerged under the weight of the question. His eyes lost the virtue of looking at the surroundings as they were. He saw himself diluting in the darkness spread by this question. He wasn't an earthen lamp which the winds could silence, but he could feel the roaring sound of the growing storm around him in the darkness of the question. The question never lasted for more than three minutes but those three minutes had the gift of longevity. They drank on his thoughts and made him feel the agony. Every time he would tell himself that his heart was a blank slate on which unwanted sentences had been scribbled. He kept reading his past from the slate and realized that the heart had become a dormant desert entering which was next to impossible. No one in Mabadmorpho had ever thought about the heart turning into an impregnable jungle of weeds. His mind would revolve around this jungle and then a sentence would leave his mouth which would bring him back from the state of melancholy. Having reached the stairs of Jamila Miss's house, he tried gathering control over his melancholy. 'Jamila Miss is also cheating on her husband.'

He smiled at that thought. He stopped and turned. There was no one behind him. Not even his shadow. He thought, at times even the shadow leaves us. When the thoughts of his shadow engulfed him, god knows from where a frame of his new shadow took shape in his heart. He liked that shadow. He told his shadow that he was part of Jamila Miss's treachery. This treachery was a vicious cycle.

By the time he reached Jamila Miss's door, he concluded that treachery and cheating were human instincts. In fact, the most important aspect of the human instinct.

Spending the night with Jamila Miss reduced his pain. This was so because his heart had found another thought to ponder.

'Treachery is the way to find one's soul.'

This short stay at Mabadmorpho had given rise to many serious questions in him. He searched for those answers within himself. His heart was a fertile field where he harvested his imagination. He was now well acquainted with the meaning and void of human relations. He felt a different sense of hardening within himself. Continuous reflection on his stay in Mabadmorpho, his relationship with Jamila Miss and the past which had been written in a blur on his heart transformed him into a different man altogether.

4

I Wish to Alter What My Words Mean
(*Mein Apni Baat Ka Mafhum Dusra Chahun*)

His friends and the frolicsome atmosphere at the kholi brought him back from the dungeons of his thoughts within a week. Sometimes these imaginings transformed into crabs and scorpions that wanted to crawl on his chest, but tiredness and sleep saved him from the pain.

So, the days spent themselves.

It hadn't rained for many days.

Clouds would gather in the sky over Mumbai, do a little sightseeing and wander off to some other place. Moosa Patel was in Hong Kong for some work. Ali was in some other part of Mumbai and Asrar was managing the counter. He was now aware of the colours, characteristics and textures of various precious stones. He had also learnt the skill of dealing with customers. Whether the customers bought anything or not, they were impressed by Asrar's style of interaction. Moosa Patel was the first to notice this.

It was around 3 p.m. Asrar was sipping tea and chatting with his mates. The clouds rose from the Arabian Sea and covered the sky over Mumbai. The sky was pitch dark. The roaring thunder and lightning created chaos among the sleeping insects that lived in the depths of the drains which ran below Mumbai. On seeing the clouds dance over the city, the mice which lived on the footpaths vanished immediately. There was a message in the sounds made by the mice which was deciphered by the pigeons, eagles and doves. The wind was strong, and it made the trees bend in surrender and move this way and that. Asrar's workplace was near Haji Ali Dargah. The pleasant weather made Asrar decide that he would go for a walk and then head to Kamathipura and meet Shanti. He had made plans to meet her many times but had not been able to do so. This time he made up his mind to surely meet her. He had been meaning to discuss a dream that he had seen some days back. He did not know why he wanted to share it with Shanti. He called Mohammad Ali up and told him that he would be leaving early. Mohammad Ali said, 'It's not a problem at all. I'll finish my work soon and return at the earliest.'

Asrar came out of the shop. The road to the right went towards Haji Ali. He lifted his head to look at the sky and could see only a small section of it which was left open by the tall buildings. The sky looked more like a black umbrella which had deep coloured spots. The clouds danced at a great speed. They rose from the Arabian Sea and fused into each other to form this umbrella. They looked like patches from the ground but were actually like large lakes roaming over a huge area.

He crossed the road when his attention was caught by the television screen inside an electronics shop nearby. He read with full concentration, 'High probability of heavy rains in Mumbai and other parts of the state.' He smiled. His experience told him that whenever there was a forecast of heavy rains, it generally never rained. He had recently bought a black umbrella from Grant Road. He held it under his arms and walked towards Haji Ali Dargah.

A few people were drinking sherbet near the signal. Right next to them a path descended into the sea. If one walked a few kilometres further on the road, one would see Haji Ali. Around that area were beggars looking like Sufis, babas, saints, rogues and notorious boys, and poor people wrapped in rags. Women, children and youngsters begged in the name of God and Haji Ali. Asrar stood at one end of the road and stared at the clouds heading towards Worli. He looked at the pilgrims and rogues who sat on the sea wall and were laughing loudly. A groundnut and pea vendor came to him; he bought groundnuts for Rs 10 and continued his walk towards the dargah. He was surprised to see comparatively few beggars on the way. The level of the sea had also fallen. He could see huge rocks behind the structure of Haji Ali. The sea beyond seemed to have a yellowish hue.

Asrar sat with folded legs in one corner of the dargah. The smell of *lobaan* (incense) was in the air. One could distinctly smell rose and mogra flowers. He tied a handkerchief around his head, remembered his father and offered litanies for him. People were offering prayers inside the dargah. Women whose prayers had been heard looked elated. A few people were busy reading the Quran. Two burqa-clad women were praying in the outer part of the dargah. A woman was beating her chest wildly and a young man was crying with dry eyes. Perhaps the sound of the cries had burdened his throat and raised his heartbeat. It was as if a huge wound had opened in his heart and dried his tears. Asrar was observing them silently. He looked at the clouds from the courtyard and realized that they had covered the entire city. He was oblivious of the fact that it was already raining cats and dogs in Malad, Andheri, Dadar, Borivali, Mira Road, Kurla, Chembur and Mumbra. Milan subway at Santa Cruz was already overflowing.

There was thunder and lightning that blurred his eyes. He opened his eyes only to see a girl standing across from him.

She was clad in a white salwar–kurta. She had two roses in her bun. A light layer of red lipstick adorned her lips. The edges of her eyes flaunted carefully put kohl. She was wearing earrings which reminded Asrar of similar jewellery in his shop. The earrings were studded with two precious gems. Asrar was sure that she belonged to a respectable family. When her facial features caught Asrar's attention, the rest of the surroundings seized to exist. It was raining heavily outside. The sun shone brightly above the clouds with all its strength, but its light could not reach Mumbai. There was a faint light in the veranda of the dargah. The girl's face looked even more attractive in the semi-darkness. She had peace, serenity and confidence on her face. She was enjoying the pitter-patter of the raindrops. The happiness of the rain spread on her face and the spray of raindrops enhanced the beauty of her face.

She had a white bag in her hand with very fine prints on it. Pink and dark wine-coloured patterns looked nice on the white bag. She was looking at the yellow sea. She wiped the raindrops off her face and bent towards the wall. Asrar was staring at her back and waist when suddenly there was a loud thunderclap and the intensity of the rain increased. Asrar thought that the girl would find shelter under the elevated platform, or her companion would get her an umbrella so that she could leave. Very few people could be seen around the grave and the dargah. Those who sat leaning against the grave were lost in their own worlds.

He looked at the smoke from the incense disappearing through the ceiling. The smell of the fresh flowers on the grave was overpowering. Asrar was feeling inspired. He closed his eyes and recited Sura'h Al-Ikhlas and ran his palm over his face. The sound of the raindrops echoed in his ears. He turned towards the courtyard knowing that the girl would no longer be there but to his surprise, she was still there. This time she had her hand raised in prayer. Her body was getting wet in the rain. Asrar kept staring at her in surprise. In fact, the beauty of the scene had taken his breath away. In the pouring rain she seemed to be the most beautiful girl in the world. The heavy rains had by now seized most areas of Mumbai, including Worli to Churchgate. The Milan subway was submerged, and traffic had slowed down in most areas.

According to the calendar, 22 September was the day of the fall equinox.

'In ancient times, especially in the civilization of Egypt, the fall equinox was considered as the celestial day. On this date, the day and night have equal hours and the time prior to night was interpreted as time of death and darkness. Another interpretation of that hour is that every organism has to die before being born, there is darkness before light.'

The maulana in Chor Bazaar read that in the *Kitab-ul-Hikmat Bain-ul-Aafaq*, and he kept pondering on it for a long time.

There was time left in the vanishing of the day into the darkness of death. Asrar was still staring at that girl. She looked oblivious of everything around her. He had never seen anyone so absent from the world before. He thought that maybe she was mad or under some spell. He said to himself, 'Which mad person dresses so well?' He noticed happiness and a smile on her face. He thought that it was possible that she had never got a chance to get drenched in the rain in this way before. Such thoughts came to his mind.

'A thought never dies. It enters into oblivion and stays there alive,' the Sufi had said to the aged man in Chor Bazaar.

Asrar got up, took his umbrella and opened it. The moment he reached the girl, the sky turned dark and the night began. At that time Mumba Devi was not in her temple. She had crossed the Arabian Sea to enter the Gwadar area of Baluchistan, to go to Chabahar, in erstwhile Persia. The two were at a distance of 720 kilometres, but Mumba Devi reached the place within the blink of an eye. Chabahar is a coastal area in present-day Iran forty kilometres from the temple of Enki, which had been given protection secretly by a tribe of Zartashtoon people for the last 1500 years. Enki means the god of earth. The temple had an idol that was thousands of years old and that had been divided into seven pieces by the tribe to save it from invaders and government officials. This clan lived only in deserts and dormant areas. They had their own holy book which had a great resemblance to Zuboor (Book of Psalms). Enki had the knowledge of soul and cultures. He was also considered the god of sweet and fresh underground water and of semen.

Mumba Devi, who was used to the saline water, wanted to spend some time in the fresh waters. It was said that Mumba Devi had already seen Enki's mother, Nammu, who lived in Bahrain where the Arabian Sea met the saline Persian waters. The fusion of the water was called Nammu by the Sumerians. It is said that Enki had had sexual intercourse with his daughter, Ninsar, as well as his granddaughter, Ninkurra. One reason for his sexual acts was considered to be his soul's loneliness. Enki was symbolic of the life generated through the fusion of water and earth. Mumba Devi was very interested in hearing his stories from his daughters. Enki would invite Mumba Devi for a visit each fall equinox. It was believed that the day would come when evening would enter the night and a red moon would shine in the sky, that is when all his daughters would appear together.

'The day when the sun will dip in total darkness, day and night will be equally divided, that is when the moon will turn crimson and shine in the sky. That will be the first day of the world's end. Albeit, it cannot be said what will be the length of Qayama'h [day of reckoning].'

When Maulabax read these lines in one corner of his room, his spirit shivered with fear.

A feeling of fear also ran down Asrar's spine when he came near the girl. He spread the umbrella above her head. When the girl looked at him, he was sure he would get scolded. He stood silently. The girl looked into his eyes. The wind was strong in the rain. There was soft music in the flow of these winds. Asrar and the girl were now unaware of the wind, the rain and the music. They just stared at each other.

Asrar noticed that the kohl in her eyes had smudged, the lipstick had come off because of the rain but her lips were still red. Beautifully red. Her eyes weren't big but had a magical flame within them. He thought that he would apologize and inquire why she was getting drenched in the rain but suddenly a strong gust came and his umbrella flipped inside out. He bent down on the floor to mend it. Seeing him struggle, the girl started laughing. He looked at her, then fixed the umbrella and stood up.

'I'm really sorry, I went into a shock looking at you.'

She said nothing in response.

'You were getting drenched in the rain for such a long time. I was looking at you from inside the dargah.'

She still said nothing.

Asrar was confused by her silence. 'I thought I should tell you that the rain is going to increase in intensity.'

'Okay,' the girl said.

'If your family members are inside, shall I call them?'

'I'm alone.' She corrected herself, 'I mean there's no one with me.'

'The television says that the rain will not stop today.'

'Why believe the television?' the girl asked.

'That is also right. I too do not have absolute trust in the television,' Asrar said.

The few sentences that the girl had spoken had given Asrar the courage to converse further. He asked her if she would stay or go back home, since the sun had set and the rain did not seem like it would stop.

The girl said that she was about to leave when he had come to her. She said, 'I got so scared. I thought a djinn had come with an umbrella.'

'How can a djinn enter a dargah?'

'The pure and pious djinns do come,' she said with a lot of confidence.

He agreed. He had heard since childhood that the pious djinns are present at all holy places and offer prayers.

It had stopped raining.

Both came out of the dargah and proceeded on the path covered by the sea. Asrar folded his umbrella. The girl said that her family was in the perfume and scent business. Asrar introduced himself as someone who worked in a jewel shop at the shopping mall. The girl told him that she had vowed to come to the dargah each Saturday.

'But today is Wednesday.'

She smiled and said, 'You were destined to meet me today.'

Asrar thought she was joking. She told him that she had come today for a specific purpose. In a while they reached the main road. It started raining heavily.

Asrar opened his umbrella and held it over the girl's head.

'Get drenched today. Who knows when we'll meet in the rain,' she said and looked at Asrar.

Asrar replied while he folded the umbrella, 'You seem quite different.'

'You too,' she said.

'Arey, I'm absolutely normal.'

'You mean to say I'm not normal?'

'No no, that is not what I meant . . .'

The girl smiled at his confusion. He stopped talking. The girl told him that her name was Hina. He told her his name and a little about his village. Hina was looking at him. Hina's expression made him feel that he was unnecessarily talking about his village. He had nothing to talk about. Hina kept looking at him. He tried staring back but looked away. There was something in her eyes that did not give him the courage to look at them. Another reason was that he feared if he brought himself face to face with Hina's eyes, the attraction would overpower his soul. The power of her eyes was so immense that he just couldn't bring himself to look at her. Two minutes passed by while he was caught in this indecision. Meanwhile, a taxi stopped near the bus stop. She sat inside it and said to Asrar, who was standing at the door, 'I liked the time we spent together.'

He said, 'I'll come to the dargah on Saturday.'

'I know.'

'What do you know?'

'That we will meet again,' she said without any hesitation.

She smiled and he reciprocated.

The taxi crawled forward. He stood there experiencing her fragrance around him and in the drops of the rain. Hina's smell was equal to the raindrops. He was going to experience the same smell after nine months, three weeks and a few days.

He would then make Hina a part of this feeling and say to her, 'The smell of your body is like that of the raindrops.'

That day would be the last day of Hina's and Asrar's lives.

After half an hour, he took a bus and got down at Nagpada from where he walked on foot to meet Shanti.

She was standing at the door and talking to girls who had the same profession as her.

She wore a red blouse and a light green lehenga. Asrar recognized her. Shanti came near and looked at him closely. She was reminded of their previous meeting. Asrar had gained weight since then. Shanti looked at him and said, 'Coming after so many days, eh?'

'Yes, the job was new.'

'Of course, we're the only free ones,' she said, making a face.

'Honestly, there were a lot of complexities.'

'I kept on reminiscing about the last time,' Shanti said, moving towards the bed.

'I thought of you too.'

'Oh liar!' she said and before he could defend himself, she continued, 'Do not lie uselessly.'

'I swear.' Asrar shook his head to make her believe him.

'Why are you dishonestly swearing? Bombay has changed you too.'

'Believe it or not, I once saw you in my dream,' Asrar said with earnestness.

'I believe you.' She made him sit on the bed and drew the curtains.

'I forgot to tell you. I'm drenched in the rain,' he said in an apologetic tone.

Shanti stood up and went away briefly while he remained seated. Before she came back, many questions and thoughts cropped up within him. The unattractive, dirty walls had made him sad. Suddenly, the appearance of Hina's face in his imagination lightened his heart. Shanti brought him a towel and said, 'Go wash your hands and face in the bathroom.' He took the towel but was hesitant to go to the bathroom. He stood still when Madhuri emerged from somewhere and steadily walked towards the bathroom. Shanti took the towel from his hand and said, 'Leave it . . . Come on, sit here.'

Asrar sat down and Shanti drew the curtains again. She sat on her knees across Asrar on the bed. She removed his clothes and wiped his chest. Asrar stood up and removed his trousers. He took out his wallet and gave Shanti two Rs 100 notes. Shanti kept one note under her pillow and the other under one corner of the mattress. Shanti smiled looking at him and he smiled back. In that exchange of smiles Shanti was much more than a prostitute and he was not just a customer. There was some relationship between the two which they had experience at their first meeting itself. Seeing Shanti wipe his body gave rise to a weird feeling in Asrar's heart. He sat up and said looking into her eyes, '*Bas bas! Itna koe karta hai kya?* (Enough, enough! Who does so much?]'

Shanti said, 'You are not like a customer.'

'Then . . .?' He stopped midway. Shanti was amazed by what he said to her after a few minutes.

He told Shanti that for the last 4–5 years he had been seeing dreams of the same kind. The dream had caused him grief each time. He felt that no one else but he saw such dreams in this world. Many a time, the dreams revealed the identity of the woman who had sex with him in various disguises and loved him too. He told her that these dreams were disturbing him. Even after opening his eyes, the pain continued. His heart wanted to cry out loud. Shanti had lost her strength to speak after hearing all this. After a few moments she said in a grief-stricken tone, 'You have forgiven the person who had hurt your soul so much.'

Asrar was astonished to hear this. He wondered how Shanti could have known the most well-kept secret of his heart. He kept looking into her eyes. Before he could ask anything, Shanti told him that she had been seeing such dreams for quite some time too. She had reported this to a doctor who worked for the welfare of sex workers and was a social worker herself. She had told Shanti that seeing sexual intercourse with a close relative is a sign that people who are closest to us give us the most sorrow, but we have forgiven them. Asrar lay down after hearing the details. She bent over and kissed his lips. It was the first time that she had kissed a customer on his lips. In this kiss there was confession of a mutual pain. It was the cause of an existential ache. Both remained silent. Both were sad in the core of their souls. Both their souls were wounded. Both of them had apparently forgiven those who had hurt them the most. Despite that, this wound bled in the darkest corner of their hearts. If in the darkest corner of the heart an unseen wound bleeds for long, the soul becomes tormented.

'Forgetting relaxes and forgiveness gives peace,' Shanti said after half an hour.

Asrar agreed.

When he left Shanti's room at 11 p.m., the rain had stopped. Cigarette butts, plastic cups, packets, paper, dead flowers floated in the puddles on the street.

He lifted his trousers carefully and crossed the dirty water to reach the road. He washed his feet in one of the puddles and a matchstick stuck to his slippers. He removed his slippers and cleaned the dirt between his toes. The slippers started floating and he immersed the pair in the water a couple of times to clean the dirt on them. He wore his slippers. He was thirsty. There was a restaurant nearby. The man sitting at the counter looked religious from his face and attire. Asrar wished him and asked him for a bottle of Bisleri.

The man called out to a servant. A twelve- or thirteen-year-old boy came out and gave him a bottle from the fridge. He sipped the water and walked towards the bus stop. A few taxis were standing there. He got into one of them. When the taxi started moving, the cold breeze touched his cheeks. The cold of the wind made him feel fresh. It reminded him of how Hina had looked at him from inside the taxi. He wondered what there was in Hina's eyes that he could not look into them at that moment. The entire encounter with Hina flashed through his mind. From the farewell to the moment when he had seen her for the first time. It was like seeing a movie in reverse. He wondered how he could talk to a stranger. From where did he gather the courage to go and stand next to her and hold the umbrella over her head? What if her relatives were around? Would they have beaten him up? Such questions kept coming to him. The taxi stopped at the JJ signal. There was a lot of traffic on the road because of the heavy rain. He looked out of the taxi's window. People were having seekh kebab at a restaurant near the signal. He thought, 'Why do people not stay at home and rest during so much rain?'

The signal turned green, and the taxi turned towards Mohammad Ali Road.

Hina returned to his thoughts. He was amazed at how bold and confident she was. Are bold and confident girls good? He refuted himself by saying, 'There is no need to misinterpret if a person talks to you nicely.' He wasn't satisfied with the answer he gave himself. Had some emotion taken birth inside his heart when he looked at Hina? Why did Hina's presence render him silent? What was it in her appearance that had made him forget the entire world on seeing her drenched? From where were these thoughts coming into his head? Why was he greedy to see her again? Why was he ready to see her face for hours in silence? Why was he seeing his completion in Hina's face? Did Hina talk to all strangers like this? Before he could get out of the net of these questions, the taxi driver stopped the vehicle. Asrar got off the taxi and started moving towards the kholi.

Mohammad Ali was standing at the paan shop.

Asrar was going towards his room but thoughts of Hina were still in his mind. Her face kept appearing before his eyes again and again. Mohammad Ali came to him and asked, 'Where did you go? I've been waiting for you so long.'

Asrar looked at Mohammad Ali as if he was woken up from a dream and said, 'Nowhere. Just exploring around.'

They stood there for some time. When Mohammad Ali was done eating his paan, they went to the kholi.

He told Mohammad Ali that he had gone to Haji Ali from the shop and spent some time there. After which he went to Madhuri's place in Kamathipura and spent time with Shanti. Mohammad Ali put his arms around his shoulder and said, 'Just spent time or fucked her too?'

Asrar smiled.

Mohammad Ali said, 'It's fine. Enjoy as much as you want, just don't tell anyone in the kholi about it.'

'I'm not mad enough to tell anyone,' Asrar responded.

They entered the room.

Asrar relaxed on his bed. He covered himself with a bedsheet and closed his eyes. In front of his eyes Hina stood drenched in the rain. He kept seeing her dripping wet for a long time. He was happy looking at her oblivious of everything—she was dripping in the magical rain. For long he kept looking at her and thus he closed his eyes. The pressure on the mind and the effects of the tiring day drowned him in the deepest ocean of sleep.

Sleep was darkness and there was peace in that darkness.

5

Neither Any News About You, nor of My Own Existence
(*Teri Khabar Na Kuch Apna Hi Ab Pata Chahun*)

On Saturday, Asrar woke up at five in the morning.

Each day felt like a thousand years. The arms of the watch seemed frozen to him.

Only he knew how he spent Thursday and Friday. He was immersed in Hina's thoughts, so much so that he cut himself off from everyone around. In fact, once in the shop Mohammad Ali had stared at him for fifteen minutes and realized that Asrar was only physically present there. Later, over tea, he had asked him, 'Tell me if you have any problem.'

After a long pause he said, 'Nothing. I've been thinking about Shanti a lot.'

Ali believed him.

Asrar realized that his emotions were manifesting in his behaviour and people had started to notice it, so he started talking a lot to other people. Sometimes even unnecessarily, like inquiring which movie was about to release; which hero and heroine were having an affair; what the latest updates in political news were; what the newspapers were printing, and so on and so forth.

In the kholi he would turn the pages of Usman's books. He would please his heart by reading poetry books. If he couldn't understand a word and asked Usman for the meaning. He went to Moosa Patel's house on Thursday evening. While returning, he told Ali that he would leave half an hour early on Saturday to go to Haji Ali. Mohammad Ali suspiciously asked, 'Be honest. You want to go to Haji Ali or to Shanti's?'

Asrar placed the fingers of his right hand on his throat and said, 'I swear I have to go to Haji Ali. I would have told you if I was going to meet Shanti.'

'Moosa Bhai is also a great follower of Haji Ali.' Mohammad Ali smiled.

'Oh!' Asrar said with a pleasant surprise in his tone.

'Do you know why?'

'No, I don't,' Asrar replied.

Mohammad Ali said, 'After the demolition of the Babri Masjid, riots broke out in Mumbai. Moosa Patel was returning from Gujarat. On 6 January, riots suddenly broke out. Dongri, Pydhonie, Nagpada, Tardeo, Mahim, Dharavi, Nirmal Nagar, Chembur, and Khetwadi witnessed skirmishes. His car was between Bandra and Mahim at around 9 p.m., where a few rioters were attacking the men before the police.' Asrar was looking at Mohammad Ali in shock. The latter took a deep breath and continued, 'Moosa Bhai had said that in front of him rioters pulled out five–six people out of their vehicles, removed their clothes and cut them into pieces with swords. A constable was also part of this mob. Moosa Bhai was blank. He closed his eyes and prayed to Haji Ali. Right then a media van came from nowhere from which a few media people got off and started clicking photos of the victims who were covered in blood. Among the journalists was Waghmare, who used to visit Moosa's shop quite often. Both knew each other well. Moosa Bhai got off his car and started walking towards the crime scene when Waghmare shouted, "Ramesh, what are you doing here?" Moosa Bhai understood the code and replied, "I had come here for some work. Want to go home now."

'He made Moosa Bhai sit in the car and said that the riots had spread to the entire city and going towards the main city would be very dangerous. Moosa Bhai told him that a friend named Yaqoob lived near the dargah in Mahim and the media van could drop him there. Waghmare agreed. He also offered to take Moosa's car to his house from where he could collect it later or else the rioters would burn it down. Moosa Bhai gave the keys to him, and he was dropped off at Mahim, where his people lived. The roads were silent, and some shops were on fire. Moosa immediately entered his friend's building. Waghmare kept standing till Moosa reached the top and waved at him from the window. Yaqoob was also there at the window. Moosa Bhai stayed at his friend's house the next day as well. The riots had worsened and spread to Kurla, Deonar, and Vakola till Jogeshwari. It was rumoured that Anuradha Bai chawl was burnt down and six people, including a handicapped girl, were burnt alive. The rumour carried with it flames. There was bloodshed in Pydhonie, Dongri, Jogeshwari, DN Nagar, VP Road, Nagpada, Byculla, Kala Chowki, Worli, Dadar, Dharavi, and Kurla–Ghatkopar. A dargah in Pydhonie, a graveyard in Jogeshwari, and temples in Byculla and Mahim were reduced to rubble. The police commissioner was attacked by a crude bomb, but he was safe. Moosa Bhai had to stay at his friend's house even when his friend's office was burnt down. Yaqoob kept on repeating, "I will fuck those who burnt down my shop!" For two weeks there was rioting, looting, burning and bloodshed.'

After listening patiently, Asrar asked, 'Is this the same Yaqoob we were talking about the other day?'

'Yes. May god give him a place in heaven. Had he not taken revenge, we would have been living in fear till now.'

Asrar did not reply.

That night he dreamt that Mumbai was burning. The flames were spreading everywhere and he was lying on one side of the road covered in blood and his soul was about to depart when Hina ran towards him and looked into his eyes. Suddenly the dream changed. Blood was oozing from one of his eyes. Hina removed a rose from her bun and placed it on his eye. He felt that the rose cured his eye and it stopped bleeding. He wanted to see her with both his eyes, but she was nowhere to be found. He was surrounded by glittering smoke. He then saw that his body had become very frail, and he was flying among the clouds. The direction he was moving towards was darker.

He tried recalling the dream many times on Friday, but he couldn't. He only remembered that Hina had placed a rose on his eye.

He woke up at five in the morning on Saturday.

He kept thinking about Hina while lying on the bed. He started guessing the colour of her clothes. Where would he see her? How would he greet her? What would he talk about? What questions would she ask and what answers would she give?

He spent the entire day looking at the clock. He felt that its arms were being deliberately lazy and slow. The time in which the watch completed five minutes that day was equivalent to an hour on a normal day. He pulled out a perfume from his pocket called mogra and applied it all over, fearing that he might forget doing so in a hurry. He had carried his toothbrush along to work. He brushed his teeth in the bathroom after lunch. He had already combed his hair a couple of times and stared at himself in the mirror for long. There was a pimple above his right eye, and he had tried removing it with his nail but unfortunately it had swollen even more. Asrar thought that Mohammad Ali might notice his anxiety and comment on it, but he was busy working.

After completing his work, Asrar remained lost in thought for some time and then went and stood in front of Mohammad Ali at around 5.30 p.m. Mohammad Ali looked at him and said, 'Do return early to the room. We will go out somewhere.'

'Inshallah,' Asrar uttered and went out of the shop.

The weather was moderate. The wind had moisture. He crossed the road. He bought a Vicks candy from a nearby shop and put it in his mouth so that his breath would smell fresh while he talked. He took out a folded paper from his pocket on which he had written a few of his favourite couplets. He read them while walking. The dargah was now before his eyes. He folded the paper and put it back inside his pocket. He decided to buy a diary on which he would note down his favourite poems and couplets. He looked at the sea and noticed that the water level had receded.

He went inside the dargah and looked for Hina where he had first seen her, but she wasn't there. Then he searched for her in other parts of the dargah but in vain. He was disappointed. He sat where Hina had got wet in the rain. He went to the spot from where he had seen Hina getting drenched but there were so many people between him and the grave that he was not able to see the grid around the mazar. He sat there for a few minutes. His psyche and spirit lightened up and he saw himself sitting inside the sanctum sanctorum. He tried looking for Hina from where he was sitting but he could not see her. In fact, he saw himself. He was the one seeing, and he was the one being seen. He then imagined himself in a boat just where he imagined he was sitting in the dargah. He was seeing all of this with eyes closed. Seven or eight minutes had passed when he opened them. Hina stood before him.

For once he thought that it was in his imagination that he had opened his eyes and Hina was also a part of that imagination. To confirm that it indeed was real, he closed his eyes again and opened them. Hina looked taller from the ground on which he was sitting. Her neck was bent towards him, and she was smiling. Apparently, she had already wished him, but he did not hear her because of the noise around and because he was so engrossed. He got up smiling. The dargah was inundated with pilgrims and it was impossible to have a conversation there. Hina proposed, 'Let's go out.'

He looked back at the dargah after exiting and saw a legion of people from the main gate till all the way inside. On the other side of the dargah were huge rocks on which people sat with their relatives; there were married and unmarried couples too. They sat there looking at the sea and enjoying the cool breeze. Probably also waiting to witness the sunset. Hina climbed up the rocks and put her feet in the water. The area had a lot of sharp rocks around. Hina carefully placed her feet while she moved forward. Asrar followed her. They finally sat on a huge rock where a lot of black and brown crabs were crawling and there were corals too.

'I wasn't sure that you will come,' Asrar said.

'I was sure that you will,' she said, spreading her handkerchief. 'When did you come?'

'Around five forty-five. I met you at five thirty the last time.'

'I come near the *maghrib* on Saturdays. That day I came early.' she smiled.

They kept talking till sunset. They were amazed at the coincidence that had brought them together. They repeated 'anything is possible in Mumbai' many times. This meeting had reduced their strangeness and hesitation to a large extent. They thought each other to be trustworthy and shared what had happened or was happening in their respective lives. They lied a little too. They veiled many stories within themselves with the objective of revealing them when the friendship became a little older. Both were worried about the impression they would make on each other. Was this boldness and openness, giving out a wrong message to the other?

There were fears, reservations and hesitation still in their hearts. These fears were overcome by a small ray of hope of ishq in some corner of their hearts which rose to the surface and cleared their hesitation. They knew in the depths of their hearts that this incidental meeting wasn't a mere coincidence, but in this moment of coincidence there was a concrete sign which had a hidden pleasure for their souls. The very first time when they had met last week, they felt like each other's mirror image. The wish to meet again had taken birth in their hearts but on the day of the first meeting they had expertly hidden their desires. Even on that day they were trying their best to veil their emotions. One more misgiving that each had was this: What if the other did not reciprocate those feelings? What if the other loved someone else? Hence, they took this meeting to be just a start of a friendship. Another reason was that their hearts, bodies and souls were not fresh pages any more. Time and desires had already written so much on those pages.

They got up to leave at sunset and repeated together, '*Time kidhar gaya pata hi nahi chala* [Time flew without our realizing it],' and laughed. They proceeded towards the main road. Asrar jumped and climbed up the rocks and Hina stayed below near the sandy shore. Asrar extended his hand in her direction. She looked at him. Their hearts paused for a second. They were trying to decipher the spark in each other's eyes. Hina handed her beautiful hands to him.

The darkness of the setting sun had found a place in his eyes and the green and yellow lights of the dargah reflected the light of his soul. He looked at Hina's fingers, which he held in his fist. He found the light wine-coloured nail polish very weird, but he could not stop himself from praising the beauty of her nails and fingers.

'You have nails like that of a heroine.'

'I am thinking of growing them.'

He smiled and said, 'Why?'

'So that if someone betrays me, I can press his throat hard,' she replied.

Both burst out laughing, even though they were aware of the seriousness of her remark.

They kept walking on the road that went towards Worli. Asrar bought two cups of tea and they sipped from the cups, facing in the direction of the cool sea breeze. Asrar asked Hina to come and meet him at the mall after visiting the dargah next Saturday. There was a McDonald's on that mall's ground floor. They could sit and talk there. After much persuasion, Hina agreed.

A little past eight, Asrar hailed a taxi and bid farewell to Hina. The moment the taxi started moving, tears fell from her eyes. She had no control over them. She took out her handkerchief and started sobbing. She wept for a long time. Her mind was blank when she had started crying. It was the result of a wave that had risen within her from nowhere. There were a few stains on her heart but for long she had forgotten them, but now out of the blue the stains had resurfaced. A little while ago she had felt a streak of love in a stranger. What kind of feeling was love when it morphed into such convulsions? Her throat had started to ache and her introspection had increased her desire to cry. Hina had never cried like this before in her life.

Yusuf Memon was a perfumer in Nagpada Junction. He had a shop there. The demand in Saudi Arabia and Qatar had made his business very profitable. He had bought this shop in 1990 after taking a loan from the Memon Cooperative Bank. He had acquired the shop in the Fort area because he was in the good books of a Muslim politician who was not only known for his ignorance, emotionality and bad language, but had also brought a bad name to the community. He had once gone to jail under a black law, but his money had helped him save himself, or else the law was such that if an innocent goat was charged of being a cruel monster under that law, she wouldn't have been able to free herself from the charge and would have been convicted. The politician had a lot of money and was known for splurging it on those he liked. He made Yusuf Memon acquire the shop in such a costly and posh area as the Fort. His business flourished in this area. He was able to repay the bank loan sooner than he had expected. He also bought a flat in an old-style building on the third floor in Madanpura and put his old house on rent.

He seemed religious from the outside but wasn't orthodox. He had studied in an English-medium school till the tenth standard and had taken admission in a famous college in western Mumbai but had failed in one subject in class twelve. This affected him so much that he dropped out of education. He worked in the community trust for some time. He was skilled and experienced in building contacts and getting his work done. He got into the business of scents. He was handsome, courageous and young by heart. Hina was his third daughter.

One day an Arab had come to Yusuf's shop. He was warmly welcomed and served juice. Yusuf was impressed to see that this man could speak Urdu. The Arab told him that he had stayed in Pakistan for some time and now wanted to travel in and around Mumbai. And he would be staying in rented rooms during his sojourn. His name was Burashid Ibn Ali Al Inheraf, and his father Ali Inheraf was a poet. He was, as of then, living at the Taj hotel. He invited Yusuf over to his room with some samples of perfumes. He reached the hotel at the appointed time carrying six bottles of perfume with him. Burashid greeted him as if he was an old friend. He sat in his room staring out of the window. The lights from the city were reflected in the rising and falling waters of the sea. He then looked at the Gateway of India, which was crowded.

This was the same window through which, a few years later, Abdul Ahmad Kasab's accomplice Abu Shoaib would look out. He wanted to keep staring at the beautiful scene but he had to complete his task. He then took out a hand grenade and threw it at the Gateway of India. Then he turned to the teak table in front of him and poured water into a glass. While staring at his image in the mirror, many thoughts came rushing to his mind, but he realized that the connection between his heart and head had been snapped! Allama Jawed, aka Iqbal Rashid Turrabi, was sharing the room with him. He sipped water and turned to him and said, 'The water here tastes exactly like it does in Al-Muridikum.'

'The water and air of both the nations are the same but the future will be different,' replied Allama Jawed. He had heard this line from Maulana Abu Hamza Lashkari at Muridikum. Maulana Abu Hamza Lashkari had a great gift of giving inflammatory speeches in front of the youth and firing up in them the desire to live in an ideal society dating back to 1400 years. He would take control of their brains and light the desire for that society in their heads. Because of this skill, he was called the leader of leaders at Muridikum. Turrabi and Abu Shoaib were killed after two days. Their souls stayed at the Taj hotel for some time and left to wander off. They were amazed to see the grandeur of the Gateway and impressed by the pleasant lifestyle around. The spirits realized that the gate of the *Barzakh* had been shut for them now. The homeless spirits decided to reside on the arches of the Gateway.

Yusuf and Burashid were having a great conversation and transcended the topics of just perfumes and scents. They decided to meet in the café of the Jehangir Art Gallery the next day. In the café, they again talked a lot including about their personal lives. They ate food together and then, while walking on the seashore, Burhashid gave him Rs 50,000 as advance payment and said that he would buy perfumes worth two or three lakh per year. Yusuf could not contain his happiness. This relationship was changing into friendship. Yusuf invited Burashid to his house for dinner one day. While eating, he told everyone that he was also known as a famous antique expert in his homeland, Algeria.

Burashid returned home. He came to Mumbai again after a month accompanied by his wife and daughter. He told Yusuf that his family wanted to spend some time around natural scenic landscapes. They were planning to rent a bungalow in some hilly area. 'Would you suggest Khandala?'

Yusuf told him that he had a property dealer friend who worked in Khandala, Pune and Matheran. He could take care of their stay wherever they wanted to go. Burashid inquired about the legal documents that would be required. Yusuf smiled and said that he would take care of all that. He called his politician friend. The politician was ready to help. The next day Burashid's family and Yusuf went to Khandala. The politician's agent showed them around and suggested bungalows. They told him that they wanted a bungalow away from the crowd, where parties could be organized. The agent informed them of two such bungalows, but their rent was very steep. Burashid's wife interjected and said that if they liked the area, the rent won't be a problem. Burashid then told Yusuf that his wife Aymal belonged to a very illustrious family of Arabs and was well educated. She was a French citizen and a bureaucrat. Yusuf stared at her in amazement and respect. She looked back and smiled.

They finally liked a bungalow on the slope of a hill. It was double storey and had good enough space for a gathering of forty to fifty people. A narrow path went into the jungle from the bungalow. They paid the rent, Rs 1.40 lakh for a month, and signed all the required papers. They returned to Mumbai after three days. Yusuf invited the entire family over to his house for dinner. It was the first time when Burashid's daughter, Wardatul Sa'adat, and Hina met and conversed for a long time standing in the balcony. Hina loved her accent but could not understand most of what she said. She had gathered knowledge of the cultures of Arab countries, Algeria and India. Through her conversations it was evident that she did not like Arabs. In fact, she hated Saudi Arabia and everything about it. According to her evil posed as good there. Hina was too young for this conversation. Wardatul Sa'adat, on the other hand, was a grown-up girl of around fifteen or sixteen years and had her own political opinions. Hina's elder sisters spoke to Aymal on various themes. Around nine, dinner was served. The guests enjoyed the spread of biryani, shami kebabs and chicken tandoori.

The next day Burashid and his wife bought essentials from the Fort area. Then they hired a private car and along with Yusuf and his wife Darakhshan reached Khandala. They did a lot of sightseeing. Burashid's daughter clicked pictures of Pavana Lake, Lohagad Fort, Bhaja caves and Bushi Lake. They then proceeded to Bhairavnath temple. Yusuf was hesitant to enter the temple. Burashid and his family entered and clicked a lot of photos and came out. They sat in a shade under a tree outside the temple when Aymal told them a story from the Maha Purana which talked about Bhairav. She also told them that Bhairav was the most worshipped in Nepal and was respected a lot in India. She also told them the meaning of the name Bhairav. Yusuf was amazed. He asked her, 'Where did you acquire so much knowledge from?'

Burashid told him that Aymal had done her postgraduation in comparative religious studies. Wardatul Sa'adat explained what

religious studies actually meant. Yusuf was very confused. He had
known since childhood that his religion was the one which was
true, everything else was evil. And what was the need to know the
evil? He wondered at these people who had acquired knowledge
about so many little things. He was intrigued by Aymal's simplicity,
immense beauty and mannerisms. The interaction with Burashid
and his wife had given rise to certain thoughts and questions within
him. It was a sort of introspection. He was unaware from where such
questions were taking shape in his mind. He had never encountered
such questions. Naturally, he was surprised. He realized that he was
just a mere husband to his wife. When he thought a bit over it,
he concluded that there was no similarity between him and his
wife. There was no passion or love that existed between them.
The laughter and conversation between Burashid and his wife
made him realize that while getting involved in running the affairs
of the house, catering to the needs of the children and trying to
live a happy life, he had never asked himself what love was. He had
thought love meant using his wife at night to produce children.
He never felt the emotion of love towards any woman. He felt that
he had missed out on something while trying to make a life and
earn money. In the light of Aymal's personality, the darkness in
Yusuf's heart started to fade.

They ate at a roadside eatery and kept enjoying the beauty
of the hills. Yusuf was lost in the maze of his own thoughts. He was
thinking that his life lacked something. Though he was aware that
his knowledge, experience and even expectations from life were
limited, he thought that Burashid and Aymal's lives were more
meaningful. When he looked at Darakhshan she seemed to him more
a *kheti* than a woman. A field that can be harvested by the plough
and now it was nearly barren. She lacked a fertile and meaningful
soul like Aymal's. Yusuf was tired and his head was a burden for
his shoulders. At lunch, Burashid gave him Rs 1 lakh for not just
the scent, but also for other important items of luxury. There was
going to be a party at their place soon, which would be attended

by their friends from various parts of India. Many of them would be foreign citizens. Yusuf thought that the perfumes could be given as gifts to them. He promised to get back in three days with the most exotic scents.

Darakhshan and Yusuf went to sleep in their room on the comfortable bed. That night Yusuf did not look at his fertile field but closed his eyes to see Aymal's face. Her bright eyes, trimmed nails, intellectual conversation, shining skin came rushing to his mind while he forgot that the wet earth lay next to him.

The next morning Darakhshan and Yusuf had to leave for Mumbai.

Aymal came to bid farewell and said, 'We will wait for you.'

This sentence kept ringing in Yusuf's ears during the entire journey.

Yusuf reached the bungalow around 7 p.m. after three days. Aymal helped him place the twenty boxes of perfume in a room. He freshened up while Aymal made tea. She told him that Burashid had gone to Delhi to invite a senior diplomat of a European country for the party and would return the next day. The daughter was reading a book on the second floor. Yusuf stared at her while she talked. She was wearing white trousers and a peach-coloured T-shirt. In that outfit, her Arab look was beautiful and alluring. She proposed they go and shop around Lonavala if Yusuf was willing. On the way Aymal told Yusuf that a shopkeeper in Khandala had told them that there was a shop in Lonavala where they would find all that they required for the party. They inquired about the shop from the local people. They reached the place. Aymal was speaking to the shopkeeper when a car arrived. A dark-complexioned fat man came out. Aymal walked towards him and handed him a pink bag. He went to the car and took out a parcel wrapped in a newspaper. Aymal took that parcel and came and sat in the car.

It was eight in the night. The sky was like a dark well, without the moon. Yusuf drove carefully on the hills. He said nothing during the entire journey. When they reached home, he couldn't stop himself from asking, 'What is there in the parcel?'

'You can taste it after dinner,' Aymal replied.

He went to the fridge and took out a bottle of water while Aymal went to bathe.

He stood in the veranda looking at the flowers outside. There was space between where he stood and the outside where there was a table and a few chairs. He sat on one of the chairs and could feel the silence. He had not experienced such peace before. Mumbai stays loud and awake till 3–4 a.m. The chaos of Mumbai drowns the sound of one's soul. This silence was very pleasing to his heart. Here nature was around him in the form of darkness. The meaning of the universe seemed hidden in the silence and darkness. It was around 9 p.m. and the silence around him touched his heart. In this silence the darkness was asking him some questions. In the air there was the smell of plants, which freshened his mood. In this freshness he repeated questions in his mind created by the surrounding darkness. He looked at the sky. It was an empty well. He stared at that empty well for long. He felt it was shrinking to the extent that it seemed he was being caged inside. He wondered why he was in the well. Was it a conspiracy? The circumference of the well was contracting. Had he been here forever? If the well was the whole universe, then could any other power reside outside it? Was there only one power inside and outside the universe? And was the power of the empty well and the darkness in it an eternal reality? The empty well could have captured him had Aymal not entered that very moment. She saw him engrossed looking at the sky and asked, 'What are you looking at, sir?'

Her voice brought him back to the earth from the vast emptiness of the sky. Aymal looked even brighter after bathing. She was wearing a black Arabian dress. The fairness of her skin was more evident in contrast with this black colour. Yusuf looked at her and thought that she looked like the *Bahishti Zevar* (the jewel of paradise). He really liked the phrase 'jewel of paradise'. In fact, he had read a book titled the same in his youth. Some lines and paragraphs of the book came flashing back to his memory. He smiled and said, 'I've never seen such a beautiful sky in Mumbai.'

She sat on the opposite chair. Yusuf praised her dress, and she liked his compliment. She told him that black was her favourite colour. Yusuf asked the reason, to which she replied explaining the relationship between the nature of a human and their choice of colours. She continued, 'The universe is black and so is God.' Yusuf did not have any problem in understanding what she was saying. She asked many questions. Yusuf answered them with patience and great reflection. He told her that he got busy with business and making a living during his youth, because of which he transformed into a typical businessman and the religion within him kept vanishing. Aymal laughed and said, 'Religion is meant to come and go.' She paused and added, 'Rashid was right. You are an interesting man.'

This conversation and praise increased Yusuf's confidence. She proposed to go for a walk. He agreed. It was safe to walk outside as there were tube lights at every few steps. They took around twelve rounds of the bungalow. Aymal told him about her parents, her home, her family's close relationship with the Saud family, about her education, childhood and youth. She told him about her permanent stay in France, and that she was a practising religious girl during her youth but while doing her PhD her perspective on religion started changing. She found herself a believer of another order altogether. Yusuf was curious and asked her about the other order. She said she would tell him about it some other time. But this order gave a lot of peace and happiness to the soul. It was a call for knowledge and sufficiency.

Yusuf asked her many questions and she answered them all perfectly. There was rebellion and wisdom in her thoughts and tone. He asked her about her thoughts on creation and the universe to which she replied that all of this we see would be destroyed and would come to an end because creation is based on the 'first betrayal'. He asked her what the 'first betrayal' was. She smiled and gazed around the darkness. There were insects crowding the lights and a mogra flower plant grew under one of the streetlamps. She bent and plucked a flower. Seeing her bend, Yusuf stepped back. She looked beyond attractive to him. Some kind of emotional wave rose within him. Desires lit up. This wave or shivering he had not felt even when looking at Darakhshan naked. The wave was an expression of the desire to copulate and its last stop was the eyes. After reaching the eyes the wave paused and fell into the soul. 'The soul is the energy of the tissues. It can never be destroyed.' Aymal's daughter, Wardatul Sa'adat, had underlined this sentence in her book. She then closed the book and headed outside.

Aymal turned and looked at him. In his eyes the expression of desire was frozen. Their eyes met and at the same moment the wave plunged into the vastness of his soul from his eyes. She said that the first betrayal was the most ambiguous of the games of the universe. Since God was a victim of his loneliness, an insecure and indecisive power, hence this insecure power defamed another great power to reduce its solitude so as to provide the insecure power with security. By then her daughter had come into the gallery. Seeing them talk, she called out to her mother. Aymal waved her to come down.

They chatted for long. After some time Sa'adat went into her room to sleep. Yusuf also left to go to the room where the perfume boxes and his suitcase were kept. He was lying on the charpoy when he decided to take a cold-water bath. While bathing he kept thinking about Aymal. He had never seen anyone talk about the order of which she had been talking. While rubbing soap on his chest he thought, 'I'm sure there is no other woman like her in this entire world!'

After bathing, he looked at himself in the mirror while combing his hair. He looked at his reflection, smiled and said to himself, 'Why do you want to have sex with her? Is that the only thing left to do?' For a few seconds he looked seriously at his image. He was a typical Gujarati Memon in appearance. Pale white skin with a yellow shine; reddish lips and light golden hair. He particularly liked his sharp nose. A hair peeped from his nostril. He pulled it out. He poured perfume over his clothes and then tried making Aymal's image in the mirror. His said, 'The jewel of paradise!' and smiled.

He proceeded to the courtyard where the doors of all the rooms on the ground floor opened. There was a sofa and a few wooden chairs. There was a statue, a flower vase loaded with flowers and a photograph of a painting on the wall. On one side was a teak table with beautiful designs. On it was kept a big television. He pressed the button on the TV, took the remote and sat on the sofa. He felt Aymal come out of her room and then go back inside. He thought that maybe she went inside seeing him there so late in the night. He kept pressing the buttons of the remote. She came out again, but Yusuf's eyes were still focused on the remote. She handed him black clothes and said, 'Black clothes are considered pure during these fifteen days and white impure, so I would suggest you change.' Yusuf went inside, dressed in black and came out. Aymal was sitting on the sofa.

She looked at him and said, 'In those clothes you look like one of the members of our tribe.' He smiled.

Aymal offered a tray to Yusuf which had something that looked like majoon (a unani formulation). He asked her what it was. She said that it was healthy and in Hebrew it is called Lakum Yakum. Having it gives birth to the desire to defeat the evil which masquerades as good. Yusuf smiled. He ate four tablespoons of it and passed the tray back to Aymal, who had seven tablespoons. She asked Yusuf to have seven spoons of it if he wanted to experience its real effect.

'If you allow it, I will eat the entire tray.'

'I wouldn't. Anything more than ten tablespoons is very harmful. It will induce in you a deep sleep.' He really liked the taste and wanted to have more but he remembered what Aymal had said. He then put the tray aside on the table and raised his feet to rest them on a chair. He saw Aymal coming out of the room adjoining the kitchen and going to her room. She took some things along with her and went back to the room adjoining the kitchen. He felt very light. His eyes and cheeks were heavy, and the fingers were stretching within. He shifted to the sofa and spread himself. It was as if he was floating in the air. He was free from all worries. He tried reflecting—there were no thoughts, no emotions, no imagination within him. He was nothing but a nullified existence, an empty existence and he was in love with his being. He felt that his existence was because of his body. Unconsciously, he touched himself all over to feel his presence. He was physically there but nothing else. The body was nothing more than the residence of that existence.

The foam of Lakum Yakum had spread throughout his brain and body and he could feel it. He could feel his lifeless body floating on a sea. The doors of paradise had opened within him. He could see the naked nymphs of heaven around a pool. The pool was full of sweetened milk, and he stood inside it, half submerged. Three nymphs stood near him, their hair shining golden. The bodies of those nymphs were white as milk and their eyes were greenish blue. Yusuf had transformed into a hefty and strapping youth. He could see the hunger for him in their eyes. The nymphs started embracing and playing with his body. He felt proud of himself. His body carried the sweetness of honey for the nymphs. One of them rubbed his shoulder with her nose and eyelashes. He could feel the passion in that touch.

Another nymph licked his eyelashes and kissed his eyes. The third one leaned against his back. The awakening in his heart and the passion of the nymph who leaned against his back, made his eyes shine blue. He might have not realized but the band of nymphs that stood surrounding the pool of heaven had noticed the light. This newborn light in his eyes gave birth to an unerring desire in their hearts. The ground around the pool was covered with sandal-coloured grass. The nymphs spread themselves out on the grass. It changed its colour to a sparkling saffron hue. The moisture around carried with it the same inspiring smell that was responsible for nature's first intercourse. 'That smell, which made two souls aware of the existence of their bodies. The smell was that of evil, but evil did never confess it.' Sa'adat underlined that excerpt while lying in bed and reading her book.

The nymphs around the pool were a portrayal of the dance of existence. Yusuf and the nymphs, submerged in the pools, were the picture of Adam and Eve's eternal dream. 'That dream which Adam, Eve and the Evil had seen at the same time, but the Evil later detached himself from it. To obtain the justification for going far away from me, this was just the beginning of treachery with me.' She copied that excerpt in her notebook from the book.

Aymal called out to Yusuf a couple of times while standing next to the sofa. Yusuf opened his eyes. Aymal asked him, 'How were you feeling?' He did not reply. Aymal sat next to him. It was dark. Aymal insisted on a conversation, 'Did you fall asleep?' Yusuf held on to his silence. Aymal realized that he was under the influence of Lakum Yakum. She kept her hand on Yusuf's shoulder. She leaned and whispered in his ears, 'Do not be scared of the darkness. Darkness is life.'

'Who's afraid? I was just amazed at the beautiful dream that I was seeing,' Yusuf replied.

'You are still in that dream,' Aymal whispered.

'What . . .?' Yusuf asked in astonishment.

Aymal slid towards him. Yusuf stared at her intently. His intoxication increased. Aymal starkly resembled that nymph in the darkness who had kissed his eyes. He floated between the embrace of reality and disbelief. He could not understand if he was alive or alive in a dream. His disbelief took over his conviction of reality. He uttered, 'Goddess.'

Aymal held his hand between hers. His fingers intertwined with hers. They both stood up. In a few moments they were in the room attached to the kitchen. In one corner of the room, a statue of Seth (Egyptian god) was kept. Aymal stood in front of it for seconds. Yusuf's hands were still in her hands. Their fingers were spying on the unusual rush of the uncontrolled heartbeats. Aymal uttered softly, 'For the end of evil and for the freedom of the songs of being.' She looked at Yusuf. The darkness had no effect on her shining eyes. She looked into his eyes and said, '*Batil haq hai, haq batil* [Evil is truth. Truth is evil].'

Aymal was also under the influence of Lakum Yakum, but Yusuf's feet were shivering. She helped him sit on the bed. The room had been locked since a long time back. She felt hot. She switched on the air conditioner and picked up a bottle of perfume from the table. She rubbed the attar at the back of her ear lobes and on her neck. This was the same perfume that Yusuf had gifted Burashid on their first encounter. The scent had effect. The moment it reached Yusuf's nostrils, he looked at Aymal. Aymal moved towards him. She fell next to Yusuf on the bed. The scent was overpowering; he turned towards Aymal. She said something to him and along with the end of the sentence she kissed his forehead. There was no moon in the sky that night.

The room was dark. Both lay naked on the bed. There was a smile on Seth's face. Aymal believed that the bungalow might be surrounded by spirits who were worshippers of Seth. They would have desired to see the thirst within Aymal and Yusuf, a thirst which would be quenched by the juice of the souls, sweat and saliva. But they had stopped themselves because they remembered the declaration of Seth, 'Wherever he is present in darkness, the spirits are transformed to smoke. They have to wander the world for thousands of years to regain their form.' Aymal had heard a pagan tale that once a girl rubbed the scent of her body on the wounds of a young man which not only healed his wounds, but the scar of disloyalty was also erased from his soul. Why did her memories bring this tale back at this moment, even Aymal did not know. Subconsciously, she touched the saliva of her rose-like vagina and rubbed it on Yusuf's lips, neck and chest. The smell of Aymal's body was so striking and strong that it subdued the smell of the perfume. The smell of her body created a storm in the flow of his blood, and he was ready to embrace yet another wave. He was in the pool of heaven, again. The heaven where the soul lives to understand the realness of amalgamation.

When he woke up at five the next morning, he was lying on the sofa.

He was surprised for a moment to see himself dressed in a white kurta and pyjama. He touched his body. Was he the same man that he thought he was? In his present state he felt no visible change or transformation. He was in his preceding state. He pressed his memory. He could not remember anything clearly. He just felt that the night before Aymal had made him consume something after which his consciousness had travelled to another world and after some time Aymal had also joined him. He looked at the room next to the kitchen. It was locked. He remembered Aymal had taken him to that room. She had rubbed attar behind her ears. She had turned towards him and said, 'The human being is a mere animal. It will remain an animal even after slaying desires. Hence, do not kill your desires.'

All this came back to his mind like a blurred dream he could not trust. His was experiencing déjà vu. He could not understand on what basis he should believe all that was coming back to his mind. Was it possible that whatever he was remembering was not reality but just a dream. It had happened with him before he had assumed the incidents to be real, when they were actually a dream. Despite that his heart had kept on convincing him to believe in their reality.

Many thoughts kept floating in his heart and mind and eventually sleep overcame his senses. He slept like a dead man. He woke up in the afternoon when Aymal came close to him and said, 'The goddess wants the prince to wake up.'

Aymal's words kept swirling in his ears. He was now sure that all that was coming to his mind was absolutely real, but a reality that was dreamlike. Aymal was sitting on a chair and eating chocolate in front of him. Yusuf looked at the time on the wall clock and told Aymal, 'It's already noon. I have never slept for so long.'

Aymal peered into his eyes and remarked, 'Have you ever slept like you did last night?'

He stared back at her without uttering a word.

Aymal was in a mischievous mood. She continued to tease him, 'Would you like to have chocolate? Remember last night you were saying, "Aymal, you are just like chocolate"?'

He could recall saying that to her while making love. He smiled.

'You're incredible. You don't belong to this planet!' he said.

'And you're now part of an incredible truth,' she replied.

They talked for a while when Yusuf said he wanted to freshen up. He went towards his room. Aymal went to the kitchen. Wardatul Sa'adat was sitting under the shade of a tree watching squirrels.

Yusuf removed his clothes in the bathroom. He was about to shower when his eyes fell on his reflection in a full-length mirror. He looked at his chest intently. There was something stuck in the hair on his chest. He remembered what it was and smiled. The smell of Aymal's body still lingered in his nostrils. While bathing he rewound everything that had happened the night before like a film in his mind. Waves of gratification and enjoyment rose within his mind. He had never felt so fulfilled and satisfied with himself in so many years. He had never encountered himself in such a way before. Whatever had happened was still a mystery, a riddle but in this was hidden the beauty of his life.

He wanted to remain submerged in that pleasure. When Aymal came into his room after an hour, he was still lost in his thoughts. She could read his soul through his eyes. She had also been through that experience before. She knew when to reveal her skills. She wanted to change his mood and so she said, 'Get ready as soon as you can, we have to go to Pune to buy a few things.' He got dressed and came out. By then Aymal had already prepared toast and coffee for him. They left for Pune after having breakfast. Wardatul Sa'adat refused to come along. She was engrossed in reading her book.

The car left the bungalow. Wardatul Sa'adat went back to reading her book. She read:

> Around 1 lakh European and 20,000 Americans are involved in the religion of Satan. By the end of this century, 3 lakh humans are expected to become a part of this religion. The Church of Satan, Temple of Seth, Satanic Freedom Church are a few well-known organizations of this religion. Anton Szandor LaVey had founded the Satanic church in 1966, though evidence of Satan worship predates this event. For example, in 1948 Herbert Arthur Sloane founded a group called Ophite Cultus Sathanas in the American state of Ohio. Satan worshipping cults that came into being after the 1960s were very different from each other. There were two distinct ideologies that could be noticed in them. The first one is an atheistic cult whose understanding of Satanic worship shows that it is not a religion but an ideology or a perspective and this group, instead of worshipping Satan, believes in following the preachings in their day to day lives. The second cult is that of the theist amongst whom Satan enjoys a position of God and creator who is ritualistically worshipped.

As the car was leaving Khandala, Aymal told Yusuf that when she was researching for her PhD thesis, she lived in a small district in East Germany called Reichenbach. A few youths had committed suicide there by jumping off a historical bridge. This incident of collective suicides had garnered a lot of attention. Her supervisor had asked her to find out the details of the suicides.

The information that she had collected showed that the youths were all members of the Satanic church. They had been incapable of bearing the burden of the truths that had been inflicted on them. It was quite possible that either they could not stay firm on their belief or the new belief that they were introduced to had completely taken over their consciousness.

'What is the Church of Satan?' Yusuf inquired.

Aymal gave a brief introduction of the Church of Satan and told him that the ancient discipline was founded by Anton LaVey and that it was quite possible that the youths who committed suicide had been attracted towards Satan worship after reading LaVey's book *The Satanic Bible*.

Yusuf immediately asked, 'Who was LaVey and what is *The Satanic Bible?*'

Aymal continued, 'LaVey was a charismatic man with a magical personality. His followers referred to him as the "Black Pope". He founded the Church of Satan in San Francisco in 1966. His house was called the "Black House" where he delivered lectures for those who were interested in Satan worship. He used to charge fees for his lectures.'

Yusuf kept looking at Aymal with curious eyes while driving. Seeing his curiosity, Aymal stated further that LaVey dressed up in special attire to perform various Satanic rituals. Many a time he was seen wearing a horned headgear to prove his resemblance to Satan. After the foundation of the Satanic church, he started writing a book on Satanic rituals and beliefs called *The Satanic Bible*. The book was published in June 1969.

'Oh. Okay.' These were the only words that came to Yusuf. He took a gulp of water from a bottle. Aymal took the bottle from his hand and drank a little herself.

Aymal told him that on Satanic worship LaVey's book was supreme and comprehensive. The book contained all the required information, analysis and compilation of beliefs, rituals and philosophies of Satanic worship. Aymal also said that LaVey's next book, *Satanic Rituals*, was published in 1982 and explored the history of Satan worship in past cultures. He wrote many books to popularize his belief, which included *Satan Speaks*, *The Devil's Notebook* and *The Satanic Witchcraft*.

'So weird. It is becoming difficult for people to believe in God and LaVey is propagating the worship of Satan,' Yusuf said.

Wardatul Sa'adat came out of her room and looked down from the gallery. Beautiful butterflies danced on the creepers of the bungalow walls. A koel perched on the tube light. On the latch of the gate a chameleon sat enjoying the warmth of the sun. Wardatul Sa'adat came into the western part of the gallery. The sky was covered with clouds because of which a few dark black blots could be seen on the nearby hills. She kept gaping at those dark spots for a long time. She sat down on a nearby chair. She held the book in her hand, leaned her neck on the gallery and started reading again. 'The Temple of Seth was founded by a member of the Satanic church named Michael A. Aquino in 1975. Aquino had declared that the reason behind his differences and conflict with LaVey was the latter's greed for money. According to him, Satan was a living being whom he called Seth. LaVey became the reason of dishonour and bad name for Satan worship because of his love for materialism.'

Aymal smiled at Yusuf's remark. 'LaVey asks the same question—why should god be worshipped?'

'What does LaVey say?' Yusuf inquired.

'In the darkest and deepest parts of our soul, all humans are nothing but animals of a kind. We might be very intelligent and civilized on the outside but in the lowest part of the iceberg of our soul, there are such animalistic instincts and desires that, many a time, prove to be dangerous or horrid for us. Thus, most people tend to ignore or suppress these desires. But this suppression increases the intensity of their horror,' Aymal told Yusuf in one breath.

Yusuf looked into Aymal's eyes for a moment and said, 'Thank God this is not the case here. Satan is spreading his net in the West.'

Aymal burst into laughter on hearing this. Yusuf was in love with that laughter. He smiled too. Aymal continued, 'Mister, for

your information, by the end of this century more than 45,000
people of India would become Satan worshippers. Satan worship is
spreading in Meghalaya, Mizoram and Kerala.' She repeated herself
and added that in the states where there was a dominant Christian
population, belief in Satan was spreading like an uncontrolled
forest fire. 'And in this entire community of Satan worshippers,
75 per cent are women.'

'Oh God!' slipped out of Yusuf's mouth.

'India's most grand and influential church of Satan is in Mumbai
and it has a current membership of 10,000 people. The strength of
Satan worshippers in Pune, Bangalore and Chennai is in thousands.'

'Oh.' This information amazed Yusuf.

'If Goddess Kali is considered an incarnation of Satan, then
with a strength of more than 50,000 disciples and priests of the
goddess, India will be the world's largest centre of Satanic worship,'
Aymal said with pride.

Wardatul Sa'adat turned her chair towards the gallery. She
copied the following paragraph in her diary. She thought she might
want to use the paragraph as a reference in some essay.

'According to researchers even the hexagonic star of the Jews is
an ancient symbol of Satanic worship. It was accepted by the ancient
Egyptians as a sign of Satan. The hexagonal star is considered one of
the most powerful symbols of summoning Satanic powers. *Trishul*
(trident) is also considered a manifestation of Satanic powers by
some. This was the reason when etiquettes of food consumption
involving knives, spoons and forks were being popularized after the
Enlightenment in the European states of England, France and Italy,
many plebeians and villagers refused to touch the forks because
they considered it Satanic. Even though before that the use of forks
had already started during 7 BCE in royal households of the West.'

'I never paid attention to the fact that there really are Satan
worshippers in India,' Yusuf replied to what Aymal had said earlier.

They kept conversing on this topic for a long time. Yusuf had
initially found the topic very misleading, but soon he developed
substantial interest. The primary reason for his interest was Aymal.

He felt like an uncrowned king in her presence. He wanted to go back to the magic that Aymal had introduced him to the night before. While talking to Aymal, a couple of times he found himself on the bed of imagination in Aymal's arms.

They had covered a distance of seventy kilometres but Yusuf thought that he had just driven the car for not more than seven kilometres. He parked the vehicle under a banyan tree next to the old bus stand in the heart of the city. Aymal bought a few things from the shops around the old bus stand. Then they dined at a restaurant nearby and during the meal Aymal told him that they would go to Parvati Hill. Yusuf had no clue about that place. On coming out of the restaurant, Yusuf bought a packet of cigarettes from a paan shop and got two sweet paans packed. He also inquired about the route to Parvati Hill from the shopkeeper. On the way to Parvati Hill, Aymal kept looking at Pune and reading a book on the histories of various cities of India. They climbed the hill and looked at the city of Pune from a height. The city looked exotic. Aymal pulled out her camera and started clicking pictures of the view. Yusuf took the camera from her hand and said that she should get herself clicked with this breathtaking view as the background. She smiled and got herself clicked. She also took a few photos of Yusuf. Yusuf offered her the sweet paan. She asked, 'What's this?'

'This is the Indian Lakum Yakum,' Yusuf remarked.

Aymal burst into laughter and playfully punched Yusuf's chest with her right hand. Yusuf placed his hand on her shoulder and said, 'Do not worry, the consumption of this doesn't transport the human to another world!'

Aymal looked at Yusuf. Her eyes carried a superior kind of love at that moment. Yusuf had no courage to face it and turned his eyes away.

There were five temples on Parvati Hill. Many believers came here to pay obeisance to their gods. This was also an ancient site of historical importance. The temples here were dedicated to Ram, Vaithal, Vishnu, Parvati and Kartikeya. Aymal wanted to see Kartikeya's temple. She had studied and researched intensively about Hinduism and Kartikeya was one of the dozens of gods that had aroused interest in her. Kartikeya was the god of love, war, wisdom and victory. He was the son of Shiv and Parvati. Valli and Devasena were his two wives. He was popular in Karnataka and Andhra Pradesh by the name of Subramaniam. Tamilians called him Murugan.

He was specially worshipped in southern India, Sri Lanka, Mauritius, Malaysia and Singapore. He was presented as a red-coloured god with six heads. His mount was a peacock. He was shown sitting on a peacock with his wives. A snake was shown caught in the claws of the peacock. During her research she had seen different pictures and representations of Kartikeya. She always wondered if Kartikeya was an embodiment of eternal youth and energy. She kept trying to understand the symbolic importance of two wives, and the peacock and the snake. She clicked pictures of Kartikeya's temple. Sitting on an elevation near the temple, she told Yusuf about her views on Murugan. The intensity of Aymal's knowledge and understanding was more than enough to impress Yusuf, who was simultaneously being captured by her intense love. They sat there for half an hour and when they were leaving Murugan's peacock told the snake caught in its claws, 'The woman who is sitting outside, her husband will be murdered in Pune after three years on 13 February.'

'Will he be murdered? Really?' the snake said.

The peacock smiled at the intelligence of the snake and said, 'No. Not murdered, but he will be killed in a blast.'

They climbed down from Parvati Hill.

They ate at a restaurant. Aymal told him that by the time they reach the bungalow in the evening, Burashid would also return. The disappointment on Yusuf's face could be seen. While offering him a glass of buttermilk, she informed him that the party would be held on the eighth. Exactly at midnight all lights would be switched off that night. Everyone would be free to choose a partner in the dark. Generally, in such a situation, a partner was chosen on the basis of their body's odour. 'I would have rubbed the same attar on my neck which you gave Burashid. The same perfume that you . . .' Before he could complete the sentence, Aymal gestured to him to remain quiet by putting her finger on her lips. They looked into each other's eyes. There was a naked proposal in their eyes to unite their bodies. They looked happy while leaving the restaurant. Yusuf wanted to know all the details of the party.

The car left Pune.

Aymal had conversed on so many varied topics with Yusuf that it led to chaos in his mind. Many thoughts were bubbling up in his subconscious, but Aymal's presence destroyed and suppressed them. A couple of times, waves of despair and unrest had risen in his heart. But whenever his eyes met those of Aymal, they reminded him of the night before and the refreshing smell in his soul. The waves rose and fell into nothingness like that drop of rain which vanishes without a sign in a desert as if it never took birth. He chose to remain silent.

He did not ask about the details of the party but enlightened himself with some knowledge on LaVey. Aymal told him about the basic constructs and ideas of LaVey.

After crossing 25–30 kilometres they stopped at a roadside eatery. They indulged in pat (a grass used for essence) tea at the eatery. The weather was pleasant. Those were the last days of October. The morning wind had become a little cold. The hilly region started from where they stood. Insects and mosquitoes swarmed around Aymal and Yusuf. A big, shiny, copper-coloured insect came flying and hit against Aymal's forehead and fell on the table. Aymal smiled and said, 'Oh my God! It's so beautiful.'

Yusuf looked at her, she looked back. He tried picking up the insect but before he could touch it, it flew away towards the road. Yusuf lifted his eyes to look at Aymal and as soon as Aymal felt his eyes on her, she started looking in the direction of the road. Aymal knew Yusuf was watching her closely, but her eyes were searching for the insect. It was only her eyes that were on the road, the rest of her being was facing in the direction of Yusuf. Yusuf's eyes were on the scattered hair on her forehead; he looked at her eyes, nose, cheeks, nostrils, ears and lips. Aymal's face was now registered in his heart like a dark blot of love which had a vigorous power of attraction and in which his belief was drowning itself. There were emotions that were transforming his desire for making love into a storm. Could this just be the vigorous power of attraction or was it a black cleft in which his character as well as his identity dissolved themselves?

Aymal's eyes were not able to spot the insect, the primary reason being that the eyes of her soul were busy getting acquainted with Yusuf's yearning, his madness and impatience. The physical desires were the hunger of the soul. Aymal felt that her belly was a huge crack. A tunnel-like crack in which the pages of all sacrosanct books of the world were scattered. She closed her eyes for a moment and felt that those sacred pages were now transforming into butterflies and freeing themselves from the depth of her stomach. Those multicoloured butterflies with beautiful wings had now spread themselves around her. When she opened her eyes, Yusuf was standing in front of the table. He said, 'Let's go!' His voice was weak. Aymal did not reply. She knew that if any voice escaped her throat right then, it would have been equally defeated and weak.

The car moved a little further. Yusuf turned it towards a narrow, unconstructed street running along a dried river. There were dense bushes on both sides of that street. Yusuf shut off the car engine

after covering some distance. Both had remained silent till now.
As soon as the engine stopped, Aymal bent her head and shut her
eyes. Yusuf looked at her. He kept staring for some time. Aymal's
eyes remained closed. Yusuf moved his fingers on her cheeks.
Aymal's lips spread into a suppressed smile. She was about to open
her eyes when Yusuf opened the car's door from outside.

There was a narrow path leading to the dried river. They started
walking on it together and reached the bottom of the riverbed.
There was ample space between huge rocks at the bottom of the
river. The sun was disappearing into the red twilight. A reddish
yellow shadow spread over the jungle. Aymal stood leaning against
a rock. Her white skin shone brightly in the reddish yellow light
of the sun.

'You made me wild,' Aymal exclaimed while sitting in the car.

There was happiness and contentment on her face. Calmness
had spread over her soul. Her lips seemed cherry red. Her ears
were still warm. The heartbeats had still not returned to their
normal pace. In fact, when she had said, 'You made me wild,' there
was some amount of quivering in her voice.

Yusuf smiled and replied, 'I'm wild since I met you.'

Aymal bent forward and kissed his cheek.

After a while, Aymal told him that the kind of party that was
being organized at her house was called 'Black Mass' or 'Hollow
Mass' in their circle. Such masses were most appreciated when held
during a lunar eclipse. Only people of the same belief were invited
to such parties. In the black gathering 'Evil is truth; truth is evil' was
chanted loudly. Sometimes a downward-pointing five-cornered star
and a Baphomet idol were also used. In many such gatherings, those
religions and beliefs were insulted which sabotage the freedom of
humans. Yusuf was listening to what Aymal was saying but more

than that, he wanted to just keep staring at the movements of her lips. He kept looking at her. He asked no questions. Aymal was under the impression that Yusuf was actually paying attention to what she was saying.

Burashid and Wardatul Sa'adat were having coffee in the veranda.

During the conversation, Wardatul Sa'adat informed him that Aymal had gone to Pune to buy household essentials.

Burashid informed her that the party would see the presence of a European ambassador, counsel generals of two countries from the Middle East with their wives, four Indian intellectuals, and one politician. Apart from them, intellectuals with the same ideology would also come from Mumbai, Delhi, Nagaland and Kerala. Wardatul Sa'adat told her father that even she was preparing notes and was hoping that her thesis would be over before the party. Burashid said that they would decide on the proceedings of the party once Aymal was back. The father and daughter continued their conversation for a while and then Wardatul Sa'adat went back to her room and engrossed herself in the book she was reading. She read:

> The ritual of the Human Eye is a very essential indication of Satan worship. According to Satanic belief, this is the Eye of Lucifer and whosoever is able to take control over it, will be able to control the material world. In Egyptian mythology, it is referred to as the Eye of Horus. The Satanic organization, the Free Masons, calls it the Eye of Providence or the All-knowing Eye and have made it an essential symbol of their rituals. The influence and power of the members and ideas of this organization in the American society can be understood with the presence of this symbol on the American dollar notes.

She reflected on those words for a moment, took a deep breath and continued reading:

> The Snake is also one of the most revered symbols in Satanic rituals. It is understood to be the indicator of such power, the awakening of which within oneself will lead to an eternal state of peace and calm. The subcontinent has witnessed snake worship for many centuries, which is also an indicator of a long presence of Satanic belief in this region. Some signs and symbols associated with Satan are: a circle with the English letter 'A', where the line which intersects the angles generally transcends the boundary of the circle. It is the symbol of governance and societal disruption. The snake is attached to a demon who is said to drive young men to suicide and deviation from God. The other symbols are Lucifer's True Grail, peacock, 666, swastika, skull, bones and the black sun. On the other hand, snake or cobra is the Satan's favourite incarnation. It also finds mention in the history of the great civilization of Iran and Mesopotamia nested in Sumer. The Zoroastrians of Iran call that serpent Aharman (blemish-giver) which is responsible for all problems, sorrows and grievances in the world. The Egyptians called it Apophis who swallows the sun god every night. The Mesopotamians know it by the name of Tiamat.

Aymal told Yusuf that Lucifer was really a victim. He was deceived. A conspiracy was hatched against him. When Yusuf heard all of this, he smiled and looked at Aymal with interrogative, wrinkled eyes. On seeing his curiosity, Aymal told him that Lucifer was actually called Hilal-bin-Sehar in Hebrew which translates to 'The Morning Sun'. When the priests translated the Bible into Latin, he was named Lucifer. According to the followers of

Luciferism, he was thrown out of paradise unjustly without any legitimate reason.

'At that time, the skies were swallowed by the darkness of the end of the world. The ceiling of the sky remained deprived of light for the next forty days. The angels Harut and Marut sat atop Sidrat al-Muntaha (Lote tree that marks the end of seventh heaven) and beat their chest. When the warm rivers of blood that flowed from their eyes dried up, an angel with green wings descended upon them and said, "I want to see you."' The elderly Maulabax, after reading this from the book *Kitab-ul-Hikmat Bain-ul-Aafaq*, filled his chillum with fresh hash.

Aymal, without looking at Yusuf said, 'Lucifer will inflict an insulting defeat upon the one who has made wrong claims.' This prophetic statement that Aymal made seemed dangerous to Yusuf. He slowed down the car. The sun had already set. Everything was covered in darkness. Along the road, there seemed to be a field where a few vehicles were parked. There was a restaurant nearby. He turned the car towards the field. He parked the car under a tamarind tree and switched on the lights in the car. Aymal continued what she was saying. 'In the Middle East a few centuries back, a secret community in Iraq was given a holy treatise, *Bil Haya*, which means the Book of Life and Existence from Lucifer. This was probably the first treatise ever given to Satan believers by the one they worship. This community, which had many similarities with the Zoroastrian, still exists and believes Satan to be one and divine. They worship him in the form of a copper peacock. It is called *Mulik Taus* or the prince peacock. This community finds Satan's decision to not bow down before Adam absolutely appropriate. I . . .'

She stopped speaking and looked at Yusuf, meeting his eyes. There was belief and confidence in her. Yusuf seemed to be lost in her eyes. There was a deep darkness that surrounded the car. A tube light outside the restaurant attracted a lot of insects that were now flying, crawling and dying around it. On the other hand, the things in the area engulfed by darkness seemed to be at peace.

Darkness was the reason of the satisfaction of their being, whereas the light was the reason of the conflicts and disturbances among the self, ego and the soul. On seeing Yusuf peek into her eyes, she lowered her gaze and said, 'I mean to say that I am a part of that community.'

The tamarind tree was old, and its bark had expanded quite a lot. There were mice holes near the roots. A snake had crept into one of them during noon. Had the car not been parked there, the snake would have already left the hole and climbed up the tree. Hundreds of doves sat on the branches of the tree. These doves were attractive prey for the snake. Since the time the car had stopped there, the smell of Aymal and Yusuf was reaching its sense of smell. When Aymal's words sent vibrations through the air, the snake flicked out its tongue to feel the vibrations.

Wardatul Sa'adat copied the following paragraph from the book she was reading and when she started writing her thesis, she began with the same paragraph:

> Lucifer's favourite day is Monday. Blue, black and red are his favourite colours. He is the EA deity of the Sumer. Many cultures refer to him as EL. His prime constellations are Capricorn (the incarnation of a goat) and Aquarius (water utensil). His stars are Uranus and Venus. His directions are east and south. The most important day of the year for him is 23 September when the sun is in the first house of Capricorn. Capricorn is the tenth constellation and the first ascent brings the sum to eleven. The day after the one when the sun reaches its zenith during the winter season is the day of Satan and every true believer should celebrate it.

When Aymal looked at Yusuf after completing what she had to say, he observed, 'I cannot understand a lot of these things but . . .' He paused and looked at the tamarind tree outside the window. The wind was still. The snake had felt the stillness more than them. Some words came to Yusuf's throat and stopped right there. Aymal's tongue was going to instinctively ask 'What?' but she stopped herself. They sat in silence. This silence was irritating the snake. It was as if the darkness around the car was restlessly trying to seep into the car through the windows. All the light of the world that emerged from the womb of darkness one day had to go back to its own truth. Yusuf lit a cigarette and took a puff. Aymal took a drag as a formality and slowly released the smoke from her lungs. This act pleased Yusuf. Aymal passed the cigarette to Yusuf. He took it and while putting it to his lips uttered, 'You're my Lucifer, and I worship you.'

Aymal kept laughing and in the process opened the door of the car and stepped out. The intensity of Aymal's laughter made Yusuf happy. Albeit he was not able to understand why Aymal was laughing so much. He finished the entire cigarette trying to answer this question. The laughter had caused tears to come out of Aymal's eyes. When she stopped laughing, she proposed to go and have some tea. Yusuf gestured to the boy sitting at the counter of the restaurant and said, 'Yaar, bring two cups of special tea with ginger!'

He smoked one more cigarette till the tea came. Aymal kept staring into the darkness, the sleeping trees in the darkness and the patches of light that could be seen from far.

They reached the bungalow at around 8.30 p.m.

Burashid had already inspected the perfumes before Yusuf came. An hour passed in the conversation and no one noticed. Yusuf asked permission to leave. Burashid took out a packet from his pocket and gave it to Yusuf. Yusuf kept it in his pocket. Burashid asked him to count the money. Yusuf smiled. When he was leaving, Aymal came to him and said that she would give details about the party over the phone. That night, while in bed, Burashid described his Delhi tour to Aymal. Aymal told him that Yusuf had no opposition to their beliefs and if they worked hard on him, he might be able to play

an important role in propagating their ideology in Mumbai in the
future. After hearing that, Burashid asked whether it would be okay
to invite Yusuf to the party in the presence of high-profile people
and ambassadors. Aymal said that Yusuf was an innocuous man.
His presence might in fact be useful. The collective could taste the
freedom of his soul and this in turn would help him to free his soul
of the 'enemy' beliefs within him.

Burashid visited Mumbai three days before the party. He invited
Yusuf to a hotel. They stayed together for three hours. During
this time, Burashid tried to learn about Yusuf's religious beliefs.
Yusuf answered in such a fashion that it seemed religion did not
matter to him much. He, in fact, said that religion was one of the
major causes of bloodshed in this world. Burashid told him about
his own beliefs and that of his collective, who had already gained
freedom from the idea of God and were in favour of spending their
lives according to their own will. Yusuf knew of those things that
Burashid was not able to convey. He was smiling in his heart at
Burashid's innocence.

Yusuf said that he would be happy to be a part of that group.
Then Burashid said that apart from the important work, he had
also come to invite Yusuf to the party, though Aymal had already
informed him this over the phone.

He thanked Burashid.

Burashid told him that some people were coming from
Delhi to Mumbai to be a part of the party. They would stay at
the Taj Residency till the evening. After telling him about their
occupations and designations, Burashid told Yusuf that they would
join the party as common people. This way, their presence would
remain a secret.

The next day, at seven in the evening, Burashid introduced
Yusuf to those people.

After briefly exchanging greetings, they left for Khandala.

An Indian couple sat in Yusuf's car. They were above fifty. During the journey, Aymal was on his mind. He was not able to comfortably hold a conversation with that couple.

Two days after the party, he returned to Mumbai with the guests. He bid farewell to them at the hotel and went straight to his house.

When he lay in his bed that night, he felt his heartbeat racing. The reason for this was the dilemma in his mind. He was thinking about his place in this world. Who was he? He was no longer the person whom Darakhshan, his daughters, his relatives and acquaintances knew. The new man that was within him was unknown to everyone else. Would he ever be able to reveal his real self to them? Would they accept him with his new identity? He thought about how he would reveal the truth to Hina and Darakhshan? How would he persuade them to follow his beliefs? He was still engrossed in these thoughts when Darakhshan came into the room. She thought that Yusuf had already slept. She switched off the tube light. In the milky light of the dim bulb Yusuf saw that Darakhshan took out a maxi from the cupboard and put it on the table, then removed her clothes and wore that maxi.

He had never looked at her body with such searching eyes. He found her shapeless. The fat deposited around her waist and stomach looked ugly. Her breasts seemed to stink like a goat's stomach hanging at a butcher's shop. He wondered why he had never felt this ugliness before. With the same thought, Aymal's body appeared in his imagination. Aymal's body seemed perfect and magnetic too. Darakhshan was a ploughed field whose use was as a necessity. Aymal had made Yusuf realize that the body was a kiln of the soul where the soul turns gold on melting and the shine increased.

On the night of the party, Aymal had said something to Yusuf in a very serious tone which now appeared fresh in his mind. She had said, 'If sex carries with it the feeling of love, the soul experiences harmonious bliss. This is the highest altitude of the soul's flight.' As soon as Darakhshan spread herself on the bed, Yusuf turned over. She seemed like an unattractive, hideous insect. Even after turning away, the existence of Darakhshan caused him pain. It was a weird situation for him. In the past, whenever he felt the need, he had sex with her. Though he had noticed that during the entire process of intercourse, Darakhshan showed no reaction. She stayed still like a dead body or kept reciting a dua, a prayer. She had memorized all the duas that had to be recited before any action—from going to the bathroom to having sex.

Darakhshan stared at his back and thought that for a month Yusuf had shown no need for sex. Maybe he had been busy. On the other hand, Yusuf realized that the hideous, stinking insect lying beside him on the bed was staring at him.

Had his senses not awakened in the past? A woman who had come from Kerala to the party the other night had given a short speech where she had said, 'The lack of desire for copulation and the lack of having intercourse creates a canker in the soul. This wound makes the body smell bad and a sort of colourlessness covers the face. To hide the discolouring and smell, people participate in divine prayers and good deeds!' He tried bringing Darakhshan's face into his imagination, but it refused to be created there. Her face seemed to have broken itself into various parts. Those parts were actually dripping holes. Reeking pus flowed from those holes. He felt suffocated in that unbearable stink.

Hina said that she was reading *Gulliver's Travels*. The book was suggested by her teacher. It was a pictorial edition of Jonathan

Swift's novel which was specially published for children. Yusuf had also read that novel during his school days. He still remembered the story. He said, 'The human looks for something else and ends up finding something else altogether. Whatever he finds ultimately is so different.' He was actually saying that about himself. Hina kept her book aside and said, 'Daddy, that's why life is an adventure.'

Hina got up and sat on the chair. He smiled.

She smiled too.

He looked at Hina and said, 'My heart also desires adventure.'

'Then take this book and read,' Hina said, but she could not hear the hidden meaning in Yusuf's words.

'Arey, no. You read on the chair while I sleep on the sofa.'

'Is sleep an adventure at all?'

'I'm sleeping to stay awake,' Yusuf replied.

Two months later she was reminded of her father's words when her elder sister Nilofer told her that Yusuf had decided to live separately. He had not given any reason for this separation. He had simply said that it was his wish, and he wanted his wish to be respected. They had no choice to disagree, hence they all accepted. He would come home at the end of the month, stay for a few hours, give more than enough money for them to meet their expenses. Slowly his absence was realized by the people living around. The word spread and reached the ears of relatives. Yusuf's separation gave birth to various rumours in his clan. The rumour that spread the fastest was that he had married a south Indian woman. It finally reached his house. Darakhshan cried silently for many days.

Her mother's condition hit Hina the worst. She kept her elder sisters informed of her mother's sorrow over the phone. Saturday evening, both the sisters came to the house with their children.

They were astonished to hear that some people were saying that Yusuf had remarried. Nilofer called him up, inquired about him and then asked him to meet her. On being asked the reason for the meeting, she said that it was a serious matter, and she would elaborate only when they met. Yusuf gave the address of his house at Pydhonie which he had bought a few months back. Nilofer, her husband and Hina took a taxi to that house.

Yusuf warmly welcomed his daughters and son-in-law. The condition of the house revealed that he was spending a lonely life. Although the carpet, paintings, showpieces on the walls, pots and thin curtains told a different story about Yusuf. This was the face of Yusuf that his daughters were not aware of and had never seen before. While the conversation was unfolding, Hina wanted to go to the bathroom. The door of the bedroom was opposite the bathroom. There was a huge painting on the bedroom wall on which was the inviting nude body of a beautiful woman. She saw the painting through the curtain in the hall, and then silently shut the door of the bedroom and came back to join the conversation.

When they got up to leave, they seemed satisfied. Yusuf had clearly said that he would never remarry in his life, nor will he ever divorce Darakhshan.

His son-in-law asked, 'Daddy, then why are you living here alone?'

'I'm not alone here, my heart is with me.'

'What do you mean, Daddy?'

'I mean that a man is alone in a place where his heart is not with him. I am happy here. If I'm not able to sustain my happiness here, I'll come back home.'

They moved towards the door. Hina was silent. Yusuf looked at her. Hina looked into his eyes.

She was sad. With the passage of time, the framed portrait of the lustful nude woman in Yusuf's bedroom kept adding to Hina's sorrows.

Yusuf was in contact with Aymal.

After a few months, Aymal introduced him into that circle of people who followed the same beliefs as her. He became a member of that group.

Yusuf kept visiting his house.

He would exchange greetings with Darakhshan but never stayed over. That rope which tied a marriage was broken in search of new perceptions of desire. He had regular conversations with Hina. Three years later, Hina passed her tenth standard examinations. Yusuf gave her a diamond ring as a present. Hina, considering her mother's happiness, asked him to stay over for lunch. He agreed. It was a pleasant afternoon. He kept talking to Darakhshan as and when required. She had still not understood how Yusuf had suddenly left her life. After lunch, Yusuf told Hina that he would take her out to see the museum. Hina immediately got ready.

Yusuf told Hina about the importance of the antiques and their historical sources. He told her about different cultures, communities, religions and their signs and symbols. They also inquired about Hindu deities. At that time Hina realized that Yusuf was no longer the same man who used to call other religions evil and his religion the ultimate truth. She listened to him in complete astonishment. The museum had a lot of displays from the Mughal era. Many pieces of art from the Mughal period delicately depicted romance and sexuality. In many miniature paintings, one could see princes and noblemen engrossed in the pleasure of lovemaking. Hina looked at them for a moment and then turned towards the other section. Yusuf was able to sense that she was embarrassed by those paintings. He called Hina back and said that those paintings had no flaw; in fact they carried within them one of the essential truths of life. Running away from that was the beginning of making one's life meaningless. He said that one must give birth to meaning in one's life. Hina was silent. She was looking at the man who had always cursed her elder sisters for having conversations with men. That man who had regularly asked them to put their dupattas in place.

Since the day Hina had seen the picture of a beautiful nude woman in his room, she had a lot of questions in her mind. As Yusuf gave her the lesson of the truth of life, those questions became fresh in her mind again.

There was a wooden slab for sitting in the middle of the museum. She sat on it. Yusuf advised her to take admission in a decent college and continue her education. Talking about higher education, Yusuf mentioned that his friend Aymal was coming to Mumbai the following week and that she would be just the right person to consult about higher education. Hina was reminded of that meeting when Aymal, Burashid and Wardatul Sa'adat had come to the house. She tried recollecting Wardatul Sa'adat's image in her mind. Yusuf told her that Wardatul Sa'adat was studying for a master's degree in international law at a prestigious college in London. Hina was listening to him carefully. While talking about Wardatul Sa'adat, unconsciously Yusuf was reminded of the party at Khandala. That night she had presented herself as the Egyptian deity Isis and had read her dissertation on 'Imagination of the World without Satan' which was greatly appreciated. Yusuf looked at Hina. She looked like Isis. He smiled and said, 'You look like Isis.'

'Who's that?'

'Oh yes, she's an Egyptian goddess. Some call her the patron of nature and others call her the goddess of magic.'

Hina laughed loudly.

Yusuf kept looking at her while she laughed.

'Daddy, how did you change so much?'

'So much . . .?'

'So much that you are no longer what you used to be.'

'Change is inevitable. I feel more alive now,' Yusuf replied.

Hina did not say anything. It was already evening. They exited the museum. Right opposite the museum was a café on the ground floor of a small art gallery. They sat and had a cappuccino there. They talked more. It was already 7.30 p.m. Yusuf said to Hina, 'Let's go!' and placed his cup on the table. 'There might be traffic on the way.'

It took them half an hour to reach the JJ flyover. Had there been no traffic, this distance would have been covered in five minutes. They did not talk during the drive. When they crossed the flyover, Hina looked out of the window and felt a cold wind brush against her cheeks. She liked it. She turned and asked, 'Are you happy?'

'Yes. Earlier I just existed. Now, I'm happy.'

She smiled at her father's words and repeated them, 'What do you mean?'

'Now I'm closer to myself and have started accepting who I truly am. Otherwise we're actually the duplicates of the society we are born in. All our actions are to please others or to copy others. Even our thought process and ideas are copies of others.' He looked at Hina once and continued, 'We simply exist when we try to copy others rather than finding ourselves.' Hina noticed that Yusuf's English had become better than before. She had never seen her father talk so seriously. She was reminded of an English teacher, Rahiya Salamat, who used to talk so deeply while teaching poems.

'Daddy,' she said and then looked out of the car. While looking at the beautiful lights in a grand building of the Bohri Muhallah she continued, 'Daddy, you never used to talk like this before.'

Yusuf smiled and said, 'Yes, you're growing up and now I can speak my heart out to you.'

Hina's cheeks turned red.

Before she could react, Yusuf said, 'We are home.'

She looked into her father's eyes for a second. He smiled.

She smiled back and got off the car.

She had dinner with her mother after the night prayers. Darakhshan was very happy. She had specially made kheer for Hina. Hina tasted it and praised it. Darakhshan asked her, 'What did you talk about?'

Hina answered, 'We talked a lot. Abba has changed a lot.'

'He has changed, yes.' Darakhshan's voice carried a sense of rancour in it.

'Now he speaks very smartly,' Hina said and looked at her mother.

'Seems like he has fed you well,' Darakhshan said.

'He does not even know how to do that. You know Abbu is a man of direct words.'

Hina had found herself taking her father's side in front of her mother after many years.

Darakhshan looked at Hina, swallowed a morsel and said, 'That is why I repeatedly say that he has been possessed.'

Hina smiled and said, 'You've been trying to break the possession for four years. So much money has gone into it.'

'That is exactly why the situation is better. Had I not been doing exorcism he would not have been giving us money for our expenses. He would have abandoned us by now.'

She wanted to laugh at what her mother had just said, but that would have hurt her, and she might have started crying. Hence Hina stayed silent and agreed saying, 'You're right, mother.'

Hina told Drakhshan that Yusuf had asked her to take admission in a good college for further studies. He would take care of all the expenses and also provide her with guidance. Darakhshan felt nice hearing this. She told Hina in Gujarati that a Sufi outside Shah Baba's tomb had told her that it was her time of *saadhey saati* (seven-and-a-half-year curse) and it would continue for the same period. Which meant that Yusuf would become absolutely fine in a couple of years or so and would return home. Hina encouraged her mother and said whatever God does, he does for our good. After finishing dinner, she watched a film on the television for some time and then went to sleep.

When she closed her eyes, the entire day spent with her father projected itself on her mind's screen like a movie. She could see her father and herself in distinct colours on that screen. She stopped at every frame to try and understand her father. Yusuf was now a stranger to her. He was a riddle yet a very attractive one. She kept repeating his words in her mind. There were so many questions that had taken birth within her, thousands of questions that she wanted to ask him. Through those questions she wanted to learn about his life but also about the coldness that he'd suddenly developed towards Darakhshan. Yusuf had made sure that all their needs were fulfilled, and in fact he had started giving more money than what was required for their expenses.

Two years back he had also bought a new fridge, a sofa, a television and a showcase. He kept calling his daughters and monetarily helped them as and when required. Probably, this was why there was no negative feelings or criticism directed towards him in the house. But still there was a wound in Hina's heart. She had seen Darakhshan weep during all those years. Those cries had knotted themselves up in Hina's throat. At times, when she was alone and talking to

herself, those knots became as painful as cancer. Grief would strike
her. Everything around would start to seem strange and meaningless.
A feeling of detachment overwhelmed her. She had found herself
in such a situation many a time throughout the past year, and had
hidden her condition from her sisters and mother.

Two weeks after the visit to the museum, Yusuf called Hina up and
asked her to be ready by 5 p.m. as they had to go and meet Aymal.

She wore a white salwar and frock which had miniature
peacock feathers embroidered on it. When Yusuf came to pick
her up, he handed her an envelope. Hina knew that the envelope
was for Darakhshan. It had Rs 25,000. Darakhshan opened it and
said, 'What is so much money for?' Yusuf looked at Hina and
said, 'Use this money for the college fees and for buying books.'
Darakhshan had got her answer. Yusuf bid farewell to Darakhshan
from the doorstep itself, 'Khuda Hafiz.' He always said Khuda
Hafiz and to these words were attached Darakhshan's hope that
someday he would definitely return to her. She mumbled back,
'Fi Amanillah!'

They were at Aymal's room on the twelfth floor of the Taj
hotel by around 6 p.m. Aymal told them that Burashid was busy
organizing a seminar in Egypt. Wardatul Sa'adat looked like a
wise adult that day, even though Yusuf had seen her when she
visited Mumbai with Aymal two years back. Today she seemed
more mature. Hina shook hands with her and was reminded of
their first meeting. She recalled that during her first meeting,
Wardatul Sa'adat had said certain things that she was unable to
make sense of.

They talked about various things over tea. Jokes were cracked.
Aymal took out a chocolate box from the cupboard and offered

it to Hina. Wardatul Sa'adat got up saying, 'Just a minute, please.'
She took out a book from her bag and presented it to Hina. 'This
is to celebrate your passing the examination. Had I known in
advance, I'd have gotten something more.' She smiled. Hina smiled
back. The chocolate box was transparent. She read the title of the
book—*Being and Time* by Martin Heidegger. Hina thanked her.
For some time Aymal spoke to Hina about her career plans and
explained many things to her. She emphasized a lot on reading. Hina
told her that she had read four or five novels as well as Whitman's
collection of poems that her teacher had given her. That made
Aymal happy. She laughingly said that even Yusuf read many books.
This was a revelation for Hina. She smiled and said, 'That is why
Abba's grammar has now become perfect.'

'Even his vocabulary has expanded considerably,' Wardatul
Sa'adat added.

Aymal gave a tight-lipped smile while Yusuf scratched his hair
dramatically.

Wardatul Sa'adat and Hina seemed engrossed in their
conversation when Yusuf said, 'You both can keep exchanging
ideas while both of us will go out and do some shopping.' Yusuf
and Aymal left.

Wardatul Sa'adat talked to Hina about her future academic
and career plans and shared information about her college as
well as the course she was pursuing. Wardatul Sa'adat gave some
important advice and information to Hina and also shared her email
address with her so that they could stay in contact in the future.
Hina had an email address but due to lack of use had forgotten
it. She promised to send an email as soon as she started a new
account. Wardatul Sa'adat felt the need to have more tea and
asked Hina if she would like some too. Hina said she would.
Wardatul Sa'adat placed the order and went to the bathroom.
Hina's eyes fell on a book kept on the pillow. Its title was *The
Book of Shadows*. The cover had a pentagon made on it, behind

which was a striking portrait of a woman with smoke coming out of her palms and an owl sitting on her shoulder. In her heart she really wanted to touch the book, but she controlled herself. As soon as Wardatul Sa'adat entered the room, Hina turned and asked her about the theme of the book. She picked it up and extended it to Hina and said that for the past one year she had madly wanted to become a Wiccan and this book was based on the theme of Wicca.

Wicca was a new word for Hina. On further inquiry, the entire history, ideology, perspectives, historiography about the Wiccan and pagan religions and their magical legacy were summarized by Wardatul Sa'adat. In between, tea was served. They talked about Wicca over tea as well. This topic seemed very interesting to Hina. Hina shared that her mother thought someone had used magic on Yusuf. Wardatul Sa'adat paused for a moment and then claimed that it was impossible for any magic to work on Yusuf. Hina asked the reason. Wardatul Sa'adat said that Yusuf himself seemed like a possessor of magical powers. This statement was hilarious to Hina. Seeing her laugh, Wardatul Sa'adat completed her sentence, 'My mother only trusts Yusuf in this entire world.'

After tea, Wardatul Sa'adat took out a calendar-like frame from her bag, which she spread on the floor.

She looked at Hina and said, 'Tell me what your wish is.'

Hina thought for a while and said, 'I want to see my mother happy.'

Wardatul Sa'adat closed her eyes and chanted something, then kept her index finger on the frame. She opened her eyes and said that nothing was possible for the next one year, after which if Hina was able to fulfil the duties that her mother gave her, something could happen. Hina felt good on hearing this. She smiled and said that she would definitely do what her mother said.

Wardatul Sa'adat asked her to spread her left hand and closed her eyes. Sa'adat kept her eyes shut for two minutes, then began speaking, 'A time when neither the day could be called a day and nor the night would seem night enough, a boy will come and stand in front of you and will try to talk to you.'

On hearing this, Hina got a little scared at first but thought that this was just a guessing game and believing in it would be stupidity. She was still thinking when Wardatul Sa'adat continued, 'The winds, the clouds and water will not agree to the meeting when both of you will be tasting the flavours of each other's soul.'

This made Hina laugh.

A different kind of awe and anger had crept into Wardatul Sa'adat's eyes and she was staring at Hina.

'This only happens in movies,' Hina said without meeting her gaze.

Wardatul Sa'adat did not say anything. She kept her eyes concentrated on the frame.

When she raised her eyes, Hina was going through the pages of *The Book of Shadows*. She closed her eyes again. She opened them after four minutes and said, 'That boy will have sex with you but I cannot see beyond that. There is darkness all around. There is lightning and rainfall.'

Hina looked at her and said, 'Be patient, Sa'adat, I will relate the rest of the story to you through email.'

She smiled again. Whatever Wardatul Sa'adat was saying seemed meaningless to her. She had full faith in Allah. She had even memorized the four *Qul*. She had decided never to do anything before marriage that was prohibited by Islam. She could not find any justification to take all that Wardatul Sa'adat had said seriously.

Hina turned a few pages of the book while Wardatul Sa'adat rested. When Hina shut the book, Wardatul Sa'adat told her that a few minutes back she was under the influence of Wicca. Rarely does it happen that the soul is able to see the scenes from the future. She said, 'How I wish you had asked whether you would be able to save yourself from the darkness . . .'

No sooner had she said this than someone knocked at the door. Before opening it, she kept the frame back in her bag. Aymal and

Yusuf entered the room with polybags in their hands. Aymal handed one of the bags to Hina and said that there were a few things for her mother in it. Hina accepted the present. After this, they came out of the hotel and started strolling on the seashore.

Hina reached home at around 9 p.m. She talked to her mother for a while, and then went up to her bed to lie down. As she lay down a lot of delusions started crowding her mind. Wardatul Sa'adat's words were coming back to her again and again. She tried sleeping, but sleep had already escaped her eyes. She remained in the same condition for many days. Wardatul Sa'adat's words had made their place in the depths of her consciousness.

This made her come face to face with melancholy. The tension about the future made her morose. When she was returning home in a taxi after meeting Asrar, tears flowed down her eyes. A wave of delusion was rising within her. The grief of the soul that she had managed to suppress a long time back had now miraculously become a dark spot within her. She felt satisfaction filling up her mind and heart because of the initiated feeling of love. But the memory of what Wardatul Sa'adat had said changed that satisfaction into wretchedness and despair. She was unable to decipher the situation. The handkerchief she had placed over her mouth while crying had made her throat ache. She had never wailed like that before.

6

This Routine Journey Desires an Adventurous Accident
(*Ajab Sapat Safar Hai Ke Hadsa Chahun*)

Hina took admission in KCP College.

The college was near Churchgate railway station. Yusuf accompanied Hina to the college on the day the merit list was to come out. He was happy to see her name on the list, and for that reason he took Hina to the famous Chinese restaurant opposite Regal Cinema to have a chicken sizzler. Hina got scared when the waiter brought the sizzling chicken to the table. Yusuf had smiled and said that this was the specialty of the dish. Hina liked the food. After lunch, they went for a walk on the seaside. She had been to the seaside near the Gateway of India many times but had never sat on the walls beside the sea. It was a July afternoon. The sunshine was bearable. There were people sitting on the wall till where your eyes could see. A girl was lying in her lover's arms. Between the road and the sea wall, there was a lot of space to walk where bhelpuri, chana and moong vendors sold their wares. The father–daughter duo also sat on the sea wall. From here, one was able to see the very unique landscape of Mumbai. It looked even more beautiful in the night. Yusuf pointed his finger and showed Hina the location of places like the Raj Bhawan, Teen Batti, Walkeshwar, Malabar Hill, Girgaon, and Charni Road till Marine Drive and Colaba. Hina turned her head to see the breathtaking view of what was called the Queen's Necklace because of its shape. The skyscrapers from Walkeshwar till Nariman Point added to Mumbai's glamour. The glass panes of the buildings shone bright in the sun. Hina looked at the sea. The surface of the water was glistening with the play of the sunrays. Hina's hair flew in the strong wind. She had put a clip on one side.

Yusuf said, 'This area of Mumbai looks like a question mark on the map.'

Hina immediately asked, 'A question mark for what?'

Yusuf smiled and looked at the waves of the sea. He could see a boat far away tossing on the waves. The back of the boat looked so submerged in the water that it gave the impression that the entire boat would slide into the sea. But the boat, riding the waves, would rise again. Then it once again gave the impression of going under and rising again. After observing this, he turned to Hina and said, 'The human himself is a question mark.' Hina looked into his eyes. Those eyes were full of seriousness, as if they were made to see the world from a distinct perspective.

She said, 'You have become so serious. You never used to talk like this before.'

'Yes, a little bit . . . Now everyone asks me whether I realize it or not.' He told Hina that he was studying those books which raised a lot of questions about the condition in which we all lived, about human existence, delusions, the being, the soul and about the world itself. Aymal had given him these books two years back. Yusuf advised Hina to try and learn about other things along with what was prescribed in the college syllabus. Hina nodded her head in agreement. He was about to say something when two eunuchs walked up to him. He took out his wallet and gave a coin to one of them. Hina was trying to control her embarrassed smile. Yusuf gauged her embarrassment and said, 'Do you know what they symbolize?'

'No, I don't, Papa.'

'They symbolize the one who has made everything.'

'What?' The word slipped her mouth suddenly. Yusuf burst out in laughter.

'In a few years you will get the answer to this "what" on your own,' he said and stood on the wall. He looked down from there. A lot of insects were crawling on the stones attached to the wall. They made Yusuf think that if someone took a look at the earth from the sky or a star up above, the humans would look like insects crawling everywhere on the buildings and roads.

On seeing him stand, Hina also followed suit. She looked at Chowpatty from the sea wall. She was reminded of the time her teacher had told the class that this area was called Queen's Necklace; Hina had asked herself why such a name was chosen. This made her accept that truly the area was like a queen's necklace. The buildings surrounding the shore were like the gems studded on a necklace.

On the first day of college, Hina met Vidhi Singh, a girl from the North-east. Their conversation turned into friendship. They started wandering together in malls, shopping centres and cafeterias of western Mumbai. Vidhi Singh lived in a government girls' hostel near the college. Her hometown was Darjeeling, where her family ran tea plantations as an inherited business. She had passed her tenth standard with distinction while studying in one of the best missionary schools in Darjeeling. Her father had published three collections of poems in English and occasionally she also indulged in poetry-writing. Hina was impressed with Vidhi's free and casual lifestyle.

Vidhi started visiting Hina's house. She loved meeting Hina's mother. She praised her home-made kebabs and chilly chutney so much so that Darakhshan went red in her cheeks. Those words made her an accepted guest for a stayover. On some days during the month, the friends were seen loitering in the Muslim-dominated areas of west Mumbai. They ate peppery snacks from roadside stalls and clicked a lot of photos. At night, they would have food made by Darakhshan followed by a late-night study session in the hall and endless conversation on various topics.

Hina told Vidhi everything that she knew and understood about her father. She told her that it was a difficult time for her when Yusuf had decided to leave the house and live separately. She used to cry alone. She had not revealed this to anyone. Not even her mother and sisters. Hina told her that Yusuf used to come and meet them regularly, especially her, but the darkness that had submerged her heart refused to leave her. This darkness walked with her even to the school. Sometimes she felt alone in the classroom. Her concentration was never on her books, the teachers or whatever was written on the blackboard. A sheet of blackness covered her eyes. Hina told her of the day when her teacher was teaching them about adulthood and bodily changes—a day before that she had herself stepped into adolescence—but she was able to listen to only a few sentences that the teacher said before falling into the depth of her own darkness. During that dark time infinite questions and thoughts engaged her in a conversation. The science teacher soon realized that she was mentally absent from the class. She walked up to her table and stood by her desk for a few seconds. When she was sure that Hina was not listening to her, she banged the duster on the desk and shouted loudly, 'What was I talking about?'

In confusion and fear, Hina's tongue slipped, 'About the characteristics of the vagina.'

The girls in the class laughed for a long time. For a moment there was anger on the science teacher's face which was soon taken over by laughter. Hina realized her mistake and immediately corrected her sentence, 'about the functions of a vagina.' Her correction was also incapable of stopping the chaos in the classroom. Firstly, her voice was very soft and secondly, the class was echoing with laughter and hence her correction was heard by no one except the teacher. Vidhi also laughed for a long time after hearing about this incident. The story broke the wall between Vidhi and Hina. It made Vidhi aware of a hidden knot within Hina.

While relating stories of her past, Hina told her friend that for the last six months she had been feeling that she was able to understand her father better and hence had no complaints against him. In fact, the changes that Hina was seeing in her father were not just unimaginable but also unbelievable. She told Vidhi that there had been a transformation in Yusuf's thought process, religious beliefs, conversational patterns, reading and behaviour. He now seemed to possess a very creative mindset and a positive thought process. She elaborated on each and every small transformation that she had witnessed in her father. This was very weird and interesting for Vidhi. She felt the desire to meet Yusuf. Till now she thought that Hina's father was very influential, but through these accounts she felt that Yusuf 's personality had a kind of uniqueness and complexity. Respecting a personality is one thing but being curious and intrigued by it is another. Yusuf seemed to be very attractive. Hina found it unusual that Vidhi wanted to meet Yusuf so badly. She promised her that she would talk to Yusuf and get him to meet her at his shop in Fort or at home soon. In fact, she also told Vidhi that till now she herself had not seen the shop.

In August, the college's department of history announced a history trip to Aurangabad. Vidhi and Hina decided to go on this trip. But when Hina asked Darakhshan, she was denied permission. That night Hina called Yusuf and asked him to meet her. Yusuf told her that he would visit the house in a few days. Hina told him about

Vidhi and how she wanted to meet him. At the end, it was decided that he would pick them up from the college the next day.

Hina told Vidhi in college that she had spoken to Yusuf at night and that he would come to pick them up in the afternoon. Vidhi was glad since Yusuf had become a star of sorts for her. When Yusuf rolled down the car window, Vidhi could not smile because of the astonishment on her face. Even after sitting in the car, she remained silent as usual. She herself did not know the reason behind her silence. When the car stopped at the Churchgate signal, Yusuf turned back to talk to them. Hina gave a brief introduction of Vidhi and told Yusuf that she wrote poems in English. Yusuf greeted her warmly. Vidhi expressed her gratitude. Yusuf parked his car in the enclosure of a beautiful three-storey building which was not very far from the university. The moment Hina came out of the car her eyes caught a black-and-white board on the first storey. On the board in simple calligraphy was written 'Land of Chinawina'.

All three entered the building. The restaurant was dimly lit. Chandeliers hung here and there. Apart from the engravings on the doors and windows there were a few Chinese miniature paintings. In one painting, a family was having dinner in a peaceful atmosphere. In another painting, a Chinese girl was shown to be chopping vegetables. Vidhi's eyes stayed at the third painting for longer than a moment. In that painting Eros's beloved Psyche sat on a raised platform. Eros was looking at Psyche with eyes overflowing with passion. Their bodies were immensely attractive. Both the deities were nude, but they were oblivious of each other's exposed bodies, and each was lost in the other's eyes. For a minute the thought crossed Vidhi's mind, 'Is the eye really the home of our souls?'

She answered it herself, 'The house of the soul is our desire that resides in someone else's body.'

Hina appreciated the service and the clean glass crockery of the restaurant. She had just moved her hands towards the glass when a waiter poured water into it from a jug. She thanked him and drank the water. Vidhi looked at her. Hina smiled. Vidhi exclaimed, 'I've never seen such an amazing Chinese restaurant before!' Hina agreed with her. Yusuf told them that the restaurant had a buffet system.

A waiter placed plates on their table along with small bowls of different sauces. Vidhi was about to say something when two waiters came and placed chicken and vegetable starters on their table. Yusuf asked Vidhi if she was a vegetarian. Vidhi said that everything worked for her. Yusuf told the waiter to bring vegetarian as well as non-vegetarian dishes. Within five or ten minutes, the entire table was covered with various kinds of starters, which left both Vidhi and Hina astonished. All the dishes were delicious. They were still trying out the starters when a waiter came and asked about their choice of soup. Yusuf ordered plain vegetarian soup. While eating the starters with the garlic sauce, Hina told Yusuf about the educational trip. Vidhi interjected and said that both of them wanted to go on the trip. Hina also told Yusuf that Darakhshan had already refused permission. Yusuf solved the problem by saying that he would talk to Darakhshan about it when he would visit home on Saturday. Hina and Vidhi were glad to hear that.

Yusuf asked Vidhi about her family and her background, and Vidhi was more than pleased to answer the questions. Vidhi told them that her great-grandmother was a German woman who had fallen in love with her great-grandfather. Their tea plantations spread across many acres. She said that her father kept attending conferences of SAARC writers and his collection of poems had won a prestigious South African award recently. His articles on literature and culture were regularly published in famous newspapers. Hina was listening to their conversation while savouring the food. When Vidhi told him about her interest in writing poetry, Yusuf pressed her to recite one of her poems. Vidhi wanted to push this to some other day, but Hina persuaded her to recite. There was no mischief in Hina's eyes; she genuinely wanted her father to see Vidhi's talent. Vidhi finally agreed:

Another Poem for You, My Beloved

I accumulate heat in my braided hair,
I unwind them when my mind unwinds,
Letting it out on you with an exfoliating tiredness,
Reposing in the alcoves you provide.
You are the sauna, also the spa,
Ceaselessly soothing me inside out.
I smoke you like my midnight cigarette,
Blending in your ashen rot.
Why so well your brain registers me?
How so fast can your cerebrospinal fluid rise?
Even when you know I'm the fanfare of unrest,
Always crumbling bread-like
I breathe in your Saturn ring-like dust specks, and the
breathing gets heavier
My lungs release the enclosed darkness, they get pinker,
I say that when you caress my braid, and you pamper my
ideas further.
One day I shall write about love. Only when this unending
ballad is over.
I clean myself like you clean the rot, and my sight gets
much clearer.
I love you like I love the coffee pot. It stays with me forever.

All three of them were silent for a while. A few words in the poem were new to Yusuf. Despite that, he had understood what the poem was trying to convey. In fact, he had never read English poetry before. Just once, when he was in Goa with Aymal, she had read out to him a few poems of Pablo Neruda and Emily Dickinson. A few verses of Neruda's poem had touched him, and he was trying to recall them but could not. He praised Vidhi's poem and then told her that he was trying to remember a few verses by Neruda when Vidhi said that he was her favourite poet! Hina took out a white rose from the vase kept on the table and presented it to Vidhi. Vidhi thanked her, though she had already read this poem out to Hina before. Yusuf realized that behind the poem was a strong, bold and opinionated mind. Yusuf was impressed by Vidhi's self-confidence.

Yusuf went on to share his perspective on the poem. Vidhi expressed her gratitude again and again. Hina said that in this exchange of thanks, they should not miss out on the main course. They went to the buffet counter and served themselves their favourite dishes. By then the waiter had picked up all the used plates from the table. When they returned to the table, Vidhi told Yusuf that Hina kept talking about him all the time. Yusuf looked at Hina and said smilingly, 'Ah! She's my sweetheart!' Hina smiled. Vidhi peered into Yusuf's eyes in the dim light of the restaurant and said, 'Can I ask you a direct question?'

Yusuf said, 'Of course!'

'What's your view on religion?'

Yusuf looked at Vidhi. Her face was very different from that of a common Indian. Her eyes and nose were small, like those of people from the North-east. Her lips were reddish and thin. On seeing Yusuf's eyes concentrated on Vidhi, Hina also started looking at her. Hina thought that Yusuf did not like the question at all and was assuming that Vidhi has asked this question on her behalf. Hina's heart began to race. The few minutes of this silence made Vidhi's heart also lose pace. She thought that the question had angered Yusuf. Yusuf looked at the waiter standing next to them and said, 'Water, please.'

The waiter stepped forward and poured water into the glass.

Yusuf looked at Hina and Vidhi's pale faces while drinking the water and said, 'I'm almost an atheist, and look, I said almost, not completely, an atheist.'

Hina and Vidhi were looking at him with complete astonishment. Both were silent. On noticing their silence, Yusuf said that the question was very pertinent, and he was happy to hear it. This explanation brought back the colour on the faces of the girls. Yusuf talked about religion for a few minutes. He said that religion was part of human civilization, but it was necessary for man to question why a particular civilization was his civilization. Could one liberate oneself from civilization? Yusuf took a few names of philosophers and said that they believed that every individual had the right to question his present state, beliefs and culture. If society took away those rights, then it would be curbing thought and insulting the individual.

Even after understanding the interest that his conversation had generated in Vidhi, he changed the topic, 'Can I also ask a question directly?'

Vidhi smiled at the mention of the word 'directly' and said, 'Of course.'

Yusuf looked down and wrinkled his eyes as if welcoming the 'of course'. He then asked, 'What is your view on religion?'

Vidhi immediately smiled at the question. She turned half her face towards Yusuf as if to assess if the question was asked in jest and to understand the mischief behind it. Yusuf shrugged to indicate that there was no escaping the question. Hina was happy to see the stalemate between them thawing. She was having fun. Vidhi looked at Hina and said, 'I got myself caught, yaar.'

Hina replied, 'You only started the "direct" questions. Now you cannot back out.'

For a moment Vidhi gave the impression that the answer to the question was difficult for her. Mischief came to her mind. She turned and saw a waiter standing behind her. On seeing her turn, the waiter

came to her. Vidhi looked at Yusuf and told the waiter, 'Water, please.'
Actually, Vidhi had just mimicked Yusuf, and very well. She drank the
water and while keeping the glass on the table said, 'I am an atheist.'

Hina and Yusuf's eyes were still focused on Vidhi. Vidhi spoke
about herself for some more time. Yusuf seemed to be impressed
with what she was saying.

After they were done with the food, they had ice cream. They
chatted while standing outside the restaurant. Yusuf told Vidhi that
he could drop her at the hostel, but Vidhi said she wanted to look
for a few old books on the roadside bookstalls in the Fort area.
Vidhi left after five or ten minutes.

Yusuf and Hina sat in the car. Yusuf dropped Hina at the JJ
flyover and went back to his shop. He went to meet his family on
Saturday. After mentioning the trip to Aurangabad, he told Hina
that she should go for the educational trip. Darakhshan was ready
to express doubts about her safety, but before that Yusuf said that
he had already spoken to Miss Thomas, who was a lecturer in the
college. She was going to be present on the trip. She knew Hina
and would keep an eye on her. This was enough for Darakhshan's
satisfaction. While Yusuf was leaving, Hina accompanied him till
the ground floor of the building. When Yusuf was about to sit in
the car, Hina asked him if he really knew Miss Thomas. Yusuf
admitted that he had known her for a few years. She said that she
could never gather that from the conversations she had had with
Miss Thomas. He sat in the car and Hina returned home.

On her way back to the house, she kept thinking of how her
father and Miss Thomas could have met and become friends. Miss
Thomas was a strict, introverted, scholarly woman.

There was a traffic jam at the JJ signal. Yusuf's car got stuck in
the jam. He looked at himself in the rear-view mirror and read
what was written on it, 'Objects in the mirror are closer than they

appear.' He smiled. Miss Thomas, wearing red lipstick, a T-shirt and a skirt, was smiling at him from the mirror.

Aymal had given Yusuf Miss Thomas's number after the party in Pune and had asked him to meet her in Mumbai. He would get into a good circle through Miss Thomas. She had told him that Miss Thomas was the head of an organization of like-minded people in Mumbai. At the time she was attending a conference in Sri Lanka or else she would have been present at the party. Aymal had called Miss Thomas up and had introduced Yusuf privately.

Before meeting Miss Thomas, he bought an English novel to gift her.

The first meeting was pleasant.

Yusuf had indulged in less conversation and had carefully answered Miss Thomas's questions on the party at Pune. Yusuf had said that it was as if the party had cut him off from his umbilical cord, once again. Miss Thomas had asked what he meant by that. Yusuf had said that every individual had a cultural identity. He was a prisoner of certain beliefs and spent his life with certain kind of people around him. This imprisonment, beliefs, restraints were like the bond between his soul and his umbilical cord. Till the time man did not break this cord, he would not be truly free. This made Miss Thomas smile and say, 'Freedom is the ultimate desire of a human heart but unfortunately, the human himself is the enemy of that freedom.'

Yusuf presented the novel to Miss Thomas before she left. She had happily accepted the gift and said that she read a lot. Miss Thomas had a small bungalow in Colaba. Her parents had passed away and she was still unmarried. Every second month she hosted a small get-together of people of the same belief. They talked, debated and discussed topics like the present religious deviations of man and the freedom of his self. Yusuf became a part of these get-togethers, where he was able to connect with some residents of the city and realize how religion had created rifts in society; to prove itself to be the ultimate truth in the pages of history, religion subverted reality and used intuitions, miracles and the paranormal as weapons to meet its goals.

These debates and conversations were filled with knowledge, references and academic authority. In the initial few months, Yusuf preferred to remain a silent listener. He borrowed books, magazines and pamphlets from Miss Thomas's library to read, and then he carefully returned them. Slowly, he became trustworthy in the eyes of Miss Thomas. One day, Miss Thomas called him up on the phone and told him that on the night of the dark moon, a 'Luciferian dance' was being organized at her place. She wanted Yusuf to attend it as well. He reluctantly agreed. He kept thinking about the Pune party for three days. Once the memory of it came with such intensity that he called Aymal up on the phone and talked to her for very long. This restlessness and sudden remembrance pleased Aymal's heart and made her proud secretively. Before finishing the call, Aymal said, 'Whenever and wherever happiness knocks at your door, you should never delay opening it.'

Yusuf loved Aymal's large-heartedness. He told her that he totally agreed with her. He also informed her that Miss Thomas had organized a special party at her place, though he did not know much about it. Aymal informed him that such parties were organized every third month in the circle where the attempt was to feel the freedom that had existed in the hands of humans before the birth of religions. The second aim was to make sure that all present were also able to interact well with each other. She told him that these 'circle' parties were a form of resistance against the laws of the evil and its slavery. It was the announcement of the freedom of the self. He felt a little relieved after talking to Aymal. She said that she had introduced Yusuf to Miss Thomas so that evil didn't cast its shadow on the freedom Yusuf had just experienced. He smiled and thanked Aymal.

He reached Miss Thomas's house on the evening of the party at the fixed time. All the guests had gathered by 9 p.m. There were four women, including a young south Indian girl whose features were spectacular. There were four men who were of the same age as him and one was an elderly person. He was well acquainted with those who regularly attended the various discussions that happened at Miss Thomas's house. He was introduced to those he did not know. All of them were engrossed in conversation. Miss Thomas had already ordered food for the guests in advance. The Luciferian dance started at ten. To begin, Miss Thomas invited the elderly man to give a speech. He expressed his views on 'the universe and darkness'. He claimed that Lucifer was the Prince of Darkness and would soon engulf the false light of the world. After which, the south Indian girl who had told Yusuf that her name was Sangarma, recited a poem in Hindi. She had written the poem in her mother tongue and had translated it into Hindi.

The running theme of the poem was that God tried to misuse Lucifer's intense love, devotion, knowledge, wisdom and innocence for his own benefits and on realizing this, Lucifer decided to trample on the footprints of God and refused those of his proposals that God had forced upon him as his will. She concluded the poem with a speech where she elaborated on the same theme. Lucifer had put his being at risk to interpret the soul of God, but on the other hand God did what was against the principles. He tried to subvert the importance of the soul over the material. To insult Lucifer, God decided to put soul within the material. Lucifer refused to become a part of this. After that, God created novel powers and organisms that would be responsible for portraying Lucifer's silence in the world as his trap. Lucifer still remained silent. Lucifer knew that one day God would have to face embarrassment in the universe because of this game. That day Lucifer would dethrone him and bring him to justice.

Miss Thomas was the first to start applauding the speech as soon as it ended. Everyone applauded after her. Yusuf also joined in. As soon as Miss Thomas stood up to present her dissertation, Sangarma presented a drink in a black-coloured glass. Everyone took a sip each. Miss Thomas claimed that the drink was to celebrate the time when there would be no evil on the face of the earth and the human soul would live in freedom. To explain herself she said that there was a time when the earth was still free from the trap of religion, when a human was nothing more than a human and the earth was in celebration all through the day and night. The knowledge and proof of this was not just present in history but its music and rhythm had been preserved in the ancient wisdoms of the world. Miss Thomas said that the odour of a girl's body had been preserved in this drink. The odour of that girl who was intoxicated with the ecstasy of her first menstruation. There were other distinct ingredients in the drink. The smell of the drink was as brilliant and as stunning as human sweat.

Within two–three minutes of consuming the drink, Yusuf felt a wave rise within his soul. In fact, the entire party was now dipped in ecstasy. Miss Thomas read out her dissertation in that intoxication. The title of her dissertation was 'The Soul Was Child to Darkness'. Everyone listened to it with full concentration. With her analysis she tried to open the knotted existence of the soul. She said that whether the soul was that of the defeated God or that of the victor of the future—Lucifer himself—all had been born of the spring of darkness. And it was only darkness where the soul could find true solace. The souls that were afraid of darkness were captured by the evil. When the dissertation was about to end, Sangarma emerged from an adjacent room, stood behind Miss Thomas and placed a crown-like thing on her head. Three or four people had worn such headgear in Pune. This crown was an indication of the love for Lucifer. Miss Thomas kept her dissertation aside and hugged Sangarma. Everyone applauded and appreciated her dissertation.

At around 11.15 p.m. a round of whisky was served. The tube light was switched off, and four candles were lit. The lights outside the bungalow were also switched off. They sat in a circle. The candles and whisky bottles were kept in the centre. Miss Thomas filled one glass with whisky. She took a gulp from that overflowing glass and passed it on to others to take a sip each. Meanwhile,

Sangarma poured whisky pegs for everyone and distributed them. All of them took a goblet in their hands. Miss Thomas stood outside the circle. She said in a high voice, 'In the name of darkness who gave life to the soul. In the name of the prince of darkness, the all-knower and exalted one who rebelled for the safety of the soul.'

Everyone gobbled down the first drink in a single breath. This was a recipe to unveil the real efficacy of the previous drink. The moment this whisky fused with the previous drink in the body, the colour of the soul brightened up. The clothes seemed like an additional burden on the body. Miss Thomas came into the circle now. She was wearing a pink nightie. The elderly man pressed two fingers on his right-hand thumb, raised it and said, 'Thomas, be the night.' Miss Thomas smiled and put off the candles. The hands of the clock on the wall shone brighter than they normally would. They held each other's hands. They raised them in the air thrice. They could hear Miss Thomas's voice. 'Close your eyes and look at each other.' They all followed the command, closed their eyes and started searching for each other in the darkness. But the drink had spread in the nerves of their eyes, minds, hearts and soul; the effect was such that they could no longer recognize each other's faces. Sangarma now kept another peg in front of each one of them. Miss Thomas uttered, 'Drink the glass kept in front of you.' All of them spread their shivering hands and raised the glasses. 'Slowly, slowly, this is the last drink.'

The elderly man said, 'I hope this is not the last drink of my life.'

Everyone smiled.

Miss Thomas instructed them to open their eyes.

They opened their eyes.

Their eyes seemed to be filled with smoke. Images of humans from ancient times were emerging and disappearing in their minds.

Miss Thomas said, 'Men and women were free in pagan traditions and thus their souls also experienced bliss.'

They sat and drank more whisky for a while and kept talking to each other, laughing and singing. Sangarma had now come and joined the circle. In the flow of the intoxication, she removed her shirt and kept it aside. She was followed by the elderly man, who removed his clothes and said, 'My freedom was terminated because of these clothes.'

All of them laughed at his claim and before the echoes of the laughter died, everyone removed their clothes and threw them hither and thither. They were now drowned in the lake of ecstasy and self-forgetfulness. They had given up the shame that clothes had brought with them and were now sitting here and there, lying in each other's laps and experiencing the feeling of a thousand-year-old companionship. Their souls were reaching their peak. The soul reaches the intoxication of its zenith only when it is no longer a slave, of either itself, a body, belief or the power of another soul. They were all what they had eternally wanted to be in the depths of their consciousness since—intoxicated in the ecstasy of their body and soul.

Miss Thomas looked at the window while drinking her glass of whisky. Four or five minutes were left to twelve. She silently sipped her drink while the others were busy conversing. They were asking each other questions about their personal lives. When someone answered, the one who questioned would get lost thinking about his or her life. In this condition the one who answered the questions was not able to hear what he had initially intended to hear. The one who was answering would share such secretive details of his or her life as are actually suppressed in a normal state and hence cause pain to the soul. The questioner would nod his head and utter a 'yes' so that the one who was answering didn't feel that he was not being heard. The intoxication was now twirling and breaking their souls. They could feel each other's body. Sangarma lay her head on Yusuf's lap. Yusuf smelt her body thoroughly and then inquired, 'Was it your odour which was mixed with the drink?' Sangarma was surprised. 'How did you come to know?'. Yusuf mischievously poured whisky on her chest, rubbed it on her skin with his fingers and made her smell it and said, 'Your odour is

very strong. Well, I have worked in this field for many years now!'
Before Sangarma could ask something, Miss Thomas announced,
'Time for a dance in the name of the prince of darkness!'

They all stood up.

The clock turned musical as it struck midnight. Miss Thomas
began dancing. The dance was very strange. Her feet were shaking,
and her body moved in various directions. It had a lot of similarities
with the dance of African tribes. In fact, it could be that very
dance or the dance which had been preserved in the collective
unconsciousness of the human mind, which resurfaces rarely. There
was a feeling of freedom in this dance. The body seemed pleasured
by it and the soul intoxicated with freedom. A woman, the elderly
man and two other men turned animalistic during the course of the
dance. They were walking on all fours. Miss Thomas was dancing
like a *nagin*—a female snake. She had raised her hands and cupped
them on her forehead like the snake shown in movies and was
stinging everyone but herself. This dance was enriched with the
consciousness of creation.

By the end of the dance, they coiled up their bodies and fell
on top of each other. Only the elderly man seemed like a dimmed
shooting star. They were biting each other like snakes on the floor.
They were entering each other's souls. The salty water of their eyes,
the odour of their sweat, their saliva had all entered each other's
body through their noses and had made the intoxication of the drink
even fiercer. In their unconscious were awakened many creatures—
crawlers, creepers, the worms of the sand and various insects and
reptiles. They could hear the sounds of the wild and could feel the
insects crawl under their skin. In the depths of the collective historical
unconscious, the sounds, faces and powers of the early humans had
embedded itself securely. It was said that in specific conditions, the
mind of the human turned into a whirlpool and reached that depth
of collective darkness where these faces and sounds had been buried.
Miss Thomas's group, under the shadow of this eternal dance of the
'self', had submerged itself in the depths of internal darkness.

Before the night subsided, the elderly man was the first to leave. When Yusuf woke up, the sun was already up in the sky. He searched for his clothes. He could not find his underwear. When everyone had worn their clothes, one white underwear was left unclaimed. It was believed that it belonged to the elderly man who had, under the effect of alcohol, worn Yusuf's underwear and left. When the others came to know of this, they couldn't control their laughter.

The signal turned green.

The vehicles started rushing and their noise pulled Yusuf out of his thoughts. He looked into the mirror again. His shadow smiled and vanished. With the passage of time, Yusuf and Miss Thomas had come close to each other. Their mental and physical compatibility had made them meet each other quite often. His attendance also increased at the parties and get-togethers of the circle. Miss Thomas had also visited his house at Pydhonie a few times. It was quite possible that someone in Pydhonie might have seen this and reported it to some of his relatives, thereby giving birth to the rumour that Yusuf had kept a Keralite woman in his house. Miss Thomas's dressing style and her wheatish complexion might have made the onlooker think that she was a Kerala Christian. Miss Thomas had given a lot of gifts to Yusuf, of which the most expensive one was a painting by Amrita Sher-Gil. The painting had come into Miss Thomas's father's hand in 1941 when he lived in Lahore for some time. Yusuf loved that painting a lot. He had put it up in his bedroom. Miss Thomas was delighted to see the painting on the bedroom wall when she had visited him. She told him about Amrita Sher-Gil that day. She had said that Amrita Sher-Gil had relationships with many men, as well as a few women. Yusuf thought about it for a moment and asked her, 'Do you love Sangarma?'

Instead of giving an answer to the unexpected question, Miss Thomas kept looking into his eyes in that semi-lit room. Yusuf's eyes had caught one secret of Miss Thomas's body. She started drowning in Yusuf's eyes. There was a rising colour of sensuality in her melancholic eyes. At first Yusuf thought that he had angered Miss Thomas. He immediately hugged Miss Thomas and whispered in her ears, 'I'm sorry.' The seductiveness in her melancholic eyes now changed into a bonfire. She was aroused and felt that there was a dried up well in her body. She undressed and saw Yusuf drowning in that well. The well was very deep and in its depth were buried the tears of innumerable souls. On one side was a dried-up rose while on the other a dangerous dream had put a seal on a spring, which was unable to flow. Despite that, at the base of the well was an acceptance of life and the centre of voluptuousness.

After a while the frozen lust in Miss Thomas's eyes started to melt. The well of her being was now magically overflowing. In her escaping breath, she said, 'You are the first man. Many women like Sangarma have come and gone in my life.'

'You are the first man in my life.' Yusuf did not react to this. He believed that every woman said this lie with confidence. After a few years, he was very surprised to know that he had truly been the only man in Miss Thomas's life. Even during parties, it was only Sangarma who used to be her choice. Yusuf, Miss Thomas and Sangarma became a triangle. Miss Thomas revealed to Yusuf one day in a fit of emotion that when she was just thirteen years old, her mother had presented her naked body to one of her lovers while sloshed. That secret had lived in her heart like a snake. With the passage of time, the venom of that snake spread to her soul. Yusuf's eyes welled up after hearing her painful story.

To answer Miss Thomas's revelation, Yusuf narrated his own secret which lay hidden in his being. Yusuf told her that his father used to lead the prayers in a small mosque in Palanpur, a town in Gujarat. His mother was a trader's daughter and was not very religious. When he was about to be born, his father was reading a book and as soon as he got the news of his birth he shouted, *tafseer ruhul maani* (the elaborate meanings of the soul). It was merely the title of the book, but he named the child that. His mother found that name very difficult, she just did not agree to keep it. After a few months his mother persisted that she wanted to change the name, but the father did not agree. His mother started calling him Yusuf. This was the cause of regular fights between husband and wife. This remained a reason for the continuous tussle till Yusuf became four years old. Once, his mother pulled at his father's beard and shouted in anger, 'God has punished you for keeping such a difficult name.' The father got red with anger; he took a hammer and hit his mother on the head. Before fainting, his mother said, 'An asshole of a man can do nothing more than hit a woman.'

After the incident, he and his mother lived with his grandfather for a while after which his mother brought him to Mumbai. However, he forgot to tell Miss Thomas that the day they had arrived in Mumbai, there was a massive blast in the dockyards which became an unforgettable incident in the history of Mumbai. Around 1400 people were killed in that blast. It haunted most people living in west Mumbai for a very long time.

Mumbai turned out to be good for his mother.

After a few days she bribed a government clerk to get a fake birth certificate made. His mother spent her life with the utmost satisfaction in Mumbai and never took the name of that man who was Yusuf's father. When Yusuf turned fifteen, malaria was rampant in Mumbai. During the epidemic his mother passed away after two days of fever. The relatives who came from Palanpur to attend the burial also included his father. He kept asking people where 'Tafseer Ruhul Maani' was. In Mumbai, his maternal uncle's relatives and neighbours were not aware of that name. Hence, everyone remained silent. When his father asked a very old religious man where Tafseer Ruhul Maani was, he answered, 'Only Imam Sahib will be able to tell you that!'

The incident made Miss Thomas laugh, which reduced the restlessness of her soul. After some time, Miss Thomas asked Yusuf, 'Did you ever go to meet your father?'

Yusuf replied that he never wanted to meet a father for whom a name was more important than his son. He sat silently after saying this. He kept thinking. But he could not decide what he was actually thinking.

The next day in college, Hina told Vidhi that Yusuf and Miss Thomas were friends and that they had already discussed the study tour. Vidhi thought about it for a while and said that it was good for them. This friendship would prove beneficial for them both in college as well as in academia.

Two buses had been booked for the educational tour.

Their room was opposite that of Miss Thomas in Aurangabad.

Miss Thomas was known as a very principled and strict teacher who had firm control over the students. No one would dare to do anything inappropriate anywhere near her room. Vidhi and Hina kept talking till late at night. They got ready in the morning and boarded the bus. After sitting in the bus, a history teacher lectured them and provided them with the required information about the caves of Ajanta and Ellora. After her speech was over, the students started playing *antakshari*. Vidhi also participated enthusiastically. Hina reminded her of some songs. They stopped for snacks. Vidhi and Hina ate idli. The sambhar was very tasty. While they were eating, Miss Thomas came to their table. They stood up in respect. Miss Thomas kept her hand on Vidhi's shoulder and gestured them to sit down. She spoke to them for not more than a minute and moved forward. She asked the students if they faced any problem or difficulty during the bus journey. After eating, Vidhi really wanted to smoke a cigarette, but Miss Thomas was standing with the other teachers in close proximity. She told Hina of her situation. Hina said everyone would see her in the open. The bathroom was the only place where she could hide and smoke, but it was not in a condition where she could enjoy her smoke. Vidhi suppressed the growing desire.

All of them had eaten and boarded the bus. Vidhi asked Hina to come and sit on the last seat. Hina agreed. The bus started. There were fields of sugarcane, durra and millet dancing outside the windows. A hilly range at a distance added to the landscape. The colour of the hills was like dried turmeric in some places and like onion peels in other. Hina was looking at the scenery outside. Vidhi told her that she would sit next to the window and smoke. Seeing her unstoppable urge to smoke, Hina exchanged seats with her. Hina warned her that a teacher was sitting right in front of them and in case she decided to suddenly come there, she would get caught. Vidhi said that in case that happened, she would immediately throw her cigarette outside. Vidhi bent and lit her cigarette with a lighter and took a deep drag. She leaned over the bus window and released the smoke slowly. When the smoke freed itself from her lungs, a sense of satisfaction spread over her face.

She took few more drags in the same manner a couple of times and then, before throwing the cigarette out, she decided to take one last, long drag but this time her breath gave away and she started coughing, and a little smoke escaped from her mouth.

A boy was sitting with his girlfriend right opposite them. He was from the Urdu medium while the girl was Christian. They had been having an affair for a few days. The boy had seen Vidhi smoke. When Vidhi threw the cigarette butt out of the window and looked up at them, they gave her a thumbs up at her endeavour. She thanked them in gesture while biting her lip. Hina smiled. At that very moment the boy said, '*Le saans bhi ahista ki nazuk hai bahot kaam* [Breathe slowly as it is a delicate job].'

Vidhi didn't hear the comment clearly. She said that she was not able to hear it. The boy repeated the couplet slowly. Hina raised her eyes and looked at the boy. Vidhi articulated what she had gathered from the words, 'Look, when you do *kaam* [work] with your partner you have got to be relaxed, then there will be no issue with your breathing.'

The boy was astonished at the meaning that Vidhi had just given to his words, and Hina burst out in laughter. The boy did not say anything after that and continued talking to his girlfriend. The distance of a hundred kilometres had been covered.

They crossed the hill and the roadway which was under construction and continued in the direction of the caves. There were a lot of monkeys and birds in that forested area. The monkeys accompanied them. The students enjoyed the presence of the monkeys. The latter seemed very excited in the presence of strangers. Some monkeys were not even able to control their excitement. They jumped on the students and snatched away eatables from their hands. Two squirrels perched on the tamarind tree were peeping at the passing caravan of college students. Vidhi took out her camera to click photos of the squirrels, but they were alerted and immediately hopped and vanished. On the very branch sat an old snail, lazing in the warmth of the sun. Vidhi zoomed her camera and clicked a few photos of the snail. The branch on which the snail sat was hollow from inside. A snake had made itself a resident inside it. One could look into the downward ravines from the tamarind treetop. A long time ago, an Englishman and a nawab had been there on a hunting expedition. There was a place where the waterfall dropped to form a pool and from there on it flowed as a river. One could see the bones of the people of the Bheel tribe who had made this place their home for centuries.

Seeing the pretty miniature paintings and sculptures in the caves, which were based on Gautam Buddha and the Jataka tales, both teachers and students forgot everything that lay outside. The magic of the caves had sent vibrations in the spectators' hearts. The souls of the spectators had been freed from the caves of their being and were finding solace in the glamorous and dignified patrimony of humanity. Apart from the beauty and grandeur of the place, Ajanta was also an example of how to worship beauty and glamour. Vidhi kept thinking about the days when the womb of these caves was first inhabited and decorated.

She clicked pictures to her heart's content. Hina clicked her picture in front of the Buddha's statues. They reached the hotel at around 6 p.m. and rested for two hours before meeting for dinner. After dinner they were both lying on their beds when suddenly Vidhi was reminded of Mir Taqi Mir's couplet that the boy had recited in the morning and said, 'When you do *kaam* with your partner, you need to be relaxed and there will be no issue with the breathing.' Hina repeated the sentence and observed how strange the answer was. Vidhi turned and asked why she had laughed when she had said that. Hina explained to her that in that couplet, the meaning of 'kaam' was work and not 'sex' and it seemed that at that time Vidhi took it as sex. Vidhi took a long drag from her cigarette and said, 'You mean to say that there was nothing related to sex in that conversation?' Hina said, 'No, not at all.'

She also said that there was a girl in her school who was the daughter of a poet and she used to recite this and many other verses to them regularly. Hina repeated Mir's verse and translated it for her. Vidhi felt a little regretful. After a minute's silence, Vidhi said that the couple had become so quiet after hearing her sentence. Hina said that anyone would have remained quiet as it was a very random and unexpected answer. Vidhi put out her cigarette in the ashtray, drank water and asked Hina, 'When was your first time?'

Vidhi's direct question stumped Hina a bit. She turned over and stared at the ceiling fan and then looked at the ashtray. Then she looked at the guava tree branches out of the window on which the light from the tube light had diffused. Vidhi was looking at her. Without meeting her eyes, Hina said, 'What for the first time?'

Vidhi understood that Hina was just being dramatic. Hence, she decided to be even more direct, 'When was the first time that you had sex?' Hina looked at her and said, 'I'm still quite young, I have never thought about it.'

This made Vidhi burst out in laughter. She kept laughing for a while. She thought Hina had lied for the first time. She rolled over the bed and kept laughing. Hina said nothing. She kept looking at her while smiling conspicuously. After a while Vidhi said, 'So you are young and hence have not thought about this topic?'

She laughed again. Hina's words seemed very filmi to her. She felt that Hina was trying to hide something. Hina swore that she was telling the truth and then told Vidhi about the rules and regulations of her religion and culture. A lot of those things astonished Vidhi. It was a huge revelation for her that in Muslim households a woman having sex before marriage was considered the biggest sin that could ever be committed. Vidhi told her that even in their society they were advised to avoid having sex before marriage, but it was not a very big deal and was considered a form of recreation. No one could be kept away from it for long. After listening to her, Hina said that there were a lot of girls in her building who had boyfriends with whom they regularly slept but had kept this hidden from their parents. Both of them talked about how there was a societal, familial and religious difference in the way they lived their lives. Vidhi smoked five more cigarettes during the conversation. When virtually nothing was left to discuss on the topic, Hina asked her, 'When was the first time you did it?'

Vidhi drew a cigarette from the packet, offered it to Hina and said, 'So what if you cannot have sex? You can have a cigarette at least.' Hina took the cigarette and started smoking. She did not know how to release the smoke from her nostrils and was taking it in and releasing it through the mouth. Vidhi told her the story in great detail.

One of her classmates used to like her since seventh grade, but it was only in class nine that they fell in love and an affair started. At the same time she had met a guy in the tea plantation who had come there to research on tea leaves and other plants. He was a Bangladeshi, and ten years older than Vidhi. Vidhi's father had allowed him to stay at the plantation on a friend's request. He was allotted one room among the ones built for the government officials. When Vidhi saw him for the first time, she wanted to keep looking at him and nothing else. But she couldn't possibly do that. Vidhi was unable to meet his eyes. She later got to know that his name was Dariush. He was the son of a very influential politician of Dhaka. He asked Vidhi a few questions and insisted that she show him around. That made Vidhi very happy, but she had to hide her excitement from him, so she said, 'Okay, I will see.'

His mother was a Bolivian journalist, and he was born with her alluring and voluptuous features. His English was admiringly filled with metaphors and idioms. The way he carried himself showed that he was brought up in an environment of Western culture. For three days Vidhi and Dariush talked about herbs, wild plants and their various uses. Vidhi had no clue about the importance of plants that grew around her. Apart from his minute observational skills, his understanding and knowledge was another reason that made Vidhi go crazy about him. Vidhi wanted to know why the presence of Dariush released a spring in her body and she found herself inundated. That had never happened to her in the presence of the boy she loved at school, and neither had he attracted her so intensely. In Dariush's presence, she would remember no one, neither her parents nor the classmate with whom she was having an affair. It was a holiday in Vidhi's school on the fourth day. She took Dariush to the plantation; to reach it one had to cross a valley and a river. On one side of the river were dense forests. Because the route to the valley was through the plantations, very few people used that way. That day was also the weekly holiday for the labourers on the plantation; so she was confident that no one would come that way. She wore a red skirt and matched it with a corduroy coat. Dariush was busy collecting plant samples. Vidhi was looking at him continuously. It saddened her to feel that Dariush seemed to have no interest in her. He seemed

interested only in the barks, branches, leaves and roots of the trees
around. He would smell other leaves apart from tea and put them
in his bag.

It took them an hour to reach the river. The water was up to
the ankles. Beautiful, small pebbles and stones glistened through
the clear water around which were swimming very small colourful
fish. Dariush asked Vidhi if it was okay to collect the clear water
from the river in a glass and drink it. Vidhi stopped him and said
that there was a stream ten minutes away where the water was very
sweet. Dariush took her suggestion. How was he to know that it
was a trap that Vidhi had set? A narrow pathway seemed to unfold
in the jungle. Vidhi walked on that path while Dariush followed
her. They had just walked a little when Dariush's leg got caught in a
bamboo bush and he was about to fall on Vidhi, but she helped him
out of it. Dariush apologized but Vidhi utilized the opportunity to
the fullest and at that moment looked into his eyes silently. Then
she said, 'It is my fault that I got you into these bushes, where
people avoid coming because of fear.'

'Why are they scared of this place?' Dariush asked and supported
himself by putting a hand on Vidhi's shoulder. At that moment he
also noticed her breasts.

He raised his eyes to look at the sky when he saw that the
branches of the tree had intertwined themselves in a way that they
had formed a sheet covering the gaps. One could not see the sky
clearly only feel its presence there. The sheet sieved the sunlight
delicately. He looked at Vidhi again, and then she said, 'There used
to be pythons here and that fear still discourages people to visit
this place.'

'Pythons! They're very interesting,' Dariush said and looked at
Vidhi. He asked, 'Can one still see those snakes around?'

'No one has reported seeing them for many years. There is a
possibility that you might see one today.'

They moved forward. Dariush guessed that somehow Vidhi
was attracted to him. Vidhi's eyes, her cheeks, her body, her

odour were conspiring together to reveal this secret to Dariush. He thought that she had just hit puberty and hence was so desirous and willing. He had seen many newly adolescent girls being rather 'kind' to him before. So, there was no way any feeling could churn up inside his heart. They moved forward and the path became narrower. After a point, to save themselves from thorny bushes they had to bend their backs and walk. Dariush was thinking that he had needlessly got himself into this situation but as soon as the thorny bushes ended, he found himself standing in a circular area covered in greenery.

The scenic beauty of the place was stunning. It made him forget himself for a while. At one end were blue, yellow and pink flowers fluttering in the wind. After the flowers was a long chain of trees, behind which were pure green hills, at the end of which was white, milky mist. Dariush found himself lost in the hypnosis of that mist. He saw how a sheet of fog was rising in the wind. The sunrays seemed to play hide and seek. Everything was a phantasm. Seeing Dariush lost in the mesmerizing beauty of nature, Vidhi told him that earlier she used to come with women workers of the plantation quite often to see the hills. Dariush looked at her and said, 'It is the fog.'

Vidhi smiled. There was a blossoming red flower near her feet. Vidhi plucked it and while putting it in her hair said, 'Yes, it looks like a fog but these are actually hills. In fact, so many people come to Darjeeling just to witness their stunning beauty.' Dariush could not believe that the milky mist and fog he was looking at were actually the hills. He looked around to capture the entire scene. Around him were saal and oak trees and the alpine jungles stretched till the borders of Bhutan and Sikkim. Everything was so enchanting that he had forgotten that he had come here after crossing the thorny bushes in search of sweet water. Vidhi remembered that. She held him by his hand and dragged him forward. At one end of the circle was a slippery slope with a pathway. Vidhi said that they need to move very slowly and carefully there. They turned after five minutes where a spring was falling from a cliff playing its natural

music. It kept flowing till it found a mountain edge to fall down as
a waterfall. The spring was falling from a height of around six or
seven feet. The place where the water accumulated was not more
than knee-deep. Dariush and Vidhi stood a few steps away from the
water. Vidhi freed her fingers from his hands and pointed towards
the water, 'The world's sweetest water awaits you.'

'Is there any danger further ahead?' Dariush inquired.

Vidhi looked at him and said, 'The danger is behind you.'

Dariush tried smiling. Vidhi held his hand again. They started
walking in the water. A butterfly, four dragon flies and an insect
hummed around them. A caterpillar slept on a rock near the
place from where the spring originated. The tiny fibres on the
caterpillar's body shone brightly in the sunlight. On seeing Dariush
and Vidhi approaching, the butterflies, dragonflies and the insects
flew upwards and vanished into the ravine. Dariush bent and
put his lips on the flowing water to drink it. Vidhi was looking
at him. Dariush collected a little water in his mouth, looked at
Vidhi and drank it. The taste of the water was indescribable.
He pulled Vidhi towards himself pleasantly and hugged her. 'I have
never drunk such tasty water before.'

She cupped her hands and collected water in it and offered it
to Dariush. He drank the water from her hand in a single breath.
Seeing Dariush happy made her face go red. When he drank water
from Vidhi's hands, he noticed the whiteness of her palms that sent
vibrations into him, but he immediately overcame the sensation by
looking at the spring. The surface of the falling water was like a
mirror that captured its own beauty. Dariush moved two steps ahead
and stood below the falling water. He was completely drenched.
Vidhi was smiling at him. He kept enjoying the water falling on
him while standing under the spring with his eyes closed. When he
opened them, the sun was at the meridian looking at him. Its rays
were brighter now. The caterpillar was still enjoying the warmth.

Vidhi's face shone and looked reddish and bright in the
sunshine. Dariush looked at her and said that the water was cold

and if she wished she could also bathe. She said she didn't want to because she would immediately catch a cold in the chilly water. In reality she wanted to bathe and drench herself with Dariush, but she could not express her intent. Unknowingly, she tried to avoid that passion. Perhaps, that day Vidhi was not aware that when a passion is suppressed and thrown into the dungeons of the soul, some day it drips out in a more ambiguous and fiery form from the surface of the body. A desire doesn't die, it simply transforms itself. She might have refused to bathe but at that very moment her desire, which she had been hiding for so many days, started churning within her. She kept thinking why so many streams burst within her in Dariush's presence. When she had held Dariush's hand in the thorny bushes, suddenly a spring had burst within her whose water had a unique smell of its own and Vidhi was aware of it. But she did not know that the smell of the springs that burst from the soul was that of the soul itself and carried with it an intoxication and ecstasy.

For a few years, she had been enchanted by the same intoxication many a time. Dariush was engrossed in the sweetness of the spring and the surrounding nature, while Vidhi was trying to decipher her own situation. Hardly ten minutes had passed when a thick fog rose from the back of the hills. Vidhi saw it and before she could warn Dariush, the fog covered the spring and the valley around. Vidhi told Dariush in a loud voice that in this place, the clouds and fog covered the valley at any time and it started to pour. There was nothing to be scared of. Even after that Dariush's heart had started beating faster. He was reminded of the pythons. He imagined that snakes were licking him all over. Dariush took a step further and spread his hands. He felt Vidhi's body. She was silent. He moved a step further. He stood very close to her now. They could feel each other's faces, though they could not clearly see each other. Vidhi held his left hand so that he didn't slip in the water. For support, Dariush put his hand on Vidhi's shoulder. Vidhi felt the heat in her body's spring was still there despite the frost produced by the weather and the water. Her lips were warm with the heat of passion but she did not have the guts to proceed. It is said that cowardice is the death of passion. Vidhi did not want to retreat from where she had reached, so she bent her neck a little and kept her cheek on Dariush's hand on her shoulder. Dariush felt the heat of Vidhi's lips. That feeling created a blur over his eyes. The colour of the fog had turned to blue. He moved forward and took her cheeks in his hands and surrendered his lips to the burning kiln of Vidhi's body. That moment seemed to be an achievement of her life for Vidhi. She had waited so badly for this moment to arrive. That one kiss opened up all the locks of her body. Behind the spring, within her was boiling lava which started overflowing. For half an hour, both lay there wrapped in the quilt of the blue and pink fog. No words were uttered. The soul was meeting the soul and the bodies were mere eternal, divine bridges. When the fog finally disappeared, they were standing under the spring of nature and smiling.

The lava that had erupted from Vidhi's body had now cooled down in the falling water and flowed down into the depths of the valley's river. They kept enjoying themselves in the water, oblivious and undisturbed by the world outside for nearly two hours. The insects, butterflies and dragonflies returned on smelling the lava. While sitting on the green grass and the rocks of the waterfall, Vidhi and Dariush, like Adam and Eve, seemed busy looking for signs of paradise in each other. All this while, the caterpillar pulled out its head from under the rock and moved towards the spring. It was also a witness to the intermingling of two bodies and souls.

Vidhi's story had astonished and surprised Hina, as well as made her happy.

Vidhi had smoked a lot of cigarettes while narrating the story and Hina had assisted her too by smoking two of them. Hina could see a film of Vidhi's account unreeling before her eyes. Many a time, she imagined herself in Vidhi's place. She realized that there was a spring within her too, a spring that had a well behind it, a well that did not contain water but boiling lava. She was still thinking about herself when she was reminded of the prediction that Wardatul Sa'adat had made. A wave of reflection and sorrow spread over her face. 'Does my story make you jealous?' Vidhi asked.

'Yes,' Hina replied.

They laughed for long at Hina's 'yes'.

When they were done laughing, Hina told Vidhi about what all Wardatul Sa'adat had said. Vidhi claimed that to be absolute rubbish and advised Hina to never believe in such superstitions. Vidhi told Hina that Dariush left after a few days, and they had not been in contact since. She said that she had also had sex with her lover from school, her music teacher and an artist friend of her father's. Hina did not feel very comfortable about that revelation. She remarked, 'This is mere lust.'

'Everything is lust, even love is a form of lust but nobody confesses it.' Vidhi paused and then continued, 'In fact, lust is desire. And it is unnatural to suppress a desire. The results of unnatural actions are unexpected.' Vidhi spoke while taking pauses. Hina was reminded of all that Yusuf had said in the museum the other day. She told Vidhi, 'But I will have sex with only one man throughout my life.' This declaration came as a joke to Vidhi. She laughed at it for a long time and then said, 'This business of one man for one woman is very cinematic. It does not happen in real life. Those who are ill might be an exception.' Hina did not react to what Vidhi had just said. She got up, brushed her teeth and then went back to bed.

They visited various historical sites in Aurangabad a day later. Miss Thomas kept meeting and inquiring after them at short intervals. The Daulatabad Fort, the road that led to the fort, the walls, the engravings on the gates were very exciting for Miss Thomas. She narrated stories about Feroz Shah Tughlaq and the fort to the students walking along with her. They returned on the third day. It was an educational and recreational trip worth remembering for Hina. The primary reason for this was her conversations with Vidhi on life, sex and sexuality. Their conversation brought about many changes within her. Along with that, her subconscious had earlier absorbed everything that Wardatul Sa'adat had said. It was not easy for her to let go of the prediction.

These thoughts had resurfaced when she sat in the taxi after her second meeting with Asrar. A wave with its origins in the greatest depths had risen in her soul. There were some fissures in her soul which she had hidden for ages and which reappeared. A few moments before she had experienced the peace of falling in love with a stranger. The feeling had taken over her mind, heart and soul. She had wondered what kind of love it was which had acquired the face of sorrow and grief. She could not fathom it!

Her throat choked, and the pain became uncontrollable as she cried into the handkerchief. The conversation with herself was intensifying her sorrow. In her entire life, she had never wept like that before.

7

My Conversation Desires Distance
(*Mein Baat Karne Mein Thoda Sa Fasla Chahun*)

Around eight or quarter past eight that night, Asrar bid Hina goodbye in a taxi near the Haji Ali Dargah signal. The taxi moved forward and in a very short while, Hina's eyes brimmed with tears. All efforts to control them went in vain. Ultimately, she started crying her heart out. Initially, there was no thought in her mind.

Suddenly, it was as if innumerable termites had attacked her soul.

The distance to her house was not more than fifteen minutes, but within that time all the distinct and old moments of her life started rushing to her mind. There were some memories of childhood which could not be forgotten as they had been captured by Yusuf in photographs. There were six albums that she used to browse through occasionally. Her school days were still fresh in her mind. The occasion of her sisters' weddings appeared and vanished. Yusuf and Darakhshan danced in white and wheatish shades in one dark corner of her heart. Darakhshan seemed to have turned into a dead body while numerous colours shadowed Yusuf's face. Yusuf's face was in front of her eyes for a longer time.

Yusuf had a smile on his lips, but he was unaware that Darakhshan was not alive any more. She kept looking at both her parents and realized that her mother's death had not created any ripples or chaos in her heart. Neither was she grief-stricken nor had sorrow touched her. In a nutshell, the changing of Darakhshan's existence into non-existence was not a painful event for her. In fact, it was the bright colours around Yusuf's face and the smile on his lips that carried a lot of meaning and attraction for her. She compared the two of them for a long time. From the termite-ridden gloomy chamber of her heart rose a thought that slipped through her mouth, 'Life is so much more attractive than death.'

She repeated this over and over again.

That line carried with it some kind of unusual strength. She felt that strength in her nerves and power in her heart. A zeal to make her life more meaningful took shape within her. For the past few years, the sorrow of Darakhshan had been making her ill. In retrospect, she asked herself why she had started crying the moment she sat in the taxi. Why did tears flow down her eyes so bitterly? Which spot was so evident and old on the pages of her heart that was eating away her soul like a pest? She also tried asking herself why she was questioning herself so much. Since when had she been doing it? Did she have answers to these questions? She was engrossed in those thoughts. After some time she thought, 'It is better to enjoy the "self" than to suppress or kill it.' On the other hand, she had seen a new meaning in the rejuvenation of Yusuf's life and the free-flowing life of Vidhi.

While getting off the taxi, she tried to figure out if there had been any change in her desires, life and aspirations that year. Had she softly walked through the phases of metamorphosis? Had she been able to cut herself off from the past and move towards the future? Was she successfully freeing herself from the anguish of the past to create a new, meaningful and happy life? Such questions kept crossing her mind. When she got off at Maulana Azad Road, her heart was cold, and her face was heavy. She slowly moved towards her house. Old clothes, boiled eggs, items of daily use were being sold on the footpath. She enjoyed the crowded streets and the hustle-bustle of Maulana Azad Road. The area was very congested. The noise pollution added to the beauty of the place. The great authors of the Urdu language, Saadat Hasan Manto, Krishan Chander, Ismat Chugtai and Rajendra Singh Bedi, had already witnessed and experienced the chaos, confusion, tumult and uproar of this place. Manto's house was quite nearby.

There were innumerable people in that area. There were women clad in burqas and also slackers who were waiting for one glance of the covered voluptuous features of the burqa-clad women. They were either standing or roaming about in different directions. When her eyes caught a glance of the human figure in the red light of the signal, she was reminded of Asrar. She was surprised. The reason which had forced her into the marsh of introspection and self was not Yusuf, Darakhshan or Vidhi, but it was her meeting with Asrar. The time of the meeting, the context and condition, the day, the moment, the feeling, the scenery were exactly how Wardatul Sa'adat had foretold. She had never imagined that Wardatul Sa'adat's prediction would ever come true. Now that she had met Asrar in the same condition as described in the prediction, a very painful possibility presented itself to her. She did not want Wardatul Sa'adat to be proved right. But was it possible?

While sitting in the taxi, this thought had not reached the depths of her heart as her mind, heart and soul were still at peace because of the feeling of love. This thought converted the feeling of love into melancholy. The depression caused by this numbed her mind. That was why she kept a handkerchief over her mouth and let the restlessness of her heart convert itself to tears. Her tears collected behind the rims of her eyes but were not falling. As a result, her neck hurt, and her throat had swollen up. In that moment she started reminiscing about some old things which otherwise made a person sad. It is believed that when the soul is saddened a sort of darkness covers the self. In such a situation monologue with one's own self creates a chaos in the melancholy of the soul. Hina's monologue made her want to cry even more. When the dam of courage was broken by the flood of melancholy, she succumbed herself to weeping bitterly.

Her house was near Maulana Azad Road, but she knew her mother would become suspicious if she went home in that condition. Hence, she kept roaming about randomly for a while. She bought an ice cream to moisten her throat and started walking home.

She warmed up her food on reaching home and ate it on the sofa. When Darakhshan asked her about her visit to Haji Ali, she gave appropriate answers. She had been visiting the dargah every Saturday for the last month on her mother's bidding. The reason was that the day she had told Wardatul Sa'adat's predictions to Vidhi and had decided to share them with her mother as well. After her return from the educational trip, Hina told her mother who was chopping vegetables in the hall that evening, 'I want to talk to you about something important.'

Her tone was unsettling for her mother. Hina had never addressed her like that before. She had decided that she would tell the entire story to her mother using a fake name of the person involved. But, when she started off, she made it out to be a dream. She said, 'Maa, I saw a dream three days back. It has really scared me. I was lying on a rock near Haji Ali when a strange woman came up to me. I was sleeping while she kept staring at me. She held my hand and started reading my palm without even waking me up. She closed her eyes after seeing the lines on my palm and exclaimed, "The time when day will no longer be day and night could no longer be called night, a boy will appear out of the blue in front of you and will try to speak with you."' Darakhshan had a knife in her hand. She kept it aside and started listening to Hina's dream seriously. Hina realized that Darakhshan was all ears. Hina said that when that strange woman was talking to her, she was asleep but it was as if she was dreaming the same thing. So, it was not just the dream but the dream within that dream which scared her as well. Darakhshan did not really understand this dream-within-dream story, but she asked, 'What happened next?'

'I remember that the strange woman had said that there is fear ahead. The skies, waters and winds will not like what will happen in that moment.' She repeated what Wardatul Sa'adat had said with more comprehensible expressions for her mother— 'That moment when you taste each other's soul it will become intolerable for the winds, the waters and the skies.' Darakhshan kept gaping at her daughter. One could sense how worried she was from her expression. Hina told her mother that she laughed a lot when the lines were said. She woke up from her dream because of her laughter and she realized that she was sleeping on a rock near Haji Ali. Hina's laugh had offended that strange woman and she cried out, 'There is darkness, darkness all around. You will vanish into this darkness.' No sooner had the woman vanished after saying that than there was darkness all around. She had never seen such deep darkness before. She wanted to run towards Haji Ali but she could not see anything at all, although she had seen lightning in that darkness. She has constructed this part of the story keeping in mind what Wardatul Sa'adat had said, 'I cannot see anything. There is darkness all around. There is lightning and rainfall.' Darakhshan was listening intensely. Hina told her that since she had first seen the dream it kept coming back to her mind again and again. A fear had established itself in her heart. Darakhshan picked up her knife and started chopping the ladies' fingers and said, 'I will talk about this dream with Peer Sahib on Monday.'

One week later when Darakhshan returned after visiting Peer Sahib, she seemed quite happy. She told Hina that he had interpreted the dream to be a signal of the spiritual powers of the Baba. Hina asked, 'What kind of signal?'

Darakhshan told her that it was a signal of an impending calamity, so she should visit the shrine of Haji Ali at least once a week at the time of lobaan which would create a circle of safety around her and would keep her away from any mishap. She wanted to laugh at her mother's simplicity but realized that she might hurt her emotions. So, she decided to obey what her mother had instructed. She really liked the advice. This would give her an excuse to take a stroll every week by the sea. She immediately agreed and said that since her college was off on Saturdays, she would visit the dargah on Saturday evenings. Darakhshan looked at her daughter adoringly and blessed her.

When Asrar and Hina encountered each other for the first time at Haji Ali, it was 22 September, the day of the fall equinox. In ancient times and according to Egyptian cultural history, the fall equinox was considered to be a celestial moment. Day and night were divided equally. The moments before the night fell were believed to be that of death and darkness. One more interpretation was that it signalled the belief that 'everything has to die before taking birth. Everything had to pass through darkness to reach light.' Hina had no clue about all this. She did not know how that day was named in the calendar nor did she have the wisdom of various interpretations and associations of that day. For her it was just another day when she had gone to the dargah with the intention of enjoying herself. Monsoon was her favourite season, and she was standing in the veranda of the dargah enjoying the raindrops soaking her.

There was still time left for daylight to succumb into the womb of darkness and for darkness to metamorphose into death. It was raining cats and dogs. The intensity of the rain had a strong impact on Hina's heart. The cold gusts of wind were making her shiver. At that moment she was free of all thoughts that generally surrounded her. She was interacting with her own self. There was no Darakhshan, Yusuf, her sisters, Aymal or her daughter in her thoughts at that time. She was engrossed in the blurring landscape of her surroundings, which captivated her. And when Asrar had seen her exactly in that situation, he had thought that this girl was disconnected with the world around and was simply absorbed in her own self. Hina's strangeness and self-forsaking had left Asrar in astonishment. He was perplexed and anxious to know if the girl had a sense of consciousness and reality. Hina had created a mixture of curiosity and inquisitiveness in his mind which had given him the strength, the strength which he used as a crutch to go and stand in front of her. The moment Asrar came and stood in front of Hina, the sun drowned itself. The day slipped into night. That time was the moment of conflict between Seth and Horus.

It was true that when Asrar had stood in front of Hina, there was a wave of fear running through his heart. To save her from getting drenched in the rain, he opened the umbrella over Hina's head. No sooner had he opened the umbrella than the tilism, which had held Hina captive, was shattered.

Hina's eyes met Asrar's. The colour of his eyes captivated her completely. Asrar's eyes resembled that of his great-grandfather. His great-grandfather was a doctor in Dasht-e-Tarmizi in southern Khorasan. He was a well known and respected figure in the Zoroastrian community of Tarmizi. He converted to Islam to save his life but grieved his misfortune till death. There was a tinge of green in Asrar's eyes, which he got as a genetic gift from Tarmizi. But it could be stated that these types of eyes could be found in at least 4–5 families of Mabadmorpho. They were descendants of those Iranian and Sistani Zoroastrians who had migrated to Sindh and later moved to the Konkan a century or two ago. The attraction and absorbing power that Asrar's eyes had was also contained in Hina's eyes. Both had eyes that made them desirable.

On the other hand, Hina was astonished at the confidence with which Asrar had opened the umbrella for her. Hina's silence made Asrar think that either she was angry or annoyed at what Asrar had just done. Hina took his silence to be a sign of his courage. She stood there staring into his eyes. The rain and the wind around them had become one with their silence. Detached from time, Hina and Asrar stood astounded.

Hina's hair was already wet. A drop of water sparkled at the end of a strand of her hair. A few water drops were still on her forehead. The green kohl on the edges of her eyes had smudged, leaving just an unclear green line on the right eyelid. Her scarlet lipstick was washed off by the rain, and still her lips were red. She had thin lips. She did not have very big eyes, but they contained a magical fire within them. Asrar could feel the flames of this fire. He was sure within a moment that Hina's personality had a different kind of power. An attraction. Hina's prolonged silence had made him conclude that he should apologize to her. He also thought that while apologizing, he could probably inquire why she was getting drenched in the rain. Those thoughts were doing the rounds in his mind when a strong gust of wind came and flipped his umbrella. He bent over the umbrella and started fixing it. Hina found that sight hilarious. He was able to hear her laughter despite the intense rainfall. He turned and looked at her. He got up looking at her laughing face and politely said, 'I'm really sorry. I just wanted to help you.'

Hina was hiding her feelings and at the same time was trying not to make this beautiful-eyed boy think that she was arrogant. To lighten the situation a little, she said, 'I thought some djinn had brought an umbrella for me.'

That kick-started a pleasant conversation between the two. The rain stopped. They came out of the dargah conversing and started moving towards the path that parted the sea.

The short encounter had made both realize the attraction they felt towards each other. Each of them wanted to look at the other's face for long. But there was a distinct energy in both their eyes that came in the way of fulfilling this desire. Both understood that the strength in the eyes of the other could not be countered or else the warmth of the soul would be dimmed. The soul's strength was its ego. If that strength faded, then the soul and the physical body would surrender themselves and the soul would break free and search for shelter in the arms of the one who was now its master. A few days back, Vidhi had given Hina a book in which she had read, 'The soul decides the password of the body. Before a body peeps into the other it matches passwords through eye contact.'

On looking into Asrar's eyes, Hina was assured that the password of her soul matched Asrar's code and that was exactly why when Hina sat in the taxi, Asrar had said, 'I will come next Saturday.' And Hina had confidently replied, 'I know.'

During the second meeting, Hina had asked Asrar questions about his private life and he had answered them with a lot of simplicity. He had elaborated on his attempts to continue his education in spite of his father's unexpected death, his mother's struggles and the unfavourable circumstances they had gone through.

Asrar's Urdu accent was dipped in Konkani. Hina's had a Gujarati touch. But this incongruity in the language was not a barrier. The roughness of their language showed that there was no pretence or unnecessary formality in whatever they were saying. Asrar told Hina that that year he wanted to take admission in the eleventh grade through distance learning but because he was new in the city and had no idea about the university system and also had to manage his work, the last date to fill the admission form had passed. Hina said that when the forms would come out at the beginning of the new academic year, she would inform him beforehand.

Asrar had told her stories about his village near the sea as well as the people there, very emotionally. A picture of his village had come alive in front of Hina's eyes. Hina realized that Asrar's English was quite weak. She then thought that when Asrar would take admission in the eleventh grade and start studying, his vocabulary would become better automatically. The conversations around family, private life and work brought with them a sense of familiarity between the two. Both knew that this new friendship was not just a coincidence but within it was hidden an indication of their soul's delight. When they had seen each other for the first time, they had come to know that they were like the other's shadow. The passion of proximity had immediately risen in their hearts. The sentiment of friendship and oneness had made their souls reach that point of bliss where they were ready to surrender themselves completely. They were of the same complexion. Their noses were pointed and foreheads were broad.

While they strolled towards Worli amid the regular chaos, the way Hina spoke made Asrar believe that she was interested in him. To estimate the passion in Hina's heart, Asrar told her that on the following Saturday, after visiting the dargah, she should go to the shopping mall where Asrar's shop was. She tried making excuses on the face of it but from the inside she no longer had any reason or any hesitation to meet Asrar. When after much persuasion she finally agreed, she was reminded of what Vidhi had told her: 'If love takes birth, it cannot be erased and if it is absent, and if it doesn't exist, then all attempts to initiate it will be in vain. Ishq does not examine loyalty, nor does it expect faithfulness. The zeal of love is accredited with the feeling of surrender and selflessness.' After rewinding what Vidhi had said, a thought came to her mind: 'Has she fallen in love with Asrar?' She laughed at the very thought of this possibility.

She kept asking this question to herself, repeatedly, for the next 4–5 days.

She skipped college.

Her heart, for the first time, was filled up with loneliness and was asking her innumerable questions. At the same time, she kept remembering Asrar's courage when he came and opened an umbrella over her. She remembered the rain at the Worli sea face during their second meeting when Asrar had bought tea and handed it to her with shivering hands. When it was time to bid farewell and she sat in the taxi, she had looked at Asrar with a glance of desire. She had seen a friendliness on Asrar's face. That feeling seemed to contain warmth. That warmth caused Hina's heart to melt. Such small instances would light up her heart and play in front of her eyes like a movie clip. These reminiscences illuminated her brain which in turn sent shivers down her spine. That feeling of happiness was proving to be a labyrinth in which Hina's heart seemed to have lost itself. Her soul was restless. Its horizon seemed to have misplaced its ends.

Amid all this Wardatul Sa'adat's prophecies poured grief and fear by overshadowing her existence. She had never imagined that Wardatul Sa'adat's predictions would cast a horrific shadow over her life. The sudden appearance of Asrar proved Wardatul Sa'adat's was correct. Hina was coaxing her heart into believing that all of this was just a coincidence. This was her best defence mechanism to escape the fear that haunted her, and then she would again travel into that part of her memory where Asrar was talking to her seriously and she was happily replying to all the questions he asked. On seeing her so lost, Darakhshan tried inquiring if there was anything wrong with her.

Hina would always find an excuse in front of her mother. For instance, she'd say she was bored, her head ached or her mood was not fine. Every time she went to the bathroom, she forgot to come out. This happened six times in a row. When Darakhshan knocked at the door, twice she said she had fallen asleep, just to hide what was going on within her. Darakhshan laughed at her answer. Once, during lunch, she poured the curry in her plate but ate a roll of chapati without dipping it in the curry. When Darakhshan pointed this out to her, she replied, 'Sometimes eating dry chapati is an attempt to imitate the Prophet.' One day she was sitting in front of the television and was so lost that she did not realize that the movie was over and a teleshopping advertisement had been running for more than half an hour. Darakhshan was sitting right next to her. She found it astonishing. She finally asked, 'What are you watching?' Hina replied, 'The film.'

Darakhshan was irritated because the teleshopping advertisement was selling an Ayurvedic product that enhanced the 'lost strength' of men and women. She got up and switched the TV off. The third day, they got ready to go to the market. Hina was to lock the door, which she did. Upon returning, when Darakhshan took the key from her to open the door, she was left dumbfounded. Hina had put the lock but not on the latch—the door was not really locked. This infuriated Darakhshan. 'Look how you have locked the door!' she said admonishingly. Hina looked and realized her foolishness. A faint smile played on her lips. She apologized. After that she immediately backed her apology with, 'Whatever, Mother. Even if it was in the wrong way, I did lock the door.' Darakhshan looked at her and said, 'Where is your mind these days? You're not doing anything properly!' Hina said nothing. She went to her room and stood in front of her mirror. 'Where is your mind these days? You are doing nothing properly,' she repeatedly asked her reflection in the mirror.

The reflection replied, 'Your mind is only focused on yourself.'

She smiled and kissed her image and moved away from the mirror to see the sign of the kiss vanishing. The vanishing mark instigated her to kiss even more. She put her lips to work and kissed her mirror image for a very long time.

She went to college on Friday. Vidhi had a lot of complaints about Hina which she wished to tell her friend. But before she could open her mouth, Hina interrupted her, 'Wait, first listen to what I have to say.' Hina suggested that they go and sit somewhere after the first two lectures. A lot of things needed to be talked about. Vidhi gave her a sharp look. This made Hina smile. She said, 'I know, I know you are really angry at me for not calling you up. It is because what I have to tell you could not have been told over the phone . . .' She had not completed her sentence when the bell rang for the class. They proceeded to the class. Vidhi was still angry, and it showed on her face. But one thought gave her a weird feeling. So, what if Hina did not call her, why didn't she call Hina up? She kept thinking that if Hina's absence angered her so much, then why did she not make an effort to reach out? She kept pondering this for quite some time.

The English lecturer, while teaching, was wondering what was wrong with Vidhi. Usually, during the literature class, Vidhi made remarks or asked enthusiastic questions. But today when he was discussing Emily Dickinson's poetry, she seemed to be lost somewhere. What thought had taken away the focus of her mind? His patience broke a few minutes before the end of the lecture and he said, 'Vidhi, what made you not ask any questions today? What happened?'

Vidhi suddenly tumbled out of her thoughts. She fumbled, 'Sorry, sir, I love Charles Dickens very much.'

After seeing her classmates break into laughter, she looked at the blackboard and on it was written 'Emily Dickinson'. She scratched her nose and lifted her neck to look at her teacher and then uttered, 'I meant . . . Sir . . . Emily . . .' The teacher was aware of Vidhi's capabilities. He smiled. She smiled back. Hina smiled at this exchange of smiles. They left the college premises after attending one more lecture. Hina pulled Vidhi's leg mischievously over the answer Vidhi had just given in the class and asked her,

'What thoughts were you lost in?' Vidhi asked her to be patient. She said she'd give details when they found a place to sit comfortably. They reached Churchgate station. There was less crowd than usual in a restaurant opposite the station, so Vidhi suggested that they sit inside.

Hina drank cold water and then ordered samosa and masala dosa. Vidhi looked at her silently.

'What happened?' Hina asked.

Vidhi took a deep breath and asked, 'Come on, tell me quickly. Where did you vanish for the past few days?'

Hina smiled, but this smile was very different.

Hina had just started to speak when she was abruptly stopped. She looked into Vidhi's eyes. They reflected the dark-green light which hung on the opposite wall of the restaurant.

Vidhi looked at Hina's face on which the colour of a faint, shy blush had fixed itself. Vidhi raised her finger towards Hina and gestured, 'I think you're in love.'

Hina pursed her lips and looked at Vidhi like a small child confessing her mischief. Her eyes moistened, as a sign of the honest expression of passion. Vidhi smiled and said, 'That's okay. Is there something serious?'

Hina said, 'How's that possible. I've just met him. But I'm afraid.'

Before she spoke further, the waiter came and served them masala dosa and samosa. Vidhi ordered tea. While eating the samosa, Hina described to Vidhi her first meeting with Asrar. She told her about how that meeting had made her feel. She also talked about their second meeting. After giving all the details to Vidhi, Hina reminded her about Wardatul Sa'adat's predictions that she had earlier narrated in Aurangabad. Vidhi remembered that conversation. Hina told her that Asrar had turned up in exactly the same unexpected way as was predicted. Vidhi thought over this for a minute, and said, 'It's just a coincidence, anybody could have come towards you to talk. Nothing much to be worried about.'

Hina said that it was even more astonishing because her mother had allowed her to visit Haji Ali to prevent any bad omen or time that awaited her. Her mother believed that the evil would be destroyed. Vidhi took a spoonful of sambhar, drank it and said, 'People always invent justifications for all kinds of superstitions. One should not pay much attention to it.' Hina also tasted the sambhar. Vidhi remarked that both the sambhar and chutney were delicious. After that, many thoughts surfaced in her mind, and she gave a nice, long lecture to Hina against superstition. Vidhi concluded by saying that one should make his/her life as delicious as the sambhar they just had. Superstitious and conservative ideas should not be taken to heart. This open-mindedness of Vidhi loosened the knot in Hina's heart which had held her captive for so long. When they were leaving the restaurant after having tea, theirs faces were pleasant and chirpy. Vidhi lit a cigarette and put her arm around Hina's shoulder. While walking she told Hina that she had been angry with her earlier but when she went to the class, a thought struck her that she too had not called Hina to inquire about her well-being, even though she had her phone number. Hina said that it was better that she had not called. Those days she was just not in the mood to talk to anyone.

Vidhi stopped to look at her. She grinned and said, 'This is the magic of love! Earth starts to feel like paradise.' Both burst out laughing at this overly dramatic and filmi line that Vidhi had just delivered. They had enough free time at hand. They reached Azad Maidan on foot. Some young lads were playing cricket at one end. On the other side, there were a few tired-looking, distressed men in very bad shape sitting under a tree. There were banners around them. Vidhi asked Hina about them. Hina told Vidhi that people from all over the state gathered here for protests or to put forward their demands to the government. Vidhi looked at them from afar and said, 'The poor are born to go on strikes.'

'What else can they do?' Hina asked.

Vidhi was in a mischievous mood. She said, 'Instead of protesting for bread, they should demand cakes.'

They started giggling. They were still giggling when a young girl in a sorry state extended her hands before them. Vidhi looked at her and asked, 'What do you want?'

The girl gestured towards a stall across the road where a man was selling vada pav. 'Please buy me that. I'm very hungry.'

Vidhi said, 'Fine. I will give you fifty rupees, but you have to do something for me.' The girl looked around and then said, 'If you want drugs and all then don't talk to me.'

This unexpected answer astonished both Hina and Vidhi. The girl stood there, peering into their eyes. She thought that her guess was right. These girls wanted to lure her into buying hash and opium from the dealers. One of her companions had been behind bars for the same crime for the past few months. Since then the police had started using petty excuses and reasons to put beggars behind bars so as to save the real drug dealers. And the beggars had detached themselves from these dangerous networks and doing such errands for their safety. Vidhi placed her arm around the girl's shoulder and said, 'We study in college. We don't do drugs.'

The girl snapped, 'I've supplied a lot of material to college-going girls. I know better.'

'You might have done it, but we don't want any drugs,' Hina said.

There was a shady gulmohar tree nearby. Vidhi asked the girl to sit and talk under the tree. All three of them sat in the shade. Vidhi told the girl that they had simply wanted to hear the story of her life and in return of an honest story, they would give her Rs 50. The girl agreed immediately.

The girl was around fourteen years old. Her complexion and accent indicated that she might be a south Indian. The girl looked cunning . She started narrating her story. During her entire narration, she did not sound very emotional, nor did she seem to have fallen prey to self-pity. She was talking about the harsh realities of her life. If her story was described in the words of Hina and Vidhi, then it was a story of pain and exploitation. Her story numbed Hina and Vidhi. Their faces were no longer able to carry the burden of expressions. The girl was not looking at them. In fact, she sat there looking at the grass in the field while narrating the lament of her life. The girl said that Hina and Vidhi were not much older than her and that was why she was sharing her story with them, but they should promise not to repeat it to anyone ever. They agreed.

Then she fixed her eyes on the grass and revealed another incident to Hina and Vidhi which made them drift into absolute silence. They were not ready to accept what the girl had just told them. She told them that her father, who was an opium addict, had been raping her for the past four years. Her mother also lived with them, but another man was doing exactly the same thing to her mother that her father had done to her. The girl's lament caused intense pain to Hina and Vidhi. Before they could even digest what she had said, the girl remarked, 'At first it used to hurt, now it does not.' Hina stood up. She had reached the limit of her ability to listen. Vidhi looked at her and said, 'Don't get emotional. It is her life.'

'It's a crime!' Hina was unable to hide her feelings. The girl sat staring at them.

Vidhi put her arms around Hina and explained to her how immorality could make humans stoop very low and to acquire an understanding of them, one had to be aware of the realities. Hina sat down. She stayed mute for a minute or two. The girl continued, 'The first time my father penetrated me, he had made me consume opium. I did not understand anything at that point. In fact, I was feeling as if my beloved was making love to me.' The girl told them that a Muslim beggar loved her. His name was Sultan, but people called him Tipu. Tipu had promised her that he would take her to Karnataka and marry her. The girl blushed and said that she also loved Tipu but had not told him anything about what her father did to her. The girl finally said, 'Till the time Tipu does not take me away from here, my father will keep doing this to me.'

Hina and Vidhi looked at each other. There was no expression on the girl's face. She was quiet while there was anger brimming in Hina's eyes. It seemed as if Vidhi did not possess a tongue at this point.

Vidhi took out a Rs 100 note from her purse and gave it to the girl. She thanked them and left after being reassured that her secret would not be revealed to anyone. Both of them saw the girl crossing the road that ran parallel to Azad Maidan. She vanished from their sight. Hina said to Vidhi, 'We should have done something, instead of acting like the media by just hearing her story and doing nothing to save her.' Vidhi patiently heard Hina's emotional outburst and then added that there were, not thousands, but lakhs of girls in the city who went through this. 'What can we do even if we want to?' She paused for a minute and added, 'There is a sex market in your area. There are many girls like her over there. Who even cares about them?'

They were still talking when a bhel vendor approached them. The teeth of the north Indian bhel seller were red from the habit of chewing paan. He looked at Vidhi and said, 'Madam, I'm making fresh bhel. Don't refuse.' Hina and Vidhi could do nothing but look at him. He was fast at his skill. He prepared the bhel and handed it to them. 'Ten rupees only.'

They bought the bhel and paid the vendor. He stuffed the note inside his pocket, and asked, 'What was that girl saying?'

'Nothing much. We were just having a random conversation,' Vidhi said.

'These people are very dangerous.'

'And what makes them dangerous?' Hina asked the vendor.

'Madam, I swear by Ram . . . I've been in this vending business for many years. I know everything. They're thieves and rogues.'

Hina interjected and asked, 'Do you know her father?'

This straightforward question put him on alert. He raised his eyebrows and said, 'Oh! That bastard.' He laughed and continued, 'He's an addict of the highest order.'

'What do you mean?' Hina asked. The vendor told them that the girl's father was an avid opium user and her mother was a beggar at the VT station. On some nights she slept at the station itself. He rambled something more and then went off. After he was gone, Hina and Vidhi looked at each other. In front of them was a counter-picture of the Mumbai they had always known. They wondered if the beggar girl had fooled them. Were they cheated through the creation of an emotional story? Both were in a state of shock. A faint smile broke the chain of silence and they burst into laughter. This situation had made Hina go through a weird experience. She wondered if the young girl had made up such a terrible lie just for a few rupees. They came out of Azad Maidan from the southern exit and walked to Minerva Cinema. They conversed on various issues during the walk. Vidhi asked a few questions about Asrar. Hina answered. In spite of speaking of other things, the beggar girl kept coming back to Hina's mind. The girl had lost her childhood and had now turned into a callous adult. She had used a shrewd method to beg for alms. Hina was angry at the girl. They turned towards the Marine Drive station after crossing Minerva. They stood at the ticket counter and chatted away for a while. When Vidhi was about to proceed towards the platform, Hina said, 'The girl's joke was ugly.'

Vidhi turned and replied, 'No . . . I don't think so.'

'What do you mean?'

'The girl was not joking.'

Hina stared at her and Vidhi peeped into her beautiful eyes.

'The girl seemed honest. In fact, I feel that it was the bhel vendor who was lying. He could probably be the same man with whom her mother was having an affair.'

After completing what she had to say, Vidhi sensed grief on Hina's face. She said, 'Yaar, this is very common in India. Don't burn your heart on this. Go home and take rest. You have to meet your hero tomorrow.'

On hearing Asrar being called a hero, Hina smiled. Vidhi smiled back.

Hina descended the railway overbridge to go to the bus stop when the Ganpati idols kept in a shop in the building next to the pavement attracted her attention. She stopped to look at them. She found the idol of Ganpati standing on an elephant's trunk very beautiful. She liked Ganpati's bright and big eyes. Right then a thought passed her mind—she had never seen a Ganpati *visarjan* (immersion) yet. The scenes that she had seen on the television were astounding. She decided that this time she would see it in person. She stared at the idols for a few minutes. She saw small mice around various idols. The laddus kept in front of the mice had also been crafted skilfully. The sight of the laddus made her hungry. She looked at her watch. It was 2 p.m. Instead of going to the bus stand, she hailed a taxi, got in and took out her history book and read a concise chapter on the cultural history of Babylon. She completed the chapter in about 15–20 minutes. Before she could ruminate over it, the taxi turned into the street where her house was.

The staircase of her building was as usual dark. She paused for a minute near the stairs. When her eyes accustomed themselves to the darkness, she started climbing the stairs. She was surprised to see Peer Sahib coming down. He was the holy man whom her mother followed. As she passed Peer Sahib, the perfume from his clothes caught her nose. When she reached home, her mother was busy working in the kitchen. Hina spread herself on the sofa. She felt the smell of Peer Sahib's perfume on the sofa as well. She remained lost in thoughts for a very long time. Those thoughts were terrible and frightened her. She was reminded of the beggar girl she had met at Azad Maidan. Tiredness made her finally fall asleep.

Her sleep was dreamless for some time. Her brain was relaxed, and an unending darkness spread over her mind. It is believed that the intoxication of sleep is embedded in the darkness which softly absorbs all the burdens of the soul into itself. When the soul is accredited with this pleasure then the subconscious turns over. This was exactly what happened. When her subconscious woke up, she saw a weird dream. There was a temple in the middle of a burning desert. The wind around the temple was such that it could have burnt human skin, but the premises of the temple were so cool that it seemed that the temple was situated in a Himalayan valley. In the northern part of the temple, there was a stage where Peer Sahib sat on an elephant's trunk!

His face was the same as that of the Peer Sahib, whose disciple was Hina's mother and who was the secret keeper of all her pain and came up with novel methods to help her get out of it. Peer Baba gave sermons and read out teachings for devotees who visited the Shah Baba's tomb. The magic, prayers, consolations and new techniques of spiritual indulgence by this Peer Baba had played a very important role in giving Darakhshan new strength and confidence after separating from Yusuf. Even after various attempts made by her Yusuf did not return, but during that time Darakhshan was able to stand upright. Peer Baba had made her believe that he would definitely find a counter to the magic that had been done on Yusuf. Darakhshan had now become dependent on Peer Sahib, whom she trusted a lot. She involved him in all decision-making: big or small. Sometimes, he even visited their house. He used to say that the ceremonies and rituals performed in a house lead to prosperity and lessened the effect of the magic that had been done. He had come once in Hina's presence and had recited one verse of the Quran while sitting in one corner of the house. Hina had seen him by peeping through the bedroom door.

The Peer Baba, who sat on the elephant's trunk, had a voluminous book in one hand. The book was bent towards the east and from its pages dripped blood. But Peer Sahib seemed to be oblivious of that fact. His eyes were turned towards the sky. It looked as if there was someone in the sky with whom he was having a conversation. There were innumerable white mice on the stage which strangely had no tails! They were looking for those laddus which would help them get back their tails but there was no sign of the laddus anywhere. It seemed as if they had been on the stage for many years now and their hunger made them devour each other. The moment any of them ate the other, four mice would get added to the crowd. Their population seemed to be increasing every moment.

When Hina's attention deviated from the mice, she realized that the stage was not a usual one. In fact, it spanned the entire desert. This unusual expanse of the stage frightened her. She looked at Peer Sahib again. She noticed that the blood that dripped from his book did not have its own smell. Even the colour of that blood was yellowish red. The chaos and competition among the mice was to drink the falling drops of blood before they reached the ground. It was possible that these drops of blood would lead these mice to salvation. When a drop would fall, another collected at the edge of the book ready to fall. There was a momentary break between two consecutive drops. This short break would add up to centuries if measured in earthly hours. During that break, the mice that collected below the book would raise their necks and wait for the next drop to fall.

The scene that Hina saw next dragged her further into amazement. She saw a drop falling. The shiny drop left the book and rushed towards the ground when a mouse leaped and took it in its mouth. Hina kept her eyes focused on that mouse. She was quite far. Thousands of miles away from the scene. She saw that the mouse who drank the yellowish blood drop jumped off the stage. Below the stage was a congested, populated area. There was a difference of many years between the stage and the colony below. During the fall, the mouse transformed into a sign of the spirit. This spirit entered the body of a baby who was about to take birth in that locality. Hina transformed into a bird and started flying over the populated area. She saw the child grow into a young man.

She was amazed to see that the face of this young man had a striking resemblance to that of Peer Sahib. That young man was very accomplished. At night, his body smelt like a bright, white rose. The smell was such that virgin girls, unmarried women, married women, widows, destitute and asexual women, and even pregnant women were attracted to this smell and reached the epitome of their sexual strength. Women put in a lot of effort to protect themselves from that smell, to stay away from it and prevent themselves from getting dragged towards it. Those who feared that their will power would give up, locked themselves up in their houses. A few chained their legs. In spite of this, a moment came when they gave up and surrendered their senses to that smell. The smell colour-blinded their souls. It destroyed their sense of perception. Then their legs would drag and take them to the place where the young man was. The young man's five senses would inform him beforehand who was coming that night to drench in his smell. He was acquainted with all the women of the locality and even knew their names.

By the time he was twenty-five years old, more than 4000 women around the locality, irrespective of age, religion and class, had bathed in his smell. When these women returned to their houses, they felt as if they had just awoken from a dream. There was some magic around the young man. When a woman proceeded towards him, she would vanish from the eyes of other residents of the locality. She would walk through the lanes and streets to reach the young man but no one would see her. All the women were under the vain impression that it was they who had been honoured and blessed with this opportunity and nobody else, and hence had kept it as a secret.

Hina saw that the night when the last young woman surrendered to the power of the young man's smell, the next drop fell from the pages of the book which Peer Sahib held in his hand. The moment the drop fell, the enchanted woman drilled a dagger into the chest of the young man and cut and pulled his heart out.

It was not a normal human heart; it resembled a laddu. The laddu-like object was the source of the magical smell. Hina was looking at this from the sky. She saw that as soon as the woman tasted the laddu, the body of the young man transformed into that of a greenish-black snake. The woman caught the snake and left. Hina sat on a tree in the form of a white pigeon. She remained awake the whole night. The next day, she saw that the enchanted woman was no one else but Uttu herself. Uttu was the daughter of Enki and Ninkur. She was considered to be the goddess of the moon. Enki herself had sent Uttu on the errand. Enki had guessed that the young man, after consuming the last woman, would send a message to the residents of the locality and pose as a messenger and separate from Enki.

The scene was partly concealed. The stage in the temple was still hosting the stampede of the mice when Hina's eyes fell upon the Peer Baba's left hand. What she saw filled her eyes with tears. She felt the warmth of tears on her cheeks. She was sobbing. That was a moment of extreme conflict and breakdown for her. She turned into stone on seeing that Darakhshan's slaughtered neck was held in Peer Sahib's hand. Darakhshan's eyes were closed and the skin on her forehead had wrinkled into a line. Her mother's severed head had driven her mad, and in the madness she could not think or do anything else apart from crying. She was sobbing profusely.

'Get up . . . Wake up . . . Are you having a bad dream?' Darakhshan shouted.

When Darakhshan came out of the room, Hina had already fallen asleep. She thought that since Hina had just returned from college, she'd let her rest for a while and then give her food once she was awake. She took a bundle of methi leaves and sat near the sofa. Fifteen or twenty minutes would have passed when she saw that Hina was sobbing in her sleep. She realized that Hina was having a bad dream which was making her cry. To wake her up, Darakhshan softly slapped her a few times on her cheek. 'Get up . . . Wake up . . . Are you having a bad dream? Get up.'

Hina's eyes opened.

They were red. The moment she woke up, she realized she had seen a dream. Darakhshan sat next to her on the sofa. Hina put her head in her mother's lap. Darakhshan told her daughter that even she had been having bad dreams since the past few days and that was why she had called Peer Baba and told him about them. Peer Sahib promised to share with her the interpretations of the dream after a week. He was also going to give a pattern chart the next day that she had to put up in the house. Hina was listening to her mother. Darakhshan warmed up the food after a while and they ate together.

That evening, Hina read the remaining chapters on Babylonian culture while sitting in the balcony. She was intrigued by the history of the Tower of Babel. A curiosity to know more about the tower arose within her. She wanted to know why God had divided people on this planet. Why was a monolinguistic culture changed to a multilinguistic one. Her interest increased on this topic. She decided that when she would go to college on Monday, she would get a library book on the topic and also have a talk with Vidhi.

She kept the book on the table and bent over the balcony to see the passers-by. Her eyes were focused on the strange faces that were moving below but her mind had the image of Asrar on it.

She was continuously refreshing those few moments in her mind that she had spent with him during the last two meetings. The presence of love made the memories delightful. The last four or five days had been difficult for her. The pain of those days had now changed into an underlying bliss. Her heart was asking her to be careful, but now she couldn't care less. Everything seemed like a wave, and she wanted to flow with it. She kept thinking about Asrar. And kept carefully repeating his words in her mind. She was not aware that two hours had already passed. Her heart had become a spring of memories and thoughts in which she was drowning. Darakhshan shouted from the balcony door, 'It's already sunset. Shut the windows or else the mosquitoes will storm in.'

Hina picked up the book from the table and went and sat on a chair inside the room. She took the remote control and switched on the television. Darakhshan put her teacup next to the chair and told Hina that Yusuf had called a while back. He would come and visit them on Sunday evening. Hina said, 'It's good that Abba has started visiting us more regularly now.'

Darakhshan immediately added, 'All because of Peerji's blessings.'

'Yeah. You're right,' Hina replied.

Darakhshan seated herself next to her daughter and asked Hina, 'Turn the TV to the serial *Saas Bhi Kabhi Bahu Thi*.'

'There's still half an hour left for it to begin,' Hina said.

'Okay, then turn the TV to that comedy show.'

'Fine.' Hina sensed that Darakhshan was in a good mood.

Hina turned to the channel her mother wanted.

They watched the comedy show while drinking tea. The daily soaps on the television provided Darakhshan with her best leisure. Hina used to watch them too sometimes, but she preferred English movies more, especially love stories. She had recently watched *Autumn in New York* and *Notting Hill*.

When she watched those movies, her heart turned rogue with dreamy emotions. She had fallen in love with Julia Robert's giggle and Richard Gere's smile. She was not interested in the serial which Darakhshan was watching with full concentration. She was thinking about her meeting with Asrar the next day. Her eyes might have been on the TV screen, but her mind was preparing for the next meeting with Asrar. She was worried about what she would wear and what beauty-enhancing products she would use. She was wondering at what time she should leave. She imagined herself dressing up in front of the mirror. The contents of her make-up kit were scattered all around. The very picture of her getting all decked up increased her excitement.

She was deciding whether she should go to the dargah first or to the shopping mall and then go to Haji Ali with Asrar. She kept making plans in her head. The body had also involved itself in this process along with the mind. The flames of desire and the excitement induced by the thoughts had given rise to a distinct feeling within her body. The reaction made the body express its wishes in a sort of wetness. Her heart was ready to burn in the kiln of thoughts because in it there was a pleasure she had never experienced before. A warmth whose pleasure was felt by the heart. She kept immersing herself in her thoughts and her body enjoyed the warmth produced by this process. This pleasure added a spark to her eyes.

After bidding farewell to Hina, Asrar kept standing at the Haji Ali signal for a while. He closed his umbrella to enjoy the drizzle. He was so happy that he could not decide what to do next. Where to go? Whom to talk to? Whom to share his heart's condition with? How to keep this secret of his heart and from whom? An ambiguous and undisclosed secret. He did not want anyone to be a part of that secret. The ambiguous and undisclosed secret had a unique odour that was difficult to hide from the world. He could not understand why the emotion of love was such that it was not in the control of the heart to hide it from the world. All the strength of the heart turned feeble in front of the emotion of love.

It started pouring heavily and so he stood under the shelter of the bus stop. It was dark. He lifted his eyes. The raindrops looked like a fountain of bright colours in the lights of the city. Was it that everything around was sharing his joy? He felt that the beautiful colours, the lights and the beauty of the buildings of the city, this rainfall, the cold wind, were all party to his secret. He looked at the raindrops and said, 'I love her. I do not know why I love her, but I still love her.' After murmuring these words he immediately lifted his head to look if there were people around him. What if he had said that out loud in a state of oblivion? No, there was no one around him. There were only two boys and an old woman standing in front of the bus stop, probably waiting for a bus to come. A brown dog sat curled up near his legs. There was a mango tree behind the bus stop. A crow sat drenching on one its branches. Asrar stood there for a while. He remembered that Mohammad Ali had said that they had to go somewhere. At that very moment, he saw a bus en route to Mohammad Ali Road at the signal.

He climbed on the upper deck of the bus and occupied a vacant seat. It was now his habit to enjoy the city scenes from the seat of a double-decker bus. It was always difficult to find a front seat. It was just a mere coincidence on that day that there were very few people on the bus and the front seat was vacant. A woman sat three seats behind him with her children. The conductor had not come on the second deck yet. When the bus moved, the spindrift of the rain poured inside from the front. He pulled down the windows and started looking at the city from the window on the right. Mumbai had a special attraction for him, and he liked everything he saw. There was hunger in his eyes and restlessness in his heart that made him want to see the city. He passed these roads very regularly but every time he would come face to face with something new. Asrar was a keen observer. Life's varied perspectives invited him to be their witness. He wanted to be an onlooker of every street, every road, every building, every turn and every direction of the city. Mumbai was a net that had now entrapped him. In the company of Mohammad Ali and Qasim Dalvi he had visited almost all the important places in the city and its suburbs. He had enjoyed all the recreational spots and beaches, from Juhu till Virar.

When the rain slowed down, he opened the window in front of him. The conductor came. Asrar bought the ticket. The conductor asked him to shut the window. He said that initially he had closed it, and if the rains increased he'd shut it again. The conductor seemed like a decent man. He didn't say anything. He turned and seated himself on one of the back seats. The bus stopped at the Mumbai Central bridge stop. Asrar saw that there was a traffic jam ahead. The black-yellow taxis and red buses were all caught in the rain. The yellow-red colours soaked in rain were a pleasant sight. A few trains passed under the bridge and Asrar's eyes followed them till they disappeared into the rain. Some boys were smoking cigarettes and chewing mawa nearby and a beggar girl, soaked in rain, had spread her hands in front of one of those boys and was asking for something. A boy took out a coin and put it on her palm. She moved away. The signal was a short distance ahead. On the footpath that stretched from the station to the signal were stalls of second-hand clothes, iron tools, handkerchiefs, bags and plasticware, locks, caps, etc. Sometimes a group played a game of cards called Aadi Jodi on the footpath. In this game, three cards are used, of which one is the queen. One player shuffles the cards and then spreads them on a handkerchief. The people hovering around would bet their money on the queen. The game is nothing but a sleight of hand or a trick. People win in the beginning, but their increasing greed destroys them ultimately.

The bus reached the signal. On the left of the signal was the Mumbai state transport depot from where one could catch buses for Mabadmorpho. He saw a red state bus crawl out of the depot like a

snake. Those buses were also called *lal dabbe* or red boxes. The red
box reminded him of his village. Along with the village, came the
memories of Jamila Miss. He smiled. Those memories flashed back
into his mind which had gradually fallen into forgetfulness because
of busy work schedules, dearth of time and the fast life of Mumbai.

Jamila Miss's memories created a maddening feeling in his
heart. At that moment, he intensely missed her. He remembered
those moments, those moments that could not be spoken of, which
he spent with her. Those moments when the music of his body had
combined with the melodious compositions of her body and had
given rise to a new song within him. That song was melancholic.
Sexual intercourse was a sin for him in the beginning, which soon
seemed like a reward for the soul. It was this sin that was the sole
reason for the existence of life. Jamila Miss had taught him about
the pleasure of lovemaking and how flesh participates savagely in
this game of pleasure. Despite that, he had fallen prey to confusion
a number of times.

Having made love with the savageness of the flesh and quenched
the thirst of the body's desert, when the dance ended, Jamila Miss's
face would blossom like a rose. Her smell lingered in the room for
a long time while Asrar's heart remained restless. He felt that even
though his body was loyal and sincerely involved in the lovemaking,
there was a branch of his soul that was detached. He did not want
to express his condition to Jamila Miss. In fact, he was not fully
acquainted with this strangeness and its meaning, although he had
realized a flame was missing in this relationship. Or else why would
that branch of his heart keep away from the gaiety of lovemaking?

The traffic signal changed and the bus started moving. He
came back to the present from the blur of the past. He decided
that he would call Jamila Miss up some day and inquire about her
health. Since the road was clear, the bus reached Sahil Hotel quite
fast. The traffic extended from there till the Nagpada junction.
When the bus halted at Alexandra Cinema, he looked through the

window at the road which led to Kamathipura. There were places on Falkland Road, Playhouse, Bachchu Ki Wadi and Chhota Sonapur where thousands of unfortunate and distressed women lived and sold their bodies as if they were drains for men to release their bodily heat.

There were many localities of such unfortunate and under-privileged women, but this area was a very old one. For Asrar, the lanes in this area, the old buildings, the decomposing walls of those buildings, the women who stood leaning against the wall bargaining for their bodies, their mischievous faces, the extra powder and painted blush on those faces, their poses, sparkling clothes, pale bodies wrapped in those clothes, and the brave and strong heart inside those pale bodies were all like exhibits in a museum. He had no knowledge of the fact that this locality belonged to labourers, most of them from Telangana, who were called Kamathis. They had given their blood and sweat to build the bridge—which brings together the seven islands of Mumbai—in 1793. In the eighteenth century, there were more sex workers in Goregaon, Fanaswadi and Umarkhadi than in Kamathipura. But during urbanization and due to an increase in the city's population, they had to migrate to limited areas.

He did not know that in a few years even Kamathipura would overflow with the rise in urban population and the increase in property rates would make the government displace these women from there. Two or three centuries ago, women from Europe to Japan had come here to satisfy the sexual needs of British soldiers and Indians. But now there were only Nepalese, south Indian and North-eastern women. It seemed there was a huge black sheet spread over the skies of this area so that even God was unable to see the plight of the women. Asrar thought that under this sheet awaited the souls of thousands of sex workers for the sky to allow them to enter the other world.

The conductor sitting at the back had fallen asleep. He was a worshipper of Mumba Devi, and for the last three years he had been on that route. He saw a dream which took him to Kamathipura. A black bird was sitting on his shoulder. The bird narrated a story:

Once, Mumba Devi had visited this place. When she took a look, she noticed that more than one lakh departed souls were trapped under the black sheet and waiting for salvation. She saw many souls crying out loud. She saw that a white, lit-up soul was sitting in a corner and busy penning down something about the sex workers. This surprised Mumba. On the other side, an exhausted angel was taking rest. The angel told Mumba Devi that this mad soul had been writing something for seven decades now. 'It is not yet willing to come with me to the other world.' Mumba Devi told the angel that the will of the souls was not considered in this world. The angel said that this was a special soul. In fact, when it was about to die, it was intoxicated and had wished to God that it should remain free till it had consumed all the poisons of the world. The angel had held it and said, 'What more poison do you want to drink? You have already consumed alcohol.' The soul had replied that it wanted to drink the poison of the sad souls. Then, the commandment came that it had been granted permission!

The angel continued, 'I told it that it had been granted permission.' It then flew and came here. Since then, I've been following it and waiting for it. The long wait under this black sheet has made me tired. It feels as if I have become the black sheet.' His last sentence made Mumba Devi smile. On seeing her smile, the angel told her that the day this mad soul came here, fifteen or twenty other spirits surrounded it and started talking and laughing with it. Maybe they had been waiting for this mad soul. A few minutes after meeting it, they got the invite for the other world. This astonished Mumba Devi. She knew that this power lay only with the Sufis and the saints. The angel continued, 'What all should I tell you, Mumba Maa? A rabies-affected dog's soul had also come to this mad soul and cried its heart out. The mad soul rubbed its hands on the itch and the soul of the dog departed to the other world.' Mumba Devi looked at the black sheet for a moment and then fixed her gaze on the white soul. Mumba Devi had seen and witnessed a lot of unusual and extraordinary things and events in this world, but this white soul left her worried. She asked the angel, 'What has the soul written in so many years?' The angel replied, 'It has already written seventy lakh pages but keeps saying that more poison is still left.'

Mumba Devi remembered Shiva in her heart. Mahadev appeared in front of Mumba Devi. He was aware of Mumba Devi's astonishment. Shiva told her that this enlightened soul was an Urdu litterateur. Mumba cast a glance at the soul of the writer and then told the angel, 'You should return to your own land. This soul had been blessed to stay here till eternity and give nirvana to the lost souls and to pen down their poison on these pages.'

The angel dissolved and disappeared. He knew that Mumba Devi's words were a form of command.

The dream of the conductor continued. The black bird narrated another story to him in which the conductor was also a character.

The streetlights were off, and hence the road was dark. The darkness was able to hide the dirt from his eyes. He saw a couple of people in the paan shop at the turn. Nearby, three women stood under a peepal tree. Their clothes suggested that they were sex workers. Asrar stuck his neck out of the window. He could see a few more girls on that dark footpath. Two young lads stood near those girls. Probably they were devising ways to move forward and talk to the girls. When the bus moved forward, he saw ten or twelve people at the entrance of Alexandra Cinema. This cinema generally screened English movies, but their posters were more titillating than the actual scenes in the films. Right next to the cinema was a restaurant on which a *jahazi*-sized board read 'Bismillah'. Opposite to that restaurant was another paan shop. Two girls stood there as well. One of them was of a wheatish complexion

and was not more than seventeen or eighteen years old. She was
laughing at something.

An old man sitting at the counter of Bismillah restaurant was
looking at the girl. He was an Urdu poet. This poet had no interest
in reading out his ghazal, and had this habit of rejecting ghazals
of other poets saying that they were not *Ahl-e-Zaban*, the people
of the land of Urdu, i.e., the north Indian states. The old man
had seen those days of Alexandra Cinema when posters of English
movies were published in Urdu. He had jotted down in his diary
many Urdu titles of English movies. For example, *Kiss the Girls and
Make Them Die* became *Chumma Chati ki Zeenat, Bose Ki Qeemat* in
Urdu. *Blow Hot, Blow Cold* became *Kabhi Narm Narm, Kabhi Garm
Garm*. The English title *Flying Skirt* was translated to *Ghagre Mein
Dhum Dham*, and *The Girl with a Rifle* became *Bindya Gadi Mein,
Bandook Sari Mein*. He was of the opinion the Urdu titles were the
best examples of creative expression.

The bus moved forward.

He shut his eyes for a moment. Shanti's face surfaced in
his eyes. The touch of Shanti was refreshed in his memory.
He opened his eyes. The bus now stood at the Nagpada signal.
He would have got off the bus and met Shanti had Mohammad
Ali not asked him to meet so early. He leaned on the window
and looked at the road below. Routine life went on. The noise
and the crowd was the same as usual. He was reminded of Hina.
It was possible that she was somewhere around here. Hina had
told him that her home was just five minutes away from Nagpada
and she sometimes visited the place at around 9–9.30 p.m. for
food and buying things.

Asrar tried looking for Hina's face in his mind's eye. If he
had Hina's photograph, he would've kept looking at it. Recalling

the features of Hina's face calmed his heart. It was the attractiveness of Hina's face that had given him the strength to go and stand before her at Haji Ali the other day. When he thought of that now, he could not believe how he had mustered up the courage for that act. He had praised his guts a thousand times over and said to himself, 'Whatever happens, happens for the good.' It was true that he was extremely happy to meet Hina, to know her and to see her. What added to this happiness was that Hina had accepted his friendship. Many a time, he thought that he would never see her again. As if she was like a gust of wind that just passed by, never to return. That was why when he initially did not find Hina at Haji Ali at their second meeting, he was disappointed.

At the end of the second story that the black bird narrated, the conductor was brutally killed. Some members of the upper caste in Ahmednagar of his state of Maharashtra had chopped off his hands and legs and thrown him in a gutter. His sin was that his shadow had touched a man of the upper caste. His dead body was left there to rot. Seeing his body rotting his olfactory system woke up and he shivered with the unbearable stink of his own dead body. He woke up and looked around. He tried to control the fear and terror he was experiencing.

'Your stop is here,' the conductor came and said to Asrar, who was still lost in his thoughts.

Asrar climbed down the steps of the bus and stood near the door. The rain had caused a traffic jam. The bus was so slow that one could easily get off while it was moving. He got off the bus. The rain stopped. He walked steadily to the kholi. When he entered it, Mohammad Ali was sitting with his friends and chatting. Asrar wished him and went straight inside. Then he remembered that he was so lost that he forgot his umbrella in the bus. He decided to buy an umbrella after a while since it would be difficult for him to go to work in the rain. He came out and wiped his face with a towel and joined his friends. The group comprised Suleiman Vanu, Qasim Dalvi, Saleem Dhamaskar and Aslam Dhamaskar. Saleem mischievously teased him, 'Was it overtime at the office today?'

Asrar smiled and Mohammad Ali smiled looking at Asrar blush.

Asrar remembered that he had lost his umbrella. He told his friends that he had fallen asleep in the bus and when they reached the stop, the conductor woke him up. He left his umbrella in the haste.

Suleiman immediately replied, 'Eyes were shut or did they meet someone else's eyes!'

Saleem added, 'Ah! It's okay, lad, umbrellas keep getting lost in Mumbai.'

Asrar could not understand how to respond to the sarcastic and mischievous remarks of Saleem and Suleiman. He was wondering if they had got some sense of his present condition. On seeing Asrar look at Suleiman so inquisitively, Saleem said, 'We sense a speck in the thief's beard, eh?' Haider burst out laughing and rubbed his beard. The other boys in the kholi joined in the laughter. Mohammad Ali could sense Asrar's situation. He knew that it was the usual assumption that if anyone was two to three hours late to the kholi, he definitely might have gone to release his warm blood in one of the rooms in Kamathipura. And this was reason enough for friends to crack jokes and make fun of each other. Asrar was unused to this kind of humour. Seeing Asrar's condition, Mohammad Ali said, 'If you have lost your umbrella, let's go buy a new one. Moreover, I also have some work with you.'

Both got up and left the kholi.

There were umbrellas put on show in a shop near Minara Masjid. Asrar bought a black umbrella. After buying it, he asked Mohammad

Ali, 'You had asked me to come early. Something important?'
Instead of responding to what Asrar had asked, Mohammad Ali
stopped a taxi. 'Get inside the taxi, then we will talk. D'Mello
Road,' Mohammad Ali told the driver.

The taxi moved. Mohammad Ali told Asrar that for a couple
of days he'd had this desire of sitting in a dance bar and drinking
beer. Asrar was aware that Mohammad Ali drank beer sometimes,
but he did not know that he enjoyed going to dance bars as well.
In Asrar's head was a filmi concept of the dance bar where women
in skimpy clothes danced around drunkards who showered money
on them. But he had never seen a dance bar. He was glad that they
were going to one. Certain doubts were churning in his heart,
making his face go blank. Seeing his silence, Mohammad Ali asked,
'You seem shocked?'

'Not at all, yaar. Just that one has to shower money on the
women in the bar. I have only a few hundred rupees in my pocket.'

'*Abe chutiye*! Who told you that you have to shower money?'

'I saw it in the movies. People shower notes on the dancers.'

'It isn't compulsory. Whichever asshole has the guts to do
so, can very well do it. We'll just have fun. We will just have the
beer. Understood?'

Asrar nodded and started looking out. The yellowish halo of
the streetlight looked beautiful in the rain. They had passed the
halo, but it stayed in Asrar's head and at the centre of it emerged
Hina's smiling face. This was like the moment when they were
standing on the road outside Haji Ali which led to Worli when
Hina had a teacup in her hand and was staring at the sea while Asrar
gaped at her. Hina kept looking at the quiet waves for a minute or
two. She could feel Asrar's gaze on her and she was glad that he was
looking at her with such desirous eyes. She didn't want to destroy
that magical moment by reciprocation. If she had the feeling that
Asrar was looking at her with eyes filled with love and was happy
doing so, then she was also aware of the fact that Asrar's eyes on
her were causing a wave of happiness in her. Many boys stared at

her at school, but they were unsuccessful in producing the waves
that Asrar's stares had. Now she was experiencing transformations
within herself. She felt a kinetic vibration and sensitivity within
herself. Those vibrations and her colourful imagination were
together causing chaos inside her. Asrar had touched that vibration
with his eyes for a moment. That look of the eyes had freshened up
her face and made her look relaxed.

Hina's face floated before Asrar's eyes like a paper boat on the
water. He was ecstatic. The scenes from outside the window were
fading as Hina's face overshadowed his mind. Even if the journey
lasted for a thousand years, it wouldn't have mattered to him. He
was captivated in the magic of Hina's face, and in that spell of magic
time disappeared as if through a black hole.

The taxi reached D'Mello Road.

Mohammad Ali asked the driver to stop before a four-storey
building. The taxi stopped and Asrar came back from the lightness
of the black hole to the heaviness of the real world. In the courtyard
of the building was a neem tree, in the shade of which grew
bougainvillea and roses. Colourful bulbs lit up the branches of the
neem tree. There was a door in the courtyard which was made of
sangwan wood and attracted attention because of its huge size. The
light-brown door was decorated with flowers and designs made
out of copper wires. A well-built sardar, dressed in a white safari
suit and a black turban, stood guard. The sardar wished them and
opened the door for them.

The opening of the door was like being ushered into a
different world altogether. There was a small dark room. But this
darkness carried with it a romantic novelty. Multicoloured lights
were scattered from the ceiling till the floor, making the dimness
pleasant. There was another door at the other end of the room.
Two guards stood there. When the guards opened the door, the
sound of music and film songs came drifting out. They entered and
the door closed behind them. Three suited men welcomed them.
Mohammad Ali and Asrar sat on the sofa attached to the wall.

On the left, four girls were seated on a small stage. Behind them was the music system. There were four tables in front of the stage. Four or five people sat drinking around each table. The smoke from their cigarettes spread across the room. The girl who was singing was very beautiful. She was dressed in a sari. Asrar saw that there was a counter filled with alcohol bottles. Three waiters stood outside that counter and were carrying whisky and beer bottles to their respective tables. Mohammad Ali ordered Kingfisher beer. He ordered a mild beer for Asrar.

They started drinking at around 10.30 p.m. and continued till midnight.

Asrar observed that many men would get up in between to dance in the middle, go near the dancers, and shower notes on them or put a garland of notes around their necks. Mohammad Ali had consumed two bottles, whereas Asrar had refused the second one. He could already experience the intoxication with one bottle on his nerves. Mohammad Ali talked about many things at a go. Asrar noticed that Mohammad Ali was missing his mother a lot and desired to meet her but had very little information about her.

Over the past many years, Mohammad Ali had tried to forget the woman that his entire family had forgotten but all his efforts were in vain, and the passing time made it more difficult for him to forget her. He wanted to accept his mother with all her weaknesses. But he didn't know where his mother was, or what happened to her, if she was alive or dead. He did not visit his village very often, the reason being that the village added to his pain. In Mumbai, this pain became an oblivious shadow that did not disturb him much. That night, for the first time, he had spoken his heart out to Asrar on this. It started off because the effect of alcohol had made Asrar talk about how good his family was and that their mothers had known each other.

The effect of two beers flung open the cellar of Mohammad Ali's heart. The realities, secrets and complaints buried deep inside it were now revealed. Slowly and steadily, everything that had been suppressed now started coming out. He felt very close to Asrar and there was no hesitation in sharing his secrets. Mohammad Ali drank one more small can. The intoxication was overpowering his diction. Some swear words had found their place in his speech. His lips were shivering, and his eyes had turned heavy. Something seemed to have touched his heart. He told Asrar, 'Get up! Let me show you a different colour of Mumbai.'

Asrar got up. Mohammad Ali went to the counter and paid the bill.

Vehicles moved at short intervals on D'Mello Road. There were few pedestrians around. They walked for fifteen minutes and entered a dark lane. A little into the lane was a big old bungalow where an old Parsi couple had lived at some point of time. Now, the bungalow was used by dogs and cats as their maternity home. An owl lived in the facade. There was so much wild grass growing in the courtyard that it was impossible to distinguish the door. A tamarind tree leaned on the broken gate of the bungalow. The tree seemed a century old. There was an eagle's nest on the tree. The eagle sat in the nest every day and looked at the ships at the Mumbai Port Trust and wondered that someday she would also sit on one of these and go across the sea. The daily flights over Crawford Market and other areas of south Mumbai seemed ridiculous and useless to her.

Mohammad Ali stopped near the trees and started peeing against a trunk. Asrar's bladder was also bursting, and he could no longer bear it. While urinating, Mohammad Ali exclaimed, 'Ah! What pleasure it is to urinate under the open skies. What say?'

Asrar replied, 'You're absolutely right. In fact, I've also been defecating under the open skies since childhood.'

Mohammad Ali found that humorous.

Asrar raised his head and looked at the sky. The sky was blank. There were no stars or moon till where his eyes could see. The dark empty sky devoid of specks of light stimulated a thought in his heart. He looked at Mohammad Ali. Today, he could see the void and darkness inside Mohammad Ali. Sometime back, under the influence of alcohol, Mohammad Ali had stopped and had irritatingly said, 'The biggest mistake that my mother made was to leave me behind. Why did she leave me behind, what harm would have come had she taken me along?'

'Forget it. It has been years now,' Asrar said, putting his hand on his shoulder and trying to console him.

Mohammad Ali just looked into Asrar's eyes without saying anything.

Asrar understood that Mohammad Ali wanted to tell him how that grief was entering his heart every day and spreading like cancer. It was a wound which worsened with the passage of time. Asrar realized that if a mother chooses to be with someone else in times of difficulties, problems, need or desire, it can be accepted but the pain of leaving the child for those reasons had a lasting impact.

Seeing Asrar lost in thought, Mohammad Ali said, 'Eh, leave it. Let's go and enjoy!'

Mohammad Ali's suggestion didn't allow Asrar to ponder further on why the idea of 'sexual disloyalty' made him sad. His heart wanted to incinerate itself. It was possible that if he had clutched on to this thought for long, the patches that had been put on old sorrows would have come off. The reason was that he had not seen anything which would cut through his heart. He just had a suspicion. He had started telling himself that it was just his misconception and delusion.

After urinating Mohammad Ali told Asrar, 'Just enjoy yourself at the place I'm taking you to now. Just enjoy without uttering a word.'

'Yes, boss!' Asrar said and zipped his lips in a gesture that suggested silence. They felt better after emptying their bladders. The intoxication had mellowed down. They proceeded and had barely walked for a minute when they reached the bar where Mohammad Ali wanted to take Asrar. A watchman stood outside. Mohammad Ali shook hands with him. He looked like he knew Mohammad Ali.

This bar was different from the previous one they had visited. Although here too there was a door inside the main door, the place was very quiet. The lights were dim. It was difficult to see who sat on which table. When the door closed, Asrar felt that a woman and a man stood in front of them. Mohammad Ali murmured something to them and ordered a beer. The boy escorted them to a vacant table. The back of the table was so high that it was difficult to see what was happening on the next table. When Asrar heard a few whispers, he realized there were more people in the bar. After a few moments, he observed that there were only women serving in that bar.

'One girl is fixed for each table,' Mohammad Ali informed Asrar. He then mischievously said, 'If you do not like the service, you can call another one.'

Asrar did not understand what Mohammad Ali was saying.

In the middle of this conversation, a Nepalese woman served them two cans of beer. While pouring beer into the glass, she bent and asked Asrar, 'What else do you want?'

'Boiled peanuts and papad,' Mohammad Ali replied.

The Nepalese woman went away.

While clinking their glasses Mohammad Ali said, 'This is in memory of my mother, whose whereabouts I do not know.'

Asrar could feel Mohammad Ali's grief. To temporarily soothe his friend's wounds, Asrar said, 'A mother always remains a mother, irrespective of all contexts.'

They started drinking cold beer. As they sipped, something else was boiling within. Asrar tried to hear what Mohammad Ali had to say in spite of the intoxication. While talking they had emptied their glasses. The Nepalese woman returned with the snacks. Mohammad Ali asked her to sit down. She sat next to him and started pouring beer into the empty glasses. Then Mohammad Ali touched her cheeks and withdrew a Rs 100 note from his pocket and murmured, 'How much for French?' The girl made a mischievous gesture, bent and pressed her lips against his ears and said something softly. He smiled and replied, 'Sorry, I'm already drunk hence I forgot.' Before he could continue, she kept a finger on his lips. Asrar was continuously grinning at them.

The woman went away.

Mohammad Ali told Asrar that when he had been here three months back, she was the woman who had served him. He had forgotten this, but she still remembered. That night he had told her, 'You are solid in both serving and drinking beer.' Asrar kept nodding his head. A little beer was still left in the bottle and Asrar poured it in his glass. Beer suited him. He felt at one with himself, such was the impact of the beer. In that feeling he remembered the moments when he sat with Hina on the seashore and watched the setting sun and answered Hina's questions.

High on alcohol, he told himself, 'I fell in love with Hina at first sight.'

He remembered that he had gone to Shanti after that first meeting. He had sex with her very passionately. Under his lips, he uttered, 'Why are you fooling yourself? That very night you went and slept with a prostitute, and you call it love at first sight?' He found the word 'prostitute' inappropriate for Shanti. 'You call her a "prostitute". What makes you think you are not one yourself?' He paused and added, 'Jamila Miss used you as a prostitute.' He immediately brushed aside his own words. 'No. She actually loved me, and I also had fun. It wasn't a commercial transaction.'

Asrar had never anticipated such a monologue while sloshed. He wondered if this condition was similar to intuition. He was not able to understand three things, but he was trying to see them separately from each other. He reasoned: firstly, love and sex were two different passions and independently exist. They should not be taken as interconnected. Secondly, consensual sexual relationships were different from prostitution because they were based on two people liking each other. Their purpose was pleasure, freedom from the restlessness of the soul, a search for satisfaction of the heart. Thirdly, love was that relationship in which a man and a woman adored each other unconditionally to the extent of surrendering themselves. This adoration, he thought, evolves with time. Love is not a constant emotion. It's like belief, and it flickers, increases and decreases with time. If it evolves at all, the relationship deepens or else the passion dries up. When the passion dries up, a situation comes when it takes the shape of an incurable disease.

He was still engrossed in talking to himself when the Nepalese woman returned. This time she looked more refreshed. Probably she had powdered her cheeks. Mohammad Ali introduced Asrar, and she looked at him and smiled. He smiled back. Her teeth shone in the dark. The woman pulled his hands towards her. He immediately took out a tissue from the box kept on the table, wiped his hands and shook hands with her. While shaking hands, she said, 'My name is Pashupati.'

'Good,' Asrar said. His eyes were burdened with intoxication and now Pashupati seemed even prettier than she was. He told her his name and said, 'You look very nice.'

Pashupati smiled. Mohammad Ali said, 'He has been in Mumbai for five months . . . this is his first time.'

'First time!' She exclaimed.

Pashupati came and sat at Asrar's table. She picked up Asrar's glass and made him drink the little beer that was left. She brushed her lips on his ears and seductively said something. He probably didn't hear it clearly. She put one of her hands around his waist. She kissed his neck and tasted the salt of his sweat. She liked it. The salt had a pleasant smell. Asrar felt the rush in his veins while sitting in that small dark heaven that the bar was. It was as if ants crawled on the sole of his feet, his palms and in between his fingers.

The tipsiness in his eyes blurred everything around. For a minute he felt darkness spread in front of his eyes. He felt himself vanishing in that darkness. For a moment he thought he did not exist. He did not exist anywhere. The oblivion of existence was relaxing, but such moments do not last long. In that moment, Pashupati had swallowed Asrar's salt and the heat of his being. The taste of Asrar's sweat, enveloped in the smell of her lipstick, entered Pashupati's body. She was ecstatic. The feeling of satisfying sad hearts gave her a lot of satisfaction. Her body was a sacred bowl in which deprived, defeated, lonely and melancholic souls would pour their poisons and gain momentary happiness. A bowl in which even those who suffered from tuberculosis would leave behind their infections.

Mohammad Ali had noticed a static moment of happiness on Asrar's face at the time when he appeared to have slipped into oblivion. The things which were blurred seemed to have disappeared completely. In fact, he himself did not exist. Pashupati picked up the beer bottle kept on the table. Before keeping it aside, she drank the remains of the beer. She started to get up when Asrar held her hand and said, 'magic'.

'This is the pleasure of your first time, remember it,' Pashupati whispered. He smiled. An obscure picture of Jamila Miss emerged in his eyes. In the deep darkness he felt that Jamila Miss was not Jamila Miss but Pashupati. Pashupati was no longer Pashupati but Jamila Miss. Both were compassionate and tender, and both loved to experience the ecstasy of the salt.

A smile stayed on his lips for long.

They had paan on coming out of the bar and walked for a short distance down the lonely road. A lorry was parked on one side of the road, and they pissed in its shadows. Their eyes were heavy, and their hearts were free from the chaos of the world.

They staggered while walking. And they reached a corner where there was a Chinese food stall. The road ahead of the food stall was comparatively better lit up. The drink and the bright light moved Asrar's heart. The insects swarmed around the warm streetlights. The rain had stopped. Weed had grown around the streetlight on that road. Two creepers had grown around the light poles and were intertwined in various curves. While standing under the light, a tipsy Asrar narrated his encounter with Hina to Mohammad Ali.

Ali patiently and quietly heard him for ten minutes. Three or four people were having chicken fried rice at the food stall. Even though they themselves were absolutely sloshed, when they saw Asrar and Mohammad Ali talk so loudly, one of them remarked, 'The alcohol has struck their brain.'

On hearing this, the Nepalese fried rice vendor smiled.

Mohammad Ali and Asrar were lost in their own world. Mohammad Ali was happy to see Asrar so happy after a long time, albeit he was angry at the fact that he had hidden Hina's story from him for nearly two weeks. Even though he was drunk, he tried explaining to Ali that he had met Hina only twice. Nothing that could reflect an established relationship could be seen in merely two meetings. When Mohammad Ali saw that Asrar was putting a lot of effort in justifying his feelings, he said, 'Whatever it was, why did you not tell me before?'

Asrar didn't say anything. He looked at the creeper clinging to the streetlight. He found the encircling light very pleasant. He touched Mohammad Ali's cheek and apologized, 'Sorry . . . but listen, I've started loving her deeply . . . from the heart.'

Mohammad Ali looked at him intently. He had never seen Asrar get so emotional. Asrar continued, 'I've started loving her very, very much.'

On overhearing what Asrar had said, one of the boys standing at the food stall inferred, 'It seems like a case of a love affair.'

'This is what happens when you fall prey to love,' the Nepalese vendor added while handing over a plate.

This made the drunkards giggle. One of them said, 'God save us from love affairs. I've been a captive once, since then I pulled the ears and said never again.'

'Whose ears did you pull?' the Nepalese vendor asked.

'Pulled your ears or your arse?' one of them added mischievously.

All of them burst out laughing. The Nepalese vendor also tried putting on an embarrassed smile.

Their laughter caught Asrar and Mohammad Ali's attention. They smiled at their giggles and moved forward. While walking Asrar could feel that Pashupati had added wings of pleasure to his soul. At that moment, he wanted to be free of his own burden. That subtle feeling of lightness made him happy and blissful. It opened the locks of his heart and he could reveal his secrets to Mohammad Ali and tell him about Hina.

It seemed the intoxication had entered his veins and settled there. After passing through the dim light, they entered the area where the light was yellow and warm. A taxi halted. They boarded it.

When they got off the taxi, Asrar looked intently at Mohammad Ali. He noticed that tears always rushed down his eyes in the darkness of the taxi. His eyes were moist, and his cheeks were red. Asrar did not react. He kept his arms around Mohammad Ali's shoulder. Instead of going towards the kholi, they proceeded towards Pydhonie. All shops had already shut down in Pydhonie but there was still a little bustle on the streets. A man was selling tea. Both had tea and roamed in that area for nearly ten minutes. The tea had lessened the effect of alcohol. They reached the kholi at around two in the night and quietly slept off.

Asrar knew the reason behind Mohammad Ali's sorrow, but he did not want to start a conversation around it. It was an unhealed wound in Mohammad Ali's soul and Asrar thought it would be better if he let it pass and hope that the smoke of melancholy would subside soon, and Mohammad Ali would return to normal. That was exactly why he had taken Mohammad Ali to Pydhonie. The moment he spread himself on the bed, sleep engulfed him. The deep sleep covered his mind with black clouds. He slept as if lifeless.

In the afternoon, the next day, Asrar's heart was pining for Hina. An entire week was left before he could meet her again and it seemed like forever. He kept looking at the time and it was as if the hands of the clock had stopped. Asrar wondered that if the hands of the clock were taking so long to finish a circle, how much time would it take for a week to pass. Every passing second was as long as the time it would take for the Day of Judgement to come.

The condition of his heart worsened with every passing minute. He was not able to connect with anything and it was as if everything wanted to move away from him. Even in the kholi, his friends indulged in funny and interesting conversations, but he no longer found them interesting enough. Sometimes, he smiled a fake smile, but the absurdity of it proved that his heart was no longer in that place. It had cut itself off from the conversation and had travelled to another world. That world only had Hina and an Asrar who was captured by the desire to keep looking at her.

The secrets of love were unfolding in front of him. He realized that love was the magic of the desire to see the beloved. And to be trapped in that magic was a sort of intoxication for the lover. A distinct feature of this intoxicated condition was that the infected lover would cut himself off from the world around him. Although he was well aware of what was happening around him, he was oblivious to the world around him.

Asrar asked Haider to give him his brother's book, the pages of which he had read last week and had copied a few poems from. It was Rajinder Manchanda Bani's poetry. He started browsing through the pages. He read one ghazal four or five times:

Libas us ka alamat ki tarha tha
Badan, roshan ibarat ki tarha tha
Ada Mauj-e-Tajjus ki tarha thi
Nafs, khushbu ki shohrat ki tarha tha
Tasawur par hina bikhari hui thi
Saman Aghosh-e-Khilwat ki tarha tha

(Her clothes were like an indication
Body, an illuminated phrase
Grace, that birthed a wave of curiosity
Soul, was like the popularity of the sweetest smell
Henna was sprinkled on his imagination
The scene was like the ecstasy of the bare lap of solitude)

He felt as if those lines were written for Hina to show her what was going on in his heart. He read the last lines repeatedly with full concentration: 'The scene was like the ecstasy of the bare lap of solitude.'

Jamila Miss had once explained it to him. He tried to think and feel Hina in his solitude, but all his attempts failed. He was unable to understand why the person in whose thoughts he was lost would not stay still in his imagination. He turned a few more pages. He liked another ghazal. He marked two couplets with his pen. While reading the ghazal, he realized that it was essential for him to continue his education to understand such poetry better. He continued to flip through the pages. He read a new ghazal which blew his mind completely. He took out his diary from the attaché case and began copying:

Tere badan mein chingari si kya shai hai
Aks zara sa aur chamkne wala mein
Tere lahu mein bedari si kya shai hai
Lams zara sa aur mahekne wala mein
Teri ada mein purkari si kya shai hai
Baat zara si aur jhijakne wala mein

(What, in your body, is like a spark
The reflection is going to shine more
What, in your blood, is like wakefulness
The sense of touch will be more fragrant
What, in your grace, is like an expertise
The conversations will turn more shy)

Haider saw him copying the ghazal. He went up to Asrar and said, 'Why are you putting in so much effort? Get it photocopied later!'

On hearing Haider, Asrar suddenly surfaced from the world he was lost in.

His face was pale. Haider looked at him and said, 'Let's go and get it xeroxed. Then you can comfortably sit and read it. You will not have to write it down unnecessarily.'

Mohammad Ali was ironing his clothes. He had been observing Asrar for quite some time and he said to himself, 'This idiot has caught the illness of love. Now he will read out poems, sing songs, will remain lost in thoughts and at the time of meals will declare that he is not hungry! And later his eyes will soon open, and he will say that love is nothing more than madness and a mistake that should not be repeated. But he will still fall in love again. Every human repeats this mistake even after deciding not to.'

Asrar looked at Mohammad Ali. Mohammad Ali kept his iron aside and said, 'Haider is absolutely right. Go get it xeroxed. Till when will you keep writing?'

'I was thinking the same,' Asrar said, getting up.

'I know exactly what you were thinking,' Mohammad Ali said, at which Suleiman and Saleem Ghare smiled.

Asrar did not respond. He smiled and left the room with Haider.

At around 6 p.m., Asrar, Saleem Ghare, Suleiman Vanu and Mohammad Ali went to buy daily essentials from Null Bazar. The sun had shone pleasantly throughout the day and the mud on the streets had dried up. Saleem Ghare carried a list of things that had to be bought. Whenever they spotted anything from that list, they would stop. While the others were busy shopping, Asrar stood and gazed at the girls roaming in the market. In his mind he thought that there was a small probability that Hina might have come to the market with her mother for shopping. At times when he saw a girl from afar, he was sure that it was Hina but when she came closer, he was disappointed. Mohammad Ali was observing this. Finally, he could not control himself and told Asrar, 'Stop behaving like a fool or else you will get one nice smack.'

'What? What did I do?'

'Stop staring at the girls.'

Asrar was befuddled. He looked at Mohammad Ali and said, 'I was hoping I'll spot Hina here.'

'Now you'll spot Hina in the moon as well!'

Asrar lifted his head to look at the sky. Mohammad Ali was bemused because the sun had not even set properly for the moon to be visible. Out of amazement he said, 'There's still time for the moon to rise.'

Mohammad Ali laughed at his own wit. He said to himself, 'It is true to say that love blinds a person.'

Asrar realized his folly. He became more conscious of his actions than required. He did not lift his head up. He entered a small utensil shop but was looking down. At that moment, Hina came out of the cloth shop next to the utensil store and crossed the road with her mother. She had been shopping for the last one hour. A number of times the thought crossed her mind that Asrar lived in that area, but she could not imagine that he would be in the market at that time.

Saleem Ghare was to give a golgappa party.

They were standing around the golgappa stall on the footpath. Mohammad Ali mischievously suggested to Asrar, 'Look inside the golgappa as well . . .' Asrar turned towards him and Ali continued, 'It is possible you will see her inside it too . . .'

Before Mohammad Ali could complete his sentence, Asrar stuffed a golgappa in his mouth.

It was difficult for Mohammad Ali to control his laughter, and the golgappa he swallowed would have stuck in his throat had it not melted immediately.

Everyone kept laughing. And Mohammad Ali kept coughing.

At night, after dinner, he read Bani's poetry for some time. He underlined those lines which reflected the condition of his heart. He did not pay much attention to those lines he didn't comprehend. He would read the ones he found easy, repeatedly. He felt that his thoughts carried him away. He roamed in worlds that were far away. He took Hina to new places with him. In the deep valleys of his imagination, Hina would accompany him, every time in different clothes and new hairstyles, and full of splendour. He would hold her hand in his hand and tell her about all the new things they saw. Once he took her on a sea voyage on a magnificent boat. They talked about the speed of the waves, the distinct shades of the water, its stillness, the birds flying around. He wanted to tell Hina about the numerous fish and their heartwarming colours which she had never seen.

When, for a moment, the chain of his imagination would break and he would return to the real world, he would remain lost for a long time. And then regret having come out of the tilismic circle of his imagination. All pleasures had stationed in those thoughts where Hina was with him.

He kept the book near his head and closed his eyes.

Everyone in the kholi was busy doing their work or chatting. Saleem Vanu had bought a new phone and most of them were looking at it. The mobile was still a luxury and out of reach for most people, especially because calls were very expensive. Asrar was not feeling sleepy, but he wanted to keep his eyes shut. He wanted to close his eyes so that he could drift into a dream. A dream where he was with Hina. After a while, a dream did come to him. A dream that he had seen some time back. He tried remembering it. In that dream he had forgotten his way in a jungle. The trees in that forest were black in colour. The floor of the jungle was also black and a few tufts of grass and weeds around were also black in colour. The butterflies were also black.

He remembered that even the colour of the water flowing in the brook was black. He sat on the bank of the river in disappointment. After a while, a boat came towards him. A woman was sitting in that boat. Did he forget the dream, or did he not remember it in the same way he had seen it originally? He pushed his brain to recollect that there was a circular mark of kumkum on her forehead. The woman told him that her name was Mumba and she had the knowledge of all the routes of the jungle. He tried recollecting the conversation he had had with that woman earlier. He was still trying very hard and was able to recollect the conversation partially when Mohammad Ali came and whispered in his ears, 'Are you thinking about Hina?'

He opened his eyes. Mohammad Ali was now lying next to him and smiling. He looked at Mohammad Ali and said, 'No yaar, I was not thinking about her.'

'Do not lie. I can read your face,' Mohammad Ali said.

'What is my face telling you?' Asrar asked.

'That you are seeing Hina everywhere.'

Asrar said nothing. He remained silent. Seeing no response, Mohammad Ali picked up the spiral-bound book kept near Asrar's head and exclaimed, 'A book of poetry!'

'Yes . . . so?' Asrar said.

'Nothing, you seem like a true lover now,' Mohammad Ali said softly with the required pauses.

Asrar did not know what to say. A couplet came to him which he had read a while back.

Tum kya jano ajab ajab in baton ko
Aag kahin ho, yahan hun jalne wala mein

(How will you understand this strange condition
Wherever the fire be, here or not, it is me who burns)

On hearing this, Mohammad Ali broke into giggles. He could not control his laughter. The other boys present in the kholi were now looking at them and smiling. They thought that Asrar might have cracked a joke. He mockingly repeated the last line, 'Wherever the fire be, wherever the fire be . . . here or not, it is me who burns . . .' And kept laughing. Asrar, still as a statue, was gaping at him. There was a small smile on his face too. When Mohammad Ali's laughter mellowed down, he bent towards Asrar and whispered, 'The real fire was lighted by Pashupati last night!'

Asrar now grinned from cheek to cheek. He had a full and natural smile on his face. Pashupati's face came before his eyes. Mischief could be seen in Mohammad Ali's eyes. It struck Asrar that the thought in his head was not Jamila Miss's body nor Shanti's, but it was Hina's face. He wondered how much pleasure there was in that one moment devoid of any explanation. Hina ruled his soul. She had concealed it. In fact, she had become a powerful blow shaking his nerves. Seeing him drowning in his thoughts again, Mohammad Ali said, 'When the ghost of love leaves you, we'll go to Pashupati. She has a cure for all sorrows . . . and yes, Shanti is also there. How can I forget her?'

Asrar was still silent. His eyes were on Mohammad Ali. Mohammad Ali kept saying things. Asrar was hearing them, but was he really listening? He was lying down on a cot of romance, talking to Hina. By the time he came out of the palace of romance, Mohammad Ali had already slept. A couple of boys had also gone to sleep. Saleem Ghare was chewing away on his paan. Suleiman Vanu was chopping vegetables for the next morning. Asrar turned away and covered himself with a sheet up to his head. In the darkness, he kept thinking about Hina with his eyes open and soon fell asleep.

He woke up when the alarm clock kept near his head rang at 7.30 a.m. He was not sure if he had slept or was thinking about Hina with his eyes closed. When he could not come to any conclusion, he decided to simply smile and proceed towards the bathroom and started brushing his teeth.

For the next four or five days, his condition stayed the same, although he remained alert while in office. But there as well, when he visited the bathroom, he would sit and get lost in his thoughts and forget where he was, what he was doing and why he was sitting. In fact, once he started talking to himself while looking into the mirror and combing his hair at the office. Coincidentally, Mohammad Ali was standing right next to him. He immediately realized what Asrar was doing and whispered, 'Oye, Romeo, please spare the mirror! You can imagine her in any other place you like.'

Asrar immediately came back to his senses and fumbled, 'Uhmm . . . nothing, just like that . . .'

Mohammad Ali mimicked Asrar's tone, 'Nothing . . . nothing at all.'

From Thursday onwards, a little transformation could be seen in Asrar's condition. One could say that he was successful in controlling himself to an extent. He repeatedly reminded himself that he had to keep his emotions in check. Even after those attempts, when he lay down on the bed after a tiring Friday, Hina's memories came to his thoughts. He started thinking about their next meeting on Saturday. He decided to just look at Hina to his heart's content while she sat in front of him in McDonald's. He would try to look at the colours of her soul by peeping into her eyes. He would keep gazing at her nose, her forehead, her hair but would still be very conscious of the fact that she did not realize that he was looking at her. Such thoughts kept passing through his mind.

He woke up with the call for the morning prayer on Saturday. Everyone in the kholi was still fast asleep. He kept turning from side to side for a long time. Suleiman Vanu was regular with his morning prayers. The moment the azan ended, he got up, wore his kurta and went to offer namaz in a nearby mosque. Asrar got up and sat leaning against the wall. He felt a restlessness in his heart. There was fear in this restlessness. He had never given a thought to the fact that if their relationship did start off, how would it culminate? He did not even own a house in Mumbai and buying one was a Herculean task. Could he take her to the village? How would a girl from the city adjust to village life? These thoughts troubled him for a long time. To console his heart and escape this feeling of doubt, he told himself, 'Worry not! For those who do not have anything have the help of god. If he is benevolent enough to get me to her, He will also take care of everything else.'

Finally, he was able to put aside his fears. Suleiman returned after offering prayers. He was opening the windows when his gaze fell on Asrar leaning against the wall.

He asked Asrar, 'How did you get up so early? Are you fine? Is there some pain or trouble?'

'No, no. I wasn't feeling sleepy,' Asrar replied.

Mohammad Ali was sleeping right next to him; he opened his eyes and asked, 'What happened?'

'Nothing. I'm not feeling sleepy, that's it,' Asrar said.

'He has gone senile in love,' Mohammad Ali muttered while pulling the sheet over him.

After talking to Suleiman for some time, Asrar came out of the kholi. The sun was about to rise. The pigeons on the minarets of Minara Masjid were spreading their wings in the first rays of the sun. The roads were littered. Asrar thought that it might have rained for at least two or three hours the night before, making the litter float on the surface. A piece of newspaper caught his eyes. Even though it was soaked in the rain, one could still read what was written on it. Asrar bent to read it: 'Khwaja Yunus killed in police custody. The crops of hatred are ready to be harvested.' After reading the heading and the subheading, he wanted to read the entire report, but it was not possible. He walked ahead. A kitten lay dead at the opening of a drain. One of its eyes was out of its socket. The blood of its body had flowed away in the rainwater. The scene was awful. Although it was a very disturbing sight, Asrar still spared a glance at the dead kitten. Its skin was a light hue of yellow and it had a black mark near the neck.

There were garbage piles on both sides of the road. People were buying bread, bun, milk and rusk from the small shops nearby. The entrances of the shops were covered with dirt and the customers stood on top of the litter. There was an open drain of excreta flowing on one side of the road till wherever his eyes could see. A thought passed his mind that if the litter turned into a storm, it could destroy the entire city. If such a huge city was engulfed by garbage, the death of the people would be so icky and dire. In the excreta and dirt, the body would decompose and become part of the grime. This thought evoked a dangerous picture of the city in his mind, where the entire city had turned into a cemetery. A cemetery which was a humungous pile of garbage—humans, cats, dogs, rats, crows, pigs, hens rotting together in it. He could feel himself rotting in one grave. One of his eyes had been pulled out. Probably his dead body would be left floating in the water for many days, resulting in his chest and stomach getting bloated. After some time his stomach would possibly burst open and the muck, made of decomposed ladies' fingers, rice and moong dal, would flow out and mix with the soil and dirt. The eye which popped out would seem to be alive and looking at the other dead parts of his body. His heart would be dead, but a minuscule part of it would be still alive and connected to the eye. It was astonishing to imagine that his brain was dead but a part of his heart and the eye still living. Why?

The pigeons on the Minara Masjid were welcoming the morning sun. The sun's rays had not yet spread completely. His eye hanging outside the dead body was witnessing the expanding cemetery of garbage. Suddenly, there was no sun in the sky. The sea around had also vanished and in its place was empty space. His eye wanted to see the space closely. It seemed like a never-ending abyss, which ended at the end of the earth. He was amazed to see a blue sea in the heart of the earth. The expanse of this underground sea was far bigger than any on the earth's surface. On the shores of this sea, he saw many holes and burrows. In those lived a species of rat-like humans. The last of what his eye saw was these rat-like beings swallowing each other up. The one who swallowed the vomited blood after a while. Coincidentally, out of that blood, twelve more were born. Till where one could see there was blood and gore on the shore. This was how the rat-bodied human species was able to reproduce and increase its population. Before the black out and death of the eye, it told the last surviving cell of the heart, 'One day this species will also eat up the wall behind which are Gog and Magog.'

A pigeon came and sat among the ones sitting on the dome of the Minara Masjid.

What had happened was that Mumba Devi had told a monster that a human-like organism would appear from below the ground and would communicate with humans in their own language. And from then onwards, suddenly, the sun would rise from the west. Then the humans would bid farewell to earth and go and live on some other planet. Just like what had happened 80 million years ago when humans had left a dying planet to come and live on earth. At that time, earth was a heaven. The monster memorized what Mumba Devi had just said. After a while it transformed into a pigeon, flew and settled on the dome of the Minara mosque.

Asrar raised his eyes to look at the mosque. The pigeons were playing. The sun had risen. There were no clouds in the sky. The sun shone brightly. His eyes were dazzled. The imagination that had kept him captive vanished from his mind. He turned towards Dongri.

He returned to Minara Masjid after half an hour.

In the lane of the mosque, a barber sat with his small case outside a closed shop. Usually, Asrar would shave his beard on his own every three or four days, but today he had something else on his mind. He went to the barber for a shave and a trim.

When he returned to the kholi, his face shone, and his hair was well trimmed. Mohammad Ali was drinking tea. It was the first time that Asrar had got ready so early in the morning and had also trimmed his hair. Mohammad Ali offered him a cup of tea and said, 'You look good.'

He smiled and started drinking his tea.

While going to work, he told Mohammad Ali that he would be meeting Hina that evening.

Hina reached the mall fifteen minutes before time.

She wandered through the mall, looking at the glamourous shops selling clothes, home decor, electronics, etc. On seeing a shop with colourful bedsheets and curtains, she wished that her mother had come along. Then she could have bought a sky-blue bedsheet and pillow covers. She bought a big chocolate bar, kept it in her bag and proceeded towards McDonald's.

Asrar stood on the other end of the shop from which she had bought the chocolate. He had also bought something. He went to the washroom after returning from the shop. He washed his face, looked into the mirror and ran his fingers through his hair. There was no one in the washroom. He bent towards the mirror and spoke to his reflection, 'Let's go, dude! Don't waste time here needlessly!'

The reflection smiled at what Asrar had just said.

Hina was looking at the sprightly young people working at the counter while sitting alone in one corner of McDonald's. They were around the same age as her. Whenever anyone approached the counter to place an order, they would welcome them with a fake smile on their face. The moment the money was taken, another young worker would place the ordered food on a tray and give it to the customer with tissue papers, ketchup, soft drink and straws. The customer then carried that tray towards a table. Their eyes would never meet anyone else's but they were aware that many eyes were focused on them. People across the economic strata felt they belonged to the upper class in this environment. Those present thought they were privileged and superior. They were aware that many were deprived of this luxury of eating at a fast-food joint. A cartoon film was playing on a huge screen on one side at a very low volume. On the other side, pop music flooded the environment. A song from Paul McCartney's album *Flaming Pie* was being played in the backdrop. It was a song which Hina had heard many times. She listened to the first few lines of the song:

Some days I look,
I look at you with eyes that shine.
Some days I don't,
I don't believe that you are mine.

It's no good asking me what time of day it is,
Who won the match or scored the goal.
Some days I look,
Some days I look into your soul.

She was lost in the lines of the song. Music had its own magic. The song found a way into her emotions. When the song ended and she came out of her thoughts, she saw Asrar standing next to her table, smiling at her. For a minute she didn't even know what to say. She started smiling and stood up when Asrar said, 'Sit, sit . . .' He sat opposite her. It was the first time that he had come to McDonald's. He used to see people eating different kinds of food from the outside. He had also read about the different kinds of burgers in the advertisements, but he had never had one. He asked Hina, 'What do you eat?'

Hina looked at him and smiled. Asrar realized that he had asked the wrong question in a wrong tone. He immediately corrected himself, 'No, I mean what do you like eating at McDonald's.'

Hina was looking at him as usual. Asrar fumbled a little and made a mistake. He said, 'This is McDonald's. You do not get samosa and vada pav here. This place sells burgers!'

It became increasingly difficult for Hina to control her laughter. Her eyes were focused on Asrar. In fact, she was continuously looking into his eyes.

Asrar said, 'You'll have to eat something or the other. There's no need to be so formal.'

Hina bent towards him and said, 'I want to eat vada pav.' After saying this, she sat back to notice Asrar's expressions. Asrar looked at the people sitting around them and whispered, 'Everyone's eating a burger here; nevertheless, I'll still go and inquire at the counter.'

Hina smiled at his answer and said, 'There's no need to ask here, let us go out and eat.'

Asrar gave her proposal a thought and said, 'Okay!' In that way he could also hide his confusion.

Both exited the mall. There was a street stall nearby where people were having freshly made vada paav. Asrar bought four. They ate while walking down Peddar Road. On either side of the road were huge buildings and glittering shops. Cars rushed down the road. The ambience of the area was pleasant and clean. The crowd walking on the footpath seemed decent. Many college-going boys and girls were chatting and giggling in front of the shops. A boy kissed his lover in the middle of the road. Asrar kept looking at them while Hina turned away her gaze. When they had moved a few steps ahead, he said, 'People in Mumbai are so casual.' Hina knew the context of Asrar's remark, and so she replied, 'They're not casual, they're shameless.'

'Yes, absolutely shameless.' Asrar agreed.

'Why do people do this? I just don't understand.'

'They love each other. It happens when you are in love,' Asrar justified.

'Pathetic people!' Hina said after a silent pause.

'What's wrong with it?' Asrar asked.

'Isn't it pathetic to do all this in public?'

'Love is blind,' Asrar said.

Hina smiled at this philosophical rendering by Asrar. She wanted to enjoy the conversation further and so she asked, 'Why is love blind?'

He had said it out of the filmi wisdom he had acquired, but he had not anticipated such a question. He started thinking. He spoke what his mind had just explained to him, in his own words, 'It's the heart which is the decision-maker when you're in love, not your eyes. And that's why we call love blind.' Hina did not expect this answer. It was as much a surprise for Asrar. He could not understand if he had said something meaningful. Or was it just a fine attempt at answering her question? After this answer, Hina had no option left but to continue the conversation, so she asked, 'Why does the heart take decisions?'

'The heart is the home of the soul,' Asrar answered immediately. He was amazed to hear his own words. He wondered what had got

inside him that was giving such answers! At that very moment, he
was reminded of Bani's couplet that he had decided to recite for
Hina. He looked towards Hina and asked for permission, 'May I
recite a *sher*?'

Hina smiled.

Asrar began:

Ye bisat-e-arzu hai is ko yun assan na khel,
Mujhe se babasta hobat kuch daw par mera bhi hai.

(This is the chess of desire, do not play easy here,
  Not just me, but so much of mine is at stake here.)

Hina wrinkled her eyes and looked at him, 'You seem like a
fine poet.'

'No. I'm not. I know nothing at all. This is a couplet by an
Urdu poet.'

They turned and started walking towards Haji Ali.

Hina told him that she had once read a collection of Urdu
poets in Hindi when she was in class ten. Asrar coerced her into
reciting something if she remembered. Hina said that she could not
recollect anything. Asrar tried to persuade her. Hina was enjoying
this persuasion. She jogged her memory only to recollect a couplet
she had copied in her diary in roman script. She repeated the
couplet in her mind and then started reciting it to Asrar:

Na karda gunahon ki bhi hasrat ke mile daad.

(The desire of unfulfilled sins and crimes should be
  appreciated too.)

Asrar stopped to look at her. She tried recollecting the next
line and said:

Ya, rab, agar in kardo gunahon ki saza hai.

(If there is punishment, O Lord! for the sins that have been done.)

Asrar found Hina's Urdu accent clearer than his own. He also remembered that Jamila Miss had recited this couplet to him many times. When she had recited it for the first time, she had also explained its meaning. He told Hina that this sher was written by a very famous Urdu poet called Ghalib and he had heard it from his teacher before. Hina asked if she had recited it correctly? Asrar answered, 'Even Ghalib couldn't have recited it better than you.'

Hina laughed at this hyperbole and said, 'I didn't know you are an exaggerator too!'

'Honestly . . . ! I meant I enjoyed listening to this couplet in your voice.'

They reached the courtyard of Haji Ali Dargah while chatting. Hina covered her head with a dupatta and stood in the outer circle and started praying. Asrar stood in a corner and stared at her. It was as if her eyes were closed, her lips were chanting but her mind had transformed into an illuminated portrait gallery. In that gallery she could feel Asrar standing and looking at her with longing. All the hues of love were glowing in his eyes. Those colours were fashioned in a way that they evoked a natural attractiveness on Hina's face. While chanting her prayers, unexpectedly, the words that Asrar had spoken came to her lips, 'The heart is the home of the soul.'

She wanted to smile but controlled it because she was aware that Asrar's gaze was focused on her and she knew that the face was the foremost page of the heart. She wanted right then her face not to reflect the condition of her heart. In their conversations for the past hour, she had noticed that Asrar was a coward as well as gutsy, kind-hearted and aggressive too, disconnected from the world, yet sensitive towards it, a little eccentric and yet a little wise.

The portrait of Asrar that was sketched in her mind was very attractive. Her heart pulled her towards him. She finished her prayers and moved her hand ritualistically over her face. Asrar was still looking at her. As soon as Hina looked at him, he immediately did the same with his hands. She smiled in her heart on seeing him do that. They came out of the dargah. It was the time of sunset. The sun was touching the waves of the sea.

Both of them stood on the road to see the setting sun. Hina suddenly said that if he remembered more verses by the Urdu poet whose work he had recited earlier, she would love to listen to them. This seemed like an opportunity for Asrar. He had memorized Bani's poems over the past three days so that he could recite them to Hina someday. He did not expect that a day like that would come so soon. They sat on the sea wall and Asrar recited a poem:

Din ko daftar mein akela, shab bhar ghar mein akela.
Mein k eek aks-e-muntashir, ek ek manzar mein akela.
(Alone, throughout the day at the office, alone, throughout the night at home.
Alone, not just me, but also my scattered reflection in all the scenes around.)

He tried explaining the meaning of 'scattered reflection' to Hina. Hina had nearly grasped the same meaning that Asrar had just explained. Birds flew towards their right while the red light of the setting sun engulfed the sea. Asrar recited another couplet:

Ud chal o, ek juda khaka liye sar mein akela.
Subha ka pahla parinda asman bhar mein akela.

(It flew away with a new draft in its head.
The early morning bird, alone, in the entire sky.)

Asrar tried explaining those lines too, but Hina said that she knew
that much of Urdu and that the lines sketched a new morning. She
said that the sad scene of the evening could also be captured in a
sher. Hina's seriousness towards the ghazal gave Asrar more power.
He recited the third couplet. While reciting it, his tone was filled
with despair:

> *Us ko tanha kar gai karwat koe pichle pahar ki.*
> *Phir uda, bhaga o sara din, nagar bhar mein akela.*

> (A turning from the past saddened him.
> He then roved in the entire city, alone.)

When he had read this couplet for the first time, he could feel
as if it was an elegy for not just his stay in Mumbai but also for
others who lived with him in the kholi. He continued to
recite further:

> *Hubahu meri tarha chupchap, mujh ko dekhta hai.*
> *Ek larzta, khubsurat aks, saghar mein akela.*

> (Exactly like me, it silently stares back.
> A lonely reflection from the goblet.)

'Exactly like me.' After saying this, he paused for a moment to look
at Hina. Hina looked away at the last rays of the sun melting into
the ocean but her heart was still under the effect of his words—
'exactly like me . . . It silently stares back . . . silently'. Hina could
not stop herself from turning towards him. She could feel the
suppressed spark in Asrar's heart which if kept hidden for long
could turn into internal grief. Asrar tried smiling. Hina joined in
to make it a collective attempt. There was a faint smile on their
lips. Asrar completed the couplet with a smile on his face, 'Exactly
like me, it silently stares back.' Hina could feel the influence of
those lines on her heart at that time. He completed the couplet and

started looking at the sea. The last yellowish-red line of the sun had also vanished from the horizon.

The ghazal had seeped into her. Her heart had restlessly churned. For a moment she wished that Asrar would intertwine his fingers with hers, which would have been a significant consolation. Later, this thought made her laugh. Innumerable thoughts were rushing to her heart, but none of them was able to articulate itself well. Darkness had spread itself on the sea surface. The lights from the areas around tried to rush and scatter on the water. Soon, the wall on which Hina and Asrar sat became crowded. They sat silently in the midst of the crowd but within them there were rivers that were overflowing and flooding. Both looked relaxed as if they had discovered each other. Theirs was an adoration sewed together by love.

Asrar was impatiently thinking of ways to learn what there was in Hina's heart. He could not come up with anything. Finally, he gathered courage and asked, 'Do you know?'

Hina looked at him. She was always amazed and didn't understand why people in Mumbai always said, 'Do you know' before initiating a conversation. Whenever someone used this phrase she would answer, 'Yes, I know.' And the speaker would fumble. When Asrar asked, 'Do you know?' Hina said, 'Yes, I do.'

'I knew that you would know,' Asrar answered unexpectedly.

Hina expressed happiness through the flutter of her eyelashes. 'What do you know that I know?'

This was the only opportunity that Asrar had. 'I missed you the entire last week.'

Hina tried hiding her surprise and happiness that these words had brought with them. She did not want Asrar to know how meaningful these words were for her. She was craving very deep inside her that Asrar would utter something in which she would trace a map of love needed for the journey of love. She tried to give the impression that the words did not matter much to her. She said, 'All right . . . But how do you know that I knew this?'

Asrar answered with complete simplicity and without any inhibition, 'I'm sure you missed me too. Isn't it?'

It was not an answer to Hina's question, but it was an inquiry in itself. A question that Hina never expected to be asked so soon. She wondered how to answer it. She was perplexed. She wanted to reply honestly but was lacking in courage. Asrar immediately realized her situation and said, 'I knew you would know.'

'What?' Hina asked.

Many people sat or stood at short distances around them and were chatting. But their presence didn't concern them. They were sincerely a part of their own conversation that was bringing their hearts' restlessness face to face. This conversation was also a balm to their heart's agony. Asrar gave an answer to Hina's 'What?' by saying, 'I've been thinking about you every day, throughout the past week.'

Hina smiled. He smiled back. Hina realized that this simple-looking lad had the skill of manipulating what he wanted to say but at the same time, he was sensitive and knew the etiquette of talking. This quality of Asrar had managed to impress her. She had been in a good mood since the evening. One could see the bliss on her face. Before this evening, she did not know that a confession of what was in their heart could be made so easily, without much drama. As gentle as Asrar's entrance was into her life were the confessions of their love to each other. No filmi or traditional lines were spoken.

They talked for half an hour. Asrar bid farewell to Hina at 7.45 p.m. after seeing her off to the taxi.

Hina sat in the taxi, extended her hand out of the window and shook Asrar's hand. The intensity of love flamed in Hina's eyes and the same reflected in Asrar's eyes too. Both the hearts were drowned in love, and it was evident from the glow on their faces and the spark in their eyes. Both had gone through the same emotions in the past week. In that feeling the intensity of love was veiled. She turned and looked at Asrar from the taxi. Asrar waved his hand and said goodbye. The taxi moved forward but Asrar stayed there, as if he was a statue on the road. He was thirsty. He wanted that evening to be very long. He wanted time to crawl. But that did not happen. Today, time was in such a hurry as if it wanted to meet someone who was waiting for it. Despite the thirst that was still within him, that day was the most important day of his life. Today Hina was his. Hina's smile had confessed that she was going through the same feeling as he. Asrar could not understand where to go, what to do, whom to meet in these moments of extreme happiness. From whom to keep this secret safe in his heart and whom to reveal it to?

He kept thinking. He could not understand. He crossed the road and went over to a paan shop. He got himself a paan and after eating it, he went back to the same sea wall where he had sat with Hina a while back. The light from a distant boat cast a line on the waves of the sea. He looked at that line for a while. He kept wondering what he wished to think about. He did not want to think anything at all. There was no particular issue, no particular thought or specific thing that was in his mind. He was just happy. In that state of bliss everything else seized to matter. It was him and his heartbeats. He felt the vibrations in his heart. He could feel the rush of blood in his veins and the catalyst which was responsible for it.

He kept his right hand on his chest and thought, 'If I exist in my heartbeats, then today I write down Hina's name on them. Hina is my heart. She has created a storm in my heart.' He introspected for a while and said, 'Love is no less than a storm.'

He kept looking at the relatively noiseless waves of the sea. He had a childhood habit of conversing with the waves. The sea had disconnected from his life since the time he had come to Mumbai. He did not get enough leisure time to sit on the shores of the sea and converse with the waves. Today, his heart was brimming with the zeal of love. Amid the chaos of the city, the hustle and bustle, the garbage piles and dirt, Mumbai had finally placed on his palm a moment of eternal happiness. A moment that encapsulated the pleasures of a thousand years. In the last month of the tenth grade, nature had given him a chance to explore the intoxication of sexual pleasures and desires, but he had not experienced the self-forgetfulness and the passion of love.

Then it was sexual pleasure which had taken over his consciousness and his subconscious. Many a time, undoubtedly, sexual pleasure seemed a rather powerful emotion than that of love and it was so too. Love was a gentler emotion than sex, but in this gentleness there was the possibility of ferociousness. The simple emotion of love carried such sparks that it could turn the body, heart, mind and soul to ashes at one strike, especially if the sparks had the same intensity in both the hearts. These sparks could be seen in the eyes of Hina and Asrar at the same time and both had felt the intensity of the flames that day.

Probably Asrar still did not know that the entire story of love lay in a moment of love. Sometimes that moment of love covered years, sometimes months, days or just a few hours, but that moment was free from the passage of time and was a complete moment in itself. In fact, Asrar had entered the circle of forgetfulness of love that very moment when he had spread his umbrella over Hina at Haji Ali dargah's veranda without any hesitation. The circle was growing bigger. It was an enlarging shadow over the heads of Hina and Asrar, cutting the wings of fear and distance.

He kept looking at the silent waves of the sea. A few questions occurred to him. He asked the waves about love, body and nakedness. The sea replied to each of his questions. He told the sea about Jamila Miss and Shanti. He said that they were the safe havens of his sexual desires. They were worthy of his respect, but he did not love them. He told the sea that for the emotion of love you do not require the intensity of sex. The sea added to his knowledge by saying, 'And sexual desires are also not dependent upon love. Sex is as self-dependent as love is self-sufficient.'

He smiled and proceeded towards the bus stop with the smile still on his face. The taste of the paan was still fresh in his mouth.

When he reached the kholi, he found Mohammad Ali waiting for him impatiently.

In those days, dinner was cooked very late in the kholi. The boys whose turn it was to cook dinner reached the kholi around 9 p.m. from work, hence dinner was served after ten. Before Mohammad Ali could ask him questions, Asrar said, 'I'm really hungry right now, let's go out and have ragda patties or something.' Mohammad Ali proposed to have kebabs instead while changing his clothes. Saleem Ghare and Mukhtar Thakur asked them to get some kebabs and tilli packed for them. Asrar asked Saleem Ghare, 'If you want to eat anything else, do tell me. I'll get that too.'

'Why? Have you won a lottery,' Saleem asked.

'No. But there's a party. Will tell you when we return. Okay?' Mohammad Ali jumped in.

On hearing that there was a 'party', the other boys added the food that they wanted to the list. Mohammad Ali took out Rs 500 from his suitcase and slipped it in his pocket. Asrar and Mohammad Ali headed towards the JJ flyover and kept talking on the way. During the conversation, Asrar seemed to have forgotten the intensity of his hunger. On seeing a batata and ragda patty stall in one corner, Mohammad Ali reminded Asrar how hungry he was. They ate warm ragda and had a bowl of khichda. Asrar told Mohammad Ali that Hina had indicated that she too loved him. After hearing what Asrar had to say, Mohammad Ali said, 'If that girl did not have an interest in you, why would she meet you for the third time?'

'What do you mean?' Asrar asked.

'It means that if a girl in Mumbai is meeting you for the third time, it should be understood that she has something for you in her heart. Or else, who has so much time here?'

Asrar said nothing. He kept praising Hina. Mohammad Ali could feel the exaggeration in his tone, but he was aware that when in love, the lover praised the beloved with such elaborate adjectives. He did not think it right to interrupt Asrar. He was happy that finally there was a solution to Asrar's loneliness in Mumbai. In this way, he would be able to adjust well in the city and if things went well, he could even become a son-in-law of Mumbai. After listening to Asrar, Mohammad Ali advised him, 'Do not praise your "item" so much in front of others.'

'Why do you say so?' Asrar asked looking at Mohammad Ali, 'There's no one but you who is my secret-keeper.'

'It's quite simple,' Mohammad Ali started while keeping his hand on Asrar's shoulder. 'Do you believe in an evil eye or not? *Chutiya log ki nazar bohat kharab hai* [Idiots generally cast the evil eye]. I'm warning you in advance.'

Asrar did not respond.

Three Bohra girls, dressed in pleasant-coloured burqas, were having kebabs. Mohammad Ali whispered to Asrar, 'The Shia girl, with whom I have an affair, has asked me to meet her tomorrow.'

Asrar looked at the burqa-clad women and asked Mohammad Ali, 'Does your girl wear a burqa?'

'Yes,' Mohammad Ali replied, paused and then continued, 'She looks most sexy in a burqa.'

The kebab vendor overheard a part of what he was saying. He smiled. Asrar was also smiling.

After buying seekh kebab, shami kebab, tilli and kheri, they headed to the bakery. They ordered naan. Some unfortunate, distressed people were begging outside the bakery. Two or three of them were sitting and eating something. Near the footpath drain, a mouse lay covered in blood. The blood that had dripped out of its mouth had dried up. Probably a car had just run over it. Its stomach had burst open and the intestines had fallen out. There were flies all over it. While buying naan, Mohammad Ali told Asrar that Moosa Bhai was happy with him. 'He has increased your salary by two thousand.' The increment added to Asrar's excitement. He didn't know what to say. He uttered, 'Why did you hide this from me till now?'

Mohammad Ali took the bread from the shopkeeper and paid him. Then he turned towards Asrar and said, 'You did not give me a chance. I have been hearing about your Hina since . . .' A grin spread on his face before he could even finish the sentence. Asrar smiled too.

Mohammad Ali said that he was happy that the salary had been increased. That was why he was hosting a party for the boys in the kholi. 'It's difficult to find a friend like you,' Asrar said emotionally.

'Come on! Do not butter me,' Mohammad Ali said in a carefree tone.

They returned to the kholi. Asrar was aware that an increment of Rs 2000 had happened at Mohammad Ali's request, or else it would not have been possible. On hearing the good news, everyone shook hands with Asrar and congratulated him, then they immediately attacked the food. The party went on for quite some time.

When Hina reached home, she was surprised to see Yusuf sitting on the sofa and reading a newspaper. The happiness on her face that could be seen from the taxi to the door of the house. She wondered if Yusuf had seen her with Asrar at McDonald's or near the sea. If that were the case, what justification would she give? She entered the house, wished her father and sat next to him. Darakhshan was making tea in the kitchen. Yusuf asked, 'Where are you coming from?'

This question turned Hina's face pale. Before she could answer, Darakhshan entered with a tray in her hand. In one plate there was chuda, a dish made from flattened rice, and in the other, four pieces of barfi. On seeing Hina, she asked, 'When did you come?'

'I've just come.' Hina got up to take the tray from her mother's hand. She served Yusuf a cup of tea and went to the kitchen. She knew there was something wrong. She immediately prayed to Haji Ali and vowed that if no one got to know what happened, she would present a sheet of red roses to the dargah next Saturday. The prayer gave her a little courage. She poured some tea in another cup and came and sat next to Yusuf again. Darakhshan was sitting opposite to them. Yusuf was drinking tea silently. Innumerable reasons for his silence rushed through Hina's mind. On seeing him so quiet, Darakhshan asked, 'I hope your health is fine.' Yusuf said he was fine and turned towards Hina. On seeing him turn towards her, Hina repeated her prayers to Haji Ali in her heart and beseeched Haji Ali to help her.

'Bitiya, I'm going to America for a few months.'

This made her smile. The colour on her face returned. Yusuf thought that the news had made Hina glad. He said, 'I knew this would make you happy.'

Hina responded, 'Of course, I'm happy.'

'Won't the trip be a huge expense?' Darakhshan asked.

'It's a business trip,' Yusuf said.

Yusuf sat there for around 20–25 minutes. He primarily spoke to Hina during that time. When he was about to leave, he took out a packet for Darakhshan. Hina took it from his hands and gave it to her mother. Yusuf told them that there were Rs 40,000 in the packet. The amount would be more than enough for three or four months. While taking his leave he shook hands with Darakhshan at the door. Hina accompanied him till the main gate downstairs. Father and daughter stood and talked for around five minutes near the car. Yusuf told her that he would go to a few trade centres with Aymal to talk about expanding his business. Hina was happy. But there was a knot in her heart that made her wonder if there was something going on between Aymal and Yusuf. She, however, brushed it aside by calling it her own misconception. She bade farewell to her father warm-heartedly and requested him to call home from America every 10–15 days. Yusuf hugged her and promised that he would.

When the car had gone, Hina climbed the dark stairs to her house and while doing that she realized how big a coward she was. Her fear had made her promise votive offerings to Haji Ali. Then she told herself that everything went well because of her votive promise. She was unsure and restless for some time and finally decided that when her father returned from America, she would make him meet Asrar.

She talked to Darakhshan for a while after coming back and helped her chop vegetables. In her mind, fragments of Asrar's conversations and the ghazals that he had recited were doing the rounds. She decided that one day she would ask Asrar to write them down in the Devanagari script so that she could also memorize them. The mother and daughter had dinner and immediately after having food, Hina went to her room and lay down.

She relaxed for a while and then got up to change her clothes. She came back to her bed in her nightie. She wanted to replay and refresh the entire day that had passed in her mind. She wanted to recollect every moment, every word that Asrar had said. She knew that the rewinding of those romantic moments gave a lot of pleasure. The sequences would get mixed up and she would start all over again. She fell asleep in the process.

A dark blue smoke floated in front of her eyes. That was sleep. It made her descend. In fact, it pulled her into its depths. She dreamt she was floating in an unlit tunnel. In a minute she was falling and floating in that tunnel at an immense speed of lakhs of kilometres. When she opened her eyes, she found herself lying in a garden on soft grass. She immediately stood up. She was naked. Her nakedness did not cause her any hesitation or embarrassment. She had no reaction towards her body. She lifted her eyes to see trees of fruits and flowers till the extent of her sight. Pink and blue creepers were twined around their barks. She took a few steps. On one side there was a grapevine on which small birds seemed to enjoy hopping. The fruits on the pomegranate and fig trees seemed very inviting. She was not hungry. She moved forward. A herd of deer was parading nearby. A panda sat on the tree and was looking down. The tree was very tall. The sky was in its place, but it wasn't sunny. Probably it was that place where there was no night. She kept walking. Her hair swayed till her waist. She saw a river on the banks of which colourful pebbles shone brightly. Anyone could mistake them for precious stones and diamonds. No sooner had she taken a sip of water from the river than her thirst was quenched. She was not acquainted with that taste. She proceeded into the knee-deep water and sat in the river. The river floor was clean and small white stones shone on it. She thought it was possible that there were snow-topped mountains nearby. She looked all around only to see a long stretch of grasslands. There was no sign of mountains.

The water touched her as it flowed. She was elated.

The feeling of loneliness did not arise in her, though she wondered why there was no one around. She was still in thought when she saw Asrar coming towards her from the shade of the trees. Then she remembered that Asrar was her companion. It was a specialty of this place that one would remember the memories attached to anything only when it appeared in front of the eye, or else all the information of any association or relationship got pushed into oblivion. Asrar could also remember that Hina was his companion who had been away from his eyes for so many days only after seeing her. He came closer and sat next to her in the water. He told her that he had been searching for her for many days, but he didn't know what he was searching for. Now that he had seen her, he remembered that it was Hina that he was searching for. When they sat with each other, they remembered that they had been living together for many years.

This place was called the House of Souls.

Their souls were cast into bodies for the first time at this place. They were neither aware nor acquainted with the characteristics of the new mould given to them. And on the other hand, everything in the House of Souls was created to give them pleasure and make them happy. This was done so that the feeling that was in the heart of their creator should not affect them. To get rid of that feeling, the creator had created them. Within their bodies, they had become a song of their own life and were unknowing subordinates of evolution. The things inside their bodies were also trying to get used to their own forms and functions gradually. And seeing them so involved in figuring out things, the creator was enjoying itself.

It was the day when the key rival of the creator decided to sabotage the experiment of creation. The rival did not want the creator to achieve success in the feeling he was trying to create. Hence, he took the help of his loyal subjects to find the blueprint of the creator's strategy. He studied it for thousands of years and one day he invited the left hand of the creator, Jabaraan Zumani Khaliq. During the sleazy conversation, he was able to make Khaliq drink from a goblet where he had mixed the sap from his eyes. Khaliq lost all his senses for some time. While he was unconscious, the rival transformed him into a very beautiful green snake and sent him on a special mission. To reach the river where Hina and Asrar were sitting was a part of the mission and he had been on it for many hundred years. A few hundred years were nothing more than a moment for Zumani Khaliq.

He saw Hina and Asrar talking from behind the white flowers.

He smiled for a while on seeing them.

When he realized that Hina and Asrar were going to come out of the river, he started floating on the water's surface and reached them. They looked at him in amazement. They praised his beauty. Zumani Khaliq told them that they had been forgetting each other again and again and he had been noticing this for thousands of years. So, he wanted this never repeated and them to stay together always and not forget each other even for a moment. On hearing his convoluted talk, Hina asked, 'How is it even possible?' He said, 'It's easy but the knowledge of it lies with the creator.' Since he was Jabaraan Zumani Khaliq, the creator had shared the secret with him. Asrar said that if he was able to tell them how to save themselves from this forgetfulness, they would always remain grateful to him. The transformed form of Zumani Khaliq said, 'But there's a condition.'

'What is it,' Hina asked immediately.

'It's very easy. If the creator inquires about this, you will not remember my name.'

Hina and Asrar thought over this for a while. Then they said in unison, 'We agree.'

Zumani Khaliq told them that they should lie down on the grass next to the river with their eyes closed. A tree would bend its branch towards them. There would be a fruit on that branch which they should taste a little. And when they would open their eyes after eating a bite from that fruit, 'The House of Souls' would be a new world altogether.

Zumani left.

Hina and Asrar followed his advice. When they opened their eyes, there was a change in the form of their bodies because they had tasted the fruit.

Hina and Asrar, drowned in bliss, kept looking at each other for years. The passion of intermingling had acquainted them with a unique intoxication. They touched each other's body and then intensely kissed with their lips. The body of the other was very dear to them. In fact, since the time they had been acquainted with the wisdom of this body, nothing else in the 'House of Souls' seemed to impress them any more. They spoke about each other's body and that gave permanence to their memory.

The House of Souls was witness to Hina and Asrar making love an act in which for the first time their bodies were participating. The bodies were the source of their song of love. The entire creation and the objects were all dancing in this song while the creator seemed to be distressed at the failure of his experiment.

Hina felt Asrar taking in her body. The feeling led to the birth of shyness.

When love reached its limits and tasted the juices of completion, the magic in which they were captive, broke. They looked at that branch and started weeping. The branch was of the same tree whose fruits were forbidden by the creator.

There was darkness for a while.

Hina felt *huzn* (sadness) for the first time. She was crying in her dream. Sleep had overtaken her mind. Her soul was coming back to her body from the dark tunnel. She was putting pressure on her mind so that her sleep would break and she would be able to see the world around her.

When she opened her eyes to the dim lights, there were tears at the edges of her lashes.

She switched on the tube light and looked at her body in that light. She kept looking at herself for a long time. She touched herself and tried remembering the dream she had just seen, but in vain. The dream had drifted into oblivion. She could only recollect a few things. But she remembered that there was a brief moment of intercourse in that dream whose intensity and heat could still be felt in her body. She touched the delicate parts of her body and felt the juices in which was laden the passion called love.

Next day in college, she filled Vidhi up with all the details of her meeting with Asrar, and also about the dream that she had seen but did not remember any more. She said, she remembered the taste of lovemaking that she had indulged in during that dream. Vidhi understood her condition and encouraged her by making her understand that the body had its own needs which it expressed in various forms. They bunked college that day and sat at Chowpatty, discussing this topic and other similar ones.

8

I Do Not Want the Winds Over
My Head to Be My Guide
(*Na Sar Pe Rah Dikhati Hui Hawa Chahun*)

The sea that had its arms around Mumbai was ferocious. It desired to win the centuries-old battle, gulp the island and be victorious, finally. Tall waves rose and fell, rose again and banged their heads against the shore. It had been raining for the past three days, so much so that the dark alleys, narrow lanes, the wide roads and the crumbling streets of the city were all submerged in knee-deep water. Black clouds veiled the sky. The city no longer remembered how the rays of the sun felt and looked. The sky was leaking through huge holes in its being, as if the sky had transformed into a never-ending waterfall. The water of the sea had found a comfortable entry into the drains running below the ground. The drains were a battleground for the unstoppable rainwater and the roaring sea, in a continuous struggle to make space for themselves. This war had caused great damage to the concrete sides of the newly constructed drains. The streams of water merged together and made way into the deepest layers of the soil.

The localities around the inundated drains were submerged and the residential population was struggling with the flooding. The Mithi River overflowed and the areas around it lay submerged in deep water. There were power cuts in most areas. The condition of low-lying areas in the city reflected the wrath of rain and the destruction that it had caused. All communication between the city administration, government and the public had snapped.

In the last ten months they had met seventeen times. Initial meetings happened at crowded places like Haji Ali dargah, Worli Sea Face, Chowpatty, Marine Drive, Churchgate, Hanging Gardens, Colaba and the Gateway of India. One February evening, it was the first time that they went to the beach near Dadar station where there wasn't much crowd. The shore had shrunk and the ground seemed to bend towards the sea. Getting into the water in this area was equal to putting their life at stake. There were vendors who sold bhel, ragda patties and coconut water, but there was no suitable space to sit. Both did not like the area. They got up and walked towards the road. Seeing a crowd gathered at Chaitya Bhoomi, they proceeded towards it. Hina had told Asrar about the Mahaparinirvan Day, when a huge crowd of Dr B.R. Ambedkar's followers gather annually on 6 December. Asrar was glad to gain some information about the Chaitya Bhoomi.

After reaching there, they sat in a restaurant and drank tea. A middle-aged man was sitting and having tea at the other end of the restaurant. Asrar observed that a few couples came and inquired about something at the counter and then headed towards an area adjoining the restaurant. Asrar thought there was exclusive space for couples beyond the wooden partition. There was a Malabari man at the counter. Asrar spoke to him. The Malabari man told him that they served tea in the cabin on the other side. Asrar ordered tea to be sent into one of the cabins for them. The Malabari man said, 'The charge is Rs 150 per hour.' Asrar agreed to pay this. He asked Hina to join him for tea in the cabin. They got up. The Malabari man called a waiter who showed them the way.

It was slightly dark and in the dim light, Asrar saw that there were ten or twelve cabins. There were blinds put on them. The waiter rolled up one of the blinds and showed them in. The waiter said that he would get them tea soon. It was darker inside the cabin. Hina said, 'It was better outside.'

'Do not say a thing. Stay quiet.' Asrar put his finger on her lips.

There was very little space to stand in the cabin. A small divan was kept in the corner for sitting. There was a rack opposite the divan. Asrar had gestured to Hina to stay quiet, but she still spoke, 'There's no place to sit here.'

'You sit down,' Asrar insisted. She had not even seated herself when someone knocked. It was the waiter. Asrar took the cups from him and kept them on the rack. After that he latched the blinds. Hina was looking at him. She was a bit confused. Asrar bent down and whispered in her ears, 'I love you, Hina.'

Hina smiled.

He had repeated this sentence in the last few meetings. Hina was impressed by the romantic delivery of the line. She always reacted with a smile. Her answer was in her smile. In the dim light of the cabin she said, 'I love you too.' The vibrations of her words penetrated Asrar's heart. He kept gaping at her for two minutes, and then gathered courage to put his palms on her cheeks. In the dim light, they peered into each other's eyes. They could feel the infinite love in their eyes. They kept looking at each other for a while. Looking at each other was bliss, the greatest bliss of the world at that moment. They were lost in the moment when God knows from where Jamila Miss and Shanti entered Asrar's thoughts. Jamila Miss was angry. The brimming love for Hina in Asrar's eyes seemed to anger her. Maybe her heart was wounded. In his mind Asrar saw Jamila Miss drowning in a tunnel-like pit. The pit was full of dense blood and the blood belonged to no one but Jamila Miss herself. A spring of red blood was emerging from her chest. While drowning, she looked at Asrar and cried, 'I loved you. I thought you were mine.' Shanti stood at a little distance from the pit. She was holding a plate which fell on the ground. Vermilion and haldi kumkum were scattered on the floor.

Shanti lifted her eyes and looked at Asrar. 'You're fortunate to have found love. Ah! What is there for the likes of us?'

Jamila Miss and Shanti came before his eyes and vanished like a film sequence. Now, his eyes could only see Hina. He felt the magic of her bright eyes. Hina felt the same. There was a sense of self-forgetfulness in which she was lost as she looked at Asrar. The hidden emotions of the heart reflected in her eyes. The two couldn't see anything in the cabin but each other, though there were things strewn on the floor. Possibly, six or seven couples had spent time in this cabin since morning. Amid the confusion of the small space, darkness and the intensity of passion, people usually left behind their belongings in such cabins. A pink handkerchief lay next to Hina's feet. A used red lipstick was kept inside that handkerchief. An unused packet of Kamasutra condoms was behind the dustbin. A small cockroach was snoozing on that packet. A comb, which seemed to have been used for years, was near Asrar's feet. The teeth of the comb were broken at many places and between them layers of dirt had accumulated. A blouse hook lay in one corner. A few rose petals were strewn around. In the other corner, a bead from a rosary lay on the floor.

'Ouch . . .'

There was a plywood partition between the cabins. Hina's back was leaning against the plywood. The moment she heard the sound of 'ouch', the plywood started shaking—*khad khad khadak*! She was scared. She had not yet gathered what was happening when someone from the adjoining cabin said in an apologetic tone, 'Sorry.'

Asrar smiled. He had guessed what was happening in the adjoining cabin. The 'ouch' had been uttered by an adolescent girl. It was clear that the sound of 'ouch' had escaped the girl's lips in the middle of her ecstasy, although it was the boy who had said 'sorry'. Even after the apology, the plywood kept shaking. Hina could clearly hear the 'ah, ahs', the 'O my gods' and the moans of the girl. The girl uttered some words which made Hina laugh: '*Tu jitna chhota hai, utnach tere hathyar bada hai* [You're small, but your weapon is big].'

Hina guessed that sex workers might also be bringing customers to these cabins. She was still thinking when Asrar bent and kissed her lips softly. He was scared that Hina might get angry at this. She felt the light touch of his lips on hers but because she wasn't present there mentally, she did not understand what happened. She stayed silent. Her silence added to Asrar's confidence. He held Hina's hand and pulled her towards him. They stood opposite each other. They had never been so close before. Both wondered—what was the novelty in the attraction between a man and a woman? Where and why was this strength born which pulled two people towards each other with the same force? Both had never paid attention to this, but they were captive to the same feeling at that moment.

Their bodies moved towards each other. They put their arms around each other and kissed passionately for a long time. This was Hina's first kiss while it was Asrar's longest kiss, as well as the longest kiss that the darkness of that cabin had ever witnessed. This was because usually this cabin saw less visitors who were love-struck than those who were mostly interested in sex. It was a very special characteristic of Mumbai that there were affordable meeting places for all kinds of lovers. The cabins were the cheapest in temporary lodges where, even though the space was constricted, lovers as well as those driven by sex could fulfil their desires. It was just a coincidence that Hina and Asrar happened to be there. They were not even aware that such cabins existed in the city.

The gravitational pull of each other had reddened their tongues and the colour had rushed to their faces. As soon as Asrar removed his hands from Hina's shoulder, she sat on the table again. She sat silently with her head hanging down. She felt embarrassed. In the middle of her boldness and kissing she was amazed at her involvement in the act. Many would say it is this astonishment that transforms one day into the astonishment of love. Her mind was like an empty room at that time and Asrar was the lone, illuminated lamp in it. Hina desired to see all the colours of her life within the circle of that lamp's light. There was nothing meaningful for her outside that circle and she had control over everything that was within it. She had chosen this control for her own self. Asrar also stayed silent for a minute or two. He had guessed it right that Hina would be amazed at her own courage. He was happy. After a while he said, 'Aye . . . are you blushing?'

Hina said absolutely nothing.

'Aye . . . speak up,' Asrar insisted.

She lifted her eyes up.

'*Solid lag rahi hai, meri jaan* [Looking solid, my dear]!'

She smiled. She held Asrar's hand and put her head in his palms. Asrar was silent.

After a while, he felt his palms getting moist. He got up. He straightened Hina up. Hina had tears in her eyes. He took out his handkerchief from his pocket immediately and wiped her tears. He was not able to understand what was happening. He wondered if she was crying because of their kiss. A few drops slipped from Hina's eyes again. Asrar wiped those tears with his handkerchief and said, 'I'm really sorry.' Hina looked at him. She smiled. Asrar had never seen anyone cry and smile at the same time. That situation dragged him into a wavering in his mind. He could not understand the situation. He was getting confused when Hina said, 'I love you, darling.'

That one line changed the entire situation. Asrar also sat on the table. Hina rested her head on Asrar's chest and closed her eyes and moved her fingers over his face. Asrar sat silently, although there was a lot of sound in that silence, which echoed in his soul. There were only three or four minutes left for the hour to be over when the waiter knocked at the cabin and asked, 'Do you require more time?'

Asrar replied, 'No.'

They reached the Dadar railway station on foot.

The coach of the local train that they had boarded was not crowded. They stood near the door and chatted throughout the journey. After seven or eight minutes, the train reached Mumbai Central. They got off the train. Asrar hired a taxi for Hina at the Mumbai Central bridge, and he proceeded towards the bus stop. He stood there and waited for the bus that would take him to Mohammad Ali Road. The bus came after half an hour. He reached the kholi at 8.15 p.m.

They went to Juhu Chowpatty in the last week of February. The beach at Juhu was quite large and spread over a wide area. It was considered the most pleasant beach in Mumbai. All kinds of people went there for recreation, fun or to simply take a stroll. There were many stalls and makeshift shops for snacks, juices and sherbets that remained opened till late in the night. Asrar and Hina reached that place at around 5.15 p.m. As they ventured to one end of the beach the crowd got thinner. The point where the beach ended, the walls began. Across those walls were four- and five-star hotels, high-rise buildings and old bungalows. They kept walking for half an hour while talking. Asrar saw that couples sat with hands around each other at short intervals on those walls. Although he had visited this beach with his friends from the kholi a year back, he had not seen

this part. He suggested that they should sit in the shade of one of
the walls and talk.

They found a place for themselves. It was not too hot. The
wind coming from the direction of the sea brought with it some
relief. Asrar told her that he would be going to his village in March
and then he would tell his mother about her.

'What will you tell your mother?' Hina asked immediately.

'I'll tell my mother that a girl has done black magic on me in
Mumbai,' Asrar replied.

'Black magic?' Hina repeated the words and laughed.

'Yes. Black magic.' He spared Hina a gaze and looked at the sea.
'The spell of the black magic of Bengal which cannot be broken.'

Hina heard him and then said, 'Will you tell the truth?'

'Sure?' Asrar said.

'Have you done black magic on me?' Hina looked meaningfully
at Asrar. He could see the mischief in her eyes. He said, 'I had to do
it, or else you would have never looked at me.'

Hina smiled at his answer.

They chatted for the next fifteen minutes.

During this time, the number of couples around them increased.

The twilight spread in the sky. The rays crawled on the water.
The sea was sparkling. Some couples were lost in each other's arms.
There were some who were kissing and sharing the sweetness of
their love. They were caressing the foreheads and cheeks of their
beloved. There were two or three burqa-clad girls too. One of
them covered her face and that of her lover's with her veil so
that no one could see them kissing. At a distance, a maulana was
kissing his girlfriend but had hidden his skull cap inside his pocket.
Either he was very smart or very scared. He sat hidden behind
a coconut palm while the woman had her back towards the sea.
It was quite possible that the couple might have come from the
Juhu Galli area which was near the beach and had a substantial
Muslim population. It was also possible that the maulana was
involved with a married woman of that area. This was common in

Mumbai. Women of the city did not believe in suppressing their emotional or sexual desires.

Hina and Asrar were having a conversation while the number of love birds around them increased. The sun had spread itself on the surface of the sea. There seemed to be colours splashed on the waters. The darkness descended from the wall and moved towards the couples and then proceeded to engulf the sea. Asrar turned his neck in that darkness and saw that a girl was sleeping in the lap of her lover. At that moment, coincidentally, Pashupati came to his mind. With the memory of Pashupati, the story of that night became refreshed in his mind. That night was one of the most memorable nights of his life. He smiled. He folded his legs and took Hina into his arms. He touched her lips.

'Recite a sher, please, of the same poet whose sher you had recited earlier . . .' Hina requested lovingly.

Asrar wanted to say something, but he could not avoid the request which was made in such a loving tone. He had read Bani's work a thousand times over. Bani's best ghazals were embedded in his mind. He exerted his brain a little and recited two couplets:

Mein kyun na dubte manzar ke sath doub hi jaun,
Ye sham aur samandar udaas pani ka.
Mein dar raha hun hawa mein kahin bikhar hi jaye
Ye phool phool sa lamha teri nishani ka.

(Should I drown with the drowning landscape,
This evening and the seas filled with sorrowful waters?
I am afraid that in the wind will be scattered
The flower-like moments that carry your signs.)

Hina's eyes were focused on Asrar's face. Asrar's were looking at the rays of the sun, which the waves desired to reach. They were rushing towards them so as to touch them. The entire sea changed to yellow and dark red. The sun vanished from the sight within a minute. Asrar looked at Hina and said, 'The sun has finally set after giving us all these beautiful scenes.'

Hina found what Asrar had said very creative. She put her hands around Asrar's neck and pulled him towards her. 'The flower-like moments that carry your signs,' she said and smiled. Asrar smiled back. Hina said, 'Let this moment be a memorable one,' and then she placed her lips on Asrar's. The darkness that crawled on the evening sea was getting deeper while Hina and Asrar were present like illuminated dots in the dark depths of each other's soul.

Asrar went to his village on 15 March.

During his stay, he visited Jamila Miss at least three or four times. He stayed over one night.

Miss had borrowed a porn CD from a friend. She had already seen it thrice, but she had decided to enjoy it while lying in Asrar's lap. Her emotions had awakened when she had seen it for the first time. She had whispered Asrar's name. The echo of Asrar's name had spread through her body, stretching her nerves. Her heart had stopped beating for a moment. It was almost still.

The night Asrar stayed over, they conversed for a long time. They had dinner at 11 p.m. An hour later, Miss shut all the windows and switched on the dim lights. In the dim light, she looked at Asrar with eyes full of longing. Asrar could feel the desire in the natural spark of

Miss's eyes. She plugged the cable of the DVD player into the TV port. Asrar thought that Miss was going to play a romantic movie. He rested his neck on the pillow and started looking at the television. He saw nude bodies on the screen. He was astonished. Miss looked at him again and before lying on the bed, she switched off the dim lights too. Even before Asrar could utter a word, Miss lay down next to him. Asrar had heard about such films from Mohammad Ali, but he was watching one for the first time.

The blue and red light from the TV screen incited flames in Asrar's doused heart. Jamila Miss's heightened responses added to Asrar's amazement. Miss turned into the nude, attractive and hot protagonist from the movie. She had made Asrar bleed. The next morning, Asrar saw that his neck, forehead, fingers, stomach and other parts of the body were covered in Jamila Miss's bite marks. Despite this ferociousness and the complete involvement of his body, his soul was still coloured in Hina's hues. He remembered that the night before when Miss had undergone that transformation, he had felt that he was not with Jamila Miss but with Hina.

It was summer. He used to go and sit on the beach in Mabadmorpho every evening lost in thought. He often found himself in a dark room where he would see his uncle smiling. In the same room he saw a woman, but his heart refused to recognize her. He felt as if there was even more darkness outside the room and his father was standing there and crying. Whenever he was in a thoughtful mood, he would get up and walk towards the sea and talk to the waves. The cold water awakened a new zest within him. He would look at the waves coming from afar and would wonder where they had started their journey, why they had undertaken the journey and when it had started. He tried getting rid of these thoughts that were bothering him.

He returned to Mumbai on 1 April.

The next day he met Hina at a restaurant near the Nagpada junction. Asrar placed a bag in her hand which his mother had given as a gift. They talked for a while and decided that they would meet on Sunday, sharp at 11 a.m. at the Mumbai Central ticket counter. From there they would go and visit a place that they had never been to.

Hina went home. She opened the bag to find that Asrar's mother had sent her home-made pickle, papads and a dozen hapus mangoes.

Darakhshan asked her, 'What is it that you have brought?'

Hina said, 'Vidhi's father had come to meet her. Vidhi has given me some things from what he had brought for her.'

Darakhshan was satisfied with the answer but whenever she ate that pickle, she would say, 'It tastes like Konkani pickle.'

Once Hina finally asked her, 'Maa, how do you know what the taste of Konkani pickle is like?'

Darakhshan told her that before her marriage, she lived in a Kolsa mohalla. A lot of Konkanis lived in that area. Whenever they visited Konkan, they would bring pickles and papad for their neighbours. Darakhshan said that she ate a lot of Konkani pickle, and her mother would scold her for overeating. Hina laughed at this and said, 'True, Konkani pickle is definitely very tasty.'

'When did you eat it?' Darakhshan inquired.

'You just said that this pickle tastes like Konkani, so I guessed it might be good.' Hina made it up.

'All right, sweep the house a little.'

She was going to get the broom from the kitchen when the phone rang. Hina thought it was her elder sister's call. She picked up the receiver and said in a loud voice, 'Speak up.'

'Salamwalekum.' It was Yusuf at the other end.

They talked for five or six minutes, and Yusuf informed her that he would stay in America for three more months. Yusuf gave her a number and said that in case there was an emergency, they could contact him on that number. After keeping the phone down, Hina told her mother that Yusuf would be in America for three more months because of business. In case she needed more money, they could call his shop. Darakhshan did not give any answer. She sat silently on the sofa. Hina missed Vidhi. Vidhi had bought a new mobile a few days back. She wondered how easy it would be if Asrar started using a mobile phone; it would become easier for them to stay in touch. She immediately thought of a plan and soon put it into execution.

They reached the National Park at 12.30 p.m. on Sunday. The population of wild animals had decreased in the National Park, but people regularly spotted poisonous snakes in that area. Some even claimed to have seen a cheetah and a bear. Those who reported these sightings were usually regular visitors to bars in and around the Borivali area. They used to get drunk and wander near the National Park. People heard their claims attentively, but once they were gone they would say, 'Does this man take us to be fools? Who will believe such drunkards?' Once a twenty-foot-long python had come out of the forest. There was a large poster of a famous and influential politician fixed to a pole near the gate of the park. The snake slept on it till the sun reached its meridian. When the pole started heating up, the snake came down. Before descending, it licked the politician's face with its tongue. Thankfully no one captured the scene on camera or else the media would have created a sensation. It was the portrait of the same politician who died of mouth cancer a few months later.

Asrar and Hina walked for 20–25 minutes.

They reached that area of the park which was not visited by many people. Couples sat and chatted away under the trees next to the road. Those whose love was fresh had hidden themselves in the bushes and others were behind the trees, away from the road.

A narrow path from the road led into the dense forests. They proceeded on that path. A few steps ahead, there was a dried-up rain duct. They crossed it and reached a slope. It seemed like a safe spot. There was no chance of anyone coming there. They sat on a rock. The branches of the trees around touched them. Hina told him that her annual examinations would be starting soon. She would remain busy with her studies for about a fortnight. Asrar advised her to study sincerely. They would meet after her exams and would again visit a place they had never been.

The sun shone brightly but there was enough shade over their heads. There was greenery all around and a reflection of it could be seen on Hina's face. Asrar held her hands and said, 'The thought of staying away from you for such a long time makes me feel bad.'

'Don't think too much, you won't feel bad.' Hina smiled.

'Who has control over his thoughts?' Asrar said.

'The control does not work in the jungle,' Hina said as she laughed.

She was trying to lift Asrar's mood.

They kept talking and it relaxed them.

They came out of the National Park at around 3 p.m. They proceeded towards the Borivali station and then boarded a train to Bandra. They took a rickshaw from the Bandra station for the Bandstand. In the long list of Mumbai's beaches, the Bandstand was a popular one. Around this beach were bungalows of film celebrities. Rough, black rocks were spread across the beach. The rocks were of various shapes and sizes and many couples sat in their shade, expressing their love without saying a word. Vidhi had once explained to Hina that the tongue is an essential instrument to communicate what the heart feels. She had said that it was foolish to use the tongue only for eating food. The openness with which Vidhi had shared her sexual encounters and her love stories had initially scared Hina, but they now seemed to give her courage and made her comfortable about those things as well as removed her fears and doubts.

Asrar and Hina looked at each other after seeing the sights at the Bandstand. They smiled. There were a thousand things in that smile, and both were aware of it. Asrar held Hina's hand. They crossed the rocks and proceeded towards the sea. While crossing the rocks, they

saw many couples kissing each other in the shadow of the rocks.
They moved ahead. An adolescent couple was making out near a
rock. The whole scene was so 'unclothed' that Hina was astonished.
She looked at Asrar. Asrar pressed her hand and gestured to her to
remain quiet. They walked for a while and then sat on a rock. They
turned and saw a huge skyscraper staring at the sea with pride. It
was as if the other buildings around were a part of a background to
that scene. The sunrays were playing hide and seek with the glass
on those buildings.

They sat there till sunset. They repeatedly expressed remorse
and grief on the fact that they would not be able to meet for a
long time. Their passion led them to kiss, touch each other's lips
with their fingers and feel the warmth of love in the eyes. When
they got up, many other couples were also getting up and walking
towards the road. Their faces shone with the colours of bliss that
had been evoked by meeting the beloved. Hina noticed that the
same couple who had astonished her a while back was walking in
front of them. That girl who had removed one side of her salwar
to have sex under the open sky. She was now walking in a burqa.
Hina had recognized the couple because of the boy's shirt. Hina's
shock knew no bounds. She did not know what to make of it.
She stayed silent.

They came to the road from the beach and wandered for a
while. They were looking at the Bandra–Worli flyover that was
under construction over the sea. Hina said that when this bridge
would finally be ready, it would become easy to drive from Bandra
to the main city. Asrar said, 'Ready for difficult journeys with you.'

Hina immediately said, 'Does this line also belong to your
favourite poet Nani?'

Asrar smiled and said, 'No. This is my own line. Moreover, my
favourite poet's name is Bani not Nani.'

They laughed together.

They reached the Mumbai Central station at 7.45 p.m. Before
boarding the taxi, Hina took out a small box from her bag and gave
it to Asrar. 'This is for you.'

Before Asrar could say anything, Hina could feel his surprise. 'Open it only after you have reached home,' she instructed.

Asrar thanked her.

'Thank you,' Hina mimicked him.

He smiled.

After saying goodbye to Hina, he walked to the Mumbai Central state transport depot.

Suddenly something came to his mind. He bought half kilogram of aflatoon from a nearby sweet shop and went straight to Shanti. She was with a customer at that time. Asrar told Madhuri that he would return in half an hour. He went towards Bachchu Ki Wadi. He ate kebab from a stall. Once Mohammad Ali had taken him there for kebabs. The taste of the kebab still lingered in his mouth when he desired to have tea. There was a restaurant at the head of the road. He went there. Flies thronged the place. A plastic jug was kept at a table. Two beggars were drinking tea and sitting opposite each other at a table. One of them had a dirty, green cloth on his shoulder. Asrar had seen such beggars in his village who put a green cloth on their shoulders and begged in the name of Allah and the Prophet every Thursday. Hence, that was nothing new. While drinking tea, he started eavesdropping on what the beggars were saying. They were talking in the distinct Mumbai dialect. From their conversation he guessed that they found fault in most things and were very disappointed with the administration of the country. They looked aggrieved. They were also talking about the destruction of the world. The one with the green cloth on his shoulder claimed in a loud voice, 'The Ghazwa-e-Hind (Battle against India) was predicted by the Prophet. That day is not very far.' The beggar who sat opposite him did not express any opinion on what was said. Probably he had already heard this innumerable times. He waved away the fly sitting on his cup and then started talking about some diseases. The other beggar wiped his face with the green cloth and claimed, 'The cure for all illnesses is in the Quran. Do not send your wives to English doctors. It is haram.'

Asrar was amazed at the seriousness of the conversation the beggars were having.

The beggars chatted for some time and then suddenly left without paying the bill.

When Asrar went to pay his bill, he asked the boy at the counter, 'You allow beggars to sit here too?'

The boy replied, 'No. Not at all, who said so?'

Asrar pointed at the table and said, 'They were sitting right here . . .'

'Abhe! They were not beggars. One of them heads the prayers at the mosque nearby and the other was the *baangi*.'

He came out of the restaurant scratching his head.

He proceeded towards Shanti's building. Shanti stood at the door. They shook hands and talked for a few minutes. He told her that he had come to inquire about her well-being. Shanti was pleased. She insisted they have a cup of tea and Asrar agreed. Asrar gave the packet of sweets to her. Shanti asked, 'Why? Are you getting married?'

Asrar softly tapped her forehead and said, 'My salary has increased again. I'll invite you when I get married.'

Shanti laughed.

When he was leaving, Madhuri said, 'Ask your friend if he still remembers me. He hasn't come around for a long time.'

Asrar nodded and turned towards the stairs.

On reaching the kholi, he freshened up and rested for a while. Mohammad Ali had gone out with Qasim Dalvi. Saleem Ghare and Mukhtar Thakur had gone to the cinema. Suleiman Vanu had gone to visit a relative. There were two boys in the kholi with whom Asrar only had formal interactions. One of them was listening to film songs over the radio, while the other was reading

a book. Asrar had not opened the box that Hina had given him
yet. He thought that it could be an attar bottle as Hina's father
was a perfumer. He kept the box aside and thought that he would
open it when Mohammad Ali returned. If it was a perfume bottle,
he would give it to Mohammad Ali. Asrar took out a box from
his attaché case and started eating chiwda. A song from the film
Bazaar played on the radio:

> *Dikhai diye yun ke bekhud kiya,*
> *Hame aap se bhi juda kar chale.*
> *Jabin sajda karte hi karte gai,*
> *Haq-e-bandagi ham ada kar chale.*

> I lost myself seeing you,
> You took away everything, including myself.
> I kept praying continuously,
> Paid off the debt of devotion.

He only listened to the first two couplets, after which he was lost
in another world. The picture of Hina drenched at Haji Ali came
back to him. The song ended and at the same time Mohammad Ali
and Qasim Dalvi returned. They talked about work for a while.
Asrar seemed lost. Probably, he was still under the spell of the song.
Mohammad Ali saw the box kept next to Asrar. He guessed Hina
had given Asrar a gift. He asked, 'Abhe, what's in the box?'

'You open and see,' Asrar said.

That was enough for Mohammad Ali to open the box. There
was another box inside that box which had a Nokia 3310 mobile in
it. Everyone took turns to take it in their hands. On seeing them so
excited, Asrar said, 'A girl has given it to me.'

Qasim Dalvi looked at him and said, 'Why are you making a
fool of us?'

Everyone started laughing and Asrar also joined in. They
discussed the girls of Mumbai for a long time. They believed that

Mumbai girls fool men for money in the name of love. Asrar looked at them sympathetically because they had not seen the light of love in his eyes. At dinner, Asrar told Mohammad Ali that Madhuri was asking about him. Mohammad Ali looked at him with curiosity but did not ask him anything.

Saleem Ghare also returned by that time. He softly informed Asrar, 'Your mother is suffering from malaria. If you can manage an off from work, you should go to the village.'

After dinner, Asrar and Mohammad Ali left the kholi and sat on the makeshift stalls that were now closed. Asrar told Mohammad Ali that Saleem Ghare had just informed him that his mother was ill. He required an off from work. He hesitated while talking about taking an off because he had just been to his village a few weeks back. Mohammad Ali was looking at him. He said, 'Your luck is in place, dude. Moosa Bhai is going for Umrah day after tomorrow. Don't worry. You can go to the village.'

Mohammad Ali told him that he would inform Moosa Bhai when he would go to drop him at the airport. Asrar's face lit up. After a while, Mohammad Ali said that he would buy a SIM card the next day at the office address. Asrar inquired how much that would cost. Mohammad Ali explained that it wouldn't be as costly as before because the rates of mobile connections were falling regularly. He also advised him to use the mobile phone sparingly in the village or else a lot of money would be charged due to 'roaming'. Asrar was excited about the mobile phone. On seeing him look at the mobile again and again Mohammad Ali smiled and finally said, 'Hina has gifted you this mobile phone for her own self.'

'What do you mean?' Asrar asked.

'Dude, you'll now be in her control. She'll call you whenever she wants.'

'I would like that. What could be better than that?' Asrar said.

Mohammad Ali put his arms around his shoulders and said, 'You love her a lot, yes?'

Asrar did not say anything.

'Make me meet her sometime,' Mohammad Ali requested.

'I will, once I return from the village,' Asrar said with earnestness.

His mother was fine, and the medicines were showing their effect. Asrar plucked ten or twelve coconuts from the neighbour's tree, dehusked them and kept them next to his mother's bed. He spent the entire first day at home. The next day his mother was feeling much better.

He was not at ease in Mabadmorpho. He tried sitting on the seashore attempting to establish the old familiarity with the waves, but his heart was still restless. He spent an afternoon with Jamila Miss, but he felt a disconnect with her. Although he had showed a lot of enthusiasm in front of her, showed off his new mobile phone and promised to keep in touch, something was missing. Miss showed him her new mobile phone that had a camera. Asrar praised it. Miss noticed that Asrar was a little dull that day. She thought that he might be worried because of his mother's illness.

Asrar spent some time at Mohammad Ali's house on the third day. His elder sister told him about Rashida, Mohammad Ali's mother who had left her husband and son. The news was that she had married the man she had eloped with in Sangli and had lived in a colony on the banks of the Krishna River. The man had loved her immensely. He died of a heart attack ten years back. Rashida chose to spend her life on the banks of the Krishna River instead of returning to Mabadmorpho. She cultivated vegetables on the riverbank. Rashida lived on the money she earned by selling those vegetables. When she died, her dead body kept rotting for two days and no one came to know about it. There was a neighbour who was her friend. When she did not see Rashida come out of the house for two days, she got concerned. She gathered the people of the locality and broke open the door. Rashida lay dead on the floor. The blood that had oozed from her mouth had dried. People say that at that time, Rashida held Mohammad Ali's childhood photograph in her hand.

Mohammad Ali's sister started crying while narrating the story. She did not know why she was crying but she cried for a long time. Asrar's eyes were also moist. He tried controlling his tears but in vain. He stood in one corner and cried while looking out of the window. He cried for a long time. After a few sobs, Ali's sister said that they had found phone numbers and the address in Mabadmorpho in Rashida's diary. The police had called to inform them about her death.

Asrar was in a state of shock.

He sat on the seashore late into the night, silent, sad and restless. He felt the absence of alcohol that night. He was thinking about the sorrow that would strike Mohammad Ali and what he would go through after hearing the news. On the other hand, when Mohammad Ali's father had heard about this tragedy, he had dismissively said, 'As you sow, so shall you reap.' But Asrar knew that Mohammad Ali's soul was anxious about his mother. He wanted to accept her, to meet her. In the life that he had known, his mother's disloyalty was not a big issue. He respected his mother's choice. He had realized in a very short time that sex was as blind as love. The one who drowned in it would also be allowed to resurface.

On the fourth day, when his mother started feeling better, Asrar returned to Mumbai.

Hina was busy with her exams.

They met at the Nagpada junction in the first week of May. They stood at the side of the road and chatted for a long time. Before she left, Asrar gave her his new mobile number.

The following week they met at the Gateway of India. They took a stroll along the beach and a small ride out on the sea. Hina was excited to see the sparkling waters in the middle of a summer day. Asrar was happy to see her happy. He was reminded of the day when he had taken his first trip to the sea. He had looked at the Taj hotel and the adjoining buildings religiously. This belief in Mumbai had now turned into love for the city. And the love he had for Hina had become his religion.

The boat was returning to the shore when something struck his mind suddenly. He said to Hina, 'Let us get married.'

Hina could not hear anything because of the noisy wind. She asked, 'What?'

'Let us get married,' Asrar looked into her eyes and repeated confidently.

'All right. Let's do it as soon as we get off the boat,' Hina replied.

Asrar became thoughtful.

Hina smiled and said, 'I'm not kidding. Let us go to my father's shop after getting off the boat and get married.'

Asrar thought Hina was not serious. He was looking at the waves.

Hina put her arms around him and said, 'What happened? Are you not ready yet? How much time do you need?'

Asrar looked into Hina's eyes and said, 'I am ready.'

'Are you mad?' Hina said.

'Yes. For you,' Asrar replied.

Hina didn't say anything. She started looking at the waves again. She was trying to avoid meeting Asrar's eyes because at that moment at least, she didn't have the power to come face to face with the flame that she had just seen in Asrar's eyes. On the other hand, her soul was ecstatic. An idea occurred to her. As soon as she got off the boat, she asked Asrar for his mobile phone and then dialled a number while standing in a shade near the Gateway. Asrar was buying peanuts, but his mind was still focused on Hina. After talking over the phone for a minute or two, she said, 'I've spoken to Abba. Your wish of getting married shall be fulfilled today.'

Asrar looked at her with astonishment. To add to his surprise, Hina said, 'I want to marry you too.' Asrar didn't know what to say because when he had said 'Let's get married' he had not meant that he wanted to get married that day itself. It was said in the zest of love but at this moment he felt as if he was in the middle of a difficult exam. He looked at Hina and said, 'I am ready.'

'I am ready too,' Hina said. They walked till the road in front of the Taj hotel and took a taxi. 'How should I explain to this mad woman what I actually meant?' Asrar said to himself. Hina thought that Asrar was an adamant man. He never retreated from his decisions and that was why he was absolutely ready that day as well. No sooner had they boarded the cab than Asrar took Hina's hand in his. Her palms were moist.

'We're getting married. Why are you sweating?' Asrar asked mischievously.

'This is the sweat of happiness,' Hina answered.

'You fool, there are tears of happiness not sweat of happiness,' Asrar corrected her, though Hina knew that she had said that in her confusion. She smiled at her mistake. They got off at Eros Cinema opposite the Churchgate station. Asrar was sweating at the thought of meeting Hina's father and the prospect of getting married there and then. What would he do? There was worry writ large on his face and the sun had made a few drops of sweat ooze from his forehead.

Hina paused at the entrance of a restaurant and looked at Asrar, 'Kindly wipe your sweat, or else my father will think I have kidnapped you from somewhere.'

What she had said was enough to make Asrar believe that Hina had taken the marriage bit seriously.

'Hina, you took it too literally. When I said let's get married, I meant we should get married soon. I didn't mean today itself!'

'I'll marry you today. Who knows what will happen tomorrow?' Hina said.

'Arre pagal! Is this the way marriages happen?' Asrar asked.

On seeing Asrar's hesitation, Hina became adamant. She said, 'I'm blind in your love. I can no longer remain patient. Abba will also find us a room.'

Her words made Asrar think, 'Love is definitely a cyclone.'

'Your father will take care of everything, but my mother should also be present. She is not against our marriage.' Asrar tried to make sense.

'Whatever you have to say, say it to my father,' Hina said this and entered the restaurant. She was followed by a scared Asrar. Pleasant music was playing in the dim lights. A girl was sitting at the table on the left. Hina went and sat next to her. Asrar stood near the table. Hina gestured to him to sit opposite her. He sat. Hina and Vidhi looked at poor Asrar for some time. Hina introduced Vidhi as her father's secretary. Her father would be a little late. During that time, Vidhi interrogated Asrar. He answered every question carefully as if it was his marriage interview. Vidhi and Hina were having fun bullying Asrar. Vidhi mischievously asked him, 'Have you guys done anything before marriage?'

'I had suggested once but she didn't agree.' Asrar's reply embarrassed Hina. She remembered what he had said in the National Park, 'I desire to kiss your entire body.' And she had said, 'That is done after marriage.'

'Do not say this in front of her father,' Vidhi warned him while looking at Hina.

They grilled him for a very long time. At last, Hina took pity on him and revealed that this was her friend Vidhi, about whom she had told him earlier. Asrar could relax now. He laughed. They were still laughing and teasing Asrar. Asrar also participated in the fun. He enjoyed meeting Vidhi; she also liked him. It was Sunday. After coming out of the restaurant, Asrar called up a friend in the kholi and spoke with Mohammad Ali. The three of them boarded a taxi and went to Crawford Market. Asrar had called Mohammad Ali there. Vidhi cordially welcomed Mohammad Ali. During the conversation, Ali told Hina that Asrar kept talking about her the whole day. Asrar looked at Hina and smiled.

Vidhi said they should take a look around Crawford Market and Mohammad Ali Road. Mohammad Ali volunteered to be the guide. It was 6 p.m. when they reached the JJ signal. They were tired of walking and stopped at a restaurant to drink tea. While having tea they debated about which beach was the most beautiful. Mohammad Ali claimed to have seen nearly all the beaches in and around Mumbai, but found that the most beautiful was Kalamb beach, which was around eight kilometres from Nalasopara station. Asrar found Manori beach the best. Vidhi gave the final judgement that all of them would go to Kalamb beach in the last week of June.

Hina told Vidhi that she would stay at her place that night. They stood and chatted outside the restaurant for a while after which Asrar and Mohammad Ali bid farewell to them. Hina said that she would call Asrar at 10 p.m.

Mohammad Ali and Asrar went back to the kholi, talking on the way. Ali praised Hina and told Asrar that he was fortunate to be with such a decent girl. Asrar said, 'I've heard your *item*, I mean the girl from UP, really adores you.' Mohammad Ali paused and looked at Asrar, then said, 'Yes, she's undoubtedly sexy.' Something came into his heart; he thought for a moment and then said, 'Listen, her father had a pickle shop earlier. She likes sampling the pickles and she also asks me to do the same, but she never says that she loves me.' Asrar kept smiling and listening to Mohammad Ali. Today, after days, Mohammad Ali was in his spirit. This brief outing had made him feel better, otherwise there had been a permanent crease of worry on his forehead for the past twenty days. Asrar knew the reason behind Mohammad Ali's unease, but he never initiated a dialogue about it. His experience had told him that wounds were healed not by talk but by time. On meeting Vidhi, he was immediately reminded of Mohammad Ali and that was why he had called him to Crawford Market.

Vidhi had come to Hina's house after a very long time. Darakhshan decided to cook mutton pulao for her. Hina and Vidhi helped her put the ingredients in place and helped her as much as they could, then they went and sat in the balcony to chat. They talked a lot. Vidhi shared her opinion of Asrar. She felt that he was innocent and loved Hina a lot. Hina was happy to hear what Vidhi had to say. While talking about Asrar, Vidhi repeated what he had said that afternoon, 'I had suggested once but she didn't agree,' and said, 'There's so much innocence in what he said.' Asrar's words had made Hina blush even in the restaurant. When Vidhi repeated it, a weird feeling passed through her. Before she could drown herself in that feeling, Vidhi asked, 'Tell me, why did you not agree?'

Hina put her hands on Vidhi's shoulders and said, 'I'm scared. If we do everything now, then there will be nothing left for retaining his interest in me.'

'Are you mad? He loves you with all his heart. Everything can be sacrificed for this emotion . . . then why not this one . . .' Vidhi stopped in the middle of the sentence.

'But this one thing is also . . .' Hina wanted to say something, but she stopped. She wasn't sure what Vidhi had in mind. Vidhi continued from where she had left, 'I mean to say that sex is an expression of the heart. So, when you give your heart to someone, you should not suppress the desire for sex. Especially because of the uncertainties of the future. This is an insult to love!' Vidhi lectured her.

Hina listened quietly.

'Sex is the natural shelter of love. Denying it is a denial of the soul, as well as your own being,' Vidhi said.

Hina was still silent.

'Sex opens those windows of our bodies through which light enters. This light cures many diseases of the soul.'

Hina was silent.

'Copulation is an easy cure of *rohzin*—the soul's melancholy.' The old man in Chor Bazaar loudly read this out from *Kitab-ul-Hikmat Bain-ul-Aafaq*.

Then after explaining it to the Sufi-looking man, he added that if a child witnessed the sexual indulgences of his or her parents or one of them, it caused *huzn* or melancholy in the child's soul. This huzn drilled a hole in the soul. The circumference of the hole kept expanding with time. The emptiness of the hole turned it into a disease. The tried, tested and easy cure to this disease was the ecstasy of lovemaking. Lovemaking had so much power that it could slowly heal the invisible hole in the soul. That was why a patient of rohzin, the melancholy of the soul, automatically bent towards copulation and wanted to burn in the flames of making love. The burnt flesh reduced the size of the hole in the soul.

The Sufi-like man was listening to him silently.

After hearing Vidhi, Hina said, 'Are you reading sexology these days?'

'I'm reading Osho's books,' Vidhi told Hina and for the next fifteen minutes she filled Hina up with the basic information on Osho and his philosophy.

Vidhi talked about sexual pleasures for a long time. After listening to her patiently, Hina said, 'It scares me.'

Vidhi laughed and said, 'Just do it once, then your heart will want more.'

'More, more, more,' Vidhi repeated.

'More, more, more,' Hina joined in.

They kept chuckling for a long time. There were no clouds in the sky. The illuminated moon with its light spread all over the sky was announcing its rule.

They finalized Sunday for the trip to Kalamb beach. The bus journey from the Nalasopara state transport stand to the beach was memorable. The road was rough. There were small localities at short distances. The conductor would ring the bell and the bus would stop. People boarded or got off. The clothes of the commuters showed that the majority of them belonged to the Koli caste but most of them had converted to Christianity. They had crosses hanging around their necks. A few girls were conversing in broken English.

All four of them felt that they had come thousands of kilometres away from Mumbai. The passengers in the state bus were very distinct from those in Mumbai. They had their own dialect and accent. There were fields and shanties along the road. Life seemed serene. There was no hustle. No one seemed to be in a rush. Someone was smoking a cigarette, while someone else was rubbing tobacco on their palms. Some seemed so tired and distressed that their faces looked burnt and black like roasted potato. An old woman had a sari-like cloth tied around her. She probably didn't even know what a blouse was. There was a substantial tribal population around Mumbai, especially in Thane district. The lifestyle of the new generation was changing, but the older men and women in these tribes were still closely tied to their local culture. Vidhi saw that the old woman took out a bottle from her bag and had three sips from it. The smell of the sherbet in the bottle was very strong. Asrar was acquainted with both the smell and the drink. He immediately informed Vidhi and Hina that it was called tadi. It was a kind of brew derived from the local palm trees.

Hina asked, 'You've had it before?'

'Everyone drinks it in the village,' Asrar answered.

Hina smiled and looked out of the window.

Kalamb beach was big and the colour of the sand was black. Vidhi looked at the sand and said, 'This beach should be called the Black beach.' The area around was sparsely populated. There were few people around.

All four of them kept playing in the water.

There were vegetable fields adjoining the shore. On the other side of the fields was a string of coconut trees. Asrar wished he was alone with Hina. While playing in the water, the same thought struck Hina. How she hoped that one day she would be alone with Asrar on this beach. They would stand in front of each other while it rained heavily and darkness engulfed the surroundings. In that magical darkness, she would move towards Asrar and kiss his lips. The thought came and went away in a moment, but she kept sailing on the waves that this imagination had left her on.

They had fun at Kalamb beach till 2 p.m. Vidhi was carrying her camera and clicked photos. They sat on the sand and talked for a while.

At 4 p.m. they decided to return. They reached the Mumbai Central station at 7 p.m.

Hina called Asrar up at 10 p.m. They shared the hopes and wishes
that had sprouted in their hearts at the beach. One thing that
was clear was that both were in search of privacy and seclusion.
Their affinity had entered that phase where the other parts of their
body wanted to have a conversation with each other more than
their tongues.

A sort of darkness would appear in their eyes, which was born of
the moisture of the hormones in the body. They talked and their
conversations expressed how much they desired each other. In the
middle of the conversation, Asrar said, 'We'll go to Manori beach
during the monsoon.' That was followed by an elaborate description
of Manori beach.

He had gone to Manori beach some months ago with Qasim
Vanu and his friends.

They met again in the early days of June. Yusuf returned from
America in the second week of June. He seemed to have changed
a lot. He stayed at home for a day. Hina's elder sisters and their
children came over. Yusuf was very hospitable towards his sons-
in-law. He had brought gifts for all of them. He announced during
dinner that a branch of his shop would soon open in New York.
Everyone congratulated him. He spoke to Darakhshan a couple of
times. One could notice a few changes in Darakhshan as well over
the past few months. Peer Sahib called her over the phone, and she
would go and meet him once every fifteen days. The void in her
heart was now starting to refill.

On Friday, 25 July, at 8 p.m. Hina called Asrar and told him that it
had been raining non-stop for the past three days, and they should

postpone their programme of visiting Manori beach. Asrar insisted that all the fun was in getting drenched. Hina was reminded of Kalamb beach where she had imagined heavy rainfall and the darkness around while she stood in the sea and kissed Asrar's lips. That reminiscence brought to life the other buried feelings in her heart.

She sat on the sofa after hanging up. Some ambiguous thoughts rose in her mind like bubbles and then drowned in the depths. She started looking at the rising bubbles in the light of her closed eyes. She imagined she was sitting on the beach, and it was raining heavily. A slight darkness had spread around. There were grey clouds till the eyes could see and the rain fell incessantly on the sea. The waves looked ferocious in the dark. There was romance in looking at those dangerous waves. She could now see Asrar. He stood in knee-deep water. He looked at her while standing in the sea. Their faces were blurred in the dark, but this blur was making them all the more attractive. Asrar looked at Hina and opened his arms. Hina moved towards him.

The gushing wind seemed to be in a rush. She tied her dupatta tightly around her waist. She was moving forward and simultaneously her footprints were being erased from the beach. All her footprints had vanished when she placed her foot in the water. The sea was quite cold. She felt a wave in her ribs. The wave infused intensity in her heart. When she came closer to Asrar, the rainfall around them became wilder but it was drizzling slightly in the small circle where they stood. They looked at each other, then turned their eyes to see the rain around them. The intense rain had veiled the nearby sights from their eyes. Hina put her arms around his neck and rubbed her nose against his. Asrar place his lips on hers. In that moment, their bodies could feel the warmth of each other. The surrounding rainfall now approached them from all sides and reduced the circle. The intensity of the rain lessened around them, but it continued to rain heavily over them.

Hina opened her eyes. Darakhshan was sitting on one corner of the sofa, watching a drama on the TV. Hina turned on her side and closed her eyes to resume the same scene in her mind. Even after much effort, the scene could not be created with the same intensity. She wondered if it was time to cross all the limits. Was she ready? Had her fear vanished? Why should she put limits on her own desires? She kept interrogating herself. Her heart told her that she was not just ready for it, but her love had converged and reached its zenith. Vidhi's words came to her mind, 'Sex is the zenith of love.' Hina concluded that she loved Asrar today for today. Loving him today for tomorrow would be a lie. She stayed silent for a minute or two.

She was again in the world of her imagination. It had stopped raining. At the same time, the black clouds were raining on the city and the suburbs. In her imagination, she saw that she was lying on the beach with Asrar. It was night and stars blinked in the sky. Their lights were dim but there was fervour in that dimness. Their bodies were cold after bathing in the water but suddenly, a fire within took over them. They soon realized that it was no ordinary fire but was like radiating uranium. There was a pleasure in burning in the radiation. She wanted to remain ablaze with the pleasure throughout the night. On burning in that fire, a human could be reborn from his or her own ashes, like the phoenix.

She was lost in her thoughts when she suddenly heard a loud thunder. She stood up. Darakhshan exclaimed, 'See, how heavily it is raining!'

'Yes . . .' she said and went to the balcony.

Water had clogged the road. She saw thick raindrops fall in the light of the streetlight. Only a few buses and taxis could be seen plying. She was looking at the rainfall when Asrar's words came back in her mind, 'All the fun is actually in getting drenched.' She smiled at that.

It rained cats and dogs till 4 a.m. Most areas of the city were waterlogged. The rain stopped just before daybreak. The sun shone in the sky. All the water collected in the four hours of rain, flowed into the drains. The ground drank the water accumulated on the train tracks. There was an ebb in the sea. All the drains that were carrying the rainwater had vomited it into the sea. Life came back on a normal track.

When they boarded the train next morning, it looked as if it had rained many days back. They got off at Malad station at 10 a.m. The bus stop was near the railway station. They took a bus to Marve Beach. On the way Hina made Asrar listen to two songs of the film *Veer Zara* on her Walkman. She also told him about the heavy rains the night before and said that she thought if the rain continued then the train service might be temporarily halted. Asrar told her that when it had seemed that the rain wouldn't stop he had actually prayed. Hina chuckled at his exaggeration and said, 'So, God is controlling the rainfall as per your instructions?' Asrar said, 'Of course! It's possible. You never know what act of yours impresses God.'

They talked on the way and the half-hour bus journey ended in a jiffy. Marve was the last stop. The bus emptied out. They could see the bay right in front of the bus stop. The bay of Marve was a narrow sea strip that surrounded Manori on the left of which was the sea. The boat came to the shore in two or three minutes. The rain had stopped but the clouds were collecting in the sky. They got off the boat and sat in a horse cart. There was an umbrella of clouds over them, and the breeze was a little nippy. The horse-cart man was humming a song in the local dialect. On both sides of the road were bamboo racks where fish were dried during the summers. Small prawns, big prawns, mandeli, bombil and other small fish were dried in the spaces between the fields around the end of May. The fish easily dried up when spread on the roads made of coal tar.

When the horse cart moved forward, Hina could feel the smell of fish in the fresh air. The pathways on the sides of the bay entered into the village of Manori and would end at Manori beach a kilometre or two ahead. The beach was spread over ten to twelve kilometres. On the right, many small boats floated on the water. People stood in waist-deep water to unload the fish from the boats and take them to the shore. There was considerable amount of movement on the beach, although the big boats were tied to wooden planks at a little distance from the shore. Makeshift shelters were built on the boats to keep them safe from the rainfall. Innumerable bamboo racks were constructed between the beach and the village which were used to dry the fish. In the net-like shades of these racks, the Koli men sat for rest or weaved nets.

Hina and Asrar got off the road and took a narrow path to the beach.

The Koli village was not more than a kilometre away from where they stood. The beach in front of them was covered with huge rocks. These rocks continued a kilometre into the sea. For centuries, the people of the Koli samaj had used these monstrous rocks to make enclosures. These enclosures were used to capture the fish. When the tide came in, small fish got entrapped in these spaces. On the left, the beach seemed to shrink and at one place, a chain of hillocks could be seen. There was a graveyard from the point where the hills began. There was a hill near the graveyard but very few people climbed it to go to the other side. Asrar pointed at it and said, 'Let's go there. The sea looks amazing from there.'

It was 11.15 a.m. They walked towards the hill.

In Mumbai, it rained heavily over Ghatkopar, Karla, Sion, Bandra–Kurla Complex, Andheri and Santa Cruz. Although it had been raining in Mumbai as well as the suburbs since 8 a.m., no one had imagined that with the passage of time, it would become dangerous. People had left for work or were leaving.

Hina and Asrar's umbrella was overturning repeatedly in the gushing wind. They decided to close their umbrella and get wet in the rain. Asrar kept his mobile, watch and wallet in Hina's purse. Hina took out a polythene, wrapped her purse in it and held it between her arms. They were enjoying getting wet on the beach. Hina raised her head towards the sky and felt the raindrops fall into her eyes. Asrar collected the raindrops in his palm for Hina to drink. Hina was impressed with Asrar collecting the raindrops in his palm. When they turned and looked back after walking for fifteen minutes, the beach on the right could not be seen. They stopped. There was no one near or far. They stood silently enjoying the noise of the sea while the raindrops echoed in their ears. This sound was accompanied by a huge wave of warning, but they were too lost in pleasure to take notice. They could not decipher the warning in the weather. The mobile was disconnected from the network as it was inside the purse or else the warning issued by the weather department at least would have reached them that there were chances of very heavy rains in the next twenty-four hours. But people always took such warnings with a pinch of salt and were hopeful that the rain would stop.

Asrar pulled Hina towards him and kissed her lips. Hina was impressed with this unexpected kiss. She participated and reciprocated. They walked further. The direction of the rain was towards them. The raindrops were hitting their bodies along with the cold wind that slowed them down. On the other hand, the sea level was rising. It was 12.15 p.m. when they reached near the hill. By now water had started collecting on many roads and lanes across Mumbai where it had started raining early in the morning. All the lakes around Mumbai were already full to the brim. The water from last night's rain still clogged the drains. The huge drains which poured the water from the city into the sea were unable to do so because of the pressure from the sea water rushing in at high tide. As a result, the water from the drains flowed back into the city.

A narrow path along the graveyard led to the foot of the hill. Asrar stopped near the gate of the cemetery and recited, '*Assalam o alaikum ya ahlal qubur, yaghfiralla lana o lakum anta salafna wa nahnu bil asar.*'

Hina asked him what he had recited in Arabic. Asrar told her that it was a small prayer through which he conveyed his salaam to the dead. Hina looked at him and said, 'Maybe the dead souls gave you an answer, but you did not hear it.'

A djinn was reciting some prayers near the gate of the graveyard. He was impressed by what Hina had said and he remarked, 'Yes, I'm astonished that all those under the graves unanimously replied walekum as-salaam, but you couldn't hear it. You'll also not hear what I'm saying but given the loudness with which the souls have replied, it feels that they want to stop both of you from going towards the hill.' Right next to where the djinn stood, there was a plant with purple flowers. One of the spies from Mumba Devi's court sat on the plant in the form of a spider. Mumba Devi had sent him to gather information about the 'Water of Eternal Life' or '*Aab-e-Khizr*'. Mumba Devi called this spy by the name of Farishta Firqa-e-Mau'tazilla. He knew that after a few weeks, Mumba Devi would definitely ask him about what he had just seen. Mau'tazilla saved the scene he saw in his memory.

He also saw Hina from behind a branch when she had bent down to pluck a flower.

Hina plucked the flower. Then she held Asrar's hand and started climbing the hill. After five minutes they stopped near a tree of wild sugar-apples and kissed each other. For the first time, Hina tightened her arms around Asrar. They kept kissing each other's forehead, lips and eyes. Raindrops were falling on them and they looked like a blur from afar. The hue of the rain falling on them was light pink. Mau'tazilla was looking at them. He had seen the rain turn pink for the first time. He was amazed.

At 1 p.m. they reached that spot on the hill from where they could see the sea. They were able to look at the waves banging their heads on the rocks of the shore.

Black clouds had spread over Mumbai and the surrounding areas. It was raining heavily on the city. Milan subway was waterlogged and vehicles had stopped moving. Water had collected up to the knees in small localities and the water of the Mithi River had

flooded the areas around it. Both Asrar and Hina were looking
at the sea and enjoying the beautiful sight. In a moment the sky
above the sea was covered with black clouds and it turned dark all
around. They looked at each other in that darkness. Their hearts
were beating fast, and their eyes sparkled. This spark resembled
precious diamonds in the dark. Hina kept her purse aside and put a
few stones on it. The grass had grown sparsely on the hill. The soil
below the grass had turned brown due to the rain.

They sat down. Asrar held Hina in his arms. They kissed for a
long time. They were shivering because they were drenched in the
rain and because of the cold wind. Hina wanted to say something;
she felt her teeth chattering. She was shaking. Asrar laughed at
her condition. She smiled. Asrar pulled her to his chest and this
time he started moving his fingers over her entire body. The gentle
touch of Asrar's fingers on the sensitive parts of her body gave her
immense pleasure. There was a distinct magic in that touch; in fact,
it was intoxicating. This feeling had spread over her soul. It was as
if her body had transformed into a spring which resulted in novel
desires. She wanted to close her eyes and see the light within. She
was attempting to see the bubbles that were bursting inside her.
There was a feeling of surrender and self-pleasure involved with the
urge and a song of ebriety. She found her existence getting a new
fragrance in Asrar's proximity and in his arms. Mau'tazilla noticed
that the pink circle of rain which was on top of Hina and Asrar had
now spread further. His amazement increased. He came out of his
hiding place behind the stem and sat on a leaf. He saw that the pink
had taken a deeper hue.

The heat that was produced in her body the other day while
she had sat on the bed of her imagination, today multiplied. Its
intensity was spreading to her pores. The pink raindrops fell from
her silky hair on to her back. The drops from her forehead fell on
Asrar's chest. She saw Asrar in her lap and they kissed each other's
forehead and eyelashes in the fervour of their emotions. She felt
ablaze, like an oven, and that reflected on her face. Her face was

getting darker while two red lines had risen in the white of her eye. Her face looked pink in the pink rainfall. A weird thought passed Hina's mind. She embedded her teeth behind Asrar's ear. Asrar was stunned and intoxicated. When Hina's sharp teeth bit Asrar's skin, the waves rose higher in his veins. He felt courage rising in him. The courage magically brought the blissful emotions to the surface of the mind. His face shone. He was quiet. He was looking at Hina's drenched body in the pink rain and amid his silence.

It was 1.30 p.m. The destruction had been started by the rain. Trains were running with irregular pauses and stops. Offices were shutting down. Mohammad Ali had tried many times to reach Asrar's phone, but it was out of reach. The phone service was also halted after some time. The routes of airplanes were diverted. Most roads and slums seemed to be floating on water. Four or five dead bodies floated towards the sea on the Mithi River. Of these, one dead body was spotted by the municipality's rescue team. Many houses had fallen in areas around Dharavi, Andheri, Kanjurmarg, Matunga and Saki Naka. To add to the destruction, hazardous black clouds started gathering over Santa Cruz. The wind was uprooting trees and carrying away roofs with it. Animals and birds were hiding in fear. Cats and dogs were turning mad. Many wild snakes were spotted near areas around Borivali, Aarey Milk Colony and in Dahisar. Three or four people had died of snakebites. A drain flowing from Borivali towards the sea carried the water from National Park. The people living along that drain had seen a bear, two deer, and a snake flowing away in the water. The bear was alive, but the flow of the drain was so fast that no one could attempt to save it. It rained heavily from Andheri to Vasai. The locals had never seen such intense rain in their lifetime. Many slums and huts next to the railway tracks were demolished by the winds and the rain. People had collected under the trees opposite the railway tracks and were praying to their respective gods to stop the rain.

Asrar and Hina stood on the top of the hill and looked at the sea. The dark, black clouds ruled the sky above the sea. Huge waves were rising in the sea, but the beach strip spread deep into the area and hence the waves were away from the shore. The black stones on the shore looked beautiful. The intensity of the rain was increasing. A blur had spread around. Hina told Asrar that she had seen the same view in her imagination the night before. They were standing at the shore. Black clouds had gathered above their heads. A slight darkness spread around and Hina hugged him in that darkness.

Asrar kept his hand on her shoulder and said, 'It seems you'd seen today yesterday itself.' Asrar's words left Hina puzzled. Was it déjà vu? Or was it just an illusion which had taken the form of a picture in her head instead of being a memory? She had read a brief book on déjà vu a few months back. She had read that déjà vu meant 'seen before'. It was that mental state when a person thinks that what they are experiencing in the present has already happened in the past, irrespective of whether it has actually happened. Probably that was why she was puzzled. Seeing her lost in thoughts Asrar said, 'Let's climb down and sit on the rocks to enjoy the sea better.' She picked up her purse and once more peeped below the hill to look at the sea. The sea water jolted around the beautiful black rocks. She stared at the rising waves, the seashore, the black clouds in the sky and the rain that fell into the sea. She had never seen a view more beautiful. She was lost in the lap of nature. She held Asrar's hands in hers tightly. She imagined that the entire scene before her eyes was looking at her. Hina was now a part of the scene's soul.

Black clouds had gathered over their heads, resulting in darkness all around. They stayed there in each other's arms. A few teardrops collected in Hina's eyes, but Asrar could not notice them because of the rain. Those drops in Hina's eyes were the expression of the bliss that every layer of her being was experiencing. Asrar was her life's greatest happiness and achievement. She was seeing that person in Asrar which was the antithesis of her father. Her father was a very good human being but had failed to love his wife. This had become a knot in Hina's heart. She didn't want herself to be the continuation what her mother went through. She was in search of a life of her own with her individuality. Sometimes, when she looked at her mother, she thought that she would only spend her life with the man who would love her infinitely and whom she could love infinitely. Her adoration for Asrar had soon changed into love.

The breakdown in her mother's marriage and the resulting emotional turbulence had pushed her into the dark gulf of mental convolution and depression. She rose from the dark marshes of that mental state with the assurance that she would choose that man as a companion who would be the reflection of her being. Their souls would be the same or as if in the same cage. She took Asrar to be the interpreter of her feelings and the reflection of her self. Asrar's craving and passion had created a sense of completion in her. This feeling of being complete had risen from the layers within her in the form of tears.

Her tears infused with the rain turned pink. A drop of her tears touched Asrar's tongue and spread into his veins and reached his heart to dissolve into his blood. He was unaware of her tears, albeit his heart had acquired a pink hue.

It was 1.50 p.m.

When they reached the graveyard, the djinn had already completed his prayers. He saw Asrar and Hina going and sitting on the black rocks on the lap of the hill. Through the sound of the sea, he had guessed that it would take not more than fifteen minutes for the waves to reach the beach. He was suddenly reminded that he had to attend Dawrat-e-Aayat-e-Quran organized by the Rahmat-e-Haq O Jamat-ul-Murabitun in the coastal areas of Karachi and the interior of Sindh. He immediately flew away. The moment he flew away, Mau'tazilla transformed into a saffron snake and crawled to the place where the djinn had stood a few moments back. After sensing the smell of the djinn he was able to guess where the djinn had gone and why. After gathering the required information, Mau'tazilla turned into a white pigeon and flew away.

Heavy rains continued in the suburbs of Mumbai, like Virar, Kalyan, Thane and Panvel. It was also raining in Mumbai Central, Churchgate, Colaba, Masjid Bunder, VT, Vikhroli, Dadar, Bandra as well as Mahim. At some places the colour of the rainfall was greenish and at others it was saffron. Powai Lake was overflowing, and its water had started descending into the Mithi River. The colour of the raindrops here was black, as if coal tar was raining down. The Mithi River was above the danger mark. The government machinery, police and sewage experts were all out on the roads trying to fix the drainage. People were instructed not to leave their houses and efforts were being made to help those who were already out. By 2.15 p.m., all local trains were halted. Highways thronged with vehicles, cars and bikes as well as pedestrians. In many places the water had accumulated waist high and a lot of people were caught inside their cars. Those who were fortunate were saved, while many died in their vehicles.

The clouds that had accumulated over Santa Cruz burst open at 2.15 p.m. Clouds fell on top of clouds and a huge blast was heard in the sky. In an area of about ten to fifteen kilometres, the rainwater poured in huge volumes, as though an angel had overturned a lake on top of the city.

Kalyan, Thane, Mumbra, Badlapur, Borivali, Malad, Andheri, Santa Cruz, Bandra, Kurla, Sion, Ghatkopar, Dharavi, Choona Bhatti, Dadar and other areas were flooded. Around 3000 people had lost their lives, and no one knew about them. The corporation, the media and the welfare organizations could have never imagined that the death toll would be so high. All means of communication and transport had snapped. All were disconnected. On the other hand, the Mithi River had turned into a well of death. This well of death had already pulled 500 souls inside it like a magnetic force and had eliminated them. The widely expanded seashore around the city had turned into Koh-e-Nida, a mountain in epics which attracted people and erased their existence like a brutal assassinator.

Asrar and Hina sat on a huge rock. Small, brown crabs were crawling around it. Their presence scared the crabs away. Ten or twelve snails were smelling them from the cracks in the rocks. There were larger rocks ahead which had enough spaces between them so that one could stand there. Asrar looked at the glistening, clean and transparent water below. He said, 'Let's go further down.' Hina smiled. They carefully stepped down. They stood between two rocks and madly and passionately kissed each other. This madness was coupled with the passion and madness of love. This madness had freed them from the worries of time and place. They looked at each other's faces in detail. It is said that when carefree love, liberated from the worries of time and place, dwells in the retina, it makes one see the complete face of the beloved. Their lips were as red as burning coal. Their eyes looked infinitely attractive in the dim light. There was musk in Hina's heart that burst open at that moment. She could feel the fragrance spread within her. It was difficult for her to veil that smell.

'Let's go a little further. Someone might come here,' Hina said.

They walked over the rough rocks and moved even closer to the sea. After five minutes, they stood on a rock and looked at the hill from where they had seen these rocks before. The tip of the hill seemed to have gone missing in the blur created by the rainfall. They looked till where their eyes could see but there was no sign of any human around. They were sure that there was no one on the beach except them. They moved forward. The rainfall was intense. Darkness had spread on the surface of the sea. They turned and looked at the beach. Even the rock on which they had stood earlier was barely visible. Hina looked at the sky. Black clouds had become umbrellas over her head. Those umbrellas had millions of holes from which cold waterdrops were falling on her. She was transforming into an oyster—an oyster that wanted to fill itself up with the healing drops of spring rain. The trapped fragrance of restless musk inside her had now travelled to the depths of her mind. A different kind of strength, maturity and audacity had evolved within her which gave her confidence to not betray her heart's desires. Behind her temerity was her immense trust in Asrar and the motivation she derived from Vidhi's very happening life!

Vidhi had also showed her two movies with ample sexual content in them. These movies had reduced a lot of anxiety and unnatural fears from her heart. Now she wanted to deeply feel the lusciousness and fragrance. Asrar's desires had revealed themselves to her already. When Hina had asked him to walk away from the shore towards the raging sea, Asrar had realized that his eyes were destined to have a glimpse of the most beautiful of human bodies. Along with the heart-gripping features of her face, Hina's curves triggered a distinct intoxication within him. Today he had deeply felt the touch of Hina's curves and in that touch there was a spellbinding magic. A darkness emanated by waves of desire had spread into his eyes and his soul was soaked in it. In this passionate soaring of the spirit, he felt that it was raining rose petals around them along with water droplets from the sky and in the atmosphere the fragrance of *Arq-e-Gulab*, rose water, was dissolved.

His soul was under perpetual happiness since the day he had met Hina. All the doubts intertwined with the branches in the depths of his soul had been dissociated. Even those doubts that he had about his mother. Falling in love with a woman and the presence of desire of copulation with her had made him a little vagrant. This vagrancy had made him capable of letting go of things easily. There was no place in his heart for any regrets. Hina ruled over each province of his heart. Probably one of the reasons why love was synonymous with lunacy was that it removed all concerns from the lover's mind and deployed the lover to worship the beloved.

The umbrella of clouds was showering water over them from its cracks while they lay making love on an oblong stone hiding behind a larger rock. Asrar slowly whispered into her ears, 'I love you more than I love my mother.' Hina immediately responded: 'And I love you more than I love my father.' They were aware that they had freed those words from the depths of their subconscious. Or maybe they just knew nothing other than the fact that they loved each other more than any other person in the whole world. There was a spark through the contact of their drenched bodies and in that moment their clothes seemed like an enemy. They had to be forfeited. Now they were free from the cotton threads which had become a burden on their skins.

The wave which had turned their lips into burning red cinder had now spread into their nerves. Their intoxicated souls were ready to merge into each other in the heat of this passion. They were aware of the flames emanating from their hearts. Now their eyes were increasingly traversing the curves of each other's skin. How a pale pink rose gains its brightness fully after being soaked in the rainwater! Hina's skin had acquired the brightest hue of pink after being drenched in the continuous rain and the wildness of love. Asrar had felt the fragrance of rose rising from her glowing skin. That smell had slyly entered his brain and filled all its corners. It had now proceeded to fill up his chest. He whispered, 'Your body smells like the drops of rain.' Hina could not hear it in the noise of the rain and the softness of his voice. That fragrance had the ability to soothe the soul! Asrar could not help but think for a moment that both Jamila Miss and Shanti were deprived of this fine perfume. Asrar did not know that when love overtook the passion of sex then the fragrance of the body expressed its colours over all the desires. This colour raised lovemaking from the status of sinful devotional worship to that of a mixing of selves with devotional worship.

Hina had put her ears to Asrar's chest. His pounding heartbeat took over Hina and she intertwined herself with his body. She was like a female serpent which was looking forward to an intercourse with the chosen male snake but had become tired after the love-dancing for hours. Overcome by passion, she was like the serpent which wrapped itself around its partner. In the intensity of passion, Hina kissed Asrar's heart. When Asrar felt the touch of those lips on his chest, a storm arose in the blood vessels that were travelling towards his heart from various corners of his body. The flaming blood drove itself towards his mind and on reaching it, metamorphosed into a thousand fireflies. Every iota of his mind was now lit up. There was a unique brightness and vibrance in that light that boiled the volcano in his soul.

It was at the same moment that a bunch of clouds had burst over Santa Cruz. The waves of the ocean rose five feet high with the winds of the storm and were moving towards the coast monstrously, as if a tsunami had erupted in the seas. But for Asrar and Hina there was no fear of the rising waves or their ferociousness because of the storm in their own hearts. In fact, they had not even given a passing thought to the fact that the rain could churn the ocean into a tsunami, even though the images of destruction caused by the tsunami in southern India a year ago were fresh in Hina's mind.

Hina and Asrar were lost in the pleasures of intimacy and togetherness. This moment was the zenith of their love. They were alive not in their own selves but in the eyes of each other. Their abode was no longer within themselves, but they had found residence inside each other's being. Their souls were enlightened but they were oblivious of the world around. Rain, ocean, coast, rocks, nakedness—none of it could find place in their minds. They were no longer aware of their own selves! This moment was also the time when their souls were lost—a moment which is called nirvana by some. Beyond this submission of the soul, another short moment was yet to come. A moment where, with the desire of their souls, they would reach the highest altitude of their being's pleasure. The moment would be blinding. That moment would be closest to the taste of the death of the self. In such a state the being would experience its presence and absence alternately.

The high waves of the ocean had launched a war on all the coastal areas around Mumbai. Some waves had also entered the city. Whosoever got caught in the labyrinth of these waters could not escape even after much effort. Six million cubic metres of water of the Powai Lake had broken the banks of the Mithi River and destroyed all the areas at a distance of about twenty-five kilometres. The rising waves of the sea had added to this devastation. The clouds that burst in Santa Cruz had caused immense chaos. Mumbai had transformed into a Shehr-e-Ashob—a lamenting city. The length and breadth of the city was submerged in water. It some places the water was seven feet high, in some it was six and in some it was five or four. In the areas where the water had reached a height of five to seven feet, there were many fatalities. In the entire history of the island, the sea had never been so hungry before.

Unaware of the sea's unveiled hunger, Hina and Asrar still lay on the rock, lost in enjoying the moment with their souls engrossed in each other. They had not yet come out of their trance when a huge wave hit against that rock with full force. The moment the wave pulled Asrar away was the moment when he had reached the surface of the blinding stage of his being's pleasure. He could not understand anything. He did stand up, but the very next wave attacked immediately. Hina wrapped her hands around his legs when he stumbled and fell. They held each other but before they could establish balance another satanic wave engulfed them. Wave after wave crashed on them, which made it impossible for Asrar to swim. Hina had put her arms around Asrar and was holding on to his neck very tightly. Asrar tried to remove her hands so that he could swim but Hina could not understand his efforts and anxiously tightened her hold like a lover who was wounded and was about to be sacrificed. The sea threw them to the surface twice, to show them that the coast was far, far away and the pink rains had transformed into black till wherever their eyes could see. On both occasions they had looked into each other's eyes for a flash. In their eyes there was love, unconditional and intense love for each other and nothing more.

Acknowledgements

Without the guidance and insights of Milee Ashwarya, publisher, Penguin Random House India, this journey of mine would not have been possible. I am grateful and thankful for her devotion towards the project of translating this novel.

Special thanks to Nabina Das, Zafar Anjum, Jayapriya Vasudevan and Tarique Eqbal.

Basic information about various kind of diamonds and stones was taken from the *Daily Ummat* (Karachi), November 2013. A few details about the concepts of Satanism, its history and current status in the subcontinent, were also taken from a series of articles published in the *Daily Ummat*.

The poem on page 178 by Utsavi Jha. The couplet on page 20 is by the Urdu poet Akhlaq Mohammed Khan 'Shahryar' (1936–2012).

Couplets by the Urdu poet Rajinder Manchanda Bani (1932–1981) have been used in the novel. The original chapter titles were also derived from a ghazal by Rajinder Manchanda Bani.